MENDED

BELLMARE HIGH
BOOK 2

MARY

TRIGGER WARNINGS

The book contains emotional and physical abuse, grief due to the death of a loved one, trauma, panic attacks, anxiety, graphic violence, and mention of domestic violence and cancer.

PLAYLIST

Family Line — Conan Gray
Blue Light — Mazzy Star
we fell in love in october — girl in red
A Message — Coldplay
Careful — Michelle Featherstone
Lay By Me — Ruben
Glue Song — beabadoobee
Cigarette Daydreams — Cage The Elephant
18 — One Direction
Drown — Bring Me The Horizon
Pretty Girl — Clairo
broken cd — beabadoobee
Hold Your Breath — Chase Atlantic
You & I — One Direction
The Cuddle Song — Jae Seven
The Elevator — Lizzy McAlpine
Our Night Together — Jason Alvarez
Pretty Boy — The Neighbourhood
Guidebook To Healing — Jamie Miller
Matilda — Harry Styles

CONTENTS

1

HEATH

WHAT THE FUCK?

Sebastian is messing with me. It *has* to be a joke. There's no way he meant the words that left his mouth.

"What did you just say?" I ask again, just to be certain that my hearing hasn't gone impaired recently.

My best friend stands across the cell, shoulders drawn taut, and his face a mask of seriousness. There's not even a microscopic hint of amusement on his facial expression—which is a rarity for him. He's always smiling and teasing me.

"Your dad is flying down from Toronto with a lawyer." He chews his bottom lip before continuing, "He said he'll be here soon. Your mother is coming too."

I grip the metal bars firmly. *No fucking way.*

My parents are coming to Bellmare. After more than a year, I'll get to see them. The last time they were here, it was Emery's funeral. My mom wept herself a waterfall of tears until she didn't have any left. Soon afterward, she fell into depression, and Dad thought it'd be wise for them to leave. Well, there were also the everyday fights between the three of us. They were feeling... I don't know what they were feeling, but I was raging at them. I blamed them for Emery's death—*I still do.*

The three of us were mourning in our own way because there was nothing else left to do. Emery, a daughter and sister, was gone after a fierce battle with cancer. *She lost. We all did.*

"You shouldn't have called him," I murmur, thinking about all the ways it will go. Almost every possibility ends with a big fight and them leaving. Something I'm used to. They never stay.

"I know," he says quietly, "but it was the only way. I talked to the officer and he told me that Alex Hanson pressed some serious charges against you—by the way, hold your tongue and don't speak to anyone here. Also, don't you dare raise your fists. We don't want to make this situation *any* worse than it already is. You hear me, Heath?"

I'm not a fool. I'm aware of the gravity of the situation. As much as I hate to admit it, I am in a fucking mess—which I'm fine with, because I don't regret hitting Hope's shitty father. Not one bit. Given the chance, I will attack him again, and this time I'll do permanent damage.

"I'm fucking serious!" Sebastian gets in my face—as much as he can with the bars between us. "Don't do it. *Please.*"

We stare at each other and the realization slowly sinks in.

I can't fuck up.

I have to wait for my father.

"I won't do anything. I promise," I tell him to put his worry at ease.

"Please don't. I don't want you to—" Agony flickers through his green eyes at the mere prospect of me getting into any more shit.

In this moment, I understand how he feels my emotions. My anger, pain, and frustration are mirrored in him, and while I already know that, it's my first time fully understanding it. I've always thought Sebastian knows I'm sad but he won't understand. Apparently, I've been wrong all along.

"I won't go to prison. Relax." I glare at him to erase the ripples of tension between us.

He shakes his head, a confident smile taking over his face. "Like hell I'd let you."

I smirk. "You'll pull me out from the depths of hell?"

"I will, because you're my best friend."

I nod, which is equivalent to 'You're my best friend too.' Sebastian grins and I feel content that he knows how I feel about him.

Without him, I wouldn't have made it this far. *Without him,* I'd be all alone. *Without him,* life would be a canvas of darkness and boredom.

An officer rounds the corner and stops next to him. He casts a displeased scowl my way before addressing Sebastian. "You're his buddy?"

Sebastian nods.

"Then it won't be long before you're sharing the cell with him. It's been a long time coming with how this one—" he points his thumb in my direction "—has been wreaking havoc since last year. I thought changing schools would knock some sense into him, but his ways haven't changed."

I glare at the officer but Sebastian pins me with a glare of his own. *Keep your mouth shut.*

"Is there any way I can spend a few more minutes with him?" Sebastian asks politely, dismissing all the previous nonsense even though his nose is flaring.

The officer sends him a wicked smile. "I can throw you in with him. Would you like that?"

Before Sebastian can agree to it, I grab him by the collar of his shirt and pull him to me. "You need to fucking go. Now!"

"Heath—"

"I'll be fine. Just go."

"But—"

"Please," I grumble.

Giving me a stiff nod, he backs up.

"Let's go." The officer leads him out and he looks over his shoulder to make sure I'm okay, but I roll my eyes and flip him the finger. He laughs and disappears around the corner.

When he's gone, it's then that the reality of the situation dawns on me.

I'm locked in a fucking cell.

For the first time, I'm facing the consequences of my actions.

My parents donate money to the school, so it hasn't held me accountable for all of my inexcusable actions. I get into fights, miss classes, and talk rudely to every teacher. They let me get away with a lot when deep down I know I don't deserve it.

I should be punished, and maybe this is my punishment. I deserve it.

Pulling away from the bars, I sit down on the cement floor and lean my head against the wall. The cold surface permeates chills through my body. It cools my anger and rationality starts to whirl into my thoughts.

There's an eerie quietness around me, which should haunt me, but instead, I feel calm. Faint light from outside seeps into the little room and I soak it.

It's cold, silent, and dark here.

With my head leaned back, I stare at the ceiling. I think about the person who's been living in every corner of my mind since the first time I met her.

Hope Hanson.

Is she okay?

Fuck. I can't help but worry about her.

I'm always worried about her.

I wonder if she's safe.

My heart squeezes tightly as if someone has plunged their hand into my chest and has that damn organ in their fist. I'm in agony just because I can't envision her in pain, let alone watch her bear it in real life.

Every emotion that she feels, I feel ten times more.

In the silence, it's my heart that speaks first.

I want that girl.

In a way that I want her to be all mine.

After the fair, the kiss, the ferry ride, and everything else that happened wasn't enough, I decided to go up to her room and spend some time with her. Okay fine. The real reason was that I wanted to ask her out. Like guys do in her romance books.

So imagine my surprise when I was about to ask her on a date and tell her how I felt, and her dad knocked on the door in a way that left me confused and angry. I was going to fling the door open and pummel his face, but Hope asked me to hide. So I did.

While listening to their conversation, every piece of the puzzle fell into its place. I saw the full picture she had been hiding from me at every instance, despite the number of times I asked her or assured her.

Like a switch being turned on, my brain put together everything, and I knew without a doubt that the man—her father—was her tormentor. He was the one who was hurting her mentally and physically. He was breaking her piece by piece as if she wasn't his own flesh and blood.

I know parents are shitty, considering I have such a brilliant pair as an example. But the fact that some are so fucked in their head, they abuse their own kid, is something even I can't understand.

When her dad hit her, my mind went blank with rage. I didn't wait or think, I acted.

My fist hit his face in the darkness of my thoughts and anger. I don't remember much other than fighting him, and Hope getting worried for me. She was terrified of what he'd do to me. I finally understood why she didn't tell me about him. She wasn't worried about herself, she was worried about *me*.

In my defense, I don't regret it one bit. I'm glad I got to hit him.

However, I'm also not sure how I'll get out of this problem.

I never wanted a record and now I have one.

My reputation is already bad, and now it just took another hit.

Despite these thoughts, I'm more worried about Hope. I can't imagine what hell she's going through. Her pathetic piece of shit of a dad must be taking out his frustration on her, or maybe he's left her alone. Whatever the case is, I feel helpless and useless because I can't save her.

I hate it.

I want to be with her, not here.

Time passes slowly when you're trapped in your head. Seconds take minutes and minutes take hours to slip away.

At some point, my eyes close and exhaustion weighs on me thick. The adrenaline rush finally disappears, but my mind can't stop worrying about her.

I just want to make sure she's okay. I don't even care if I get to ask her on a date or tell her about my feelings. I just want to see for myself that she isn't hurt or crying right now. I want to... There's so much I want to do.

My thoughts crumble and unconsciousness tickles my head. Before I can fight it off, I'm already falling through the darkness.

2

HEATH

THE RATTLING SOUND OF THE LOCK AGAINST THE BARS wakes me up.

"Good. You're awake. It's time to go." The shrewd officer from before, who escorted Sebastian out, is back with his scowl and hatred for me. I've never crossed paths with him, but he certainly has a grudge against me.

"What do you mean?" I rasp out, my throat dry from being parched for hours. Standing up on my feet, I stumble a little. Looking down, I find the cut on my leg that needs medical attention. The wound I totally forgot about in the heat of the events that took place afterward.

"Hurry up!"

Ignoring it, I walk out of the damn cell where I don't want to be again.

The officer, tall and sharp-looking, narrows his eyes at me. "There is someone who paid for your bail and everything else. You're going home even though you don't deserve it."

My fists are clenched tightly beside my sides, rage coursing through me like a stream of molten lava. My teeth grit together.

He's here.

My father came for me.

Like most kids, I should feel joyous or relieved to know my parents care for me. He came all the way from Canada to bail me out. I should be happy, but I'm not.

I'd rather spend another night here than see that man. The man I hate so much.

Quietly, I follow the officer. He continues to tell me how I'm spoiled and don't deserve the privilege. At some point, he tells me his son goes to the same school as me and has told him a lot about me. Talk about stalking. Seriously? Doesn't that guy have something else to talk about besides keeping tabs on me and discussing me with his dad?

"I hope you change yourself and grow up," he says before turning to his left. "There's the man who bailed you out."

Reluctantly, my gaze jumps from his face to the one he's staring at.

Gray eyes. Cold face.

Xavier Travon awaits me, dressed in a black suit that fits him perfectly—custom-tailored, straight from Armani. He has a taste for the finest things: the latest phone, laptop, and car are always in his grasp. The Rolex on his wrist catches the light, its gleam reminding me to check the time.

I glance at the clock in the corner. 5:30 a.m.

It's too early in the morning to deal with him after a year of not seeing him.

"You're free to go. Hurry up, leave." The officer gives me a nudge, and I shoot him a glare.

Striding toward Dad, I realize we're the same height now. In fact, I might be a couple centimeters taller than him. I remember the last time I saw him—last year, just a week after the funeral. He hasn't changed much.

Under the suit, he's still packed with muscle and has a defined body made from hours of exercise and a nutritious diet. He has the same hair as me, and his face is sharp, with features strikingly similar to mine. His displeased scowl is in its rightful place and his piercing eyes are busy cutting everything in its way.

Without a word, he turns around and walks out of the police station.

8

I follow him since he's holding the bag that has my phone, wallet, and wrist watch in it.

Climbing down the stairs, we stop in the middle of the parking lot where a shiny, new black Mercedes is waiting for us. Opening the back seat door, he throws the bag inside and gestures for me to get in.

Like fuck I would.

I need to check up on Hope. I need to make sure she's okay. I'm worried sick about her.

"I'm leaving," I tell him as I approach the car to get my phone and text her.

"You're not going anywhere but home." He closes the door and keeps his hand on the handle.

That voice. The deep, stern voice that loves to command me.

My heart clenches at the sound of it. *I've missed it.* Fuck. I hate saying it. I hate it. But I can admit it to myself as long as I don't say it out loud.

"Those are your first words to me after seeing me for the first time in more than a year?" I ask him, my eyes set on him in a glare.

He returns it with one of his own. "Get in the car, son. We need to have a long talk."

I smile dryly.

There's so much I want to say to him. I just don't know where to begin.

I want to be angry at him. Hit him. Curse him. Hurt him. But there's also a part that just wants to give him the silent treatment and make him suffer.

I'm torn between the two.

"Heath—" he starts.

I shake my head. "No! Don't say my name. Just don't."

My hands shake in anger or perhaps sadness. I have no clue. All I know is my head hurts and my heart is crying.

Seeing his face reminds me of the hospital visits and the long discussions with the doctors. A time in my life I'd rather forget, but can't, because those were the last days I spent with my sister.

The past is not only made up of bad moments, it also has good moments. The ones you don't want to forget about. As much as it hurts to remember it, there's also joy in remembering it because you get to relive those good moments.

Instead of lashing out at me, he softens his response, which is a first. "Let's go home."

My mouth opens in surprise, but I soon realize I don't have time for this.

"I have to be somewhere," I reply, even though I shouldn't. I don't owe him anything.

"It's five in the morning. Where do you have to be?" he asks calmly, but his gray eyes burn with annoyance.

For fuck's sake. Why is my phone in the backseat of his car and I need to get past him to get it?

"None of your business." I move to open the door but he holds the handle.

I glare at him, and he returns it with one of his own.

"Get in the car. This is my last warning." His serrated tone surprises me.

"What will you do—"

Taking a step in my direction, he says, "Carol is inside the car, and I won't have you disrespect my wife and your mother. So get your ass inside and talk to her."

I freeze. "Mo-Mom is here?"

I've never stuttered in my life before.

He nods slowly and opens the door.

My body folds inside the car. The moment the door closes, the woman in the passenger seat turns to me, and I'm struck by the sight of a teary woman.

"Heath! Oh my God. You're okay." Her hands cup my cheeks and she brings my face close to hers as she places a damn kiss on my forehead.

I'm so stunned I barely resist or show my disgust.

"I told you he'll be fine, Mia Cara," Dad assures her in a gentle tone as he joins us.

Mom continues sobbing and feeling my face to assure herself that I'm here and okay.

It takes me five minutes to get a grip on myself and break free from her hold, pushing back from her so she can't touch me.

What the fuck just happened?

"Heath—"

"He's fine. Give him space." Dad lays a hand on her back and rubs as he pulls her to him. He kisses her temple as she cries into his chest while speaking words that don't make any sense.

My parents are here.

Right in front of me.

"I told you I'll take care of it. Now stop crying. You know you look awful when you cry."

I stiffen at hearing those words.

What the fuck? I said the same words to Hope.

"He was in a cell—" she sobs into his chest.

He kisses her head. "Not anymore. I got him out. Now will you please stop crying? You're breaking my heart."

Reluctantly, she pulls back, and he wipes away all her tears and presses a kiss to her forehead. He whispers something to her I can't hear, or perhaps I don't want to hear, when I'm busy staring at the woman who's my mother.

The first thing I notice is that she's significantly lost weight. She looks thin and weak, as if she hasn't eaten in days. There are dark circles under her eyes and a hollowness to her cheeks that wasn't there before. Her bony face is still beautiful without makeup, but there's a sadness to it. Her hair is dark brown and curly—so different from mine. When she looks up, her ocean-blue eyes meet mine, which are a replica of hers. They're sad and filled with worry.

"I missed you so much," she says on the brink of tears.

Dad sighs heavily and tips her chin so she can look at him. "No more tears."

She nods, but a tear slides down her cheek. He brushes it away. "I told you to stay at home. You never listen to me."

She shoots him a mean look. "Our son was locked in a cell. There was no way I was going to stay at home. I'm right where I'm supposed to be."

Dad purses his lips, displeased, before giving her a nod. "When we get home, you'll rest as you promised me."

She gives him a quick nod, then turns to me. Her eyes run all over me and she smiles a little. "You've grown up and you look well."

"I've been eating healthy and working out," I tell her instead of being mad at her. Something is wrong with her, and until I get to the bottom of it, I can keep my attitude in check, I suppose.

Despite not wanting to do anything with her, my eyes assess her, and I end up saying, "Are you sick?"

A frown embeds between her eyebrows. "No, I'm perfectly fine." She smiles. It's fake.

"Don't fucking lie to me."

Dad sends me a cold stare. "Watch it."

With a sigh, I grumble, "You look really weak."

Waving her hand in the air, she brushes me off. "I missed a meal. It's nothing serious."

From the looks of it, a hundred of them. "It looks fucking serious."

Dad glares at me again.

So I face him and point my finger at her. "Tell me, what's wrong with her?"

Before he can answer, Mom puts her hand on his arm. They share a look that speaks thousands of words I can't hear, yet they understand each other perfectly.

A minute later, he turns to me. "She's fine."

My stomach tightens into a series of knots, wrapping around my gut with worry.

I know it. Something is wrong. I just can't put my finger on it.

It happened with Emery.

It happened with Hope.

Now it's happening to my mother.

Hope? Fuck. I need to contact her.

In a haste, I take out my phone and switch it on.

There's one message from her that makes my heart drop into my stomach.

Hope: I'm fine. I'll see you at school.

My fingers tighten around my phone and I'm seconds away from cracking it.

I'm fine?

She's never fine. That's the problem.

See you at school?

It's Saturday today. How am I supposed to survive two days without making sure she's okay?

"Are you okay, Heath?" Mom asks.

"I'm fine," I reply, looking out of the moving car. I didn't even realize Dad started driving. I'm bewildered that he didn't drag a driver with him. Usually, he has one who drives him everywhere, but not today.

"You look mad," Mom says.

I glare at her.

She smiles, which reminds me of Hope. Fuck. I can't survive not seeing her until Monday. I need to be at her house.

Mom frowns in worry and it punches my heart. Seriously, where did my anger go?

"Can you tell us what happened? What did you do?"

I swallow hard and look away when I catch Dad's gaze in the rearview mirror.

Unfortunately, we're stopped at a red light, so all the attention is on me.

A minute passes. Then another.

Five minutes later, I still haven't answered them.

I can't tell them about Hope. They won't understand it. My feelings toward her are so strong and real, I feel them in my chest and the rest of me. She consumes me deeply *and* completely. There's no escape from her, not that I want it.

I'm falling for her. It should be scary but I'm not afraid. I want her. I don't care that she comes with an abusive father and a controlling mother. I want her troubles, her problems, her issues. I want everything she can give me, and I'll take care of her. I *want* to take care of her.

Fuck.

How did I get here?

One day, I collided with her in the hallway, and the next, I was searching for her in crowds just wanting to see her again. Even if it was a mere glimpse. Whenever I'd see her, I wanted to be close to her, talk to her, and just stare at her for hours, not only because she was beautiful—that she is—but there's such softness to her face that I want to protect her and hold her. *Yeah. Me.* I like hugs now. Every little moment with her is a shot of comfort, light, and peace. I want to take it and get drunk on it. I want her like I've never wanted anyone. Talking to her about my sister is easy, not only because she listens to me but also understands me. I feel like I can lower my walls around her and she'll quickly reach for me and wrap me up in herself. She's my safe place.

The car ride continues in silence as we reach the mansion. Dad parks in the driveway where Derek is waiting in his prim and proper uniform and opens the door for me.

"It's good you're back, sir."

That's a fucking snide remark.

"It was one night," I grumble as I get out.

He shuts the door. "It could've been more. Be grateful that Mr. Travon got here on time."

I'm about to answer him when I hear my parents talking.

"I'm fine. You don't need to worry," Mom says to Dad, who's helping her out.

"You don't look fine," he protests.

Wrapping his arm around her tiny frame, he holds her to him. Against him, she looks small and breakable, but he looks at her and holds her with such delicateness.

This is the first time I'm really seeing them. Don't get me wrong. I'm mad at them and hate them—for abandoning me and Emery and never visiting us—but I also see them in a new light today.

"Stop fussing over me." She taps his chest and then looks around as if searching for someone. "Where's Heath? Did he leave? Xavier—"

The sheer panic in her voice makes me come around, so I'm standing right in front of her.

Before I can say a word, she's breathing heavily and her hand is gripping her diamond necklace.

Dad frowns. Shooting me a glare, he says, "Go inside and wait for us."

"I'm not your fucking dog."

"I said go—"

Mom holds his hand and leans against his chest.

"What's wrong with her?" My feelings betray me as my voice comes out weak and low, thick with worry.

Dad sighs and keeps rubbing her back. "Just go inside and wait for us. Please," he presses in a pleading tone.

Casting a last glance at them, I leave them.

Instead of waiting inside, as he told me to, I go up to my room and lock the door.

Plopping on the bed, I grab my phone and stare at her text before typing the words.

Heath: Are you okay?

I wait for her reply. It's early in the morning, so I don't expect her to answer me.

Ten minutes pass and no response comes from her, which drives me crazy.

I'm seconds away from marching down to her house, dragging her father out, and beating the shit out of him, but it'll cause problems for her. I'll be put away in a cell—again—and then nobody will protect her. At least, when I'm out, I can do something.

Well, not fucking something, apparently.

With a groan, I slump on the mattress and stare up at the ceiling.

My head is exploding. There's so many things, all happening at the same time. Hope is back home with that monster; she doesn't know I planned to ask her out on a date; I can't visit her or contact her; my parents are here.

My life is a mess, and for the first time, I feel the weight of it pressing down on me.

My breathing slows and deepens as thoughts in my head swirl in chaos.

I'm having a panic attack. It's happening.

Just as that realization comes, my hands start trembling. I wiggle my fingers, but they won't stop shaking.

Air packs tightly into my chest. I can hardly breathe.

It's been weeks since I last had one. I was certain I wouldn't have them again.

I was wrong. So fucking wrong.

A knock sounds on the door loud enough to distract me.

Pulling every bit of energy out of me, I sit up and clutch my chest.

For fuck's sake.

I hate this.

I just want to be normal.

"Heath, are you inside?" Mom says from the other side in a panicked tone.

"He's inside. Derek said he spends all his time here," Dad explains. A few seconds later, a much louder knock greets my door. "Open your fucking door."

Sitting back on my hands, I close my eyes and take control of myself by doing the five-things technique I read online.

Five things I see: ceiling, floor, door, my phone, and Hope.

Four things I touch: duvet, my jeans, pillow, and my chain.

Three things I hear: my parents, my thoughts, my heartbeat.

Two things I smell: my cologne and the disinfectant.

One thing I can taste: Hope's lips.

"Son, open the door. Now!" Dad commands.

Getting up, I walk to the door and fling it open.

Mom stares at me in distress, and Dad looks slightly anxious and pissed.

"I'm here because I want to be alone," I tell them.

Dad narrows his eyes. "Your mom and I want to talk to you."

I arch an eyebrow. "About?"

"Why were you locked in a cell?"

I'm surprised that he doesn't already know. "They didn't tell you?"

"They told me you beat up a man. They didn't tell me why."

Right, of course, they didn't. Because that bastard spun the narrative and made it look like he was the victim and I was the abuser. What a fucking asshole.

"What happened, hon?" Mom asks in a fragile voice that makes it hard not to lie to her. Worry marks her face.

"You don't need to worry about it," I say.

She takes a step toward me. "How can I not? I was asleep when I heard your father getting the news that you were locked up in a cell. It was Sebastian and he was really worried about you. I was worried too when I pulled the news out of your father—who didn't want to tell me." She glares at him before turning back to me. "We flew down here and I was thinking about you the whole plane ride. So don't say I don't need to worry because I can't stop worrying until you tell me what's going on!"

"Carol—"

Tears pooled in her eyes. "What happened? Why can't you just tell us?"

I grind my teeth. "I just can't."

"Why not? What did you do?"

"I didn't do anything that I wasn't supposed to do."

"What does that mean?"

"Exactly what I said."

"But—"

"I need to be alone."

I reach for the door, but Dad puts his hand on it and keeps it open.

"Your mother is not done yet," he warns me.

I glare at him. "I am."

He shoves the door and it hits the wall with a thud. "You will be done when she's done."

"Xavier, it's fine. Don't talk to him like that," she says to him softly.

His gaze shifts from me to her. "He doesn't get to disrespect you."

She looks down and fidgets with her necklace as she mumbles, "I deserve it. God knows I do."

My throat feels thick with the cocktail of emotions that I can neither swallow nor retch up.

What am I to do? I can't just forgive them for everything they've done just because they showed up to save me. It doesn't measure up to the years they were not here. It doesn't erase the sick feeling that made me think they hated me or didn't want me. They checked up on me, sure, but it wasn't enough. Nothing they did was enough.

They are strangers to me. I don't know anything about them. Little things, like how they take their coffee, when they leave for work, what their day is like, and all the other little details. I also don't know if they love me, care about me, or want me—that bit makes me feel pathetic.

Dad turns to me, his stormy gray eyes fill with fury. "Is this how it's going to be? You fucking disrespect your mother?"

Mom grabs his arm as tears stream down her face. "Please, calm down."

He looks at her. "Calm down? If it were anyone else but my son, I'd have that person six feet under dirt for disrespecting you and making you cry."

She quickly wipes her tears and plasters on a weak smile. "See? I'm fine. No need to be angry at him."

His gaze softens, and he mutters a few curses before taking her hand. With his other hand, he pushes me back into my room, stepping in with Mom beside him. Turning around, he locks the door and stands in front of it.

What the actual fuck?

I glare at him, but he's matching it with his own.

"Now, you will talk," he tells me.

Mom pulls away from him and walks over to me. She's short compared to my six-foot-two frame, and thin against my muscular, lean body. Still, the sadness in her eyes and the sorrow on her face manage to disarm me like an arrow hitting me straight in the chest.

"Would you like to sit with me?" she asks hesitantly.

"No," I deadpan.

Dad intensifies his glare on me.

Mom slowly nods. "Right, of course. I understand." She takes a long breath, then says, "Perhaps I can hold you for a few seconds? I need to assure myself you're okay and here with me."

I frown hard. "I'm right here."

Her blue eyes plead. "Please."

Fuck. Her eyes remind me of Hope. Big and soft like a puppy. The one person in the entire fucking world I can't refuse to.

"Fine," I agree.

In a second, her slender arms wrap around my waist and she presses her face against my chest.

Something strange happens. *I like it.*

"I don't know what I'd do if..."

On instinct, my hand rests over her back. "Nothing happened," I assure her.

I find Dad staring at Mom. As if he can feel my stare, he looks up at me. There's tension and anger in his eyes, but also worry for me and her. Something has changed about him. He's still cold, but it's like his defenses have weakened.

It's been a year since I've seen him, and that little change is quite prominent.

Mom pulls back and there's color to her face. She looks better just because she got to hug me.

"I'm so glad you're okay. I was so worried—"

I cut her off quickly. "I'm fine." Somehow, my tone comes out gentle.

She nods.

"Now, will you leave me so I can rest? I spent a night in a cell. I need to sleep."

She backs up. "Of course. We'll talk when you wake up."

I frown. "Aren't you leaving?"

Both of my parents freeze and exchange a look.

It's Dad who decides to answer me. "We're moving back home."

My jaw hangs open in surprise.

Mom joins in with a warm smile. "Permanently."

My parents are going to be here. They are moving back home.

For fuck's sake.

"Why?" I whisper..

A heavy look passes through Dad's eyes. "Because of you. We've already lost one child. We are not losing another."

Tears build up in Mom's eyes as she sniffles. Dad wraps his arm around her and pulls her to him.

You lost her because you weren't here. I want to scream those words at him, but seeing my mother become small and weak does something to my heart.

I move to walk away from them when a wince leaves my lips and catches their attention.

Mom looks at me and slowly her gaze settles on my leg. She steps away from Dad and starts moving closer to me. "Oh my... What's that? Why is there blood?" Her hands start shaking.

Dad stares at the wound on my leg and then at me. "Care to explain what happened?"

I run a hand through my hair to gather myself. "It's just a cut."

"There's a cut?" Mom whispers, her fingers playing with the diamond necklace. I notice how hasty her movements get and how hard she's staring at my leg.

I glance at Dad and he's noticing the same thing. Getting closer, he puts a hand on her back and says, "I'll call a doctor."

Somehow, those words make her pale.

"Relax," Dad tells her as he cautiously brings her to him. "He will be okay. I promise."

I don't know about that.

3

HOPE

THE STRANGEST THING HAPPENS. *NOTHING* HAPPENS.

Dad drags me home. After thanking the officers and offering them smiles and sweet words, he goes to his bedroom and doesn't come out.

I stand in the hallway for five minutes until deciding I need to escape before he changes his mind and comes for me.

Turning the lock on, I lean my back against the door of my bedroom and take a deep breath. It doesn't calm my racing heart or quiet my loud head. It does nothing.

I step away from the door, looking for my phone so I can talk to Sebastian, since I can't talk to Heath, but something on the floor catches my eye.

Blood.

The wood is marked with dry spots of blood that I know belong to Heath.

I clench the material of my shirt as I try to contain my heart, which starts beating wildly and uncontrollably.

Heath bled because of me.

The reminder is all I need to realize that if he stays by my side, only the worst will happen to him.

I can't bear that.

He's someone I care deeply about. And it's not just because he's the guy I like, but because he's also my friend. He's done so much for me, and all I've done is give him worry and distress.

He said he doesn't deserve me. He's wrong. *I'm the one who doesn't deserve him.*

He's too good to be caught up in the mess that is my home life.

With my heart in my throat, I near the blood stains and kneel on the floor.

The longer I stare at it, the more awful I feel.

My chest packs with air and it feels full. Yet I can barely feel any oxygen flowing through my blood and reaching my cells.

I can feel myself getting dizzy.

No! You can't crumble now.

Get yourself together.

Standing up, I get my phone and search online on how to get rid of blood stains. The article says to use water and vinegar—both of which I need to get from downstairs.

As much as I don't want to go, I can't have the stains on the floor. They'll haunt me.

For the sake of my sanity, I need to clean it up so I don't overthink and drive myself crazy—which I know I will. Just by staring at them, I'm spiraling.

I grab the stuff from the kitchen. It's quiet in the house, which is rare. The mere presence of Dad is loud enough to raise goosebumps on my arms. Seems like he left because I can't sense him in the house.

I hurry back into my room.

As I sit on the floor to clean, my hands start trembling.

My world turned upside down a few hours ago.

And it all happened so fast.

One minute, Heath was getting over the windowsill because he wanted to talk to me, and the next, Dad was knocking on my door like a madman. What occurred afterward is a blur. A film of events I keep pushing back because as soon as I remember, my heart hurts and I feel terrible for causing Heath all the trouble.

Because of me, he's locked up in a cell right now.

I wonder if he's okay.

That's another thing I'm forcing myself *not* to think about because I don't trust myself not to run the seven blocks so I can get to him.

I hope he gets out. He has to.

I'll do anything to get him out of there. Anything.

Scrubbing the floor with more force than needed, I try not to let my mind wander, but it does. I keep thinking about Heath and prepare myself for the moment he'll break things off with me. I mean, any sane person would do that. He doesn't need to bother himself with me, no matter how much he likes me.

In fact, now that he is locked up in the cell, he must have already made up his mind to break up with me.

Which should be fine.

We weren't in a relationship or anything, but there was—is—something between us that maybe isn't worth the trouble.

At that thought, I hear the cracking sound of my heart breaking into pieces.

I want him like I've never wanted anything.

I really, really, really like him.

I'm falling in love with him.

But now I have to abandon all these feelings because after what happened, Heath wouldn't want to do anything with me.

It takes me far too long to clean the stains.

Putting away everything, I step into the bathroom and turn on the shower. When I stand naked in front of the mirror, it's then that I notice the red cheek and a small gash on my temple. The blood has dried and the wound has closed, but it appears fresh.

With my fingers, I touch it and wince as it hurts. I clearly remember the worry on Heath's face when he saw it, even though he was the one who got stabbed. My pain bothered him more than his own. Just like I forgot about all the aches in my body when I watched him get hurt.

Gathering every bit of courage from within me, I push myself away from the mirror and step under the shower. The warm water cascades down my back and soothes me.

I stand there for a long time before I start washing myself.

Thirty minutes later, I return to my room, dressed in a new pair of sweatpants and a sweatshirt, and sit on my bed.

Picking up my phone, I text Heath.

> Hope: I'm fine. I'll see you at school.

I know he'll worry about me. I hope this puts him at ease.

I set my phone aside so I don't reach for it and spam Heath with messages and calls.

After what happened, I don't know where we stand. I'd be okay with whatever he decides, even if it means leaving me.

I hear the door downstairs open, and it makes me sit rigid on the bed. Chills race down my spine and my body turns cold. I don't think I'm breathing because I'm so scared.

I start counting to distract my head, but the sound of the footsteps climbing the stairs makes me stumble over numbers. There's only my room on this floor. The attic is filled with dust, cobwebs, and piles of used stuff that Mom doesn't want to throw away because she's sentimental to the core.

Wood creaks outside my room and I know he's here.

I start hyperventilating, and no amount of breathing exercises that Heath used to do with me helps.

The doorknob turns, and Dad steps in, looking and smelling drunk. In one hand, he's holding a bottle of Scotch, and in the other, he has a cigarette.

His eyes lock on me and I quickly jump to my feet.

I'm tall but he makes me feel like the smallest woman in the world.

"You're alone," he says, as he walks into my room. I move back but my legs hit the mattress. There's no escaping. I'm trapped.

When I don't say anything, he adds, "Because your boy is spending the night in the cell."

"I told you to stay away from him, but you didn't. He's there because of you," he reminds me.

He's there because of you. Those are the only words I hear.

I clasp my hands together and fidget with my fingers as the ball of anxiety starts rolling around in my stomach.

"It's all your fault. You're the reason why bad things happen to people."

I stay quiet, listening to him intently.

Dad walks to the book wall and stares at it. He takes a long swig from the bottle and then takes a puff from the cigarette. "First, you ruined my marriage and now there's a boy suffering because of you." He faces me. His dark eyes bore into mine and all I see is darkness. "Hope, you're nothing but a bad omen."

Bad omen.

I cause people problems.

They get hurt because of me.

I'm a problem.

My chest aches as those words fill the spaces inside me.

I find all the pieces of the puzzle that I've been trying to put together for years.

The reason why my parents fought.

The reason why I didn't have friends.

The reason why I've always been empty and lonely.

It's because I'm the problem.

Dad watches me closely as he drinks the last bit of the bottle and then tosses it away. It clinks on the floor then rolls away into a corner, stinking my room with its pungent smell.

"I told you to stay away from him, but you didn't listen to me," he says in a low, quiet voice.

It's past midnight and the world is sleeping at this hour. There's a silence and peace in the air that almost feels eerie.

"A boy was in your bedroom when you know you are not allowed to have boys in the house, let alone in your bedroom," he finishes and clicks his teeth in disappointment. Averting his gaze from me, he looks down at the stack of books and says, "You made a grave mistake, Hope. And mistakes have punishments."

Bending down, he picks up a book I've read more than twenty times because it's one of my favorites. I consider it my comfort read; the book I read when I'm feeling down and just want to feel something.

I stiffen as he flips through the pages, his eyes taking in the words and my notes.

My thoughts are written on those pages. Anyone who reads them will know me from the inside out.

People find intimacy vulnerable, but I find my favorite books to be read by others vulnerable. They're my most prized possessions because they contain pieces of me I'll never show to anyone.

"Books. You've loved them since you were a kid." He closes the book with a thud using both hands. The cigarette hangs between his mouth and his eyes are now back on me again.

I gulp under his fierce stare, seeing darkness swirl in patterns.

Keeping his eyes on me, he rips apart the book, making sure each page is torn out of the spine in the most brutal manner.

I stand five feet away from him like a statue. I can't move.

I watch him rip it to shreds before starting on the second one, then the third, and the fourth until he's on the last book.

While he's doing it, I only stand and watch. Tears push past my eyes and fall down my cheeks, burning my skin like acid. A few slip under my jaw, move down my throat, and slide down my chest—the place where my heart is weeping.

Dad tears all my books until the floor is a mess of pages and I have no idea which page belongs to which book.

Striding toward me, he steps onto the pages—*pages* that I turned countless times and had my thoughts written on them—and coats them in his dirty footprints. The footprints make my heart clench and more tears rush down my cheeks.

Stopping in front of me, he says, "That'll teach you a lesson as you're so determined to disobey me."

I meet his gaze and all I see is anger. For what, I don't know. I haven't since he first raised his hand to me. "Remember, I straightened your mother into obedience, making sure she doesn't forget that she belongs to me."

My heart pounds in my ribcage as I hear those words.

"Now, will you stay away from that boy or not?"

I nod, trying my best not to stare at the pages on my floor.

"Good, otherwise you won't like what I do," he warns me. His face is grim and his eyes are filled with hatred.

With that, he leaves and closes the door with a loud thud. The sound shakes me and I gasp. Suddenly, I find the room too suffocating to breathe.

Rushing toward the windows, I open them and lean over the sill as I try to get air.

A thorn seems to prick me in the chest. With each breath I draw in, pain spreads through the nerves. It hurts. *It hurts.*

I try to regulate my breathing when I see Nadina looking up at me from her window. She's sitting in a rocking chair, knitting what appears to be a sweater but it's small and red in color.

She stares at me and I feel like she can read me better than Heath does.

I push back and close the windows. When I turn around, the utter mess of my torn books awaits me.

With each step I take, my stomach churns.

I crouch down on the floor and pick up a few pages. My hands shake as I hold them. Some pages are torn so badly that no amount of glue or tape will ever put them back together. They won't be the same as before.

4

HOPE

"Oh my! What the hell happened here?" Mom's alarmed voice enters my ears, and her touch sweeps over the top of my head, pushing away the hair from my face. "Hope, wake up, honey."

Her face is the first thing I see. It takes me a whole minute to realize my head is on her lap and I'm lying on the floor.

Lifting my hand, I bring it to rub my eyes, but pages smack me in the face. Pushing my hand away, I study the pages. Slowly, it all comes back to me what happened.

Bright morning light streams in and fills the room, highlighting the mess. Pages are scattered in every direction. There are small piles amidst the mess—that was me trying to align pages to make the books complete. The bottle of glue is open and the tape is undone beside the pile closest to me.

I don't remember when I fell asleep *or* how I fell asleep. I was sure sleep was the last thing that would happen to me after everything that took place.

Mom cups my face, her thumb caressing the graze Dad gave me on my temple. Her eyes are heavy with remorse.

"What happened?" she asks.

"Dad," I tell her, brimming with hope that maybe this time she'll believe me.

Her gaze searches mine, disbelief lingering in it, as if I'd have the audacity to lie to her.

"Your dad did this to you? Are you serious?" she asks, her thumb touching my cheek where he slapped me. I bet it's still red and swollen.

"I'm telling you the truth. He did this to me," I say. My throat bobs with emotions that I try my best to throw down.

Mom stares at me, the wheels turning in her head in thought.

A whole minute passes and she doesn't speak a word, so I pull my head out of her lap and sit up. Every muscle in my body screams. It hurts everywhere. But strangely, it doesn't matter anymore. In the past few months, pain has become a normal thing for me.

It's surprising how much a person can change in a small amount of time.

"Hope..." Mom reaches for me but I grab her hand and put it on her lap.

"It's fine if you don't believe me."

"That's not true. I believe you... I just... Your dad would never... He never hit you." Her voice breaks as she speaks. A second later, her sniffle eats away at the uncomfortable silence in the room.

I turn my head and catch sight of her crying.

"Alex would never do it to you. He *promised* me. He *told* me." A sob breaks out of her. "I begged him to never go near you. I asked him so many times. He told me."

Her tears fall like raindrops, hitting the floor and creating a puddle of pure despair and heartbreak. Her body shakes as she sits kneeling next to me and completely breaks down.

My hand itches to reach for hers and hold it to provide comfort, but the past few months flash through my mind. All those moments when I tried to reach her in the hope that maybe she'll do something, and when I did, she broke my trust. When she rejected me, she shattered something deep inside me. Making me believe that no one would believe me if I told them.

Mom cries while I listen to her. Until I can't.

My absolute resolve crumbles and I reach for her, because at the end of the day, I love her. Ever since I was a kid, she's the only one who's been there for me. With no friends or siblings, she's stuck by my side, and we used to do everything together. She loved me, cared for me, and protected me. Despite the distance that has come between us in the past couple of months, what she's done for me over the years is not something that I can ever pay back.

"I'm sorry for letting this happen to you," she whispers.

"It's not your fault."

"It is. I should have believed you when you told me. I just never imagined that Alex would hurt you."

Yeah. Me too.

"Dad has changed a lot. He's not the same person anymore." Not that he was good before. He used to abuse Mom. I watched things I shouldn't have. Everything he did changed my perspective on love and relationships.

Love starts off as a bright shade of red, but with time it turns maroon and then black. Darkness encapsulates it, and it morphs into something that only brings pain and emptiness.

That's the definition of love for me.

The kind of love I've watched my whole life.

One that I don't want for myself or anyone.

"He feels the same to me," she murmurs, touching her wedding band with a tenderness that reflects her deep love for him. "When he walked through the door that morning, my heart started beating the same way it did when he first set his eyes on me. There was something about him that pulled me to him, and in one month, I fell in love with him."

Mom smiles sardonically. "I had promised myself I wouldn't get involved with a guy until I had completed my studies and was working, but all my plans went down the drain when I met your dad. His bad reputation attracted me. He was the complete opposite of me, yet we fit together so well. I knew I was with the wrong guy, but he felt right in all the right ways. I was a different person with him. So, I didn't hesitate when he suggested we get eloped. I was in my last semester of med school and I had a lot going on, but the idea of spending the rest of my life with him was more appealing than getting a job and achieving my dreams."

My heart is in my throat. This is the first time Mom has ever told me their story. I've known parts here and there, but never the whole thing.

Her cheeks turn red, and she looks younger. As if I'm seeing the old version of her who met Dad in college. "Then we had you...and...I... We were overjoyed even though we were young and had nothing."

I clear my throat. "Then how did you manage everything?"

Mom cups my cheek—the one that isn't bruised—and says, "I love you more than anything in the world, Hope."

I frown, purely surprised by her words, because her actions toward me have been completely opposite.

"Now, tell me what happened? Why did he hurt you?"

I pull away from her touch and fidget with my hands in my lap, my anxiety multiplying by a factor of a hundred. But I give her a brief summary of everything that happened. The moment I mention Heath, she sighs as if it justifies why Dad hurt me.

"I told you to stay away from that boy. What was he doing in your room so late?"

I freeze under her scrutinizing gaze. "He wanted to talk to me."

"What could he have to say?" Mom presses, long gone are her affection and softness.

"I don't know," I blurt in panic. I can feel the strong and rapid drumming of my heart in every corner of my body. The anxiety that had ebbed before returns now in full force.

Mom watches me intently. Her gaze is so sharp and fierce that it tears down my walls and looks at my heart that contains all my feelings for Heath. Like, care, worry, and fondness. It's all laid out in front of her in the open and I've never felt more vulnerable in my life.

"Hope, do you like this boy?" Each word is spoken slowly and carefully, as if she's scared to hear my response.

I'm equally scared to reply because I know what'll happen.

My gaze averts from her to the pages covering my bedroom floor. The books I cherished so much are now torn pages. The one thing I love the most in the world was damaged by one parent, and now I'm standing on the precipice of allowing another thing that I like—a person—to get ripped apart from me because of the other parent.

The irony makes my heart ache. It physically hurts to even think about Heath bearing any more burden because of me.

"I don't." My voice is steel as I lie to her face.

Mom stares at me. "You do. I can see it in your eyes. Perhaps, you feel even more than just like for him." She shakes her head, disappointment glistens in her eyes. "I never thought you'd lie to me, especially for some guy."

He's not some guy.

I want to scream those words at the top of my lungs.

"Feelings are a passing thing. Whatever you feel for him is invalid. You can get rid of it."

I don't want to get rid of it.

"It's all hormones, honey. You're at an age where your body is going through many changes and this infatuation—or whatever the hell you want to call it—you feel toward this boy can be ignored. Your feelings can be ignored."

I look up to her.

My feelings can be ignored.

It means they hold no value worth treasuring, but rather to be tossed away or erased completely because they are invalid.

Mom clasps my hand and I jolt at her warm touch. She cups my face with the other and looks deep into my eyes. "It's your first time with a boy. It's the thrill and excitement that's pulling you toward him. He doesn't care about you or love you. He's just playing with you, and before you know it, you'll fall in love and get eloped—"

We both stiffen at the same time.

Mom is seeing me in her.

She thinks Heath and I are the same as her and Dad.

I refuse to believe that. Because what I feel for Heath and what he feels for me is real, pure, and strong. He isn't playing around with me. If he wanted to, he would have made sexual advances at me. If anything, he's taking things at my pace, which is basically turtle pace.

"It's not like that with us. Heath really likes me. You have to believe me."

I know I'm making a mistake telling her about this but she needs to know. I can't let her paint Heath in a bad light. He is a good person.

"Last night, when Dad attacked me, Heath pulled him away from me and hit him for me. He protected me!" I tell her.

"It wasn't because he cares about you but because he wants to isolate you from everyone you love."

My eyes widen in shock. "He would never do that."

Mom rubs her temple. "Look, I know you don't believe me, but you have to know that I want the best for you, Hope."

"No, you don't. Because if you did, you wouldn't have let Dad live here or ask me to stay away from Heath. You would have believed me and trusted me. But you don't."

"And I have good reasons not to because I've been where you've been," Mom argues and sits straighter. "I can ask you to stay away from him, but I know you won't, so be prepared for the consequences when they come your way."

She stands up and looks down at me. "As for your Dad, I'll talk to him. What happened last night won't happen again."

She walks, stepping on every page in her path, knowing how much it hurts me. When she's at the door, she looks back at me. "If you're wise, you'll listen to me. I know what's best for you, Hope."

The thud of the door closing echoes in my ears as I contemplate what to do next.

I'm falling in love with a guy who can't be mine. Still, I want him.

5

HEATH

"You know that she's going to beat our asses," Sebastian says from the pillar where he's leaning against.

"I think you mean *your* ass." I remind him from the opposite pillar I'm leaning against.

He smirks. "I didn't forget to mention that it was *your* brilliant idea."

"You fucking asshole." I scowl.

"I told you to tell her from the beginning, but you wanted to keep such a big thing a secret." He sighs heavily and I sense how much this situation is weighing down on him. "You know how she feels about Hope. If it wasn't for her driver dropping her off here, she'd be on her way to Hope right now."

"Who says she can't bribe Elias?" Elias is Marie's driver.

"Because her dad ordered, and he would fire him otherwise."

I switch on my phone and check my messages for the hundredth time. There's no reply from Hope.

My worry is growing with every passing second. I want to spam her phone with messages and calls, but I'm afraid her dad might have her phone and he'll hurt her if he sees them.

The only thing keeping me from going over to Hope's house is Sebastian. He came to my house as soon as I told him I was out of the cell. I'm pretty sure he broke a few signals to get to me. Perhaps he knew that Hope would be the first place I'd go to.

"You're not leaving this place, James," Sebastian warns me. "Otherwise, I will tie you down with the help of Marie."

I scoff. "You're insane."

"I'm right. And you know it." He stares at me, asserting his point. "I'm not letting you go to her, especially not after what happened. You need to be careful."

I narrow my eyes. "I need to protect her."

His gaze softens. "I know and *you are* by staying away from her at the moment."

"You don't know him, Sebastian. I've seen him. I've talked to him. He is a monster." My fists shake by my side, not from fear, but from disgust. I've never seen a true monster in my life before. Someone who'll hurt their own blood with no mercy.

"Look. We both know what'll happen if you go to her. You'll make things worse for you *and* her. Your dad just got you out, and you want to go back in there?" Folding his arms over his chest, he pins me with an intense stare. "Think before you act."

Before I can reply to him, the gates open and a white Mercedes-Benz drives down the driveway. The car stops at the stairs of the porch.

Marie gets out in a hurry. The first thing I notice is, she looks nothing like she usually does. She's dressed in jeans and a white top. Her everyday jewelry is missing and she's wearing slippers when she usually has some funky shoes on. When she looks up at us, my chest shrinks. Her eyes are rimmed red and her cheeks are rosy. Her blonde hair is untamed and wild, as if she didn't even brush it.

She is a complete mess.

She doesn't spare a glance at Sebastian as she climbs the stairs in determination. Midway, her eyes get teary and I fear she'll trip over because of her blurry vision, but she stays composed. Her cheeks are wet by the time she stops in front of me.

Straightening, I step closer to comfort her. "Marie—"

A hard punch knocks my breath out. A second later, another one follows, and soon she's raining down punches on me.

I brace my arms by my side and take every single blow because I know I deserve it. She needs to let out the frustration she's feeling—frustration I caused by deciding to keep her out of this matter.

Marie keeps her jabs coming at me while sobbing. Her cries bring me physical pain. I bet Sebastian is in even more agony listening to them.

But she needs to let it out.

Marie feels happiness and joy to the fullest, but she also feels sadness and pain to the fullest. She is a myriad of emotions and she lives through them vicariously.

"Why didn't you tell me!"

Punch.

"Am I not important to you?"

Punch.

"Do you know how I feel?"

Punch.

"You hid something so big from me!"

Punch.

One after another, she throws those questions at me, and I stay silent, not having an answer to a single one of them.

After a few minutes, her fists stop hitting my chest, and she slumps her head against it and sobs heavily.

"Just why... Why didn't you tell me?" Her voice is low and quiet. Then, in an even quieter tone, she says, "I hate you."

My heart breaks inside my chest. I inhale a deep breath to let the air fill in the cracks that those words have brought me.

Marie is incapable of hating anyone. Fuck. She didn't hate the girls who bullied her, but that has changed. Because of me.

I look over at Sebastian, whose face has contorted into sympathy. His green eyes meet mine and he tries to tell me she doesn't mean that, but we both know at this moment she does.

Hesitantly, I place my hand on her back and say, "I'm so sorry that I didn't tell you."

Turning her head, she looks up at me, and the sight hurts. "Why? Why didn't you tell me?"

"Because I wanted to protect you."

She watches me for a while but doesn't say a word. Which is unusual in itself. Chatterbox is her middle name—given by me.

"But I had the right to know." A single tear drops from her eye and slides down her cheek. "You both knew and I didn't. I could have helped her."

I squeeze her arm. "It's not your fault, Blondie."

She shakes her head and steps away from me. Sebastian is in sync as he crosses the distance and wraps her in his big, muscular arms that will protect her from anything.

Bringing his face down, he talks to her as she hiccups in his chest. Her hands are fisting his T-shirt and her head is tucked against his chest.

The three of us walk inside the silent home. As we cross the living room, I find my father standing over my mother, who's curled up on the sofa. He hands her a teacup with a saucer, then presses a kiss to her temple. When he rises to his full height, his eyes lock on me and he studies me. He then shifts his attention to my best friends, who are staring right back at him.

He opens his mouth to say something, but I turn to my friends and say, "Let's go to my room."

Marie and Sebastian take the hint. As I shut the door and turn on the lock, I breathe out a sigh of relief, knowing that I can openly talk to my friends without worrying about anyone hearing us.

"Hope isn't replying to my texts," Marie announces in panic. "That has never happened before."

Her lips wobble and Sebastian quickly engulfs her in his arms. "Don't think the worst, baby."

"It is the worst when someone doesn't return your messages and calls. I know from experience."

"I'm sorry," he murmurs.

Marie looks up at him and shakes her head. "It's in the past. You're here now." Wrapping her arms around his neck, she kisses him.

Fortunately, one kiss doesn't turn into a make-out session—for which I'm so fucking grateful.

"I think you'll like my idea, Blondie," I say as I take a seat at the back of the couch. "In fact, you might be the only one who'll go with me."

"What idea?" Her interest piques. That's exactly what I need.

If Marie agrees, Sebastian will have no choice but to agree with her. He's so in love with her that he can't refuse her.

"Heath," Sebastian snaps as he glares at me.

Marie looks between us as we stare at each other.

"What's going on, guys?"

"Heath, don't do it," Sebastian warns me.

I want to scream at him that if the roles were reversed, he would have done the same thing. He would have gone to Marie no matter what. It wouldn't matter what kind of monster was in his way, he would have crossed him to get to his girl.

Yes. That's the thing.

Hope is my girl.

I lock my gaze on Marie. "You and I are going to Hope's house to make sure she's okay."

Marie gains some color in her skin. "Yes! We should—"

"No! You two are not going anywhere. It's dangerous."

Marie and I both look at Sebastian, who seems to become the voice of reason today—he always is. I hate that he's always right.

"But, Sebastian—"

"No! Marie. You are not going. I'm not letting you go to her house where that monster lives."

"But you'll be with me. I'll be safe."

"That fucker twisted the whole story and pressed charges on Heath that had him spent a night in cell. If his father didn't have money, he'd be in a courthouse today." He heaves a heavy breath. "Do you even realize how sensitive this matter is?"

Marie and I both stay quiet.

"If her dad sees us at his doorstep, he'll waste no second in kicking us out. God knows what he'll do to you. He. Beats. His. Daughter."

Marie trembles violently and presses a hand to her stomach.

My insides roll in disgust and hatred. The amount of rage consuming me is nowhere close to how he makes me feel. He drives me livid. I can't say if he doesn't appear in front of me again that I wouldn't do anything to him.

Sebastian's eyes soften. "He's been hurting Hope for months. Can you imagine how scared and helpless she felt?"

Marie sniffles. "I'm such a bad friend."

"Gosh, no, baby." He steps closer and tucks her in his arms. "You were what she needed to get through every hard day that she was having. I truly believe that your friendship helped her and she didn't do something that would have taken her away from us."

Suicide.

I close my eyes at that thought.

Fuck. I can't imagine Hope leaving this place.

I don't know what I'll do without her.

In such a short time, she's become my hope. Something I look forward to when I wake up in the morning and go to sleep at night.

That girl has changed me.

Now I can't think of a moment where she's not in it.

My feelings for her are so strong, fierce, and huge that they fill my entire chest till I can't breathe. She's what I'm filled with, and still, there's more room for her to consume me.

She's starting to own me, or maybe she already does. I'm hers, and she's mine.

That is, if she wants to. I'd never want to take away her choice in any matter. But I hope she chooses me, because I choose her.

"Then why didn't she tell me? Is there something I did that made her feel like she couldn't tell me?" Marie asks Sebastian, who looks down at her with such sadness. She always blames herself. It looks like even therapy hasn't helped her let go of that habit.

"No, baby. No!" Sebastian says softly.

"I tried to be good to her, Sebastian. I really tried."

"I know you did. I swear it's not you."

"Then?"

"She was scared."

"But—"

I intervene, knowing I have to put her head at ease. "She didn't tell me either and I asked her a lot of fucking times. Sebastian is right. She was scared."

Marie narrows her eyes at me. "I don't even want to talk to you. You knew and you didn't tell me."

"And I had a very good reason for it. Sebastian agreed."

"Hey! I did not."

"You did?"

They both speak at the same time.

I sigh and run a hand through my hair. "Fine. He wanted to tell you, but I asked him not to. Not until we tackled the situation on our own." I meet her gaze. "I know you, Marie. You would've jumped in front of her dad to save her, and I didn't want it to be you. It had to be me. I'll gladly take a hit for Hope—and I know you will too. But as I said, I was protecting you."

Marie sniffles. "I want to hug you and punch you at the same time."

My lips tug upwards in a smirk. "What will it be then?"

Pulling away from Sebastian, she comes in my direction and wraps her arms around my waist and squeezes. Then comes the punch.

I wince and glare at her.

"I think it'll be both." She smirks back.

"Maybe I hate you," I grit.

"Then I guess our feelings are mutual."

Sebastian wraps an arm around Marie's stomach and tugs her backward. "Calm down, baby."

"I'm mad at you, Heath Travon. You've got months of groveling to do."

I roll my eyes. "As if I care."

"You will when I stop speaking to you."

"I think I'll finally find peace."

"That's what you think, but I know you'll hate it."

"You can think whatever you want, Blondie."

"What makes you think I'm not. When I close my eyes—" she closes her eyes "—I see you buying me lots of cupcakes, my favourite winter drink every day for a month and trying to talk to me."

"Keep those eyes closed for a long time because that's the only place where I'll be groveling."

Marie opens her eyes and grins. "You never know. A lot of strange things happen."

"What do you mean by that?" I arch an eyebrow.

"You see, a few months ago, you were walking around with an empty heart. But now your heart is filled with love. You're always thinking about Hope. And when you're near her, you can't stop looking at her. And I saw you kissing her. You couldn't stop. The guy I knew would never fall hard for a girl, but look at you now."

My heart drums inside my chest.

Those words are not words. They're facts.

Marie knew it from day one. Just like Sebastian.

I set my gaze on Sebastian, who's watching me with a smile. Asshole. I bet he's dying to say something obnoxious to me.

Fall hard for a girl.

That's ridiculous. I'm not in love with Hope. I just have feelings for her—feelings that won't go away. The fact should bother me, but it doesn't. As long as they're here, I'm connected to her, and I crave that connection. I want her. And I want her bad. But that's all there is to what I feel for her.

Not love.

Definitely not love.

"Marie, you're annoying." I can feel heat in my cheeks.

"Maybe, but I don't care. Sebastian said what truly matters is what you think of yourself." She presses a soft kiss to his cheek and leans back in her chair.

I don't even know why she pays hundreds of dollars to that therapist when she's got a brilliant one right by her side.

Standing up from the couch, I ask, "So, are you coming with me or not?"

Marie nods. "I am."

"For fuck's sake," Sebastian murmurs. "Didn't you guys hear me? I don't want you two to go there."

"We just want to make sure Hope is okay," Marie says softly.

I stay quiet, letting her take the reins of this request because only then will it be granted.

"Me too, but—" he rubs his temple, "don't give me the puppy eyes, baby. Don't fucking do it."

A smile tugs at my lips, and I have to rub them to keep it from showing.

"Marie, you can have anything but *this*, baby," he pleads.

Marie goes a step further and grabs his hand. "Please, Sebastian. I want to make sure that Hope is okay."

"I can't have you in that house."

"Please."

"He could hurt you."

"Please."

"We don't know what will happen."

"Please."

"I'm telling you—fuck! Fine. We'll go. But only on one condition."

Marie throws her arms around his waist and eagerly nods. "Anything."

"If her parents are at home, we won't go anywhere near her house, do you hear me?"

"But how would I check up on Hope then?"

"You won't."

"But that's the reason we're going."

"I know, but you're the most important person in my life. I can't let anything bad happen to you. You're all I've left, anyway."

Marie shuts up for good and gives him a nod.

Sebastian said Marie can't go inside, but he never said anything about *me*.

SEBASTIAN WASN'T KIDDING. HE WAS SERIOUS ABOUT NOT letting Marie and me go inside. For the past ten minutes, we've been sitting in his jeep, watching Hope's house like creeps, looking for any signs whether her parents are home or not.

"Maybe we should knock on the door and check?" Marie suggests.

"No!" Sebastian quickly shuts her down.

"Then how would we know?"

"We wait."

"We've been waiting for more than ten minutes. It looks so quiet and lonely. Like no one lives there."

"That's exactly where people like them live." His voice is heavy with memories.

"Her mom would be at work. Hope told me she works a lot. So that means her dad..." Marie shakes in her seat. Her hand covers her mouth as she stares intently at the house.

"Marie, hey, look at me. Calm down." Sebastian reaches over and places a kiss on her temple and wraps his arm around her.

"Hope is alone...with him," she whispers.

"We don't know that."

She takes a deep breath. Turning her head, she looks at him. "We need to help her, Sebastian."

"We can't. This is a dangerous situation. You could get hurt."

"It'll be worth it," she replies.

He cups her face and leans his forehead against hers. "I've been through shit like this. You know that, baby. Because of me, you got hurt, and it killed me. You know it killed me." He meets her gaze. "If that man hurts you, Hope will be devastated and she will push you away to protect you. Just like she's done for the past months."

"But who will protect her? Who will save her? She's so...fragile. How can he hurt her?"

Those questions feel like arrows piercing my chest.

"For fuck's sake." Moving away from the center of the front seats, I open the door when Sebastian grabs me by my arm.

"Heath, what the hell are you doing?"

I give him an annoyed look. "What does it look like? I'm going to check up on her."

He tugs me inside forcefully. "You're the last person to be going anywhere near that house."

"I don't care, because I need to see her," I reply, my voice tense.

"I know, but I think—"

My eyes clash with his and I'm shaking in anger. "I haven't heard back from her. Not a single fucking word. I've called her. I've texted her. Nothing. I don't know if she's okay. And I need her to be okay. Because if she's not, then I..." My voice cracks and I hate how weak I'm looking in front of the two of them. "I just need to know that she's okay."

Sebastian watches me intently with worry glistening in his eyes. He's afraid for me.

Between the three of us, he's dealt with fucked up shit the most, especially with parents so he can relate to Hope. Even back when I suggested that we swoop in and save Hope, he was rational enough to think things through and not let me take a wrong step. I hate him for it, but deep down I know things are complicated and I need to proceed with caution if I want to protect Hope.

"I don't think you should go, but I also know that you won't listen to me." He sighs heavily. "You care too much about her."

Yes, I do.

I care a lot about Hope.

More than the limit. If there is any.

Without saying a word, I exit the car and start making my way toward her house. As always, I can sense that something is wrong in this place. Maybe it's the eerie silence or perhaps the lack of life spilling out of it. Just by looking at it, you can tell it's not a home.

I stand in the driveway, hoping to go toward the back and climb up to her room, when I see a slight movement in the kitchen.

A chill travels down my spine and I prepare myself to face that asshole again.

Sebastian will get so mad at me.

"I suggest you leave," an old woman speaks from nearby. I recognize that voice. I've spoken to her before.

Averting my gaze from the house, I lock it on her. She's in a pink gown, with her gray hair pulled back into a braid. She's wearing jewelry all over, and it's all types of colors and designs. I'm sure Marie will love this woman.

"I'm not leaving," I tell her.

She watches me, then goes back to moving the sticks and knitting a red sweater.

"It's better that you do. Don't get the girl into any more trouble."

My heart drops.

"I would never do that."

"Why?" She arches an eyebrow, daring me not to lie.

My hand reaches up to my hair, and I run my fingers through it, feeling self-aware. Fuck. Why am I feeling hot all of a sudden?

"Because I like her," I finally say.

Her gaze snaps up to me and she studies me. "Have you told her?"

"Yes."

"Good."

"You told me to take care of her." I remember the little chat we had when I came to pick up Hope to go bowling. She asked what my intentions were about her. I told her we were just friends. She told me to take care of her. Something she didn't need to ask me for. I'll always take care of Hope, even more than I take care of myself.

"And it looks like you do. You're here."

"I need to go inside. I'll see you—"

"Don't go. She's not alone."

My spine turns rigid. Fuck. Please don't let it be her dad she's with right now.

My tone is tense as I ask, "Do you know who's with her?"

The woman nods.

"It's her dad, isn't it?" My hands curl into fists beside my sides.

She shakes her head as her eyes fill with sadness. "Worse. It's her mother."

My eyebrows knit together in confusion. "She doesn't hit her."

The old woman sighs. "No, she does the absolute worst. She plays with her head. She says things to her that hurt her, and for years, she's done it." She breathes in a long pull of air. "I don't need to live in that house to know exactly what goes on in there. I hear and see everything and let me tell you. It's no home for a young girl to live in."

I stare at her, too stunned to speak a word. I've known Hope for a few months and I've come to the conclusion that her parents are shit and she is living in a hell house. But this woman knows so much more about this family and hearing her say all these words triples my worry.

Now I want Hope out of that house more than anything.

I want to protect her and keep her safe. I want her to feel good. I want her to be okay.

Will I be able to do that?

"I thought her dad was the worst," I confess.

She shoots me a dry smile. "Oh! He is, but her mother isn't far behind. The two of them are a toxic pair bound together by love. I've seen this film a hundred times in all my living years and I can tell you it never ends well."

"I need to see her," I say, looking at the house, specifically Hope's window. It's closed.

"She's okay," the woman replies with no hint of a lie. "I saw her with my own eyes. She is okay. You better go home."

"But I need to see her for myself."

She gives me a sharp look. "Now is not the time or the day. Go home before you create any more trouble for her. She's already had enough."

The command in her voice makes me turn around and walk back to the car. Her gaze follows me all the way.

I climb into the back, and sounds fill the space inside just as I close the door.

"Why didn't you go in?"

"Who was that old woman?"

"Do you know her?"

"What were you guys talking about?"

I close my eyes and lean my head back, granting myself a moment to take everything in.

She said she's okay.

She better be or I don't know what I'll do.

On the way to my house, I tell my friends everything and the three of us decide that seeing Hope in school is the safest way. Because none of us wants to cause Hope trouble.

Despite this, my heart and body ache to see her and hold her in my arms. I want her near me so I can calm the chaos whirring inside me, because having her away from me is unbearable. I want to spend all my time with her and get to know so she isn't a stranger to me, but a person I've known since I was a kid. And God, I want to kiss her. Fuck.

I want to kiss her until I can't anymore. My lips turn numb and my heart plummets to the ground with beating so fast.

She's all I want.

She's all I need.

Monday is so far away when I have such huge feelings for her. But I'll wait for her.

6

HOPE

My phone takes hours to charge enough to turn on. I know it's time to get a new one, but there's no way I can afford it right now. A new phone will cost a lot and if I want to stop bothering Heath with my bracelet business, I need to get a model similar to his, but I know the one he has is super expensive.

If it comes down to books or a phone, I'll always choose books. I bet Heath wouldn't think like that. He'd tell me to buy a phone because it's an investment for the business I've been running.

My business... It's been two days since I checked Heath's phone. I wonder if there are any orders. I wish there were hundreds of orders so I could get busy and stop my brain from thinking.

Since my conversation with Mom, I can't stop thinking about how little I know about my parents. All the things they told me have further stories connected to them. I don't think I'll like it when I get to know all those.

The second my phone lights up, it starts chiming with messages and calls. I quickly switch it to silent and watch the notifications bombard my screen. At this rate, my phone is going to glitch and freeze up.

After two whole minutes, the notifications stop coming, and I swipe up the home screen and click on the messages app. There are a hundred and seven messages from Heath and two hundred messages from Marie.

My heart sinks.

She knows.

The thought makes my hands clammy and the rhythm of my heart picks up.

I knew that I wouldn't be able to hide the truth from her forever, but still. The fact that she heard it from someone else, not me, breaks my heart. I know I wouldn't have been able to tell her anyway, but still. It was my truth to tell.

I'm still thinking about it when Heath's name pops up on the screen. He's calling me.

I decline the call in panic.

Is he out of the cell?

At once worry clings to me and I want nothing more than to talk to him, but it's late at night and it's so quiet in the house after the disaster that unfolded a few hours ago.

Mom and Dad had a huge fight and it ended with him smashing a beer bottle against the wall. He didn't hurt Mom, but he yelled at her. I was the centre of their conversation as Mom took my side, but Dad wasn't having it. So he did the one thing he knows the best. He terrorized her, and it worked. She stopped talking and the topic was pushed under the rug like it wasn't even there in the first place.

They returned to their room, and a while later, I could hear noises that made me sick to my stomach. I can't believe she let him touch him, let alone sleep with her.

Gosh! Just thinking about it makes me want to puke.

> Heath: Pick up my call. I want to talk to you.

I see his text and switch off my screen.

Curled up on my side, facing the window, I look out at the night sky, which is breathtaking with shimmering stars. I like seeing them.

My phone buzzes again and I flip it over and see another text.

> Heath: I know you're reading my texts. Say
> something, please.

What am I even supposed to say to him? Because of me, he spent a night in a cell and has a record now. I got him into this mess. I'm nothing but trouble to him.

It hurts. It hurts a lot. Because I don't want to be that person to him. I want to be his safe place like he is mine. *But I'm not.* I'm the storm that wreaks havoc in his life.

Another text pops up.

> Heath: Rose, talk to me.

Rose. He has a nickname for me. That wasn't supposed to happen. He wasn't supposed to give me a nickname—a nickname that gives me butterflies. Every. Single. Time.

> Heath: Fine. You don't need to reply. Just keep
> reading my texts, okay.

I hold my phone tighter.

Why is this guy so good to me? He doesn't have to be, and he isn't with most people, but he is with me. He's the sweetest to me.

> Heath: I hope you're okay.
>
> Heath: Why the fuck am I saying it? Of course
> you're not fucking okay. You must be hurt.
>
> Heath: I'm so sorry that you got hurt because
> of me.
>
> Heath: I don't want you to get hurt because of me.
>
> Heath: Like ever.
>
> Heath: So I'm sorry that you're hurt.
>
> Heath: Are you crying? Please tell me you're not
> crying. You know I hate it when you cry.
>
> Heath: You look awful when you cry.

Heath: Absolutely hideous.

Heath: No! Fuck. You're not hideous.

Heath: YOU ARE THE MOST BEAUTIFUL GIRL THAT I KNOW.

Heath: IN THE WHOLE WORLD.

Heath: AND YOU HAVE THE MOST BEAUTIFUL EYES. I LIKE THEM A LOT. NOT MORE THAN YOU, OF COURSE.

Heath: I LIKE YOU THE MOST.

I like you the most.
I like him the most too.

Heath: I hope you like me too or otherwise I don't know what the fuck I'll do.

Heath: I know you have feelings for me.

Heath: The way you kiss me, there's no faking it.

My cheeks turn red. I can't deny that I enjoy kissing him. It's one of my favourite things to do. Now I understand why people kiss and why characters love making out. For some, it's the thrill and passion, but for me, it's the comfort and sweetness.

I tap on the message bar and start typing.

Hope: You're a good kisser.

I watch the dots appear and disappear on the screen. It's like he can't decide what he wants to send.

This is the first time we've talked since the incident. No calls, no messages. Nothing. All we did was wonder about each other, hoping we'd be okay.

Heath: That's because I like kissing you.

Insecurity hits me out of nowhere. I assume Heath has kissed other girls. There's no way he hasn't. The way he moved his lips and kissed me... Yes, there's no doubt that he hasn't. And it makes me a little jealous that plenty of girls had him before me. He was someone else's, before he wanted me.

> Hope: More than the others...?

I press my hand over my chest as I try to contain my heart inside. I don't want him to think I'm jealous or anything. Just a little sad.

Heath: What others?

> Hope: Other girls...

Heath: They meant nothing. I don't even remember kissing them. It was fucking nothing.

Heath: I consider you my first kiss because I felt everything when I kissed you. It was the best kiss.

I smile at that because that's exactly how I feel about our first kiss and every other after it.

Heath: Tell me you're okay. Please.

> Hope: I'm okay.

Heath: Are you hurt?

> Hope: No

Heath: Don't lie to me. Tell me the truth.

> Hope: I'm not lying to you. I swear, I'm okay.

Heath: Did something happen when you got home?

> Hope: No.

Heath: Did he leave you alone?

> Hope: Yes.

Heath: I find that very hard to believe.

Hope: He got drunk and watched TV.

Heath: Where is he now?

Hope: Downstairs, sleeping in the bedroom with Mom.

Heath: Can I come over? I'll be quiet when climbing through your window.

Hope: No! Please don't come here. I don't want you to get into any trouble.

Heath: I'll be fine, Rose.

Heath: You don't need to worry about me.

Hope: Please, don't come here.

If he comes here, I know bad things will happen. Dad will find out, and what happened the other day will happen again. I don't want that.

I don't want him to get hurt any more than he already has.

Besides, if he were here, standing a few feet away from me and staring at me, I know I wouldn't be able to break his heart by ending things with him. Like an addict, I'd cling to him, even for a short amount of time, and would do anything that he wanted from me. Despite knowing I'm nothing but a thorn that'll prick him and make him bleed. The total opposite of the nickname 'Rose' that he calls me by.

Guilt consumes me.

Hope: Are you okay?

Heath: I'm fine, Rose.

Hope: How's the wound?

Heath: It'll heal. Nothing serious.

Hope: I'm so sorry for what happened.

Heath: Don't be. I'd do it again just to protect you.

My heart clenches seeing those words.

Heath: I'll pick you up for school tomorrow.

Hope: No. It's too risky. I'll just see you at school.

Heath: That's too much wait.

Heath: You have no idea how badly I want to see you.

Heath: All I can think about is you.

Heath: Your face, your body, your hair, your eyes, your lips... I think about your lips a lot.

I can barely breathe.

Heath: If you let me kiss you I wouldn't stop.

Heath: Unless you want me to stop.

My heart is beating so loudly I can hear it in my ears.

Hope: I only stop because you leave me breathless.

Heath: Good.

One word. *Good*. It shouldn't make my stomach warm.

Heath: Are you sure I can't come over?

Hope: Yes.

Heath: I can come over anytime you want, Rose. You just tell me, okay. It doesn't matter what time it is, I'll be there for you.

Hope: You don't have to.

Heath: I want to. So don't think too much about it.

Hope: I can't help it. I think a lot.

Heath: Then let me come over and distract you. I assure you, I can be a really good distraction.

Crimson red burns my cheeks and my entire face heats up at that message. I'm sure he didn't mean it in the way I've taken it...or maybe he did. *I don't know.* I'm new to this. Despite reading so many romance books and knowing about feelings like the back of my hand, I'm still clueless.

It's the self-doubt that keeps throwing excuses at me. I know Heath likes me. He told me himself. But after what happened on Friday night, I can't bring myself to understand why he still wants to talk to me.

Doesn't he realize that I got him hurt? He got stabbed because of me. I cleaned his blood off the floor with my own hands. The sight crosses my mind whenever I close my eyes. I can feel my hands getting wet with the stains of his blood. And the worst of it all, he spent a night in a cell because of me.

By the time I reach all these conclusions after long thought, all I want to do is shut off my phone and go to sleep.

I need courage for tomorrow because there's no way I'm letting Heath bear any more hurt and trouble because of me. He doesn't deserve it. And if he stays with me, things will only get worse, and he'll get caught up in the crossfire and eventually he'll be forced to hate me.

7

HOPE

School has never intimidated me, until today. All I want to do is run away and never come back here.

My whole body fills with dread and fear at the idea of going to school today as I make my way toward it.

I haven't even stepped into the hallways, and I'm already trembling like a leaf.

It's Monday, meaning everybody will be there. If the news didn't travel over the weekend, then it will today. By the end of the day, everyone will know what happened. This is a small town where people gossip and word travels fast.

My feet feel heavy and reluctant to move. I'm half convinced I have stones in my Converse, given how difficult it is to take a single step. One step. It shouldn't be that hard.

It's okay.

People already act like I'm invisible.

I probably won't be the headline of today.

There could be a chance they have no idea about what happened.

Like a chant, I repeat those words in my head, hoping they can give me courage. I mean, books have always helped. Why can't my own words help me?

My phone buzzes in the back pocket of my jeans. I know it's Heath. I just don't have the courage to talk to him right now. Not when I'm standing ten feet away from the school building and commanding myself to enter it.

Can I miss school?

But where would I even go?

The library is my sanctuary, but Heath and my friends will find me there.

I don't want to be found.

I want to be lost.

Today, more than ever, I wish to be alone.

But I can't miss classes. If I fall behind and get bad grades, the situation at home will become even worse.

Inhaling a deep breath, I stare at the school and the students lingering on the grounds. No one has noticed me yet. As usual, they're all busy talking and laughing among themselves, not paying attention to others. *Please act like you don't know me.*

Holding the novel open in my hands, I fix my eyes on the page and start paving my way into the school. I've only taken a few steps when I hear their voices.

'She's here.'

'Did you hear her boyfriend beat up her dad?'

'He spent the night in a cell.'

'She went to visit him.'

I was wrong. So wrong. They all know.

My skin crawls under the sheer attention of every single person who's watching and talking about me. I feel like scratching and making myself bleed because all at once, the blood flowing through my veins resembles a river of hot, molten lava.

Turn around and leave.

I can't.

I close my eyes momentarily, then stare back at the paragraphs of the long monologue that are best for this occasion. Blindly, I climb the stairs and push through the doors of the hallway. The eyes follow my movements.

Don't look at anyone.

Walk straight to the math class and take the seat in the back and pretend—

Silence reigns over the hallway the second I step inside. The air thickens and tension fills the space.

I can feel it.

The attention. The stares. The voices.

My hands start shaking.

This is too much for me. All I want to do is get out of here.

Out of all the days in my life, today I want to be invisible. I want to wrap myself in the invisibility cloak and just sit in the corner while the world moves on.

Tears build up at the back of my eyes and I truly have no idea where I'm going. At this rate, I might collide with someone—

My book jams hard into someone's chest.

"I'm so sorry—" My voice cracks. I'm one second away from having a meltdown right here, right now.

A finger settles under my chin and tips back my head. Through my blurry vision, I see him.

Heath Travon. His blue eyes stare down at me.

My head quietens. The voices subduing to nothingness.

"You never watch where you're going," he says. Lifting his other hand, he wedges his finger between the pages, closes the book, and plucks it out of my hand in one effortless move that leaves me surprised in the way that butterflies fill my stomach and dispel the cloud of anxiety.

His arm wraps around my waist and he pulls me to his body.

"Heath—"

His soft, warm lips brush against mine and just like that the whole world fades away. He is the only person I can focus on.

Nudging my lips once more, he asks for permission. I grant it to him by kissing him, wanting to get lost in him instead of the voices in my head or the whispers flying in the air.

We kiss in front of everyone, not caring one bit about the number of eyes that are fixed on us.

Wanting to be close to him, I put my hands on his chest that's burning hot and seek in its warmth. I want to infuse myself in his skin and hide.

I feel his hand open and sprawl over my back as he pulls me flush against him, just as his mouth kneads mine in a slow and long kiss that's filled with the feeling I missed you.

I meet his strokes with equal passion and longing.

People murmur around us, but I only focus on him and my pounding heart.

When we pull away, I tuck my face into his chest. My breathing is out of control.

The first thought that crosses my mind is, I will be the headline today.

Heath nuzzles his face in the side of my neck. I twist my head a little and meet his worried gaze.

Are you okay?

No.

Wrapping my arms around his waist, I snuggle into him and he holds me tightly against him. Just being this close to him makes me feel okay. It's like oxygen fills my lungs and I can finally breathe.

"I'm here. You have nothing to worry about." He presses a kiss to my head. "I've got you."

The voices around us get louder, and the scrutinizing gazes watch us with interest.

I shiver in his hold because I can hear them—or at least my head can, even when it's made up.

She kissed him.

Is she dating him?

I knew she was a freak behind those books.

My heart scratches the walls of my ribs, desperate to get out and be free. But I keep it inside, hidden under my skin and alive with my blood.

You know you have to break up with him, don't you? my brain says.

The mere suggestion makes my heart clench. I don't know how I'll do it, but I have to. It's the right thing to do. I truly believe it.

"Let's get out of here," Heath murmurs against my temple.

I give him a nod and start pulling away from him.

Grabbing my hand, he leads me out of the crowded hallway. People hardly spare us space to move and we bump into them, until Heath swipes out his arm and pushes everyone out of the way. The chatter picks up and I try to tune out every word I hear.

I expect Heath to take me to his car, but he climbs up the stairs leading to the library on the first floor.

When we pass by it, I stare at his back but he keeps going as if he has the perfect place in mind.

We climb another set of stairs, and another, before he pushes the door that opens to the rooftop. Dry, cold October air brushes against my skin and I draw in a deep, long breath, finding it easy to breathe.

Heath closes the door behind me. Leaning me against it, his mouth is on me, and I just melt.

His one hand settles on my waist and the other cups the back of my head as he kisses me long and deep, taking his sweet time with no care in the world.

Butterflies come alive in my stomach and wildly flutter around. I wonder if he gets butterflies, too? Or if the chemicals in his body mix up and reactions happen? Maybe it's only me who feels like she's standing on the edge of the mountain peak and he's in the air, asking me to jump and I do without a second thought. Because I trust him.

Because I trust him.

The realization hits me like cold water. I trust him with my body but this is different because now that he knows all my secrets, I still trust him.

Standing on my tiptoes, I fist his T-shirt into my quivering fingers and inch closer to him. The longer he kisses me, the more my hands move over the broad expanse of his solid, warm chest that resembles a rock. My hands rise and touch his skin—it's burning and there is the thrum of his rapid pulse.

I jerk back in response.

Oh my God.

I've never touched him like this before.

My head thuds back against the door but since his palm has it cushioned, he takes the brunt of the hit.

His eyes study me in detail. "What happened? Did I do something wrong?"

I shake my head.

"Was it the kiss? I didn't use tongue."

I shake my head again.

"I made you breathless, didn't I?"

I shake my head, then nod, thinking that's a better excuse than telling him what really happened.

His thumb swipes back and forth on my jawline. His touch is so soft and gentle, as if I'm the most delicate and precious thing in the world. It's an exquisite feeling, knowing someone values you so much that they are careful with how they hold you.

Slowly, he tips my head back and aligns our gazes, leaving me no choice but to stare at him.

"I'm beginning to know it when you lie to me, Hope."

I let out a sharp exhale.

He used my first name.

That means trouble.

Blue eyes search mine. "And trust me, I don't like it one bit."

"I'm sorry," I murmur.

"You don't need to apologize."

"But—"

"I'd like the truth instead."

I stare at him, then look down at his chest. The simple black T-shirt paired with the same black jeans and black Converse. Nothing is new about his attire, but he still looks so good in it. So good.

Closing my eyes, I take a deep breath. *Here it goes.*

"It was... I... My hands..." I palm my eyes as my cheeks burn in embarrassment.

"Keep going," he encourages and his touch continues on my jaw, making it harder for me to tell him. "I want to know."

"I touched your neck and felt your pulse."

His thumb stops moving.

I peek at him and find him frowning at me. "*That* made you pull away?"

I nod. "I've never felt it...before."

Heath watches me, then removes his hands from my body and instead cups my face in his warm palms. His touch is so gentle that I can't help but lean into it.

"I know this is all new for you, fuck, it's all new for me too. We'll take everything at your pace. So just talk to me, okay. Don't lie and hide things from me. Not anymore."

The only thing I focus on is the part. *We'll take everything at your pace.*

"You want to be with me?" I ask, feeling stupid, because in my head, I intend to end things with him. But that kiss, the way he holds me, and now this. No guy will ever be him. They won't care about me like he does. And maybe I'm being entirely selfish but I like him so much that I don't want to end things with him. I don't want to stop being his friend and the person he kisses and holds.

Heath stares deep into my eyes as if he can read all my thoughts. "I want to be with you."

"After everything that happened?" I ask because I need to be sure.

"After everything that happened."

He doesn't mean that.

Clearly, he doesn't know what he's talking about.

I shake my head to get out of his hold, but he doesn't let go of my face and me. So I give up.

"No! You are confused and you don't know what you're talking about," I say, my throat constricting. An ache throbs through its walls and I gulp to keep going. "If you stay with me, you'll only get into trouble. You'll get hurt. You'll bleed."

"Hope—"

I look up and meet his intense gaze. "There was blood on my bedroom floor. *Your blood*. I had to stare at it and think about how badly you got hurt because of me. I was the reason for getting you hurt."

My voice cracks. "And then I had to clean it. It took me an hour because it wouldn't come off. So I kept scrubbing hard...really hard... until my hands ached..."

Tears fall from my eyes and dampen his palms.

"And I couldn't stop thinking. No matter what I did, it just wouldn't leave my head." I sob.

"Hey, listen to me—"

I shake my head and sniffle. "And then Dad came into my room... and he tore down my book wall."

"What?" His voice rises and shock and anger flash on his perfect face.

I nod and cry harder. "He took my books, one by one, and ripped every single page out of them. There were some pages that he just ripped to shreds."

"Son of a bitch!"

"I tried glue and tape, but the pages... They wouldn't join together." A soul-shattering sob wracks through me and my whole body goes weak. He ruined the one thing I love the most in the world.

Strength leaves me and I crumble but Heath steadies me against him and wraps his arms so tightly around me that I can't remember the feeling of being alone—a feeling I've felt my whole life but it just goes away.

I cry like a baby in his chest and he lets me.

No matter what I tell myself, the tears don't stop and I completely embarrass myself in front of him.

At once, my feet are off the ground. I pull away from his chest and realize he's lifted me in his arms.

"Put me down! I'm heavy," I whisper, my voice coarse.

"I can carry you just fine, Rose," he says and walks us toward a corner.

Sitting down, he leans against the wall and keeps me in his lap. I try to get off him but he stops me by putting his hand on my thigh and squeezing hard.

Heat pools into my stomach and I look at him.

"I'm not letting you go anywhere, Rose." Lifting his hand, he wipes away all my tears and then cups the side of my face. "I told you, *I've got you.*"

"I can't sit here for long. Your legs will start to hurt and you have a wound."

"You can sit here forever and I won't complain," he tells me softly. "My legs will be just fine. The wound doesn't even hurt. Don't worry about me."

"Someone has to," I say.

His eyes soften as he leans down and kisses me. "I promise I'm fine."

He starts pulling away but I put my hand on his neck and stop him. That pulse I felt earlier is right there, fluttering under his hot skin.

"I think it's best if we stop seeing each other." Tears cloud my vision. "I don't want you to get hurt because of me."

"Maybe I want to get hurt for you."

"Heath..."

He grabs my hand that's holding his neck and brings it to his chest, where his heart is beating. "Do you really want that, Rose?"

I stay silent and look down at my lap because looking into his eyes and telling him that I don't want to see him will be the biggest lie I've ever spoken. And even if I somehow say it, I know my heart will shatter into a million pieces, right here, right now.

"You don't want it. Good. Otherwise, it would've been alarming to others that I had resorted to stalking."

That makes me look at him.

He leans closer. "What? You thought I'd just give up on the only girl that makes my heart beat this fast." He presses my palm harder into his chest. My hand vibrates with the strong thrum of his heartbeats, each one strong and fast, as if calling for my name. "I'm not letting you go and I'm not giving up on you. From now on, you're my girl."

"Your girl?" I ask, clutching his T-shirt into my fingers.

He nods, staring deep into my eyes. "Yeah."

My cheeks turn red and I quickly break eye contact.

His girl?

What does that mean?

Are we in a relationship now?

Heath Travon is my boyfriend.

No, wait. That seems too good to be true.

"Look at me, Rose."

As if he's put a spell on me, my body does as he says.

"It isn't your fault."

I shake my head. "It is. If you hadn't met me—"

"Then my life would've been miserable. I would've been alone and angry with no hope in life. Ever since you've come into my life, I have this light that casts away my darkness, and I want to bathe in it all the time. I wake up in the morning because I want to, not because I need to. And when I'm with you...I just want to stay with you. Because I like talking to you, listening to you. I even like making bracelets with you. And when you smile at me or laugh at something, I get this feeling inside me. It's like fireflies or some shit is fluttering in my stomach. There's warmth, light and this sense of nervousness because I don't ever want *this thing*—that is between us—to go away." He pauses. "Maybe you can try and stay away from me, Rose. But I can't. I fucking can't. I will not let you go, not because you asked me to and I have to be the nice guy—which I'm not—but because I know you and I know deep down you want me."

"I want you," I tell him, "but because of me, you got hurt and spent a night in the cell. I can't ever let that happen to you, because it will happen again if you stay with me."

"It wasn't your fault. Nothing that happened is your fault."

"But—"

"No! Don't fucking say it. I did it because I wanted to and I will do it again." He brushes my hair away from my face. "I have to keep you safe."

"You don't need to go to such lengths for me. I'm not worth it."

"Because you're worth far more." He caresses my cheek. "And I'll show it to you."

"With me, your life will be complicated."

"I like complicated."

"You'll get into trouble."

"I'm always getting into trouble."

"You'll get hurt."

"I'll heal."

"Your feelings will change."

"A night in the cell didn't change a single fucking thing so I know nothing else will."

"My parents will hate you."

"It doesn't matter to me." He kisses me. "Only *you* matter to me."

"You'll always worry about me."

"I already do."

"Loving me will be hard because I have anxiety. I also get panic attacks and I'm always overthinking," I tell him all my weak points, feeling like I've stripped myself naked in front of him. He can see all the marks, scars, and imperfections that are usually hidden under clothes, creating a pretty image. But now, all that's left is the ugliness.

It takes me a few seconds to realize I used the word *love*.

Oh no.

What have I done?

He only likes me.

I sit up straight in his lap, still, I'm short. Panic washes over me and I blurt. "I'm so sorry. I didn't mean to tell you to love me. I wasn't trying...to... I..."

I fumble so hard that I can barely form any words.

My hands shake and my heart beats so fast I feel like it'll tear down my chest and come out.

I stare at his chest, unable to make eye contact with him. The embarrassment is so hard, red paints my face and neck and turns my skin so warm I start sweating in my cream sweater.

This is so awkward.

Heath chuckles and his chest vibrates with a deep and husky sound that pulls my attention.

Wrapping his arm around my waist, he tucks me in his chest and looks down at me.

"You like to steal my thunder, don't you, Rose?"

My lips pucker like a fish. No sound or words come out.

"And let's not worry about love, complications, troubles, your parents, and other stuff. I want you and you want me, it's just as simple as that."

"But what about—"

He shoves his fingers into my hair and kisses me hard. So hard that all my thoughts scatter and disappear into oblivion.

By the time he unlocks our lips, I don't even know what I was going to say. All I can think about are the tingles that dance on my lips and the way they feel a little swollen.

"I see. That gets you to stop thinking."

Before I can reply to him, the door to the rooftop opens and Marie stands there with Sebastian.

8

HOPE

MARIE TAKES A STEP IN MY DIRECTION, BUT SEBASTIAN PUTS his arm around her waist and pulls her back. He says something to her in a low voice.

"She knows, doesn't she?" I whisper to Heath without averting my gaze from her, who has red-rimmed eyes and her lips are trembling. She looks like she wants to cry a river and I know it'll be for me.

"She does," he answers.

I stiffen. Shame washes over me. I want to find a corner and hide, just so I don't see the hurt on her face and the sadness in her eyes. She looks miserable and worried—both things I don't want her to be.

I dimmed her light. Her bright, warm light that is magic and suits her is now replaced by gloominess.

Now all I see is the girl who's shed tears for me, looking distressed.

Heath rubs my back and draws my attention to him, as if he can read my thoughts and knows it upsets me seeing Marie like this. "It's not your fault."

"It is."

"It is fucking not," he says harshly. "Don't blame yourself for a second. *It is not your fault.*"

I stare at him and let his words sink in.

It is not my fault. I repeat those words a couple of times but I still feel guilty.

Heath's gaze softens and he adds, "She's your friend, that's why she's worried. I'm sure if the roles were reversed, you'd feel the same. Don't you think so?"

I nod, remembering the time when Marie shared about her past with me, and I started crying, because I didn't want any of those things to happen to her.

"You know, she's been anxious about you ever since Sebastian told her. She beat me black and blue for not telling her. So just take it easy on her."

Looking back at her, I ask, "She must hate me."

"She does not."

"She looks like she cried a lot. It is because of me."

"Don't worry about it."

How can I not? My best friend looks nothing like herself.

Marie and I stare at each other for a while, until she rips away from Sebastian and runs toward me.

I stand up from Heath's lap and wrap my arms around myself. My stomach ties up into a rope of knots. It twists and turns as anxiety starts to grow.

She comes to a halt, and there's only a couple of feet between us. Too little yet too much.

"Hi," she says, her eyes filled with tears.

"Hi," I reply, my voice cracking.

No words come to me, and by the look of it, she's feeling the same. Her lower lip wobbles and she rubs her arms.

I fidget with my fingers, my anxiety kicking up.

Sebastian comes up and stands beside her but I don't look at him. I can't. All my attention is fixed on Marie, who wants to say everything and nothing at once.

Heath stands next to me. And just being this close to him, I find strength to face Marie.

"I...I wanted to tell you—" I start.

"Can I hug you?" she sobs.

Without thinking, I cross the distance between us and wrap my arms around her in a vice grip. Her arms quickly wrap around me, and instantly, I'm completely enveloped by her—everything she is, good, light, comfort, and warmth. Being this close to her is like sitting under the sun and letting its hot beams melt away your fears, sadness and loneliness.

Marie starts crying, and a second later, I join her.

I hear Sebastian and Heath speaking to us but I barely hear a thing. All I'm focused on is the girl who's my best friend, another person I've bothered and worried.

The last thing I wanted was to be a burden and it's exactly what I've become.

A mess. A complete, utter, hideous mess.

"Are you okay? Please tell me you're okay?" Marie asks, holding my hand. She hasn't let go of it in the past hour or so.

I give her a smile. "I'm okay."

"Are you hurt anywhere else?" She glances at my temple, where I've covered the small cut with a band-aid.

My cheek hurts a little, but I shake my head. "I'm fine, Marie."

Her eyes scan mine. She looks unconvinced, but I don't have it in me to tell her the truth. It'll worry her. Besides, the pain is little. I can tolerate it.

"I don't believe you, Hope. You can lie all you want, but now I see things differently."

"I'm not completely lying to you. I am fine, except for a little pain in my head and cheek." I cave in, seeing her puppy eyes. There's no way you can refuse her when she looks at you with those sad, big hazel eyes.

"Where does your head hurt and which cheek?" she asks.

I take her other hand and put it over the side of my head. Her fingers move over the surface, her touch gentle, careful not to hurt me in any way, which I find endearing. She finds a little bump and I wince. She stops.

"It's okay. It doesn't hurt that bad."

"You promise?"

"I promise."

A stare burns the side of my head. I turn and find Heath staring at me. He's sitting next to Sebastian, who's also watching me, worry thick in his green eyes. He sends me a smile and I return it.

Heath scowls hard, so I shoot him a smile too and his features relax.

"Which cheek hurts?" Marie asks quietly, which is so unlike her.

I point at my aching cheek and she gazes at it.

"I didn't even notice how it looks extra red today. I thought it was your natural blush," she says. "It stings, doesn't it?"

"A little, but it's okay."

Marie squeezes my hand. "Stop saying it's okay because it's not. You don't have to pretend. None of this is okay. It's all wrong, and I hate it."

Her sentiment tugs at my heartstrings. I used to feel the same way at the beginning, when it first happened. I couldn't come to terms with it and kept thinking it was wrong. As time passed, and Dad crossed more lines, I just realized it didn't matter whether I thought it was right or wrong. All that mattered was how I could be strong and make it through each day. Trying to be okay so I could survive each day.

I knew what fear felt like because I had watched him abuse Mom for most of my life. In the past few months, I've also learned what it feels like to be betrayed and have your trust broken. Parents are supposed to protect you and love you. Not hurt you until you have no tears left to cry.

And it's not just Dad who has played with my emotions. Mom has done equal damage, where I felt like I couldn't tell anyone about what I was going through because no one would believe me.

So, I know it's not okay. Nothing that I'm dealing with is okay. But to survive, I have to be okay.

"You're right, but if I don't pretend to be okay, then I won't be."

Marie stares at me for a long time, as if she completely understands what I said. Without saying anything, she hugs me, and I hug her back.

Tears appear in my eyes once again but I keep them at bay. When Marie sniffles in the crook of my neck, I can't help the sob that escapes me.

We cry again and I tell her everything from the beginning. I keep a few private things to myself, parts that are too ugly and horrific to share.

Heath and Sebastian also come closer and listen to me. In the middle of it, Heath sits behind me. He makes space between his legs so my back is pressed against his chest and my head is nestled nicely on his shoulder. His arms wrap around me, cocooning me in his scent, warmth and him—everything that I like so much about him.

9

HEATH

"You okay?" Sebastian asks.

"I'm fine," I lie. The truth is, I'm far from fine. So fucking far away from it.

Hope is talking to Marie, well, more like crying a river and babbling stuff. They haven't had a proper conversation since Marie tackled her in a hug and refused to let go of her. I was afraid she'd suffocate my girl. *My girl.*

What was I thinking when I said that? *I wasn't.*

That title means she belongs to me. *She is mine.*

Do I even deserve her? *It doesn't matter. Because I'll become whatever she needs me to be.*

This past weekend has made me realize I'm in big fucking trouble. Because I'm willing to go to such lengths for this person that it's insane. No one would understand it if I told them that this one girl has the power to make me do anything. I will do anything for her without thinking a single word.

And now she is attached to me. I'm not single anymore. We're together.

"If you frown any harder, you'll grow wrinkles," Sebastian pipes up, his tone laced with humor.

"I'm not frowning."

Sebastian rolls his eyes and pulls out his phone. Turning on the camera app, he brings it in front of my face and I see that I am indeed frowning.

Asshole.

I relax my muscles and the frown goes away.

"What has you frowning that hard?" he asks.

"Nothing."

"C'mon, tell me."

I lean my head back but keep my eyes on Rose. She's still crying and I want nothing more than to wipe away her tears and paint a smile on her face and plant joy in her eyes.

Fuck. What am I becoming?

"What is Marie to you?" I ask him.

"She's everything to me." His reply is fast.

"I know that. I mean, she's your girlfriend. What does that mean?"

"Why? You want to ask Hope to be your girlfriend?"

My heart races. "I told her, she's my girl."

"She's your girl, as in your girlfriend?"

"I think so."

Sebastian gapes at me. "What do you mean you think so? It's either yes or no."

A sigh leaves my lips. "I don't know. We didn't discuss the details. I had more important things to talk about."

He chuckles. "Only you could fumble around with the girl you like so much."

I glare at him. "If I remember correctly, you fumbled around a few times yourself, jackass."

That sobers him up. "Fine, you're right. But since I've gone through all these stages, I can help you." He faces me. "What do you want with Hope?"

"I want her."

He rolls his eyes. "That means a lot of things. You have to be certain about what you want with her so you don't hurt her by leading her on or confusing yourself."

I swear he's making it more complicated than it already is.

"I want her to be my..." My cheeks burn. "*Girlfriend*."

Sebastian grins like he's been waiting for this day for years.

Who knew a pretty book nerd would be the one to make me want a relationship?

"You're blushing," he teases. "It's cute."

I shoot daggers at him. "Shut up!"

He laughs and I want to pummel him.

Okay, so what if I have feelings for a girl?

It's normal.

However, all that I feel toward her doesn't seem normal. There is so much happening all at once: my heart jumps, begging to reach her, the cadence of my breathing changes to rapid breaths as if she's sucked all the oxygen in the room, and insects and fireflies fill my stomach, waging an assault that makes me nervous. I keep my touch gentle, so I don't hurt her. My movements are slow, so I don't scare her. And when I kiss her, I want to devour her, but I go at the pace she wants me to because she's all that matters to me.

Sebastian clears his throat.

I look at him, and he smirks. Clearly, I had been busy staring at Hope while thinking about all that.

"Communication is the key. Talk to her and be clear about what you want," he suggests.

"So I tell her that being my girl means that she's my girlfriend."

He nods. "Yes, and also, make sure you go at her pace. If she wants to take things slow, then—"

"I already know that."

"Did you ask her out on a date?"

I shake my head. "I haven't gotten to that part."

"What part did you get then?"

"The part where she had to clean my blood off her bedroom floor and her dad tore apart all of her favorite books."

"Fuck!" A mixture of sadness and despair flashes across his face. "He is a monster."

"He is," I grit out. "You have no idea how much she loved those books. Books are her favourite thing in the world."

Whenever I see books, I think of her.

"I hate that man," I tell him. Rage sears through me and turns my blood hot. I'm so consumed by the desire to hurt him, but the sight of Hope stops me. It'll upset her if I hit her dad and spend another night in the cell. She already feels guilty about it.

"I swear I'll break your bones if you do anything irrational. I know you want to hurt him, but think with a cool mind before you dive headfirst into this mess. You have to be careful and logical about this because you won't be able to do anything if you're locked up inside a cell."

I take a deep breath and slowly let it out. I do it a couple of more times before I'm finally cool enough to kick that monster out of my head.

Sebastian is right. What happened to Hope is my fault. Maybe if I hadn't appeared in front of her dad and hurt him, he wouldn't have touched her books. She'd still have them and wouldn't dampen my T-shirt from her tears.

I'm glad he didn't fucking hit her. Seeing Hope in bruises would have sent me over the edge and nothing would have stopped me from driving to her home and attacking him.

My best friend grabs my shoulder and gives it a squeeze. "You have a lot on the line. It's not just him you'll be hurting. He'll hurt you *and* Hope."

I curl my fingers into fists.

"Things will get worse if you lose control and just think about him. *Hope* is the person stuck in the middle of this complicated situation. You have to put her first and think it through before you do anything."

I close my eyes and try to imagine a scenario where I can stand and watch him hurt Hope.

I can't.

"I can't make any promises, Bash."

"Then don't. Because I was once in your place. I wanted nothing more than to hurt the people who hurt Marie. Nothing else made sense to me." He stares at me. "Just call me before you do anything. I'll be there for you."

I nod, knowing I can't trust myself when it comes to Rose. I can risk everything for her.

"You should take her out on a date. Make sure she has a good time," Sebastian suggests.

"I know."

He smirks. "Don't tell me you're nervous to ask her out."

I push him off. "It's not that." *It's exactly that.*

When I look back at Marie and Rose, they have stopped crying—thankfully. They seem to be engrossed in a deep conversation. I notice Rose letting Marie touch the side of her head and then point to her cheek. I know exactly what the topic of their conversation is and it pisses me off because I'm once again reminded of the person who caused the damage.

I'm burning with the desire to search him at this hour and hit him, when Rose turns her head and looks at me. Trust, affection, and care shine in those gorgeous brown eyes that I've become obsessed with in the last few months. They are not just eyes anymore. They have the capability to make me feel weak in my knees, kneel down and worship the ground she walks on.

She looks away from me and sends a smile to Sebastian.

A scowl grows on my mouth, hating the fact that she didn't send her smile *my* way.

Fortunately, she notices for Sebastian's sake—I was thinking about shoving him—and sends me a weak smile. It's nothing like her usual sweet smiles that make my heart pound, but it's a smile nonetheless. It's enough that she's managed to muster up one despite everything that has happened to her.

Marie says something to her. A few minutes later, after a hug, they start crying again and Sebastian and I make our way to them.

I help Rose sit between my legs and against me as she shares about her parents and her childhood. She then talks about her dad's return and how he started hurting her. Listening to it doubles my anger, but the only thing that keeps me calm is her. I keep her tucked in my arms and take in every detail that she tells all of us.

Marie starts crying again and Sebastian hugs her and whispers words to her.

"You didn't tell me those details," I grumble into her hair. "I had no fucking idea it was this bad."

"I'm sorry—"

"You don't need to apologize. I don't blame you."

Since her back is to me, I can't see her face and read her thoughts.

Rose surprises me when she grabs my wrist—the one with her bracelet on—and places it in her lap. She rarely initiates physical touch with me, so I'm surprised when she does. I lose my ability to speak.

"There were times—many times—when I wanted to tell you everything. I would gather the courage, but then the thought that you'd judge me or stop talking to me would just shatter that courage and I'd keep it all inside. You and your friends are the good parts of my life, and I didn't want to lose that."

I hug her tighter. "You'll never lose us. No matter what happens, you'll always have us. Drill that into your head."

I don't see her smile, but I know one is curving on her lips. "Okay."

"Good," I murmur, nuzzling my face in the crook of her neck. Her lavender scent enters my system and I can't help but lose my mind over it. That flowery scent is fucking addictive and I love getting high on it.

A shiver runs through her and her breathing becomes rapid. I tilt my head and look at her. Her eyes watch me, and she looks so innocent and pure, making me want to do dirty things to her.

But I won't because I want her to lead me. After everything that has happened, I know it can be hard for her to indulge in physical touch.

Of course I want to do things with her—things that are wicked, the kind she's read about in her romance novels—but I'd rather wait for her.

"Heath," she breathes.

"Yeah," I reply.

I wait for her, but she doesn't continue—she doesn't need to. Her pupils dilate and her cheeks turn red and it's clear that she's getting attracted to me.

Before I can tease her or steal a kiss, the shrill sound of the bell disrupts the moment.

Rose pulls away from me and clears her throat. "It's lunch break. We should go down."

Marie speaks with a grimace. "People are talking so if you want to avoid them, we can eat out."

Rose stiffens and she resembles a statue. I just know her overthinking mind has started working.

Leaning close to her, I wrap my arm around her stomach and set my chin on her shoulder.

Looks like I can't keep my hands to myself anymore.

"They...know...about...me," she pants.

Panic contorts Marie's face. "No! They don't know about you. They are just talking about Heath and you and how amazing you look together. Really. You don't need to worry about them. They know nothing about what happened over the weekend—"

The more Marie talks, the stiffer Rose gets.

I glare at Marie. "Stop talking!"

She opens her mouth to fight me, but one glance at Hope has her mouth sewn shut.

I mumble curses, knowing all that information has triggered Hope. She didn't tell us for months because she didn't want to be judged and now the whole school is gossiping about her. Earlier in the hallways, she looked like she was about to have a panic attack if I hadn't arrived. Everyone was staring at her, pointing at her and talking shit about her. While I know how to shut people up, she doesn't. All she knows is how to hide.

I cup her cheeks and force her to look at me. Her gaze meets mine and it's brimming with big, fat tears that are ready to be spilled.

"Don't cry." I grit my teeth. "It's okay."

"Everyone knows," she croaks out and reaches for my T-shirt.

"It doesn't fucking matter."

"But—" What comes out is a gasp that turns into a pant. In seconds, she's fighting for breathing, putting a tear right through the centre of my heart. The entire world be damned. I hate it when she cries. "I..."

"Listen to me. I want you to breathe, Rose."

She shakes her head but I tip back her head and make her look at me.

"Take a deep, long breath. Now." I demand.

Closing her eyes, she takes a long, deep breath and slowly lets it out. I keep talking to her and she listens to me.

"You're doing great, Rose." I caress her jawline and her eyes open and stare at me. "Just five more times."

She nods.

I move forward and press a tender kiss against her temple. "Good girl."

She doesn't react and it hurts.

I glance away from her and find that Marie and Sebastian are no longer there, but standing a couple of feet away from us to give us privacy. I almost smile at their thoughtfulness.

Two minutes later, Hope looks up at me and she looks much better than before. My palms are still cupping her beautiful face that I like so much.

"Better?" I ask, wiping away all the traces of her tears.

She weakly nods. "I'm sorry—"

I press my lips against her and sweetly kiss her. "You have nothing to be sorry about."

"Are you sure?"

"Yes."

Footsteps near us and we both look at our friends.

Marie shoots a smile at Hope. "We can eat at the diner."

Hope looks hesitant, even though I can see the way her eyes light up. She wants to be away from here.

"Let's fucking go." I stand up and offer my hand to her.

She takes it and stands up.

Ten minutes later, we're in the diner, talking and laughing about things that matter far more than our problems.

10

HOPE

HEATH PARKS AT THE END OF THE BLOCK—AS I ASKED HIM
to—and faces me. His stare burns a hole in the side of my face and
makes my neck burn.

"I should go," I say. My own voice sounds weak to my ears.

We both know I'm scared.

"It's getting late." It's not late. I have three hours until my curfew.

I made him drive me straight home from school, so we haven't
spent a single minute together other than at the rooftop.

Even after spending the whole day with him, I want to spend more
time with him. Before, there was only talking, but now our time
together includes hugs and kisses and I like those so much. I want
more. An endless supply will do.

You're my girl.

My heart leaps.

I haven't been able to ask him what it means. It could mean I'm his
girl, as in a girl best friend. But he wouldn't be kissing me, then. Or I'm
like a special girl that he wants to kiss and hug, but doesn't want to
date.

I have so many questions, but I have zero courage to face him, look
him in the eye and just ask.

I grab my bag from the floor and hug it to my chest. I reach over to open the door, but the locks click in place.

"You're not going to say goodbye to me, Rose?" Heath asks, his voice rough and husky as it scrapes over my skin and raises goosebumps.

Without looking at him, I say, "Um, goodbye. I'll see you tomorrow."

Oh my God.

That sounded so cringe.

See you tomorrow?

I want to die after saying that.

I'm still pondering over my absurd sentence delivery when his fingers brush away my hair from the side of my face and expose me to him. The intense blush that climbs up on my cheeks and clings there makes me nervous.

His knuckle swipes back and forth over my cheek, and a soft breath escapes my mouth.

Oxygen leaves the car and it feels like there's no air for me to breathe.

"You're not looking at me," he says. "I like it when your eyes are locked on me."

My grip on my bag tightens.

"Rose," he calls me and it's impossible for my body not to answer.

I sheepishly peek at him and all I see is confidence oozing off of him.

Do I even affect him like he affects me?

"There are your eyes. They are as beautiful as you."

"You have prettier eyes than me," I retort, finally finding my voice back.

His lips twitch as if he disagrees.

I clear my throat. "I have to go."

His mood changes immediately. His eyes turn dark and his face loses its gentleness. "You don't have to."

My lips curve in a sarcastic smile. "I have to. I don't have anywhere else to go."

"That's not fucking true."

"It's fine. It's not that bad. He...hasn't hurt me since Friday."

"It doesn't mean that he won't hurt you again."

I know that. "Thank you for today. It meant a lot to me."

He was my safe place today, and I hid in him, not wanting to face the world—I've never had that before. Somewhere else to go when things got hard at home. I read books for escapism, but this was different. It made me feel good in a way I have never before.

"Don't go into that house," Heath says gruffly.

"I'll be okay. Don't worry about me."

"I *cannot* do that."

I give him a weak smile. "Don't follow me, please."

Something on my face makes him unlock the car.

I get out of the car and wave at him before turning around and walking down to my house.

I don't have to look back to know Heath is in the same spot, keeping an eye on me.

THE MOMENT I SHUT THE DOOR BEHIND ME, I SENSE THE eerie silence in the house. It puts me at ease because I know he isn't home.

Most kids like it when their parents are home—I also used to when it was just mom and me—but it's the opposite for me. I like it when it's empty because it means I don't have to be afraid or careful.

Walking into the kitchen, I find everything clean and the place neat. No doubt that Mom was here in the morning and tidied up.

Instead of going into my room, I put my bag on the floor near the doorway and enter the space.

I don't know how long Dad will be out, but until he is, I want to relish every second of his absence.

Opening the cabinets, I grab a pot and set it on the stove after filling it with water. Taking the pasta from the other cabinet, I pour in about half a packet and add oil and a little salt.

I know I'm being a fool for every second that I'm spending here and not in my room, but it's been months since I've felt this light. I used to be alone in school and at home. No one to talk to or spend time with. It's taken me a lot of time to finally accept that I have people in my life who care about me. There are still times when I doubt them and their intentions, but really, I'm just doubting myself because I can't trust something this good has happened to me.

I have friends.

I think about this every day and each day the truth sinks a little deeper inside me, as if looking for a ground to land and plant itself.

A guy likes me.

Now that's a truth that seems incredibly unreal to me. I'm nothing like the other girls who are pretty, brave, funny, sarcastic, sweet, or possess a million other good traits that make it easier for guys to fall in love with them. All the female characters that I've met have everything, and it makes perfect sense when the male character can't help but fall in love with them because they are just amazing.

But in real life, things aren't like that. People have flaws, insecurities and imperfections.

Here, I am thinking about love, but it's too good a thing to happen to someone like me. Sometimes, I wonder what Heath sees in me, because no other guy ever saw it before and they all had perfectly functioning eyes. I never caught the eye of a guy who wanted me like Heath does. Someone who wants to protect me, care about me, and fight for me.

I know it's not sex that he wants.

If that were the case, he would've made advances—but he hasn't.

We've done nothing other than kissing and hugging.

The strangest thing is, he seems to be satisfied with that, as if he doesn't care if we get to the intimacy part or not.

My body warms at the thought of sex and intimacy. I've only ever read about it. I wonder if all those things actually happen.

I have zero experience in the department. I've never touched myself, let alone someone else.

So really, I don't see what Heath gets out of this relationship that we share.

I prepare the sauce for pasta as the warm sunlight of the sunset falls like a wave into the room and drowns it in golden. A calm and peace hang in the air.

I pour the pasta into the sauce and mix it well. The fresh colors of the vegetables and the vibrance of the red tomato sauce look enticing. I feel proud of myself. This pride is different than when I get perfect scores—because I work hard for them. This is me being good at something I'm not good at.

After a few minutes, I taste the pasta off the spatula and grin, it tastes heavenly. I'm half convinced that I didn't make it myself.

I pour some in the fancy white china plate that Mom rarely uses because it's reserved for special events like birthdays, anniversaries, and guests—we never have guests over.

For some reason, today feels special to me as if I've survived, although a war awaits me. When Dad comes home, all the calm and peace will sweep out of the house.

It's a worry that I'll tire myself over later.

On the pasta, I also sprinkle some unevenly cut coriander just to make it look good. Then I rush upstairs and lock myself in my room.

I turn around, deciding to read as I eat it, but I see the empty space where my book wall used to be.

The plate almost slips out of my hands, but I grip it at the last second.

All my books are gone. I don't have anything to read.

My throat bobs painfully and the reminder of what happened comes back like a bullet and knocks the air out of me.

Breathe in. Breathe out.

Heath's words come to me, and I repeat them in my head as I practice breathing and calming myself down.

I sit on the bed in such a way that my back is facing the gone-book wall. I know it'll be too hard for me to glance at the spot and not miss my books.

I take a bite when my phone pings with a text.

Heath: Do you like it?

I frown.

Hope: Like what?

Heath: You haven't checked your bag.

Hope: What's in my bag?

Heath: See for yourself.

I rush to my bag and open it. I don't see anything new in there. Just to be sure, I move my notebooks and folders around. It's at the back of them, tucked under my pencil case, that I find a book. I take it out and read the title.

Love in Hate. It's the latest and the last book in the series. I've read the first three: Love in Steps, Love in Chords, Love in Notes, and truly loved them. I can't believe he bought it this soon. It released this weekend.

I open the first page and see that it's a signed copy with my name. I've never had a personalized, signed copy before. Never. Ever.

Hope: You got me a signed copy!

Hope: You didn't have to.

Heath: I wanted to.

A smile curves on my lips and a rush of happiness flows through me.

Hope: Thank you so much.

Heath: You're welcome.

I set aside my phone when another message pops up on the screen.

Heath: Text me as you read the book.

My fingers hover over the keyboard. How can I stop myself back from falling in love with a guy like him? He's making it so hard. I can't hold myself back. Every little thing that he does makes my feelings for him stronger.

I put away my phone instead of sending him a text. I don't know what to say to him.

Grabbing the book, I sit on the bed and start reading it while eating the pasta that I made. I grin at how good it tastes and paired with one of my most anticipated reads, it tastes even more delicious.

The sun sets, painting the sky in beautiful shades of orange, pink, and yellow. Shadows dance on the walls in the canvas of the golden light. The chirping of the birds comes from the tree in Nadina's backyard. I glance over and see a meticulous nest of sticks where a sparrow family is sitting together.

Maybe, just maybe, I'll be fine.

11

HEATH

It's late at night when I get home. I let out some steam at the underground and fought two matches. The entire time, I was imagining my opponents as Alex Hanson, and I might have gone a little overboard with the punches, but I couldn't stop myself. I got hurt too. It's just bruises—they'll heal.

I step into the foyer and find the lights on and no Derek. It's the first time he is sleeping, otherwise, he's usually lurking around in the dark corners of the house. He rarely catches me sneaking out and the times he tails me, I know how to shake him off.

I walk through the foyer into the hallway when the soft notes of conversation catch my attention. They're coming from the living room.

Curiosity gets the best of me and I enter the room only to find my parents. Dad is standing next to Mom, who is sitting anxiously and fidgeting with her hands. He's holding a teacup that's steaming with hot liquid as he stares down at her.

"Drink it, Mia Cara," Dad says softly.

I find it ridiculous that Dad, who is six-foot-two, is holding a flowery china teacup with a saucer that looks so small and breakable in his hands.

"But he is not home yet," Mom argues. "What if something has happened to him?" Panic rings in her voice.

Dad opens his mouth to say something, but I interrupt. "You don't need to wait up for me."

Mom's head whips toward me, and she stands up. As she comes toward me, she looks me up and down, as if searching for injuries. "Heath—"

"I'm fine and you need to sleep." No matter how many times I think about saying something cruel to her, seeing her like this breaks my resolve.

Her eyes have sunk into the sockets and her face is sharp and bony. Also, her body looks so weak.

She is sick.

I just need to know why.

My reply makes her take a step back. "Why were you out so late? It's past midnight. School ended hours ago."

"I had things to do." *I don't like coming home.*

She frowns. "What things?"

She is worried, I get it, but I've lived my entire life without their interference. I'm not letting them control me now. We're practically strangers.

Without a reply, I turn around and leave. Footsteps follow me and I roll my eyes.

"Heath! Wait."

I race up the stairs to get rid of her, but she's persistent.

"I asked you a question."

I ignore her.

"Where were you?"

I pretend she's not there.

"Answer me!"

I don't understand why she's getting involved.

"I'm your mother."

I stop in my tracks at those words.

My heart pounds as my emotions get the best of me. Anger, frustration, sadness, and grief cloud my head and I can't withhold them from consuming me.

Looking over my shoulder, I level her with a glare. *"My mother, you say?"*

She stares back at me.

"Where were you my whole life? Why weren't you here?"

She pales.

"You have no right to ask me anything when you're just a guest. You'll stay here for a few weeks and then leave. I know you will."

She stays quiet.

"So drop the act and just do what you do best, which is to pretend Emery and I don't exist." I scowl. "Oh, wait, it's only me now. The other one is dead."

Tears fill her eyes as she reaches for her chest.

I should feel content at the sight of the damage, but I feel nothing. There are moments when I feel a tug on the bond we share because of blood. However, there's so much distance between us that reaching each other feels impossible now. I don't know her at all. She's my mother. I should love her and care about her, but all I feel are fleeting emotions for her that appear when she's in front of me and disappear when she's out of sight.

Dad freezes when he sees us.

"Heath, I'm—"

"Stay away from me and leave like you always do."

Without waiting for her reply, I enter my room and close the door with a loud thud. Leaning against the door, I rest my head against it and slip the bag from my hands.

My chest feels tight. Every breath that I draw in brings pain.

I wonder if I'll ever breathe freely without feeling like there's too much in my chest.

In seconds, I can hardly breathe.

Panic attack. Just what I fucking needed.

I make my way to my bed, lie down and stare at the ceiling. I inhale long, deep breaths and then exhale slowly. I repeat it until the weight moves off my chest and oxygen flows easily through me.

I didn't want to hurt Mom.

Fuck.

The look of her hurt and horror twists my insides now that I see it play on loop in my head.

Since they've come back, my emotions have been all over the place.

There is so much anger and frustration that makes me yell at them, but there's also sympathy because only we three share the grief that Emery's death left us.

My heart is filled with resentment, but there is a tiny corner that brightens up at the sight of them.

I'm not supposed to feel this way. But I can't help it, though.

No one's ever waited up for me. They didn't sit in the living room wishing that I would come home.

I comb my fingers through my hair, feeling so conflicted.

With a sigh, I roll over to my side and retrieve my phone from my pocket. Quickly, I pull up my conversation with Rose and see that she still hasn't replied to my last message.

I'm about to send a message to her when a knock raps on my door.

I stiffen for a moment before pulling myself up and making it to the door.

Dad stands on the other side with a resigned expression, holding a tray with dinner: a plate of stir-fry and rice.

He thrusts it in my direction. "Eat it."

"I'm not hungry."

He stares blankly. "Don't you think you've upset your mother enough for tonight?"

I hate the guilt that stirs inside me. "I only spoke the truth."

"Which is that you hate us."

"Yes, and I want you both gone."

"I told you. We've permanently moved back, so remove the idea from your head that we're leaving."

I smile mockingly. "You will leave soon."

"We won't." He presses the tray into my chest. "Eat it."

"I told you—"

He glares. "You've done enough damage for today, son. Don't push it or else."

"Else what?"

His lips thin as if he knows exactly what he wants to say but doesn't want to.

I narrow my eyes. "Say it."

Something switches in his eyes and his demeanor changes. The air of power and authority that he commands evaporates as he says, "I don't want you to hurt your mother ever again. You want to be mad, be mad at me. You want to yell, yell at me. Don't direct your cruel words or actions toward her. Nothing is her fault, it's all mine."

I gape at him in shock.

His eyes fill with pain. "What you said to her tonight broke her and I can't take it." He clears his throat. "So the next time you want to punish us, aim at me."

"I don't want to punish you," I murmur, surprised that I even said it.

Dad cocks a brow at me. "You want to. You blame us for Emery."

I scoff. "Yeah, well, it *is* your fault." *You should have been here.*

Pain and regret flash across his face, and I know I've hit the mark.

I grab the tray from him and close the door.

Things between us will never change.

12

HEATH

NEXT MORNING, I SEE ROSE COMING DOWN THE ROAD, having no idea that I'm waiting for her in my car. After the shit show last night, I barely slept. I stayed awake thinking about stuff, and when the morning came, I just wanted to see this girl, knowing that being with her would calm me.

She's holding a book close to her chest and looking down at the road, not being vigilant at all.

She takes a left, passing by me without a single glance.

People are usually aware of their surroundings, but this girl never is.

What am I going to do with you, Rose?

I press on the horn and she jolts in shock. Looking back, she studies the car and then me. Joy replaces her shock and she quickly hurries to me.

I cock my head to the passenger side, signaling her to get in.

A few seconds later, she's in the passenger seat looking beautiful in a white sweater and jeans. I swear, she makes me forget how to breathe with how stunning she looks. Her hair is down, cascading in waves that make me want to get my fingers tangled in it. And she has no makeup on, which only accentuates her natural beauty.

My hands tighten around the steering wheel. All I want to do is reach over and kiss her. But the conversation I had with Sebastian comes to my mind.

I need to make some things clear so we're on the same page.

There shouldn't be any doubt in her mind when it comes to us.

I want her. She should know it.

"Hi," she says shyly.

"Hi," I reply.

My gaze falls on the book she's holding. I put it in her bag yesterday. A few weeks ago, she told me about it and looked so excited. I couldn't help but order it for her. From the looks of it, she's read a lot of chapters. Her makeshift bookmark is wedged deep inside the book. Bookmarks are next on my list.

"You didn't text me." My voice is deep and firm.

Hope gulps, looking all sorts of nervous. "I...forgot."

She's lying.

I put my elbow on the console between the seats and lean over. "What's the real reason?"

She backs up until her spine hits the door. "I... Um..."

She is not herself today.

Raising my arm, I touch her cheek and caress. "Did your dad do something?"

She shakes her head. "I got lost in reading."

Her words are a muffled whisper as I cup the side of her face and lift it. Her pretty brown eyes stare at me. They are the reason that got me into this feelings mess—not that I'm complaining.

Brown eyes are so common. Every other person has them. I see them a thousand times throughout the day, but something about this girl's eyes is just different. They affect me. One look at her and I'm a goner.

The color dances the line of whiskey and honey, the perfect blend that makes the exquisite shade of brown I've ever seen. They are addictive in nature and filled with so much innocence and sweetness. There's no way you can say no to her or won't do whatever she says. Or perhaps it's only me who's a prisoner of her gaze.

I near her and her soft breaths graze my lips.

For fuck's sake.

Does she have any idea how much she affects me?

Blood rushes down my body into an area that shouldn't be getting aroused at this moment.

It's not the right time.

Not until she says so.

There is tiny space between our mouths; if either one of us moves even a little, our lips will meet.

But before that happens, I need to have the conversation. Even though I can hardly think of words right now. All I want is to taste those damn lips.

"Rose, I need to talk to you," I rasp.

She is staring at my lips and I'm half convinced that she's not heard a single word and just wants to kiss me.

That would be a big problem, because I don't want to talk either, and only kiss her.

She nods but doesn't look at me.

Please.

Stop staring at my mouth.

Or I won't be the gentleman that I always am with you.

I lean back her head and only then she looks at me. "You are my girlfriend."

Way to be fucking straightforward.

In her romance novels, this was a question.

Fuck me.

I screwed up.

Hope gapes. "What?"

"Yesterday, I told you that you're my girl. Maybe I should have been clearer." I run my thumb back and forth over her cheek. "I want you to be my girlfriend, Rose."

Her cheeks turn red. "Girlfriend," she repeats. "You and me."

I nod. "You and me."

She tucks her hair behind her ear and closes her eyes. "I kinda assumed that you meant that yesterday, but I wasn't sure and told myself that maybe you just wanted me to be your...special girl. Not like a girlfriend. I was a bit confused because the way you hold me and kiss me made me feel like I was more."

My breath gets stuck in my throat.

This is the first time she's spoken exactly what's on her mind without letting herself overthink and layer her words with lies.

It takes me a minute to find my voice. "*You are more.*"

She opens her eyes and stares back at me with a heavy gaze. It's filled with vulnerability and a magnitude of emotions I can barely decipher.

I can tell no one has ever uttered those words to her before.

I smile down at her. "You *are* my special girl and girlfriend, Rose."

"Are you sure?" Doubt is thick in her tone.

"Yes, I'm sure."

I've barely let those words out when her mouth is on me and she kisses me so hard my head spins.

Her hand rests on the back of my neck and her strokes get deeper and slow, devouring my mouth.

Everything about this kiss makes my feelings for her stronger.

Her fingers graze my scalp and I groan.

Chemicals mix like a fucking cocktail inside me and I grab onto every string that I can to keep my control in reins.

Vivid images of explicit activities fill my head. And I hate myself for wanting to do all those things to her when she isn't ready.

I swear, if she saw the way I have her in my imagination, she'll break up with me and be out of the car in less than a minute.

No girl has ever driven me this crazy.

My hormones are high and fanatic like a fiend.

And fuck. When she kisses me like this, I lose my fucking mind.

Hope breaks the kiss, pulls away from me, and faces the window. I lean my head against the headrest, panting like a fucking dog who ran a mile.

Fuck. Me.

Please.

I watch Hope through the side mirror; her cheeks are bright red and she's breathing hard. After a moment, she touches her lips gently and finds them a bit swollen.

"Looks like you know how to kiss now," I tease her.

Her eyes meet mine in the side mirror and she quickly turns around.

A grin curves on my mouth.

"Sorry...I..."

"I'd like it if you kiss me like that again." It's a terrible, *terrible* idea because now I'm hard.

"You liked it?"

I nod. "A whole fucking lot."

"I learned that from you."

I smirk. "I can teach you other things."

She blushes. "Okay."

Yeah. I won't survive this girl.

I'm in a lot of trouble.

THE MOMENT WE GET OUT OF THE CAR, EVERYONE STARES at us. We've been the breaking news since yesterday, and I hoped that the attention would lessen, but that doesn't seem to be the case.

I come around the front of my car and stand next to Hope, who looks at every face that's staring back at her with so many questions and judgment. She looks like she'd rather crumble to dust than enter the school and go to class. The waves of anxiety radiate off her and infuse into me, making me feel every single thing that she's feeling.

I send a glare to everyone. A few cower and avert their gazes, but some stare back at me with the same confusion and question: are you really dating her? I narrow my eyes, sending a clear warning—a declaration of war if any of them come near and talk to my girl.

I stand in front of Hope, blocking her line of vision like a shield.

The rays of sun hit my back and the thin black sweatshirt I'm wearing itches. But that thought fades away when I look at Hope, who looks breathtaking under my shade. The sunlight doesn't get to her and she stays tucked away in the shadows, exactly where she likes to be.

"Are you okay?" I ask.

She nods. "I'm fine."

"Are you sure?" I narrow my eyes purposefully.

She breaks. "Everyone is staring. They know about us and what happened on the weekend."

I clench my teeth together. "You don't need to worry about any of it. If someone says something, tell me, and I'll take care of them."

"Take care of them as in beat them?"

I don't utter a reply because we both know it would be a lie. I'll shut down anyone who tries to hurt her with their words. It's enough that she endures abuse at home.

I grab her hand and lace our fingers together. Giving a squeeze, I say, "Let's go inside."

Our walk to her classroom looks like straight out of a movie. Everyone stops and watches us in bewilderment. I shoot them a glare, but it doesn't work. The whispers and looks continue.

Rose has a different class, which annoys me. I don't want to let her go so soon.

We stand near the assigned classroom, looking at each other.

A minute passes and I make no move to leave.

Hope gives my hand a squeeze and slowly pulls away her fingers, one at a time. "I'll be fine—"

A girl bumps into her, sending her straight into my chest.

I wrap my arm around her waist and steady her.

"Are you okay?" I ask.

She gives me a nod.

"Are you—"

"Ah! Look at it. You have a girlfriend." I avert my gaze from Rose to the girl who stands with a hand resting on her hip.

I think I've seen her before. Blue eyes and blonde hair.

"You got a fucking problem?" I ask her, point-blank.

She scoffs. "Just unimpressed with your taste."

"I don't care about your fucking opinion."

Hurt flickers through her gaze. "You don't remember me, do you?"

I shake my head. "I'm glad I don't."

"I'm Shian," she tells me.

I look down at Hope. "Text me if something happens."

She nods.

I bend my head down and kiss her softly and then I'm gone.

CLASSES GO BY AND IT'S LUNCH TIME WHEN I FINALLY GET
to see Rose.

Sebastian and I wait in the parking lot to go eat at a diner. Sitting in
the cafeteria would bother all of us, but especially Rose. She had a
panic attack yesterday at the thought of facing everyone. So far, no one
has said anything to her in front of me, but I know there are comments
people are dying to make.

Fuck.

This takes me back to when Marie was dealing with this sort of
stuff. It's not as extreme now, but the effect is still the same. Words get
to people.

Sebastian crunches loudly on Doritos. "So, did you ask her out on a
date?"

I swear he's more obsessed with my date than me. I'm more
nervous about it.

"Not yet," I say, staring hard at the doors. Marie and Rose should
be out by now.

"What are you waiting for?"

"I just made things clear to her this morning. I told her that being
my girl meant she's my girlfriend."

"Well, at least you made some progress."

"She's been through a lot. I want to take things slow." I lean back
and face him. "Besides, I don't have any rush. I like how we are."

Sebastian bursts out laughing, making me feel like an idiot. "I can't
believe I'm hearing those words come out of your mouth."

I flush. "What do you fucking mean?"

"It's just strange hearing you talk about her this way. Given how
things were a while ago, I never thought you'd let anyone in, much less
a girl."

He is right. I didn't see any of this coming.

If someone had told me I'd be dating a girl and having huge feelings
for her, I would've cursed them out.

The mere thought sounds ridiculous. Yet here I am. Liking this girl
so much that it feels like it's more than just *like* at this point. What I

feel for her isn't a crush anymore. It's evolved into this anchor that has plunged itself deep into my heart. There's no way it's ever coming out. If I try to rip it out, I know I won't survive.

What's the word for this feeling or situation?

I don't know and I'm scared to know about it.

This feeling has been there for weeks. The more time I spent with her, the deeper that anchor sank. I can't tell when it happened or how it wormed its way inside me. All I know is, it happened without me realizing.

It should scare me or surprise me, but the truth is, I became obsessed with this girl the moment she looked at me from that window and made me pause. Dad's voice became a background noise as I focused on this girl who had the courage to look me in the eye and not cower.

When we collided in the hallway, she proved to me that she was brave and that standing up to me wasn't a problem for her.

My twisted head took all those cues and rolled them up in a ball of fascination that kept growing the more interactions I had with her.

Unknowingly, she made me hers.

"I like that look on your face." Sebastian's voice is low.

"What look?" Calm carries in my reply. Just thinking about Rose brings me peace.

Sebastian just stares at me with a composed, thoughtful face that says he's trying to figure me out.

Good luck with that.

"You're in love with her," he says slowly.

My stomach tightens.

My heart drops.

My mind goes blank.

"I'm not." I straighten up.

My best friend is messing with me. He's trying to freak me out. Of course, I'm not in love with Rose. I can't be in love with her.

"You are. You have been for a while now."

I glare at him. "Stop saying it."

A smile dances on his lips. "Even if I don't say it, it won't make it any less true." He chuckles. "Marie and I have both known for a while. In fact, I lost the bet."

"You placed a bet on me falling in... with Hope."

Fuck. I can't bring myself to say the L word.

"We did. It was inevitable." He shrugs.

"You're wrong. I don't love her. I only like her a lot."

Sebastian arches an eyebrow. "Liking someone a lot is considered loving them."

"You're wrong."

"I'm a guy in love. I know it when I see it."

"Sebastian, stop with this nonsense."

He laughs. "I think I've seen this film before. A couple of weeks ago, actually. Looks like you're gonna keep denying until you finally agree."

Before I can muster up a reply, I see Marie and Hope walking toward us.

Not wanting to wait any longer, I cross the distance between us and stand near them.

"...so butterflies are amazing. They transform into this beautiful thing after going through so much ugliness. I mean, I don't consider the six stages of larvae ugly but others do. I think those stages are beautiful in their own way—Heath!"

Rose turns and looks at me. What I see makes me stiffen.

Her eyes are red rimmed and her cheeks are flushed. Despite the smile on her face, it's obvious that she's cried.

My mood changes. "What happened?"

I fucking knew it.

Someone used their useless mouth to spew bullshit to hurt her.

When I get my hands on them I'll make sure they suffer.

Hope glances at Marie and a quiet conversation goes on between them. Finally, after what feels like a long minute, she answers me. "People said some things."

"What things?" I press.

"About what happened on the weekend."

Fucking hell. I only spent a couple of hours there, not a life sentence. People were eating these rumors with sheer interest and delight. It wasn't Hope who was getting the looks. I was in the spotlight. Since we were dating, people were eager to reach her to get to me.

I just hoped they wouldn't find out about Hope's dad, otherwise, it would be a mess. People have a habit of enjoying other people's misery and it would be a field day at school every day with comments she doesn't need to hear.

Especially when she is learning to step out of her comfort zone and take a step forward in my direction. She is telling me stuff now, which is new.

I am proud of her. For trusting herself and me.

"What did they say?"

Rose chews on her bottom lip. "Stuff about you spending a night in a cell and the reasons why you could've attacked my dad."

I hate people.

"What did they say that made you cry?"

Rose looks at Marie, who takes the lead. "It was Shian. She's a girl from our grade. You must have seen her around. She's bitter because she asked you out a while ago and you didn't pay any attention to her so she's spreading false rumors and targeting Hope."

"Is it the girl from the morning?" I ask Rose.

She nods. "She wants to be your girlfriend."

"Hah! As if Heath would ever date her. She's evil," Marie says. "Also, she doesn't complement him at all."

I arch an eyebrow. "What does that mean?"

Rose and I both stare at Marie.

Sebastian strolls over to us and hugs Marie to his chest. "Explain, babe."

Marie grins at him, then faces us. "People who are compatible complete each other. Like I'm loud and chaotic, but Sebastian is quiet and calm. In places I'm lacking, he completes me, and in places he's lacking, I complete him."

That makes sense. Rose complements me.

In all the places I feel empty, she fills me and makes me whole.

I only wish that I do the same to her.

"So really, Shian had no chance. Besides, even if she had somehow lured you into her trap, I would've kicked her out of your life," Marie says, determined.

I cough to hide my laugh.

"Heath deserves Hope." Marie grins.

I look down at Rose and she blushes.

"No, I don't," I murmur, not for anyone's ears.

But she hears me because she shakes her head and murmurs back. "You do."

13

HOPE

I SEE TWENTY ORDERS WHEN I CHECK HEATH'S PHONE AFTER school.

We're parked outside a department store from where I'm supposed to get the beads, strings, letter blocks, wrapping supplies, and twines to prepare the orders.

I was going to walk from school to here but Heath insisted on driving me.

"Is something wrong?" he asks when I don't speak and keep staring at the screen.

"No," I say, keeping the explanation to myself but then I remember that he's my boyfriend.

Heath Travon is my boyfriend.

Unbelievable, I know.

I truly believe I'm in a fictional world.

This is a main character moment.

Now that I'm in a relationship, I have to talk to him. I can't keep things from him anymore. All the books I've read have taught me that communication is key.

Besides, it isn't fair to him. He is here. After everything that's happened. That means something. He wants me and wants to be with me. The concept is hard to grasp, but it doesn't change in truth.

"Then we should—"

"I didn't think I'd get any orders!" I blurt. *Keep going.* "I didn't post any videos and posts as you'd told me. There's less engagement on my account." I gulp. *Speak more.* "I wanted more orders because that'd mean I'd keep myself busy and not think about stuff at home." Finally, I dare to meet his gaze.

Heath stares back with a blank look, then his gaze softens, and he says, "I like that you're talking to me more."

"We are dating," I mumble.

He shoots me a smile as if the statement makes him happy.

I make Heath happy.

That doesn't scream burden.

He gets out of the car and comes around to open the door for me. He offers me his hand, and I take it. He pulls me out and locks his car.

Together we go into the store and gather the things for the bracelets. At the counter, I take out my wallet to pay, but Heath gives the lady his credit card.

When we're out, walking toward his car, I turn to him. "I can pay now, you know."

He smirks but keeps looking ahead. "I know."

"That means you don't have to."

"I know."

"Next time, let me pay."

He opens the door for me. "Not happening, Rose."

"Why not?"

"Because..." he clears his throat, "that's what happens in your romance novels. The male character pays for everything."

It takes a minute to understand the meaning. "You don't need to be like them."

"You adore them."

I do. All my favourite fictional men are perfect.

"Yes, but I like you for you," I say.

The little things Heath does are different because they are only meant for me. It makes me feel special.

"I'm not trying to be them. I'm taking cues from them because this is the first time I'm in a relationship. I don't want to make fucking mistakes or mess up. You deserve better and I promised to be better for you."

My mouth hangs open in shock.

Heath closes my mouth by giving a nudge under my chin. "I'm aiming to be your number one. You won't even consider those men."

"They have their own girls."

"Yes, but *you* will be mine."

How I force myself to sit in the car and not have an attack from the butterflies in my stomach is beyond me.

My pulse flutters at the rate of their wings.

It's a miracle I don't pass out from being flustered.

———

By the time we roll into the driveway, the sun is disappearing into the horizon. The view behind his extravagant house in the sky is breathtaking.

The tall, wide white mansion itself looks like a piece of art.

I've been here a lot of times now, but I still can't get over how beautiful and lavish this place is and how normal it is for Heath to live in it.

For someone like me, who's spent most of her life struggling for money and living in a house with rooms that don't even measure up to a single room in this house, it's intimidating to be around things that cost thousands of dollars.

The second I'm inside, I freeze.

Something feels different.

I don't know if Heath recognizes it.

The number of times I've been to his place, I've never smelled notes of vanilla scent in the air or the aroma of freshly baked cupcakes from the kitchen. Kelly doesn't bake. Also, there are fresh flowers in the vases.

"Heath, is that you?" I hear a female voice I've never heard before.

Heath goes rigid. "Fuck!"

Quickly, he presses me to the nearest wall by putting a hand on my stomach. His touch permeates tingles under my skin and I let out a shaky breath.

Yes. Totally normal for a girlfriend to get this affected by her boyfriend's touch.

Heath keeps his hand on my stomach, unaware of the reaction he initiates in me and looks around the corner for someone.

My heart is beating too fast for me to ask him who that is.

"My parents have come back," he tells me, still keeping an eye on the hallway.

His parents are here.

Oh my God.

The first emotion to consume me is anxiety—and it's the only one that stays. No sign of excitement for me. I'm too busy panicking at the sudden bomb that he's dropped on me.

I didn't expect to meet his parents because he told me they never visit. So I never prepared myself for what would happen the day they would be here and I'd have to meet them.

Subconsciously, I tame my hair the best I can. As for my face, I know the mascara and lip gloss I applied are still there, so I look somewhat good. I glance down at my clothes and wince.

An old white sweater and faded jeans. They don't look good.

Before I can dwell on my outfit, that voice speaks again.

"You're back from school," That woman says. His mother.

Heath and I have been friends, but I've never seen a single photo of his family. I know what his sister looks like, but not his parents. I know his heart and his mind, but there's still so much depth to him that I need to dive into and explore. What I know is surface-level and it's not enough. I want to know him on a deeper level like he knows me.

A muscle ticks in his jaw at her statement and he nods. Even from his side profile, I can tell that he doesn't like her. There should be no strong feelings there for the woman who's his mother. A distance worth miles seems to be between them by the look of blankness in his gaze.

Uncomfortable silence hangs in the air like a thick fog, making it hard to breathe. Tension is so thick I fear it won't be cut with a knife, saw, or anything sharp.

Given how little I know, I interpret that things are not good between him and his parents. From what he's told me, he hates them for leaving him and Emery. The few times he's talked to me about them, there was so much hatred, pain, and disappointment in his gaze and voice that it broke my heart. It felt like he had truly given up hope on his parents and considered himself alone. For him, they didn't matter.

"I made some cupcakes—"

Heath's fingers gently dig into my flesh. "I don't eat cupcakes."

There is a long pause before his mother speaks again. "I didn't know that." She sounds hurt.

"Of course you didn't," he replies in a bitter tone that I've rarely heard him use.

"I can make you something else. Perhaps, we can make it together and—"

He quickly shakes his head.

She clears her throat, and when she speaks, there's hope in her voice. "Let's eat lunch together. I'm sure—"

"I have things to do."

"Oh, okay." She sounds wounded, as if those words slashed her skin and made her bleed.

I don't need to peek around the corner to check if she's hurt.

From the sound of it, she was looking forward to spending time with Heath, but he didn't feel the same. He doesn't want to talk to her or be near her.

This hatred is different—I didn't know there were different kinds. Heath doesn't want to physically or emotionally hurt her. He just wants to stay away from her and keep adding distance between them.

Her steps recede, and the distance between them increases.

When she's gone, he grabs my hand and leads me to his room.

The lock clicks and he slumps against the door like the weight has been lifted off his shoulders. The tightness to his face and the anger in his eyes are present as he stares past me at the windows.

Putting my bag and the stuff on the floor, I near him.

"Are you okay?" I don't know why I ask him when I already know the answer.

He isn't okay.

"I'm fine," he murmurs, bending down his head so that his face is tucked in the crook of my neck. For a long moment, he doesn't say a word and just breathes. With each inhale and exhale, I feel his breath brush against the sensitive places of my skin—ones I didn't even know about—and I try to suppress a shiver.

"You don't look fine," I say.

I reach up and tangle my fingers into his hair. The strands are soft and rough in places, exactly like him.

Heath doesn't reply. Instead, he wraps his arm around my waist and pulls me flush against him. Our fronts are pressed, and I'm infused into his warm and solid body.

"I will be, because you're here," he tells me.

A blissful feeling blooms inside me.

I've never been a source of someone's comfort—I've never been anything to anyone, really. When you've led a lonely life, you start to wonder about your place in the world. I always thought mine didn't exist. But being here with him, I realize I do have a place, and it's beside him.

In the past months, I've only seen him being my rock where I could land and crash and he'd put me back together. But now I'm starting to see that perhaps I can be his rock too. I can be the place where he runs to cry and let it all out.

"She was your mom."

"Yes."

"When did she get here?"

"This weekend. She came with my dad, who got me out and handled the case. He's the reason why I'm not going to trial and facing a new set of fucking problems." He pauses. "They said that they are moving back, but I don't believe them. They'll leave like they always do."

"What will you do if they stay?"

Heath hugs me tight. "Be very fucking mean to them so they leave."

"Do you really want that?"

"Yes. I don't want them here."

"Your mom seemed nice."

He chuckles dryly and pulls away from me to look me in the eye. "She left me."

Disappointment, anger and sadness swirl in his gaze. For the first time, I see his vulnerability in full force. Most of the time, he keeps his emotions locked away behind his hard exterior, but there are moments when they break through and escape.

I live for those moments because I get to know him more.

And if there's anything that I want more in life, it is to read Heath better than I read books.

"Are you hungry?" he asks, changing the subject. "You only ate fries at lunch."

"I'm okay," I say.

He shakes his head and makes me sit on the couch. "I'm going to grab some snacks, you open those bags and start on the bracelets."

In a second, he is out of the door as if he knew that I'd protest and ask him not to get me anything.

A smile tugs on my lips.

I'm not going to find a guy like Heath again in my life. My mother was wrong. People who are special don't come into your life so often. They are like shooting stars. Gone in the blink of an eye.

Try not falling in love with him.

I can do it.

I stand up to move to the floor when something catches my eye. There are cardboard boxes sitting in front of the large flat screen and TV unit where his gaming console is.

Curiosity piques my interest, but I dismiss it. If he wants to tell me what's inside, he will.

"Do you like stir fry and rice?" Heath closes the door, holding a large tray. "If you want something else, I can order takeout."

"No, it's fine. I like stir fry."

Heath sets down the tray on the table and joins me on the floor.

"You look sad."

I start to deny but stop myself.

Talk to him more about yourself.

"It's my favourite. Mom used to make it for me on nights she'd be home. It was the best." My smile is sad when I add, "I haven't had it in months. She's rarely home, and also, Dad spends time with her now."

I'm not jealous, just upset that things are changing and I can't keep up. Mom and I used to be so close, and now it's like there's a wall between us and I can't reach her anymore. With Dad moving back home, she's become even more distant from me.

I know she can be strict and manipulative at times, but I still love her and want her. The reason is, she stuck with me all those years when no one else did. With her, I didn't feel truly alone. I felt like I had someone.

"You sound like you miss her," Heath says, seeing right through me.

I nod. "I do. I miss what we had; it isn't there anymore."

He watches me, trying to read me like he always does.

I flush under his scrutinizing gaze and clear my throat. Looking around, I search for a reason to distract him, and that pile of boxes catches my attention.

I have no right to ask him what's inside those, but I also can't keep wondering. The last time he had a box in his room, it contained books.

My favourite books. The Harry Potter series.

Luckily, I had those slid under my bed, so they escaped Dad's wrath. But the books he destroyed were the ones that had accompanied me for years. I read them whenever I'd feel alone. They held more value to me. And now, they're gone. I can never put them back together.

I remember we ordered books on his Amazon account. I didn't ask him about it afterward and I wonder if they arrived or not.

"You should eat. It's getting cold," Heath reminds me.

I start on the food and he does too.

One bite and I close my eyes to its delicious taste.

"Kelly is so good at making food."

"She is. But she sucks at baking."

"I can relate to that. I don't know how to bake. I've tried but I always mess up." I take a bite. "But I made great pasta yesterday."

Heath's eyes drift up to meet mine as he dips a spoonful into his mouth. The gesture isn't sexy at all, but it makes my stomach tighten anyway.

"You should have brought some for me," he says softly.

Surprise hits me so hard, my mind goes blank.

He wants to eat something I make.

Butterflies take a joyful lap around my belly, filling me with an exciting feeling.

If this happened in a book, I'd be squealing and rolling on my bed. *Can't do that here.*

"I..." A shiver rakes through me. "You'd want that?"

"I wouldn't ask if I didn't want it, Rose."

Rose. He's been calling me that a lot lately.

I don't have a nickname for him.

I like the name Heath. It suits him perfectly.

However, I rarely call him by his name. It makes me so nervous because when I say his name, all his attention turns to me, and I become the centre of his world. Nothing or no one else exists. Only we do. And I haven't learnt how to deal with that.

There are so many things that I'm learning. So much that I still have to learn. With him, I can do it.

"Is cooking something you like doing?" Heath asks, breaking my chain of thoughts. "I know reading is your favourite thing in the world."

I grin. "I don't cook a lot, but Dad..." Instantly, the food tastes like rocks in my mouth, but I swallow regardless. "He's asked me to make dinner every night. I usually go with pasta or spaghetti because it takes less time and I can quickly go to my room."

I don't need to spell it out for him to understand what I'm trying to say.

I sneak a glance at him, and he looks deadly.

The blue in his eyes has turned a shade darker and his face is twisted in a scowl.

He sets down his empty plate on the table and runs a hand through his hair.

I notice the silver rings on his fingers. There's three on his right hand and two on his left hand, and of course, my bracelet on his left wrist. It's always there.

"So he makes you work, huh?" he murmurs under his breath, sounding annoyed and mad.

"It's okay. I don't mind," I assure him.

"I fucking do." He retorts, looking all sorts of grumpy.

"He has a bunch of rules. As long as I follow them, I'm okay."

Heath's demeanour changes and I quickly realize I shouldn't have said that.

"What kind of rules?" he asks in a low voice that shakes all the atoms in the space between us.

I gulp and repeat them to him. He gets stoic with every single one of them. When I finish, he looks like he wants to go on a rampage.

I set aside my now-empty plate and move closer to him.

I stare at his hands, wanting to take them and comfort him in some way.

His touch always helps me, but I'm not sure if mine will have the same effect.

"Fuck, just what kind of monster is he?" he grumbles. "I swear, if I see him again, I will fuck him up real bad. He won't be able to speak, let alone hurt you."

"No!" I panic. "Don't do anything. You'll get into trouble."

"And I've told you that I don't mind the trouble."

"I know," I whisper. "I just don't want it for you."

Heath sighs, then shakes his head. "Sometimes, I don't know what to do."

"He stays out for most of the day. I haven't seen or talked to him."

The muscle in his jaw ticks.

I've only ever read about that in books.

It is hot.

My cheeks burn as I fidget with my hands.

"Do you know why he hurts you?" he asks.

"I don't."

"Do you wonder why?"

"I used to think about it a lot, but now I just don't care. Whatever the reason is, it doesn't justify the abuse. You don't hurt the people you love. Not every day, not all the time. I used to love him when I was little. He was good to me. He'd let me watch TV, take me to the playground with Mom, and buy me chocolate. Although it was a long time ago, I remember it. It's like my brain is keeping some good parts of him, so I can't completely hate him. But I'm trying to. He's hurt Mom, me, and you. I can't ever forgive him for that. You're important to me."

Heath reaches for my cheek and cups it. "You're important to me, too. The most important."

Having him touch me gives me the courage to hug him. Unlike before, when his arms would stick to his sides, now they wrap around me and embrace me like he'd protect me and never let go.

I don't know what I'd do if I ever had to let him go.

I know I won't survive.

"If you ever feel like he's going to hurt you, call me. I will be there for you."

"You promise you won't attack him?"

His arms squeeze my waist. "Don't make me promise that."

"I need that promise."

Heath sighs and I can't help but smile in his chest.

"Fine."

"We should work on the bracelets. I want to send them tomorrow."

"Here I thought we'd be doing more boyfriend-girlfriend things."

I meet his gaze. "What things?"

Heath smiles. "You know very well what things."

Sexual things.

I quickly escape his embrace. "These orders can't wait."

He laughs and heads to his walk-in closet while I clear the table for us to work on.

Of course we'll be doing those kinda things now.

Why am I getting nervous?

If anything, I should be relaxed because I know how everything happens.

I just never thought my smut knowledge would ever be helpful.

I sneak a glance at him and he's adjusting the thermostat. He looks sexy—I can't stop drooling over him—in gray sweatpants and a black T-shirt. The sight is exquisite and I'm staring unabashedly.

The way his strong and big muscles squeeze into the material of his T-shirt, which is too tight and the chest that is hard and packed. I know he has a six-pack. I've seen it and I think about it often.

My eyes trail down to his sweatpants. Gray sweatpants. He definitely knows what they do to girls like me. It's like kryptonite. Also, they hang low on his hips.

Heath frowns when he catches me staring. "Is it still too cold for you?"

I can't get the words out.

Gray sweatpants.

Gray. Sweatpants.

Gray sweatpants.

This is it. This is how he breaks me. I'll agree to do anything with him if he asks me while he's wearing those gray sweatpants.

"Rose," he comes closer. "What's wrong?"

"Gray sweatpants." I press my hands to my mouth.

Oh my God.

I just unlocked the secret to him.

He cocks an eyebrow in confusion. "What about them?"

"Nothing," I say quickly and look at the beads.

Coming closer, he goes down on one knee beside me.

The air gets thick and my breath hitches.

He caresses my cheek. "You're blushing, which can mean only one thing."

"What thing?" I keep working the beads into the string to avoid looking at him.

"You're thinking about something dirty."

My head whips in his direction. "No, I'm not."

The arrogant smirk that dances on his lips says *I know you, Rose.*

For some strange reason, he decides to let it go and helps me with the bracelets. We make them in silence and it's the comfortable kind.

Every now and then, his fingers brush against mine, or his body leans closer in my direction, and the butterflies in my stomach go into a frenzy. Every little gesture is like a shot of electricity coursing up all the wires in my system, bringing me to life.

But nothing affects me more than when our eyes lock, and it feels like he enjoys looking at me—like he finds the mere sight of me lovely and doesn't want to look away.

In all those short glimpses, he makes me feel special.

14

HEATH

It's late at night when I stroll into Emery's bedroom. It'll be a sleepless night, the first I've had in a while.

Because of Hope.

She's the reason.

Ever since meeting her, she's all I can think about. One look at her and she's captured my mind and made a home there. It's filled with pictures of her smiling, laughing, blushing, and crying. Every emotion that she expresses, my eyes capture it and my brain hangs it on its walls. Other things exist alongside her, but they don't compare to her. Even my grief.

But tonight, standing outside my sister's room, it all gets swept away with the force of sadness that welcomes me. It's been a while since I've felt this emotion and I realize how much I've missed the feeling of it. I've lived with it for more than a year, and unknowingly, it made a home inside me. One that I had no intention of destroying or getting rid of.

Grief and sadness mix together into a strong potion. Within seconds, my veins are flowing with the concoction, and everything in me hurts.

Inhaling a deep breath, I reach for the knob and twist it. I step inside only to find Mom sleeping on the bed, holding onto a purple dress that Emery used to wear a lot. I wonder if it still smells like her? No one has touched a single thing in this room. Kelly and Derek both know this place is off limits. Kelly cleans it once in a while, but she's very careful, making sure nothing gets repositioned. It's considerate of her and I'm thankful to her.

Mom frowns in her sleep, tightly clutching the material in her hands. Distress contorts her face.

The sight tugs my heartstrings for some insane reason.

I'm at war with myself, with her and Dad being here, sharing the same space with me. For the longest time, this room, this house and all the things were mine, but now they are theirs, too. It all belonged to them anyway because they paid for it, but I felt an ownership because they weren't here.

A cry leaves past her lips, and on instinct, my feet move me toward the bed. It happens so suddenly, without a second thought. As if my body couldn't resist not comforting her.

She calls for Emery's name, her voice filled with pain as if she's being pulled apart at the seams.

I run a hand through my hair, not knowing what to do.

She is having a nightmare and I just woke up from mine a few minutes ago.

Leaving the dress, her hands drift in the air, desperately searching for Emery as she keeps calling her name. Her cries and worry grow more when she doesn't find her.

Surprise roots my feet to the ground, my body frozen in place.

I knew something was wrong with Mom, but I didn't expect her to be having nightmares. It's been a year and she lives in Canada, where places and things aren't marked by my sister's existence.

Sometimes moving away from a place makes it easier to forget the bad memories tied to that place.

However, I understand now that hasn't been the case with my mother.

She misses Emery dearly. There's no faking in the way she's calling her and reaching for her.

In my head, I'd convinced myself that my parents don't care about us. After all, I had a lot of evidence to back up that claim.

From early on, they left us and rarely checked up on us. Their involvement in our lives was scarce. Kelly and Derek are the only people we knew who were always present when we needed something and sometimes talked to us. They had chores to do and they weren't invested in listening to how we were doing at school, if we had friends, or how our day was. Those random questions felt personal and special because we would be talking about ourselves, but my sister and I realized no one wanted to hear our answers. Our parents lived far away from us and they visited once a year for a short amount of time. Even if we wanted to answer those questions, they didn't have the time.

Growing up, Dad was distant and quiet and Mom was reserved and hesitant. She tried to talk to us, but it felt like she was nervous, so she'd back away or watch us from afar. Our family dinners were filled with awkward silence and stolen glimpses. The four of us didn't know what to talk about or how to talk to each other. It felt like we were a couple of strangers locked in a room rather than a family.

It made me wonder why they had us in the first place—why they tried to conceive us if they were just going to abandon us. What was the point of making a family if you weren't going to live with it?

I feel physically sick because I don't have answers and the worst part is I'm looking for them.

Despite saying I don't care, I want the truth.

I want to know why they live somewhere else and not with us— me?

"Heath, what are you doing here?" Dad speaks from behind me.

"Mom is here," I answer him.

His footsteps near me and then walk past me as he reaches for her. She's full on sobbing and screaming.

Lost in my thoughts, I didn't even hear her. My thoughts are loud enough to tune out the world and sharp enough to dig into me like claws.

"Mia, wake up," Dad says. What he says next is in a foreign tongue. I don't know what he's saying. It's my first time hearing him speak another language.

I had no fucking idea he knew a language besides English. Are there any other languages he can speak? Does Mom also speak other languages?

How much do I not know about these people?

Dad's voice and touch wake Mom up and she quickly folds herself into his chest as she cries. She looks small and breakable against him.

I look at Dad, who looks equally fragile as he holds her in his arms and kisses her forehead. His palm rubs her back in an up-and-down motion, a movement so practiced it feels like he's rehearsed it every night, now able to do it in his sleep. It's become muscle memory.

At two in the morning, he's dressed in a charcoal gray suit with no tie. His hair looks wild, as if he's run a hand through it a million times because of stress and his face is a mirror of tiredness and lack of sleep.

"Stop crying, please," he assures her. "It isn't good for your health."

His words do nothing to her as she keeps crying.

So he just holds her.

The sight reminds me of Hope and me. All those times she hid things from me, but couldn't keep them inside—she'd cry. The only thing that helped was holding her.

Dad looks at me. "Get me a glass of water."

Without a word, I make my way to the kitchen, fill a glass of water and return with it. I realize it's the first time the three of us are together after her death and in her room.

There are no family pictures of us four, but still, that's exactly what we are.

A family.

No matter what I say or what happens, the truth can't be erased or altered.

Mom calms down after Dad makes her drink a few sips of water and tells her not to cry anymore. She half-listens to him as her tears keep spilling down her cheeks.

Looking up at him, she asks, "Where's Heath?"

He cups her cheek and wipes away all tears. "He's right here, Mia Cara."

Mia Cara. Is that his nickname for her? I've heard him say it a lot whenever he addresses her.

Gently, he turns her head in my direction and her face gains some color.

Abruptly, she stands up and loses her balance, but I grab her elbow and steady her. When I glance to the side, Dad is a second late to help her.

She erases the distance between us and wraps her arms around my waist. She hugs me tight as if she'd never let go.

But I know she will.

In a few days, she'll be gone. I'll forget how warm her embrace feels. I'll forget how she smells exactly like summer and spring—flowers and fruits. I'll forget how, when she hugs me, the child in me rushes to her silhouette, excited to reach her and talk to her.

Those little facts will fade away with time, like leaves change color in autumn and are eventually gone by winter.

"I thought you were gone," she murmurs. "That you'd never come back...like her."

My eyes shoot to Dad, who closes his eyes momentarily, and when he opens them, those gray irises are filled with so much agony it surprises me how he doesn't sink into the pain.

I place my palm on her back.

"I am here and I'm not going anywhere," I tell her.

"For how long?"

"Forever."

She looks up at me to read me. "You really mean that?"

I nod.

Mom watches me for a long moment, then says, "Your eyes are just like hers...so blue." She cups the side of my face in her shaky hand. "They remind me of her."

They remind me of her, too. Always.

Before she can say more, Dad pulls her out of my embrace and wraps his arm around her waist, supporting most of her weight.

"Let's go sleep and don't wander off this time."

So this happens frequently.

Mom sniffles. "I like sleeping here."

"C'mon now. I'm done with my work."

They walk out of the room when Mom looks back. "Are you going to stay here? I can stay with you."

I glance at Dad, who wants to take her to their room so she can sleep. The dark circles under her eyes are going to get darker if she doesn't rest.

One look from him and I know what he wants me to say. Just to go against him, I want to say the opposite, but what good will that do?

Mom will suffer, meaning Dad will suffer.

I can hurt both of them.

The question is, why can't I do it?

I've never held any feelings for them. They are not important to me. I don't care about them.

Then why does it feel like all that is a lie?

Anger and frustration sizzle through my veins. My fingers curl into tight fists, ready to attack. A second later, they start shaking.

I feel like a mess because my head is all over the place.

Nothing seems like what I thought it was.

Without saying a word, I walk past them. Grabbing my phone and car keys from my room, I race down the stairs and leave.

I don't know where I'm going.

All I know is, I can't breathe in this house.

The walls feel like they're closing in on me, and the ground is shaking.

It's the people, not the house, that's making my heart pound.

I need an escape.

Pressing hard on the brakes, I stop my car. I reach over and check the glove compartment. Two cigarette packs sit there untouched. Ever since I said those words to Rose, I haven't smoked.

The urge to light one up and forget makes my fingers tremble.

Rose won't know it if I smoke right now.

However, I'll be betraying her trust. That's the one thing I can't ever do. I can't let her down or lie to her.

I don't want to be like her shitty parents.

On instinct, my hand moves back, and I close the glove compartment.

If only I could see her right now.

15

HOPE

My phone vibrates beside my head, waking me up from a deep sleep.

I rub my eyes and pick it up.

What I see makes me sit up.

Heath is calling me in the middle of the night.

I listen closely to the quietness that clings to the darkness in the house. Mom and Dad are sleeping downstairs in their room. Things seem to be okay between them, like the weekend or the fights they've had never happened. How my parents sweep the mess under the rug and go on with their lives surprises me. They don't talk, but when they do, a fight happens and Mom gets hurt and later she forgives him. The cycle repeats every day, leaving me puzzled.

The call ends, and I curse myself for not picking it up.

My eyes waver to the door. I don't think my parents are standing outside my door right now. If they were, I'd know. The creaky floorboards would give away their presence.

I dial Heath's number and press the phone to my ear.

The erratic, little heartbeats echo in my ear.

"Rose." His voice, crisp and low, pours heat into me.

Just my name. He only speaks my name and I melt like ice under the sun.

"Heath," I whisper, my voice all shaky and breathy.

Where is all the oxygen in the room?

"You said my name. I don't hear it quite often from your lips." The hint of a smile lingers in his words. I don't need to see him to know there's a grin on his lips.

From deep within, I summon courage. "Should I say it more?"

"Fuck, yes."

I smile. "Then I will."

"You can start right now."

My confidence bubble bursts. "Right now?"

"Yes."

I gulp hard.

Saying his name shouldn't be this difficult. It's only five letters. One word.

I open my mouth to say his name, but no voice comes out.

A long moment passes between us as I fidget with the ends of my sweatshirt.

"Say it, Rose," Heath says.

I should. I really should.

It certainly wasn't a problem before. I never got so nervous or felt tingles exploding like fireworks inside me.

But now that my feelings for him have grown, every single thing tied to him means something.

"I'm trying to," I reply.

"How about you come out and say it to my face?"

I freeze. "What?"

"I'm parked a few houses down from your house."

"Why?"

Silence extends on the line, then his next words break it. "Because I need you."

Because I need you.

Heath needs me.

No one has ever needed me before. Especially Heath. I'm the one who's always needed him and he's always been there for me. He's seen me cry, have a panic attack and shake in fear, and he stayed. He always stayed. And being with him made me feel better.

"I know you can't come out and meet me. I know it's fucking late. I know you'll get into serious trouble. I know all that. Fuck!" His heavy breaths are like stones hitting me in the chest. "But I need you right now."

"Is everything okay?" Worry digs its claws into my chest. "Did something happen?"

He doesn't say a word.

I get the hint that something is wrong. "I'm coming to you. Give me five minutes."

"Okay."

Quickly, I change into a neat pair of clothes. Putting on my blue Converse, I grab my phone and book.

My parents don't know about the noisy floorboards, but I do. In the past months, I've learned which nooks and corners creak and which don't. With the stealth of a ninja, I get downstairs and then outside. I make sure I have the key with me so I can let myself in the morning. Hopefully, they won't notice my absence. No one comes to wake me up. My alarm does the job, so the only thing I need to worry about is sneaking inside without them knowing.

Cold wind brushes past me and makes my bones shake. It's late October and winter is around the corner. I'm excited about the chilly mornings, warm drinks and bundling up in scarves while watching my breath curl into the frosty air like little clouds. Autumn is my favourite season, but so is winter.

I tread down the empty road and spot a black car. Heath is leaning against it, looking up at the sky with a grave expression.

I'm a couple feet away from him, but I don't have to be close to him to realize that he is different tonight.

The sound of my footsteps makes his head turn in my direction. He abandons his spot and eliminates the distance between us. In a matter of seconds, he's right in front of me and my personal space fills with the scent of his cologne.

I open my mouth to greet him but his lips shut it. He kisses me with a desperation that makes my body weak. It's a miracle that I'm standing and not on the floor in a puddle.

Heath frames my face in his hands as he kisses me longer and harder, setting my whole body on fire. The chill of the night no longer affects me, because I'm burning up.

Only when my lips go numb does he pull back and lean his head against mine.

"You're here," he whispers. His hot breath fans over my skin.

"I'm here." I press my hands against his chest. Through his black hoodie, I feel his heart rate quickening. "We should leave before anyone sees us."

He hums in response, but makes no move.

I tug on his hoodie and he slips his hands off my face and strides toward his car. Opening the door for me, he helps me inside and then joins me.

I keep looking back, and only once we leave my neighborhood do I let out a breath of relief.

"I'll get you home soon," he adds and then gets quiet.

Leaning my head against the headrest, I study his side profile. His sharp jaw is set in a line as if he's tightly pressed his molars together. His eyes are fixed on the road, and tonight, there's an edge to them. They remind me of icy waters in the North. So cold that they'd cut you in half. I've never seen this look on him before. Annoyance, fury, joy and softness are a few emotions I've seen and come to understand, but this new look worries me.

His knuckles turn white around the steering wheel.

I fidget with my fingers in my lap as I let him drive me to his secret spot.

Ten minutes later, we're parked on the cliff. The whole town sleeps below us with only a few lights on. A quiet hangs in the air as if the whole world is resting and we're the only ones awake.

We both sit in the car in uncomfortable silence, and it gnaws at me. The silence between us has never bothered me before.

Even without asking, I know something is on his mind.

Because I need you.

Something isn't right.

"What are we doing here?"

Heath keeps staring out the window. It's so dark outside, you can hardly make out anything.

A minute passes and he doesn't answer.

I start growing anxious. "Did something happen?"

He releases a long breath before facing me. His eyes hold a distant look and his face is stern, no emotion flickering over. "My parents are home. I don't know how to deal with that."

The topic doesn't surprise me one bit. In all the time I've known him, he's told me so little about these people who brought him into this world. I don't know what they look like or what they are like. I suppose it's the same with Heath. These people are literal strangers to him.

"What do you feel for them?" I ask.

"Anger. There's so much anger inside me for them that I don't know what to do with it. Whenever I see them or talk to them, all I can remember is that they are the reason for my sister's death. Maybe if they were here and kept an eye on us, we would've been able to save her." He quietly adds, "But they weren't and she's not here anymore."

This is the first time he's openly talking to me about them, and I'm understanding why he hates them. Still, I don't know what to say.

My parents are present in my life, and that hasn't ended well either.

"You once asked me what my parents are like? I wonder about that too. I know nothing about them. They are complete strangers to me." He smiles bitterly. "And now I have to live with them and they are everywhere in the house."

"You hate that too?"

"What"

"That they are everywhere?"

"I do. The other night I came in late because I was at the underground and Mom was waiting up for me. It was strange to see her in the living room. I've never had someone do that for me before. It was past midnight and she needed sleep. You should see her, she's thin and weak. I don't know why the fuck she thought it was a good idea to wait for me."

Heath says he hates it, but the way his voice raises in worry tells me that maybe he cares about them, even if it's only a little bit.

"Every morning she wakes up early and prepares breakfast,

knowing I only drink a protein shake," he grumbles. "She also follows me around, which fucking annoys me."

I bite my lower lip to not smile at that. "What about your Dad?"

He frowns. "He isn't like my mother. He doesn't hover over me, but I find him always watching me. He knows when I leave and come back. And I know he knows about other stuff too."

"You said they are planning to stay. It seems to me that they want to know you."

He chuckles dryly. "It's too fucking late."

"Are you afraid that they are going to leave again?"

A muscle in his jaw ticks. His eyes go cold.

"There's more to it, Hope. It's not just that they left. It's that they didn't visit, call, or check up on me for years. They abandoned us and now suddenly they want to make up for it," he snaps. "Broken things don't get mended."

My heart breaks for him. "I'm sorry."

He deflates. "Me too for having such shitty parents."

"You're not alone. Mine are the same."

His gaze softens. "I'm sorry."

I nod. Shitty is an understatement for the damage my parents has done to me. I feel like I'm not the same person anymore. Something fundamentally has changed within me. I have no idea what pieces of me I've lost or if I'll ever get those back.

Leaning his head back, he says in a quiet voice, "The thing that bothers me the most is, why do I care? I don't like them at all. I hate them. It was good when they weren't here and I didn't have to see their faces or listen to their voices. I had nothing to remember them by, but now... Fuck!"

He rubs his face and groans. "Now I don't fucking know what to do."

Frustration bubbles under the surface and he looks about ready to burst and explode everywhere.

This is the first time I'm seeing him this way.

There is so much I need to learn about Heath Travon. He's like a puzzle that I need to collect all the pieces of so I can put them together and complete the picture. Only then will I truly know him.

Watching him go through such an array of emotions and a situation like this makes me want to help him, but nothing comes to mind.

Gosh. I'm the worst girlfriend ever.

I need to read more books and see how characters tackle this sort of issue.

Usually, they hold each other or distract themselves by having sex—

NO! I can't do that.

Option one it is.

My cheeks burn and my heart races.

Just thinking about sex makes me so nervous.

Heath is staring straight ahead with a stoic face and cold eyes.

Slowly, I let my hand cross over the console and take his. The silver rings on his fingers feel cold, sending a shiver down my spine.

He swivels his head in my direction and gives my hand a squeeze.

"What is it, Rose?"

"I'm trying to comfort you."

A laugh comes out of him. "Just by holding my hand?"

"Is it not enough?"

"It is, but I think you can do more."

My eyebrows pinch together. "How?"

He smirks. "Get in the backseat and I'll tell you."

My stomach flips. "In the backseat?"

Instead of answering me, he moves to the back while I stay rooted in my place.

"Come here, Rose," he says in a husky tone that makes me press my legs together.

Why did I think of sex earlier? Now I can't function normally.

Not wanting to make him wait, I climb into the back and settle down beside him. Well, not exactly beside him. There is enough space to fit a person between us—which shouldn't be there since we're dating.

Heath reaches over and turns on the ignition, but doesn't switch on the headlights. He turns on the music player and ANGELS by

Chase Atlantic starts playing at a low volume. Just enough for us to listen to the music and also talk to each other.

When he moves back, he makes sure to sit right next to me.

The thrum of my pulse increases at having him so close to me. His body, his heat and his scent are making my senses go into a frenzy. I'm clueless as to which one to focus on and how to deal with him.

I know how his body looks under that black hoodie. The strong structure of the muscles in his chest and torso and crevices that make the six-pack. I remember his upper body very vividly—I couldn't forget after seeing him in just shorts. He's beautiful and perfect in every sense of those words.

And if his body isn't enough to make me nervous, his body heat is like that of a furnace that'll keep me warm all night. He also wears this cologne that smells refreshing, yet enticing, just like him.

The combination of all these three is something I can handle only in books. But now that it's in real life, my head and heart have stopped working. No rational thought crosses my mind, just loud heartbeats that beat like a drum into my ears.

"Are you okay?" he asks.

"I'm fine," I blurt.

"You're clutching the ends of your sweatshirt a little too tight." I quickly let go and place my hands in my lap. "And you're looking at my chest."

I meet his gaze, then quickly look away because it looks so intense in the dark.

Heath cups my chin and tips my head back. "Look at me, Rose."

"Okay," I whisper, staring into his blue eyes that have softened. They remind me of an ocean on a summer day. The color is so bright, blue and beautiful that it imprints itself on my mind, making it impossible to look at the shade again *without* thinking of him.

"You look nervous. Is something wrong?" His thumb caresses my chin. "Tell me so I can fix it."

"It's nothing like that." My heart pounds.

"There is something that is bothering you."

How can I tell him it's the idea of intimacy that scares me?

Perhaps, the thought hasn't even crossed his mind and only I am fussing over it.

"Are you worrying yourself over what I said to you earlier?"

"No."

"You don't need to do anything you don't want to. We're taking things at your pace. Whatever you want, I want that." He tucks my hair behind my ear. "If holding my hand is how you want to comfort me, then it's enough. You are enough for me."

I shake my head. "I can do more, but I feel scared."

"Scared of what?"

"Not knowing what I'm doing."

He smiles down at me. "That's fucking impossible. Whatever you'll do to me, I promise you, I'll feel it."

"Are you sure?"

"Yes."

"We're only on first base."

"I'm aware."

"Don't you want to go to other bases?"

"Do *you* want to, Rose?"

Heat flushes through my body, igniting every inch of me.

"I..." I stammer.

He presses a soft kiss against my temple like I'm the most precious thing in the world to him.

"It's okay if you don't have an answer right now. Think about it and tell me later."

I shake my head and force my hands up to fist his hoodie into my hands. Despite how hard my lungs ache and how fast my heart beats, I refuse to let myself be the shy, nervous girl who can't communicate. With him, I want to share my thoughts no matter how absurd they seem. He deserves to know all of me.

He likes me. That means something.

I push him back to straddle him.

Once I'm sitting on his lap with my knees on either side of him, only then do I meet his gaze.

He looks utterly stunned. His eyes are wide and his mouth is a little open.

A flush of heat curls in my stomach, turning my insides into liquid. I can't believe I just did that, or that I'm not backing off.

"Please wait. I have the answer," I say without my voice shaking. "I want you too, but in a way no one else does. I want to know the way you like to be kissed or how you like to be touched." My skin is burning hot. "I want to go beyond the first base with you but I don't know how to do that. I want to complete all the bases with you."

This is it.

The reason why I need to fling myself off this cliff after what I just said.

I straight up told him to have sex with me. Or eventually.

Heath sits beneath me like a statue. He doesn't utter a word and only stares at me.

The growing silence makes me anxious.

So, I look down in his lap and play with the strings of his hoodie that looks too good on him—everything does. I don't think there's anything that won't suit Heath Travon.

At once, his hand cups my face and lifts it.

Leaning down, he says, "Do you have any idea what you fucking do to me?"

Before I can open my mouth to answer him, his mouth is on mine and he kisses me hard. If it wasn't for his hand holding the back of my head, I would have fallen behind by the sheer force with which he comes at me.

It's like he is talking to me with his body rather than his words.

Not that I mind this form of communication.

In return, I fist his hoodie and arch myself into his direction as I kiss him back. His hand moves down my back, bunching up my sweatshirt and pulling me to him.

The air grows thick and tension rises.

My heart beats so hard my fingers shake.

All because of this boy who consumes me like a drug.

I've never done drugs in my life, but now I understand why people find that euphoric feeling exhilarating. Every nerve ending in my body comes to life.

We kiss for what feels like hours, but it's only been minutes.

Sometimes, time slows down when I'm with him. Every second ticks by at the pace of a turtle.

Heath is first to pull away, and fills the tiny space between us with his hot breath. It dances on my swollen, numb lips that still ache to taste more of his.

It's only my labored, fast breaths that halt me from claiming his mouth.

Books have indulged me enough to know that kissing is romantic, but I had no idea how special and close it makes you feel to someone.

My lips are forever imprinted by his.

"Fuck!" Heath murmurs and moves. In doing so, the inner side of my thigh brushes against the front of his jeans and we both still.

A gasp leaves me, and I clutch his hoodie even tighter.

Don't freak out.

Don't freak out.

Don't freak out.

"Oh my God," I whisper.

Heath grips both sides of my waist and groans.

"It's fine. Don't worry about it," Heath assures me.

"I'm sorry."

He huffs. "It...happens. Not your fault, Rose."

But it is my fault.

I know enough to know that I'm the reason.

"Can I help?"

"No!"

"Let me get off you."

"Fuck no!" Those words carry a bite and he tightens his hold on me. "I like having you this close."

"But—"

"Relax," he says softly.

I nod.

"You don't have to worry about this. I've made up my mind and I won't change it. I'll go at your pace."

I melt against him, loosening my taut muscles that have stretched due to tension and panic.

"All I want is you, Heath."

His fingers dig into my sides as he drags me across his lap.

I can feel him beneath me, and for a second, it scares me because I've never been with a guy before. But with that ball of fear, there is also a cloud of excitement that swirls, brimming with anticipation.

I hear him mutter, "For fuck's sake."

And then he pulls me against him.

16

HEATH

ALL I WANT IS YOU, HEATH.

The string holding my self-restraint is close to snapping after hearing those words.

She *wants* me.

She wants me.

In the sense that I take off her clothes and see her like I've never seen her before. The pale, smooth skin that I know would blush under my touch. The body that would shake because of my kisses. The sounds that would escape her mouth because of me.

Those thoughts alone make me want to throw caution to the wind.

But only one thing stops me.

Rose.

She's been through so much, especially with her dad. He abused her for months and I know that has left emotional and physical scars on her. She felt fear and panic, shedding so many tears.

Now all I want to do is protect her and show her happiness.

That matters to me far more than my own desires.

I feel like I've finally found someone who understands me and makes me feel whole. She fills my emptiness with herself. Like a bright ray of sunshine, she casts away my darkness. Just being with her is enough to make me feel better.

I like her. I like her a lot.

But there are times when my chest expands with so much care, worry and fondness that I fear my bones will break and everything inside me will come out.

Seeing that will scare her.

The absolute fucking last thing I want.

Placing my arms around her waist, I envelope her in a hug that brings her close to me. My nose buries in the crook of her neck and I breathe in her flowery scent. *Lavender.* The sweet fragrance makes my blood race. The familiarity of it is now something I'm accustomed to.

Rose softens in my hold.

Chase Atlantic plays in the background as I keep her in my arms. The safest place for her.

When I saw marks on her body, fear in her eyes and tremors in her hands, all I wanted was to take her somewhere she would be safe. Unknowingly, I've shaped myself to be that someplace for her where the danger—her dad—can't get to her. I know I'll do anything to put myself in harm's way so it can't reach her.

"Are you feeling better?" she asks.

Her voice.

Fuck. Her voice weakens me.

I like it when she speaks to me in her gentle and sweet voice laced with worry—for me.

"I am," I answer honestly. "I told you. I needed you tonight."

"You have me."

How fucking grateful I am.

"I'm sorry for making you sneak out and be with me right now."

"It's fine," she blurts almost immediately, not making me feel guilty for a second.

A vague thought crosses my mind. A thought that Sebastian planted in my head.

"We haven't gone out on a date," I mumble in her neck.

"Date. We. No." Hope fumbles over words pulling a chuckle out of me.

"Sorry..." she whispers. "I thought since we're already dating, it doesn't matter."

Now I feel like an asshole for making her lower her standards. She reads words on papers and feels things. For fuck's sake, she's in love with guys who are purely fictional but to her they are real.

I've read the books she reads and I know how grand gestures are a big theme in all the romance stories.

Rose is a hopeless romantic. I want her to experience all the romantic things with me.

Everything she has read about, I want to make it come true.

I don't want her to lower her standards and settle down for the bare minimum. Instead, I want to set the bar so high that it makes it impossible for her to even think about those fictional men let alone love them.

My chest constricts as I utter my next words, "That night I came to your room to ask you out on a date."

Rose pulls back and stares at me in shock.

I fight the urge not to tug her back into my arms.

"Why didn't you tell me?"

I arch an eyebrow. "Because I was fucking nervous."

"You get nervous?"

"Only around you."

Even in the dark, I know her cheeks are painted in that beautiful hue of red that is my favourite.

"What about butterflies?"

"You mean those tiny insects in my stomach?"

She nods.

"I get them because of you."

Her cheeks redden further. I just know it.

Leaning forward, I find her lips in the dull light of the screen and kiss her softly. My movements are slow as I devour her.

After a second, when I know she's breathless, I pull back but not before stealing a peck.

Fuck. I can't get enough of her lips.

Kissing is not supposed to be this addictive.

"Go out on a date with me," I rasp.

She pants as she catches her breath. "Okay."

"Where do you want to go?"

"I'll be fine wherever you take me."

I smile. "I'm fine right here, right now. All that matters to me is you're with me."

"I feel the same."

I give her waist a squeeze. "Tell me the place, Rose."

"Bookstore."

"A place you haven't been to before."

"Aquarium."

"There is an aquarium in the city," I tell her. "We can visit it and then have a nice dinner at a restaurant."

She clutches my hoodie tightly. "I won't be able to go with you. My parents will find out and..."

She doesn't need to end that sentence. We both know what will happen.

"I'll take care of everything. You don't have to worry about anything."

"But how?"

"I'll figure it out and text you the details."

"Heath—"

"It'll be okay. I'll make sure that you have fun."

I know her head is running at a hundred miles per second, but so is mine. Now that I have her permission, I will find out what to do about this matter.

Since it's getting to be early in the morning, I drive her home fast and ask her to text me once she's in her room.

Hope: I'm in my room.

Heath: No one woke up?

Hope: No.

Heath: Are you sure?

Hope: I heard them snoring.

Heath: Be safe for me.

Hope: Okay.

Mary

Heath: Text me if something happens.

Hope: I will.

Hope: Are you okay now?

Heath: I'm okay.

Hope: I wish I could do more like you do for me.

Heath: You gave me a boner so I think you did a great job.

Hope: Oh my God! Please kill me.

Heath: I can't. We have a date.

Hope: I'm sorry about the...

Heath: Don't think about it.

Hope: It's hard not to.

Heath: Want me to distract you? I'm parked close by.

Hope: You should go home. We have school in three hours.

Heath: I'll come pick you up.

Hope: You don't have to. I'll walk.

Heath: I don't want my girlfriend to walk.

Hope: It's fine. I don't mind.

Heath: I fucking mind.

Hope: I just don't want my parents to see you.

Heath: I'll park around the block.

Hope: Okay, if it's not too much trouble.

Heath: It's not.

Hope: I finished the book you gave me.

Heath: What did you rate it?

Hope: Five stars.

Heath: Why five?

Hope: Because it was perfect.

Heath: Here I thought perfection doesn't exist.

Hope: That's because you haven't met Jack.

Heath: For fuck's sake.

17

HOPE

THE NEXT DAY, IT'S LUNCHTIME, AND MARIE AND I HEAD out to get food. She goes to the diner and drops me off at a coffee shop to get drinks. This is the place where Sebastian used to work. She told me how he'd personally make her seasonal drinks and give her a little extra with her orders. She always left him tips, and he'd send her a smile that made her bad day better.

Of course, she went into quite a lot of detail and I felt like I was reading a romance book with how beautifully and sweetly she described everything. She sounded exactly like someone in love.

Sebastian is special to her. Just as Heath is to me.

At the counter, I greet a teenage girl who gives me a polite smile. I hand her the note Heath gave me, with our orders written on it. He said this way I wouldn't have to worry about interacting. That small gesture gripped my throat so tightly that I said nothing, kissed him, and left.

I make a mental note to text him about it.

Passing over the note is far easier than me, staring at her and trying to get the words out as my heart beats erratically as if it's about to die. Black coffee for Heath, pumpkin spice latte for Marie, matcha latte for Sebastian, and iced tea for me.

I move over to the second lane next to a woman. She is thin and small, but looks stunning in a pastel pink dress that loosely hugs her frame. A diamond earring blinks at me as she tucks her hair back. I also catch a glimpse of the diamond ring on her finger and the necklace around her neck.

Without a doubt, she is rich.

I don't think I've ever seen diamonds in real life.

Dad got Mom a simple gold ring that she's never taken off. Over the years it's dulled in color which ironically reflects how their love has taken a turn in the past decade or so.

The woman fidgets with her hands like I sometimes do.

Are you okay? Those words sit on the tip of my tongue, but I can't get them out.

If someone asked me that question, I'd run out of here so fast.

So instead, I silently watch her panicking as she waits for her order.

The girl behind the waiting counter sends us a smile. "Your orders will take a while. I'm sorry. We're a bit busy today."

"It's fine," the woman says softly. "I'm in no hurry."

I give the girl a nod as I tightly hold onto my book.

"A table is empty over there." The girl gestures and both of us look at it at the same time. "Please wait. It'll only take us ten minutes."

The woman turns her head, and I'm met with a pair of blue eyes that look oddly familiar. Warmth and kindness shine in them, and as they gaze at me, I can't help but relax under their weight—which is new, since I usually avoid people.

"Come on," she says with a smile and walks to the table and sits down.

I take a seat across from her and place my book in my lap, making sure the cover is facing down.

My stomach rolls in discomfort, anticipating the silence that will hang between us, but she speaks up.

"It's lunch break at school, right?" she asks with interest.

I nod.

"Bellmare High?"

I nod again.

"My son goes there." She sounds excited. "You must know him. Heath Travon."

The world stops moving on its axis, and the noise in the cafe drops to pin-drop silence.

I can barely control the tremors dancing on the tips of my fingers.

Oh my God.

This is Heath's mother.

And she is right in front of me.

What should I do?

She has no idea that her son and I are dating.

I'm a stranger to her.

Also, she is beautiful. Like really beautiful.

Seconds go by as I slowly take her in. Bright blue eyes, sharp nose and thin lips. A few wary strands of her dark brown curly hair frame her face, the rest upheld in a soft bun that showcases her diamond earrings. She also has a diamond flower pendant that sits on her bony collarbone. The soft hue of pink dress suits her white complexion and makes her look young.

You should see her, she's thin and weak. Heath's words echo in my ears.

My attention drifts to her hollow cheeks, the bright flush on her face and the dark circles underneath her eyes.

Even as a complete stranger, I can tell that she looks exhausted. As if she is carrying a burden and the weight is too heavy for her.

As I stare at her for a while, I realize her eyes hold the same grief as Heath's, but where his also carry anger, hers are filled only with sadness.

When I don't say a word, she frowns.

The same frown Heath wears when he's confused or annoyed at something or someone.

They are so similar.

"Is something the matter?"

I panic. "No! Not at all. I know your son."

Her entire face brightens up. "Really? I've seen two of his friends. Sebastian and Marie. I didn't know he had more friends."

I'm his girlfriend.

"We are."

She quickly leans over the table, her eyes sparking up with

excitement. "Tell me about him. How is he at school? Does he have a lot of friends? What are his grades? Does he eat lunch or skip? Is he doing well in classes? What about sports?"

She fires off all these questions and I learn that Heath was right. His parents know nothing about him. Nothing at all.

It makes me sad, really sad, knowing that he truly has been on his own for years. His parents are alive and well, but for some reason they live in another country.

Anger simmers in my blood like boiling lava, heat enveloping me in a tight embrace.

Instead of answering her questions I want to ask her, why she wasn't there for him? Why she left him? Why she broke something in him?

The only thing that stops me is, it's not my place to ask those questions and have the answers that Heath deserves to know first. After last night, I know he cares about his parents, despite not wanting to.

When I take long to answer, his mother grimaces. "I'm sorry, I shouldn't be asking you these questions."

"It's fine, I don't mind—"

"No, it's not. I should already know all that—and more." Her voice drops. "I'm a terrible mother."

"You can ask him. I think he'd like that," I blurt.

Her eyes shoot up and they're filled with tears. "You really think so?"

I give her an encouraging nod. "Yes."

"I don't know if he's told you or not, but we're back in town and we're staying."

"I know. He told me."

She smiles. "Seems like he talks to you."

My face turns red. "Sometimes."

"Does he ever talk about me?"

Under her curious gaze that burns with hope, I fidget with my fingers, not knowing what answer to give her.

Heath wouldn't want me to meet her let alone talk to her about him. He didn't introduce me to her, which makes me feel bad, like he is hiding me. I understand that he doesn't want his parents to know about any aspect of his life—that includes me. Still, it hurts a little.

I shake my head and her face turns gloomy. I hate seeing that look on her but I can't break Heath's trust and tell her things he's confided in me.

"I see," she studies the table, "I lived away from him for all these years just to keep him safe. It was the most important thing to me that he was protected, healthy, and alive. There were so many times when I wanted to come back and spend all my days with him but I couldn't because then he'd become a target. I thought it was for the good, but turns out it wasn't."

I listen to her closely, regret thick in her voice.

"Heath is my son. He means the world to me. I love him more than anything in this world. Since the moment I learned I was pregnant with him, I have loved him. And when I held him in my arms I knew my heart no longer lived inside my chest but inside him. I just wish he knew or I'd told him. Now he hates me."

She sniffles and her bottom lip quivers.

Everything in me tells me to move forward and comfort her, but I'm a complete stranger to her. Besides, I'm not good at comforting people. I'm barely good at comforting myself.

Still, I try. "Heath doesn't hate you."

"You don't know that."

"I do."

Her sad blue eyes meet mine. "How?"

"I just do. You have to believe me." I try to sound convincing.

"I see," she murmurs, watching me.

"I know—"

A waitress stops by our table to let us know that our orders are ready.

We both stand up. Taking out a tissue from her designer purse, she dabs away the tears from her cheeks and inhales a long, deep breath. She smiles up at me. "I feel a bit better knowing he doesn't hate me."

I eagerly nod. "He doesn't. You should talk to him. I think he'd love that."

Her eyes widen and excitement rings in her next words. "Really? Are you sure?"

"Yes."

We walk to the counter, collect our orders and then walk out. A black SUV is parked at the curb with Derek waiting next to it. When he sees me, he narrows his gaze and then glances at Heath's mother.

Fortunately, she doesn't notice that he knows me.

Averting his gaze, he opens the door for her and she moves to get inside but then turns her head and says to me, "You didn't tell me your name."

"Hope."

She grins. "It was lovely meeting you, Hope. Would you come home after school with Heath sometimes?"

I'm pretty sure after I tell Heath about this interaction he'd try even harder to keep me away from her.

"I'm not sure. I have a few tests this week that I need to study for."

"You can study with Heath and when you're done, maybe you can help me talk to him." She looks so hopeful.

Seeing that look on her face pulls my heartstrings.

There's no way I can refuse her.

"I'll try to come," I reply.

A smile tugs on her lips. "Excellent. I'll be waiting for you."

With that she gets inside and Derek closes the door. He then faces me and sends me a mean glare before getting in the car and driving away.

Marie pulls over a minute later and blares her horn, signaling for me to get inside the car.

I set the drinks in my lap, careful that they don't spill, then turn to her.

"I just met Heath's mom," I blurt in panic.

She pales. "What?"

"Heath's mom. I talked to her."

"As in greeted her?"

"As in had a long conversation with her."

Her eyes gleam with surprise. "Oh my God!"

"I know," my voice comes out all panicky. "She talked to me about

Heath and how she loves him but doesn't know how to tell him. She asked me to come over and help her talk to Heath."

"Too much information, Hope. I can't process it all at once." She reminds me. "I'm still stuck on the part where you met her."

"I can't believe it happened. I met her and she has no idea that I'm his girlfriend."

She gasps. "You didn't tell her?"

"No. I don't think Heath wants me to meet his parents."

Sadness flickers through her gaze. "That's because he hates them and wants to keep his distance. He hasn't introduced Sebastian and me to his parents either."

I look down at my lap. "At least she knows about you two."

"Kelly and Derek told her, not Heath."

"And not about me."

"It isn't like he's hiding you or anything."

I can barely utter a word so I give her a convincing smile.

It doesn't work.

She frowns. "No! I mean it. He wouldn't hide you. He kissed you in front of the entire school because he wanted everyone to know that you guys are together and nobody better fuck with you."

She is right. If he wanted to hide me he wouldn't have done that. Besides, he isn't like that anyway. He doesn't care what people think about him or say about him. All that matters to him are his own thoughts and beliefs.

"Heath isn't hiding you. He's just protecting you from his parents, who have always given him a hard time."

I nod.

"Will you tell me everything that happened in the past twenty minutes that I left you? I really shouldn't have. I swear I got a mini heart attack from hearing that news."

Not wasting a second, I go into detail about everything and her face shows a wide range of reactions. She shows her feelings on the outside, making it easy to trust her because you know it's all real. There's no faking the worry, anger, happiness, fear, and excitement she feels for me, or how she always wants the best for me. I'm lucky to have her as my best friend.

"She sounds sweet."

"I think she really loves Heath."

She sighs. "Yeah, but she's done an awful job at showing him. I know my parents love me because they've shown it to me. I know they'd risk everything for me."

My mind only focuses on one bit. My parents love me.

Do my parents love me?

I mean, my mom does, but she's changed in the past few months. Our connection isn't the same anymore. She used to be my shield, my safe place and comfort blanket. Now, she isn't any of those. I told her about Dad and she didn't believe me. And when she trusted me she found a way to blame me for what happened. And my dad... He doesn't love me. Not one bit. I'm not sure if he ever did.

My parents don't love me.

A stab as piercing sharp as the tip of an arrow slices through my heart, sending jolts of pain through my chest. My breath gets stuck in my lungs and it's impossible to breathe.

"Hope, are you okay?" Marie's worried voice cuts through my panic.

"I'm...fine," I wheeze out.

Suddenly, the car becomes a cage. All I want to do is get out and be in the open.

"You don't look fine at all. What's happening?" Marie puts her hand on mine. I barely feel her touch.

I don't know what's happening.

I don't know why I'm reacting this way.

I don't know how I can help myself.

The more I think the tighter my chest gets and my breaths fall short.

Marie moves over the console and wraps her arms around me, squeezing me against her until her warmth melts my frigid state.

I gasp and she rubs my back.

"Breathe, Hope. Breathe. Just breathe."

I inhale a deep breath despite how hard it is.

"Great. You did it. Do it five more times. I'm counting."

Opening my mouth, I take long breaths and exhale them out

slowly. Marie counts and doesn't speak a word, which is something new. She is always talking.

If she spoke, I don't think I'd be able to concentrate with how distraught I feel right now.

When I've calmed down a little, she pulls back and looks me in the eyes.

"Focus on my eyes. What do you see?"

I stare into her eyes. "Hazel."

"What hazel?"

I pause and study the color like I've never done before. All my other thoughts scatter away one by one, until all my attention narrows down to her eyes. Her beautiful eyes. I've never noticed how insanely captivating they are. A sea of soft moss green with brown, the shade of autumn leaves, spreading out in waves around the black circle.

"Brown and green, but mostly brown."

"Are there golden flecks? Sebastian says there are."

I blink and look closer. "He is right. There are a few."

She pulls back and heaves out a dramatic sigh. "You are okay. Finally."

It takes me a moment to gather myself. My whole body flushes with embarrassment as the wave of humiliation washes over me, knowing that Marie saw me have a panic attack. All because of one sentence.

My parents don't love me.

I shiver as that thought comes back, so I quickly shove it to the back of my mind.

"Thank you," I murmur.

"You don't need to thank me. That's what friends do. Make each other feel better. That's one of the many rules of friendship Sebastian taught me. One day you'll know all of them."

I stay silent, not knowing what to say.

Marie's eyes soften. "What happened that made you so anxious?"

"Just my thoughts."

"About what?"

I hesitate and she senses the long pause that I take.

Reaching over, she gives me a hug. "I'm here for you always. Tell me when you feel like it. No pressure at all."

I wrap my arms around her neck. "Thanks, Marie, for everything. I just need time to think about it on my own first."

"I know. Don't worry about it."

"Are you sure?"

"More than a thousand percent." She pulls back and shoots me a genuine smile. "Let's head back to our boyfriends."

Just then, my phone starts pinging with messages, all from Heath.

Marie laughs as she starts the engine. "Heath is so obsessed with you."

"That's not true."

"The twenty messages say otherwise."

He calls and she grins.

18

HEATH

I DROP ROSE OFF AT HER HOUSE WITH A RELUCTANT HEART. She said she has a test to study for. I suggested doing it at my place, but she said I wouldn't let her focus.

She isn't wrong.

I can't keep my hands to myself when she is around.

I let her get out of my car after a five-minute make-out session and only because her lips were swollen and numb and she pushed me off because she was breathing hard.

That wasn't the only thing hard.

So was my dick that had no business getting aroused at a moment like this. Lately, it's been happening a lot and I don't know what to do about it. I've never gotten hard this fast and this bad for a girl before. It is fucking painful. It happens with kissing alone. I can't imagine what would happen if we go past second base or more. I know I'll embarrass myself because there's no way I'd be able to control myself.

Rose is beautiful. So fucking beautiful. From her big brown eyes to her lovely face. She is gorgeous.

My heart dances at a rhythm of its own whenever it sees her. I can hardly breathe or think, much less control my dick which is as much attracted to her as the rest of me.

"Fucking hell," I mutter with a groan.

We've just started dating.

Not much has happened between us apart from some kissing.

And here I am getting an erection just from breathing the same air as her.

I know the person I should talk to about this. I just don't want to because he won't let me live if he gets to know this is happening to me.

With a tired sigh, I pull out of the neighborhood and drive down to his house anyway.

Sebastian answers the door, sweating and out of breath, wearing nothing but fucking boxers. Boxers that show the outline of his erection.

The horrendous sight puts me in a foul mood.

"Don't tell me you're having sex," I grumble.

He grins. "I was in the middle of sex."

"For fuck's sake," I mutter. "I need to talk to you."

"Can it wait?"

"No."

"It has to wait five minutes. I need to finish and also Marie—"

I grab the door and slam it in his face, muffling his reply. A second later, I hear his laughter and I know he didn't finish the sentence and was teasing me.

I walk down the hallway and near the elevator so as not to hear any of their sex noises.

Sex.

They are having sex.

I wonder how he's able to control himself when Marie is in front of him.

If Hope takes off one piece of clothing...

I let out a grunt.

Stop.

I need to put these thoughts away.

Nothing of that sort is happening between us.

She isn't ready and neither am I.

Switching on my phone, I send her a text.

> Heath: Did I tell you, you looked beautiful today?

It takes her five minutes to reply.

> Hope: You didn't, but it's okay.

I roll my eyes.
Her standards shouldn't lower because of me.
I'm not losing to her fictional men.

> Heath: Well, you did. Beautiful, I mean.

She sees the message but doesn't reply.
So I send her another message.

> Heath: You looked beautiful today, Rose. You always do.

It's then that the dots appear on the screen and a few seconds later her reply comes.

> Hope: Thanks.

> Heath: I mean it.

> Hope: I know.

> Heath: You are terrible at taking compliments.

> Hope: That's because no one's ever given them to me.

My heart clenches at that sentence.
Fuck. There's so many things she hasn't experienced. Simple things that matter.

> Heath: That was before me.

Hope sees the message and goes quiet.

She's busy blushing.

That damn red blush.

It does things to me.

My phone pings.

Sebastian: You can come in now, asshole.

What the fuck? How am I the asshole?

He's the one who ditched me to have sex with his girlfriend. As if he hasn't done it a hundred times already. Fortunately, he has a brain cell to use protection and be careful.

I'm too young to become an uncle.

I march down the hallway and enter his place using the key he's given me.

Sebastian is in trousers and a T-shirt, lounging on the couch with Coca-Cola cans on the coffee table and a bunch of snacks. He lights up when he sees me, and I flip him the finger.

A sweet hum floats out of the kitchen. Marie is wearing trousers and one of his sweatshirts—thank God she's dressed decent—and is stirring something in the pot on the stove.

Sensing my gaze, she looks over and waves. "Heath!"

There's too much enthusiasm in her voice.

"Blondie." I nod.

"How are you?"

I arch an eyebrow. "We saw each other a couple of hours ago at school."

"I know."

"Then why are you asking?"

"Because a lot can happen to someone in a short amount of time."

"Nothing is going to happen to me. So stop worrying about me."

"Can't do that. You are my favourite friend after Hope and Sebastian."

For some strange reason, I feel bitter that I'm in third place. "So, I'm last on your list?"

Marie's grin goes away. "You look offended."

I narrow my eyes. "I'm not offended. In fact, I don't fucking care."

"I'm not fully convinced."

Sebastian decides to pipe in. "Neither am I. From the looks of it, you look really mad at being at the bottom."

I send him a glare. "Wouldn't *you* like that?"

He grins. "Of course, I do. I'm second on the list. But above *you*."

Marie comes over and stands in front of me. "You are one of my best friends and I love you a lot. You were definitely in second place, very close to Sebastian."

"Oh, how much I miss those days," I reply dryly.

"I miss those days too. You were always there for me and you helped me so much. I wouldn't have gotten better if you hadn't supported me. Thank you—"

"Don't start again," I grumble.

"You're important to me," she tells me. "But now I have Hope, who's my girl best friend. Something that I always wanted. She's so nice to me and doesn't judge me. She loves spending time with me and doesn't mind that I talk a lot. She has never asked me to shut up. She listens to everything I say and it makes me so happy." Tears fill her eyes. "So yeah, she's claimed the top spot now despite the fact that she hid something really big from me."

Sebastian gets up and hugs her tightly. He rests his chin on her head and squeezes her in his arms. "Shush baby, don't cry."

She cries anyway, and he turns her around, tucking her against his chest.

I grab a can of coke and walk into the kitchen to give them privacy. Their hushed whispers fly through the air, making me think of something that has always lingered at the back of my mind.

Alex motherfucking Hanson.

It's been nearly a week, and he hasn't hurt her—at least that's what she's told me and I can only wish that she isn't lying to me—but my guard is up. I know he's going to hurt her—I don't want that. It's only a matter of time.

I feel as helpless as I did before.

There's nothing I can't do other than hit him—which isn't enough.

The fact he hurts his own daughter stirs my stomach whenever the thought crosses my head. It is fucking sick.

I wish I could just take her out of that house and keep her safe at my place. I'd deal with my parents, who'd be nosy, but I wouldn't let them interfere.

All I want is to protect that girl. *My girl.*

"I'm making dinner, are you staying?" Marie strolls into the kitchen with a bright smile. Her eyes are a bit red but she looks okay.

My phone pings and I quickly check in case it's her message.

> Mom: Tonight I'm making dinner, so please come home early.

I must have been staring at the text too hard because Marie's voice comes from close.

"Is everything okay?" she asks.

"Yes," I roughly reply and sidestep her to talk to Sebastian.

"Seb is in his room folding laundry," she adds.

I take the stairs, two at a time, and enter his room. Marie's imprint is everywhere and it looks more like her room than his.

His bed has soft pink bed sheets and pillowcase—he doesn't even like pink. Makeup supplies sit on his study table, which should be occupied with books and stationery, but instead they are all on his nightstand. On the other nightstand, there's feminine perfume bottles, hair ribbons and hair clips, all in different sizes and colors. The chair in the corner of the small room has her clothes on it while his sit in the hamper. There are pink slippers near the door and a bra next to it.

I gesture to it with my eyes and Sebastian looks dumb.

"What?"

"Look down and see."

He does and grins as he picks it up. "That's my girlfriend's."

"Well fucking aware."

He chuckles as he takes care of it.

I sit on the pink sheets with a scowl and lean back as I watch him clean his room. It's a small space but he pays the rent and takes care of it. He's fucking proud of this place.

"Marie said you were folding laundry."

"In a minute."

I grow silent, watching him closely while trying to arrange the thoughts in my head. The evidence of his physical activities is everywhere and the air reeks with sex, which sends my head rolling and I can't fucking decide how to approach this topic.

He's the last person I want to discuss this matter with.

He won't let me live it down.

He will be on my ass about the details to make sure I'm not doing anything wrong.

Still, telling him I get a hard-on whenever my girlfriend is around is a bit strange.

"I don't like that look on your face."

I glance at him. "What look?"

"That constipated look."

"Fuck off."

"No can do."

"I'll do it for you then."

He laughs and walks past me and sets the basket on the bed and starts folding his and Marie's clothes.

"Something is on your mind. What is it?"

"Everything's fine."

"You just love that word, don't you?"

"You already know that."

"How many times am I going to ask before you finally tell me?"

I let out a sigh but the weight on my chest only sinks in.

His gaze burns the side of my face, but he doesn't speak a word.

Only when the silence begins to grow uncomfortable, I utter the words. "I'm a fucking mess when I'm around Rose."

"Mess?" he asks, confusion laced in his tone.

I nod.

"What kind of mess?"

"Just a complete fucking mess." I groan and tilt my head back as I stare at the ceiling. "It's embarrassing."

"And you say that you're not in love."

I narrow my eyes in his direction. "I'm not."

He smiles softly. "This is what love feels like."

My heart stops beating for a second. "No, that's not what love is. How could I love her when I just started liking her."

He stops folding and looks me in the eye. "You caught feelings for her the moment you met her. After that, your feelings just grew. You've fallen for her."

"Feelings aren't a fucking plant."

"In my head they are," he muses. "Your plant resembles a cactus. Imagine how much patience I have for watering it every day even though it doesn't require much water."

I look away, not caring about the nonsense he's spewing. All I can think about is what he said.

You've fallen for her, Heath.

As in she was a pebble on the road, and my foot stuck and I just fell. It happened all of a sudden and I couldn't save myself.

Falling should hurt, it doesn't.

Falling should make me scared, it doesn't.

Falling should make me want to save myself, but I won't.

Is this what love feels like?

The weight on my chest starts pressing down on me and I can hardly breathe.

Fuck. I refuse to have a nervous breakdown in the middle of my best friend's room. I don't want to worry him.

But the realization that I'm in love with Hope tears me apart from the inside.

It feels like the world has stopped moving and time has stood still. Everything is frozen but I'm the only one moving.

Confusion, anxiety, fear and a bunch of other emotions swirl in my head, making me nervous.

Nervous. Fuck. When have I ever been nervous in my life?

I forget all about the topic I wanted to talk about and instead ponder on what he said. This is not the first time he's told me this, but the impact of his words only hits me now.

The mattress dips under his weight as he sits down beside me. He grabs my shoulder and squeezes.

"It's okay," he tells me.

I gulp hard. "You just told me that I love her."

"Don't make it sound like I told you that you're dying."

"Then why does it feel like that?"

"Because it's something new that you've never experienced before. It's okay to feel this way."

I close my eyes and let out a long breath. The pressure on my chest moves away a little.

"We haven't even had our first date yet," I murmur.

"So what? You've spent loads of time with her and what matters is how you feel when you're with her."

"I feel calm," I answer instantly.

He smiles softly as if he gets why calm is important to me. He's seen me restless, looking for things and ways to ebb the grief and pain inside me. It's still there, but at least I have someone I can hug and find some reprieve in, if only for a short while. It's not cigarettes and alcohol that'll damage me. Every time I hug her—my arms wrapped around her and her head resting on my chest—something inside me heals.

I don't know what it is.

Love.

"This is good," Sebastian says. "You're not freaking out the way you did before when I told you."

I run a hand through my hair, trying to busy my fingers that shake a little. "What am I supposed to do now?"

"Nothing."

I look at him in confusion. "Nothing?"

He shakes his head. "Nothing."

"What do you mean by that?"

"Act natural. Don't think too much. Just be yourself when you're with her."

I scoff. "Trust me, you don't wanna know what happens when I'm with her."

He nudges me. "Now I really wanna know. What happens? You get horny?"

I quickly stand up. "I'm leaving."

"What? I meant that as a joke." He chuckles, but when he sees I'm not laughing he sobers up. "Shit."

"Shut up."

His gaze fills with amusement. "It's normal. It happens. You're insanely attracted to her. Just don't think with your dick, but with your head."

I shoot him a glare, annoyed with myself that he now knows about it. "I always think of her first."

"Don't forget to use protection."

I scowl. "Shut up."

He laughs and my anger simmers down a little. He looks so happy. So different from how he was at the beginning of the year.

Standing up, he walks over to his nightstand and takes out something. Turning around, he throws it at me and I catch it with one hand. When I open my fist, there's a condom in my hand.

"Good luck with your first time."

I throw the condom in his face and slam the door shut with a thud.

Asshole.

19

HEATH

I CLOSE THE DOOR BEHIND ME AND CHECK THE TIME.

It's past eleven pm.

Did I intentionally come home late? *Yes.*

I wasn't going to attend a fucking family dinner when we are anything but family. Plus, I knew there'd be less talking and more fighting. I wasn't in the mood to exchange fucking insults with my parents. Mom would get emotional and I'm not in the mood for that either.

I walk down the quiet hallway, noticing that my parents aren't lurking in the living room like they usually do nowadays. They wait up for me, which is the strangest thing ever. Seriously, why do they sacrifice their sleep for me? Also, why the fuck now? They didn't care before when they were living their perfect, happy lives in Canada, pretending they didn't have two children living alone in a small town like they're orphans.

As I think more, those thoughts turn my mood bitter.

I decide to turn back around and spend the night somewhere else when I hear quiet whisperings coming out of the kitchen.

Curiosity piques my interest, and I make my way toward it.

"You barely ate dinner, Mia Cara. You should eat something," Dad says.

"I'm not feeling hungry."

"Then why are you making blueberry muffins?"

"Maybe Heath likes them. *You do.*"

He sighs. "I only like them because *you* make them."

"You are always so sweet. I'm glad I married you."

"Me too. I love you with all my heart."

A second later, their kissing noises filter out of the room and I close my eyes and wince.

My parents are nauseatingly in love with each other.

Love.

The word makes my heart race.

I quickly push it away, refusing to think about it.

"Heath isn't home yet. I'm going to head out to find him," Dad says, his tone laced with worry that he rarely shows when it comes to me. "He better not be in any trouble. One record was enough to give me a fucking heart attack."

"He'll be fine," Mom assures him.

"He better be. I don't want to lose him."

A knot ties my stomach in a vice grip.

I had no idea that he cared about me. All he's shown me is indifference. I was sure that I didn't matter to him.

I lean hard against the wall as I listen to their conversation.

"You should talk to him. I think we both should."

"I would if he'd stop hating me for one second."

"He doesn't hate you."

"He does and he has all the reasons to do so. I'm the worst father ever."

"Xavier, that's not true. He doesn't—"

I emerge from around the corner—not able to control myself—and watch them stiffen. Mom gasps and Dad slips on a cold mask that doesn't let me read him, but his eyes say everything. They soften in relief and his shoulders relax.

"Heath, you're home." Mom rushes forward and hugs me. "Thank God."

I'm slowly learning that Mom loves hugging me—it's unavoidable. The way she sees me and then barrels right at me as if she can't control herself. And then she hugs me, and the emptiness inside me starts to fill with warmth. I never thought it'd fill up with anything, much less getting a hug from my mother.

I place my palm on her back.

"You're safe," she murmurs.

Before I can speak, someone else does.

"You could've shown up three hours ago. Your mother worked hard to prepare dinner." Dad's tone is accusing, but it contradicts the way he watches me as if I matter to him.

Why didn't I notice this before?

I say nothing as I separate myself from my mother and look at the island. It's filled with equipment and ingredients needed to make muffins.

"What's happening here?" I arch an eyebrow, fully pretending I know nothing.

Mom grins. "I'm making blueberry muffins."

I nod.

"I've just started, maybe you could help me make them?" she asks, eyes full of hope. "Your father has work to do so you can keep me company while he attends meetings and phone calls."

Dad tilts his head and stares at her. They share a quiet look that says a thousand words. Then, he turns to me. "Keep her company and don't be a menace."

I roll my eyes. "I'm not a fucking menace."

He narrows his eyes. "Avoid cursing in front of your mother."

I glare. "How about you—"

"Xavier, leave. We'll be fine," Mom says in a firm voice.

He sighs and looks at her with a defeated look. "After this, you're sleeping. Tomorrow is an important day."

I frown. "What's tomorrow?"

Mom smiles. "Nothing."

Before I can ask Dad, he leaves in a hurry.

I stare hard at Mom. "What is tomorrow?"

She looks down at the bowl. "Just a couple of tests."

I straighten up and near her. "What kind of tests?"

"It's nothing—"

"Are you dying? Do you have can—" My voice cracks before I can utter that word. Cancer. It isn't hard to say that word in my head, but saying it out loud is a different story—that makes it real and I don't want it to be real.

Mom pales and she erases the distance between us and holds my hand. "No! I'm fine. I don't have cancer. I'm not dying. I promise, I'm alright, Heath."

"You promise?" I croak out, watching her closely.

She nods. "Yes. I'm okay."

"Then what kind of tests do you have tomorrow?"

She hesitates for a moment. "A blood test to see if I have anemia."

"Is that serious?"

She nods. "It is, but I can treat it with medicine and diet."

"Are you sure that is all?"

"Yes."

I don't feel relieved. Worry slithers into my heart and makes a fucking home.

I hate that I'm worried for my mother. I don't want to lose her.

I make a mental note to look into anemia on Google.

My eyes narrow as I say, "If I find out that you're lying to me, I'll stop speaking to you."

She squeezes my hand that I haven't pulled away. "I'm not lying."

I nod and slowly pull my hand away.

"Are you hungry? There are leftovers that I can heat up," she suggests, not paying attention to her blueberry muffins.

"I've already eaten." Marie ordered pizza and overfed me. Sometimes, I forget how persuasive she can be.

"Right," she murmurs. "I made grilled salmon with rice and steamed broccoli."

"I hate broccoli," I reply.

She beams at me. "Me too. But your dad likes it so I just put it in there."

"I also hate spinach."

"But I saw you putting it into your milkshake the other day."

I move to the cupboard, take out a glass, and fill it with water.

164

After a sip, I answer, "Doesn't mean I don't hate it. I have to take it because it's important for muscles and overall health."

Mom watches me in wonder. "I had no idea."

"In the past year or so, I've started taking care of myself."

She catches on to what I'm trying to say. After Emery's death.

I throw the rest of the water back and place the glass down on the island.

The air grows thick with silence and awkwardness, making it hard for me to stay rooted and not leave. The grief we share is still too fresh and new to talk about and it nearly suffocates the space between us.

Mom doesn't move from her place. She looks like she's lost in deep thought.

I clear my throat to catch her attention. "Do you want to make those muffins or not?"

"Uh, yes. The muffins." She fidgets with her necklace. "Maybe I can make them tomorrow."

I shake my head, noticing the way her lower lip wobbles. If she goes to her room, she's going to cry a river and Dad will be on my ass.

I'm not a fucking menace.

"Tomorrow is too late," I grumble and sit down at one of the barstools.

She starts measuring ingredients and makes two bowls—one with wet ingredients and the other with dry, as she tells me when I ask.

"How was school?" she asks out of nowhere.

"It was fine."

She looks up at me with a smirk. "I met one of your friends recently."

"What friend? How do you even know they're my friend?"

"She said you're friends."

"That doesn't mean they're my friend."

She pauses. "She sounded like she knows you."

I frown. *Do I have a fucking stalker?*

"And you believed her?" I ask, confused.

She nods. "She was the sweetest girl and so pretty."

"What did she say?"

"Not much." She smiles. "But she said you talk to her sometimes."

For fuck's sake, who is this girl? The only girl I talk to is Hope.

"Did she tell you her name?"

Mom grins so wide, it fills her whole face with happiness. "Hope."

Fuck me.

The muscles in my body tighten and air escapes my lungs.

"You met Hope? The one with brown hair and brown eyes."

"Yes! That's the one." She grins. "She was also holding a book in her hands. I think she likes books."

Tell me about it.

Fuck! My mother met Rose out of all the people in the town. It had to be her and no one else.

What bothers me the most is that she said nothing of the sort to me.

Why didn't she tell me?

"We were at the cafe waiting for our orders when I started talking to her. She told me you guys are friends." She turns on the whisking machine. "Why haven't I seen her around?"

"She has stuff to do," I reply.

"Ah! She told me she has quizzes this week, otherwise she'd come to dinner."

"What? You invited her for dinner. *Here?*"

Mom looks unfazed as she stops the whisking machine and checks the batter. "I enjoyed talking to her and she is your friend."

Frustration bubbles under my skin. "She's not my friend, she's my —" I stop.

She gives me her full attention. "Your what?"

I stare at her, weighing my options. If I tell her the truth, she'll get invested in my relationship and ask me questions. And if I don't tell her, then I'm being a shitty boyfriend who's hiding his relationship from his parents and not showing off his girlfriend. I'm doing it to protect Hope, but she doesn't deserve to be hidden.

Nothing. I want to utter that word, but I can't get it out of my mouth.

I can't tell anyone that Rose is my nothing. It's fucking ridiculous. I just can't do it.

Fuck it.

I'll just tell her. They're going to find it out anyway.

Mom speaks. "Is she your... Well, I don't know how to say this word. I mean, I haven't even had the talk with you. And trust me, this is not how I want to find out that my son is having sex with girls and I just talked to one—"

I slip off the stool. "No! She is not someone I have sex with. Geez, Mom. Can you fucking think for a second?"

She freezes.

We both do.

I slowly realize what I've done.

"You just called me Mom," she whispers.

I run a hand through my hair and sit back down. "It's not like you are not."

"I am but you avoid using that word at all costs."

I rake another hand through my hair. "Hope isn't the girl I have sex with," I tell her softly.

"She sounds important to you."

I look up at her. "She is."

Realization hits her. "Is she your girlfriend?"

"She is."

"I met your girlfriend. Why didn't she tell me?"

I sigh. "I didn't want her to meet you guys. She is special to me."

"I see," she mumbles and mixes all the ingredients in a big bowl.

We stay quiet as she applies oil to the tray and then pours the batter into each hole. Once done, she slips the tray into the oven and sets the timer.

Moving around the island, she sits down beside me. "Do you want me to stay away from her? If that's what you want, I'll respect your decision."

I peer up at her. "I don't want you to bother her."

She gapes at me. "I would never do that. She is such a sweet girl. I already like her."

"I'd appreciate it."

Mom goes silent for a minute, then asks excitedly, "Can I ask you more about her?"

I sigh. "What do you want to know?"

"How did you meet her?"

"She bumped into me."

"Really?" she squeals. "That's how I met your dad."

I turn in my stool to face her. "What?"

She nods happily. "It was my first day at the new school, and I was frantically searching for my classroom when I bumped into him. He was a bit annoyed but helped me find it. Turns out, he had the same class, so we sat together."

"What happened next?"

"We became friends and fell in love."

I let out a dry chuckle. The irony isn't lost on me that the same happened to me. I bumped into Rose, and the next thing I know, I was crazy about her. I still am.

"How long have you been dating?"

"A week," I mumble.

"You should invite her over for dinner. I'd love to meet her."

I quickly shake my head, rejecting the idea. "No."

Disappointment fills her gaze and she says, "Whenever you feel like it."

The oven time pings and we both slip off our stools.

"I'll take those out," I suggest and grab the mittens off the rack and put them on. Opening the oven, I carefully take out the muffin tray and put it on the island.

"They look amazing, don't you think?" Mom asks.

"Yeah," I whisper.

"Would you like to eat one?"

"I don't like sweet things."

She smirks. "Then, how do you like Hope?"

I crack a smile. "She's the only exception."

Mom laughs, and the sound bounces off the quiet walls of our house for the first time in a long while.

"This is delicious," she says, taking a bite of the muffin.

I fold my arms across my chest and lean against the counter.

"Would you like to take some for Hope tomorrow?"

"She loves chocolate."

"I can make chocolate chip cookies."

"Sure—"

"We can start now."

Before I can say another word, she starts gathering stuff and I rush to her and stop her.

"You need to sleep," I tell her.

"But I'm not tired."

"It doesn't matter. Just go to your room and lie down."

She nods. "Let me clean up."

"I'll do it."

Despite me asking her to leave, she stays put and eats her muffins while I clean up.

We don't talk, but the tension isn't there. For years, we've walked on thin ice that would shatter whenever we spoke. We didn't have a common ground, a place to stand and truly get to know each other. They're my parents, but we stand so far apart that it feels impossible to erase the distance between us.

But tonight wasn't as awful as I thought it'd be.

It was nice talking to Mom.

I can't fucking believe I'm saying that.

"Would you mind if I talk to her if I see her again?" she asks.

I glance at her from the sink where I'm drying the bowls.

"Don't pester her. She is shy," I say, then quickly add, "Also, don't say anything that will hurt her. Just keep it to yourself."

Horror flashes across her face. "I would never do that." She sounds sincere.

Before I can say a word, Dad enters the room and his eyes go to her then me.

"Everything good?"

"Yes," I say.

Mom beams at him. "We were getting along."

He watches and his features soften. "Have you eaten?"

She nods. "I ate six muffins and now I might be on a sugar rush."

He smirks. "Don't worry, I'll tire you down."

I gag and both of them look at me. "Get a fucking room."

Mom laughs loud as if it's normal. Like the wall between us has finally broken down—it has.

I find it strange that I never knew what her laugh sounded like or what she looked like when she smiled. I didn't know Dad could look human and not like a stone-faced statue. He actually has the ability to soften his facial muscles and not seem robotic. Fuck, I can't believe he can even make sexual innuendos.

I'm learning stuff about my parents. Getting to know them in a way I've never before. They've stayed over before, but we didn't talk like this. We didn't talk, smile, laugh, or hang out. We didn't do anything that would bridge the gap between us.

The wall is down.

But we still have a thousand miles between us to get to each other.

Strangely, the distance doesn't bother me.

20

HOPE

IT'S LATE WHEN I COME HOME. MARIE AND I STUDIED AT THE library, where I helped her with the upcoming quizzes, specifically the chemistry one. We started after school ended, and the next time we lifted our heads, the sky was dark. I knew I had to be home, or it wouldn't end well for me.

For nearly a week, things have been too quiet at home.

Dad and I haven't crossed paths. Mom seems to handle him. She said she talked to him and what happened before won't happen again.

Of course, I didn't believe her.

I'd be a fool to believe her.

He has crossed a line and there is no going back now. He isn't going to stop hurting me. The switch has flipped and now I'm his target.

Why me?

I keep asking myself this question, but the answer is nowhere to be found.

We were never close, and I didn't love him, but at least he never raised his hand on me. He let me go. I was spared. Every single time.

Until now.

Ever since he's come back, for some strange reason, I'm on his radar.

A week has gone by and things have been going smoothly. Fear is lingering like a quiet rattlesnake waiting to attack me. The anticipation makes it worse, because I know he's going to hurt me. All I can do is wait.

Marie wanted to spend more time together, but I told her I had to be home because of curfew. She didn't say much—just stared at me with helpless, sad eyes that seemed to say, I don't want you to go home. *I don't want to go home either.*

But it doesn't matter what I want.

I'll always come home.

I have nowhere else to go.

Marie drives me home despite my reluctance for her to go anywhere near my father. She insists that she can't have me walking the streets at night.

Waving her goodbye, I wait for her to drive away before I step inside.

The second I close the door, tingles race down my spine as I take in the eerie silence and the shadows. Except for the light in the kitchen, that falls like a dim beam into the hallway, it's pitch dark everywhere and too quiet. The complete opposite of what my home is most of the time.

I hate the quiet more than the commotion. At least when the TV is playing, I know he is home or if the noises are coming from the kitchen, I can let myself sneak upstairs without getting noticed.

But this is bad, because I don't know what to expect.

Going from room to room, I look for Dad, but he's nowhere to be found—which is a good thing. It means I don't have to deal with him.

Since I ate with Marie on our way, I make my way upstairs instead of the kitchen. My heart thrums in distress despite the fact that he isn't home, but for some reason it doesn't settle down.

When I reach upstairs, I see the door to my room half open. I never leave my door open.

Chills run down my spine, and I straighten like a rod.

In fear, I move forward, push open the door and stand in the doorway as my hands tremble at the doorknob. What I see inside makes me let out a loud gasp.

The mattress on my iron bed is hanging off the edge, exposing the surface underneath where I stashed the money from the sales.

All that money—it's gone.

Every single penny.

No bills lay around, the ones I know I put there.

Something drops dead into my stomach. A weight so heavy that it sinks deep, tearing apart everything in its way as it hits the ground.

Time stills.

A freeze, cold and sharp, climbs up my body and roots me to my place. I can hardly move a muscle.

Money. My money. All of my money.

It's gone.

All gone.

Not a dime is left in its place—the spot I know where I left it.

Oh my God.

It's not there.

Air escapes my lungs as panic begins to build in the pit of my stomach.

Footsteps creak on the floorboards and a figure comes into my line of vision. The fact that there was someone in my room and I didn't notice makes sweat gather at the nape of my neck.

Dad turns his head and looks at me. His hands are full with wads of cash that belong to me. Money that I worked hard for so I could buy books. I spent hours, days, and weeks making those bracelets.

First, he tore down my books and now he has my money.

I can't breathe.

Why can't I breathe?

"You lied to me," he speaks slowly, in a stern tone. "And not just once."

I gulp hard.

"You mind telling me, how did you get all this cash?" he asks, his eyes narrowed on me.

I just stare at him like a statue.

I can't move.

Not because I'm scared, but because I'm deeply upset over losing another thing that was important to me. I was planning on buying books—the ones he ripped apart in front of me and felt no ounce of regret over. I was also looking forward to paying for food and buying things for the people who are important to me and do so much for me.

Now I'm back to square one.

But it's not that it hurts me. It's that he now knows about it, and I can't hide it from him anymore.

Dad whips the wad against his palm in a tight slap. "I asked you a fucking question."

I shudder at the raise of his voice. "I...I..."

It's a couple of hundred. Not a lot of money. But I don't work, and he knows we don't have money to spare.

He walks in my direction and I quickly back up to escape him, but my back hits the wall and he corners me.

"That boy gave you all this money, didn't he? The one who put his hands on me like a fucking delinquent."

"No."

"I know it's his money," he asserts.

"It isn't."

"Don't lie to me."

"I'm not."

"Then explain this." He whips those bills against my cheek in a sharp slap that makes my head turn. The burning sensation lights up under my skin and numbness tingles my senses.

"You're just like your mother. Whoring around with boys who are nothing but trouble and doing God knows what with them." He spits. "I wasn't born yesterday. I know how this amount of money came about. I just didn't expect it from my own daughter."

A wild mix of anger and disgust swirls in his dark eyes.

"I didn't do it," I mumble.

His eyebrows dip. "I don't believe you."

Raising his hand, he wraps it around my throat. "I told you to stay away from him but you didn't listen."

Tears build up in my eyes. I put my hands on his as I try to pry them away.

"I told you I'd punish you if you won't listen to me."

"Please..." I croak out.

"Tell me. Tell me exactly how you made this money when your mother is working day and night and you're whoring around town with that boy."

I try to shake my head, but his hold is too tight.

"I found all this money under your bed. Is that what you've been up to for the past months when I was gone. Your mother is at work and you invite boys up to your room."

"No..." I utter.

"You took advantage of her trust. You tried to hurt her." At once, his eyes turn darker. "I will kill you. Do you hear me? I will kill you if I ever see any boy around you ever again."

He squeezes tighter and I feel like I'm about to die.

Staring deep into my eyes, he says, "You are a mistake. You've always been."

With that, he lets go of me and walks out of my room.

I lean against the wall, trying to catch my breath.

His words keep replaying in my head.

You are a mistake. You've always been.

What did he mean by that?

How am I a mistake?

Those are probably words that he meant in the heat of the anger to hurt me, but something inside me says that's not true. That he meant what he said.

Shaking my head, I lock my door and adjust my mattress on the bed. I search for nooks and corners, hoping to find a single bill, but find none. He took every single penny that I made.

Like a maniac, I keep searching because I refuse to believe that I was stupid enough to keep all my earnings under my bed. I should've thought better.

Tears wet my face and I start sobbing when I realize that I have nothing.

First my books and now my money.

What's next? The people I care about?

That thought makes me weep harder.

I feel so lost and scared.

When is it going to end?

21

HEATH

"WE ARE DOING IT," SEBASTIAN SAYS THE MINUTE WE STEP out of the classroom.

"We are not," I grumble.

"C'mon, it'll be fun."

I sigh. "I'm not doing it, Bash."

"Why not?"

"It's a waste of my time."

"I can give you a hundred reasons why it'll be fun," he pleads, grinning like an excited kid.

"Not interested."

He smirks. "Hope will be excited to see your stall at the bake sale."

My head turns, and without thinking, I say, "You think so?"

A shit-eating grin appears on his face. "So, *that* got you, huh?"

"Shut up."

He laughs. "As soon as I mentioned her, the stall doesn't sound like a waste of time to you."

I avoid looking at him as my cheeks twinge a little. "I don't think she'll want to be there."

"She will." Then, he adds, "Picture this, she sees you selling chocolate cupcakes. I'm telling you, she will fall in love with you right there and then."

"Fuck off," I mutter, but think about it on the inside. If there's anything that can make Rose fall for me, it's me with chocolate.

"We both know I'm right," he says with a smug expression.

I roll my eyes. "Maybe."

"So we are doing it. Say it."

Despite my lack of enthusiasm, I agree. "Yes, we're doing it."

He grins.

We stop by his locker to grab a few notebooks. Leaning against the locker beside his, I search the crowded hallway for Rose. Girls stare and guys scowl, but I don't care about any of those people. I only want to see one person.

My body drums in anticipation. I haven't seen her since the morning because Blondie said Hope wanted to go to school with her.

Of course, it fucking bothered me, but I didn't think much of it.

Marie is her best friend. And I'm not going to be a hurdle if she wants to spend time with her. However, it bothers me how much I like to be around her all the time. We could spend all day together and I'd still want to be next to her. I can't get enough of that girl.

"Your eyes are moving at an alarming rate," Sebastian teases.

"I can't find her," I say in an annoyed tone.

"Look who's desperate to see his girlfriend."

"I haven't seen her since the morning."

"That's why you've been so grumpy."

I glance at him. "I'm not."

He shuts his locker with a thud. "You bit my head off when I asked to take your pen."

I narrow my eyes. "That's because you never bring yours."

"Because I always use yours," he shoots back.

"I know Marie buys impulsively so there's no way you don't have a pen at home."

"Yeah, she does. Because she is an angel," he states in an obvious tone. Opening his bag, he shows me the inside. The bottom is littered with pens that look brand new. "I just like using yours because it's smooth."

"For fuck's sake," I mutter as I send him a glare.

A flash of blue in my periphery catches my attention and I shove him out of the way just in time to see her rushing upstairs.

"I need to go." Without waiting for a reply, I rush after her.

My feet thunder as I climb the stairs. "Rose! Wait."

She picks up the pace as if she didn't hear me.

That confuses me.

I chase after her and call out once again. "Rose!"

Like a stubborn mule, she keeps walking.

Shaking my head, I jog down the hallway, and within seconds, I reach her. Grabbing her elbow, I turn her around. She stiffens in my hold. I tip her chin up and make her look at me.

Tension grips my body as I stare down at her face, covered in minimal makeup. It makes her look pretty, but...she's not one to wear it at school often. Also, her eyes look red and puffy.

A strange feeling tugs at my heart that something is wrong.

"Hi," she pants.

"Hi," I reply.

"I didn't hear you," she says, not meeting my gaze.

Now I know something is wrong.

I arch an eyebrow. "How do you know I called for you?"

"I..." She gapes at me, not speaking another word.

She looks stunning in a soft blue sweater and jeans, the color bringing out a beauty so striking it makes my heart race. Her hair is gathered in a loose ponytail with tendrils falling around her beautiful face.

If I wasn't already in love with her, I would be at this moment.

She is the most beautiful girl I've ever seen.

Leaning my head down, I brush my lips against hers. A soft, shaky breath leaves her lips.

"I haven't seen you since the morning," I whisper, my arm wrapping around her waist and pulling her closer. Just the feel of her in my arms makes everything right. I don't even care that I didn't spend my morning with her and how much it fucking annoyed me.

It doesn't matter anymore.

She's here with me.

"I was with Marie," she tells me.

"Are you telling me she is a better chauffeur than your boyfriend?" I tease her.

Her eyes widen. "Of course not. You are better." Then she shakes her head. "No! Not that I'm calling you a better chauffeur. I'm saying it's better with you."

I can't fight the smile that takes over me.

Without thinking twice, I kiss her like a starved man.

Heat sears through me, setting my body on fire. Our mouths move at a practiced, smooth rhythm, not missing a step or stumbling over one another. I pour all my desperation into the kiss, hoping she realizes that I missed her.

Pleasure shoots through my veins and fills me up.

I groan into her mouth as she kisses me back with equal passion and eagerness.

I pull back, cup the back of her head and kiss her again. I kiss her deeply and thoroughly, getting lost in the waves of pleasure that envelope me.

It's all good and fun until she winces and I quickly end it.

Getting panicked, I retreat. "I'm sorry. I'm sorry for hurting you —" my words vanish as I see her split lip.

There's no way I caused it. I didn't feast on her like some wild animal, no matter how hungry I am for her. I'm always careful with her. *Always.*

"It's okay," she murmurs, delicately rubbing away the blood with her fingers.

"No. It's not okay. Fuck. I didn't mean to hurt you." I brush away her hand, and instead put my thumb over the cut. "I'm so sorry."

With care, I caress her cheek to assure her, but when she winces, everything clicks into place.

I know why she applied makeup to her face.

Reining in my anger, I gather myself not to spew the theories running through my head.

She is hurt. And there is only one person responsible for it.

"What happened to your cheek?" I ask, my voice dropping dangerously low.

Rose pales. "Nothing!"

I narrow my eyes. "He slapped you, didn't he?"

"No!"

"He put his fucking hands on you. Again."

"I'm fine."

"Stop lying to me," I snap.

I break her walls with those words and she crumbles. Finally letting me see her and not hide the truth from me like she's done in the past months.

Cupping her cheek, I say, "Talk to me, Rose. Tell me what he did."

She stares at me for a long time, then whispers, "It happened last night."

"Tell me exactly what happened."

She nods and opens her mouth, but a group of girls walks past us.

When they see us standing together, they stop and stare with judgment swimming in their eyes.

I curse under my breath and grab her hand and take us to the rooftop, where we sit against the wall next to each other. My hands itch to pull her into my arms and comfort her, but I'm packed with too much anger and frustration. All I want to do is get to her house and kill that man with my bare hands.

I hate him so much. I wish he'd disappear from her life. Dead, preferably.

"No one comes here so you can talk," I assure her, eager to hear what happened that got her hurt.

She pulls up her knees to her chest and tries to make herself small like a bird. I've noticed that she often does that. As if the world is too big and everything around her is coming at her, and all she wants to do is shrink herself down to the size of a peanut and protect herself.

When I see her like this, my instinct to protect her gets stronger.

No wonder I fell for her.

It was inevitable.

The way she affects me so strongly and ferociously, it needs to be studied.

She tells me everything what happened and why she asked Marie to pick her up. Apparently, she didn't want to see me knowing I'd know right away—of course I would—and come after her dad and get in trouble—she isn't wrong. She told Marie instead, who helped her cover up the bruises and promised not to tell Sebastian or me—I will have a talk with her later.

When she finishes we sit in silence as the air around us sizzles with tension. It's so thick that it suffocates me.

I'm breathless. No air enters my system and fuels it with oxygen. I'm empty inside.

I perform the five things technique to calm myself down and not jump up to my feet and find that man.

My head is in pieces after hearing how he stole all her money and hurt her. I watched her work hard for that money. I even helped her. Now it's all gone. He stripped her of it all and left her penniless.

Fuck. What kind of sick fuck is he?

The more I think about it, the angrier I get. All I want to do is get that money back for her and hurt him ten times more than he hurt her. I keep envisioning myself hitting him until he's out cold and covered in blood.

Violent thoughts like that circle my brain, adding fuel to the embers that spark in delight.

I don't realize how hot I am until cold fingers touch me, sending a shiver through my body.

A series of heartbeats echoes through my ears, making me realize how loudly the organ in my chest can respond to her touch.

I sit completely still, letting her do whatever she wants with me.

"I'm sorry, I didn't tell you," she says, voice thick with regret.

Sighing heavily, I grumble, "You have nothing to be sorry about."

"I don't want you to hate me."

I face her, brows dipping in confusion. "Hate you? I could never hate you."

"Are you sure? You look mad."

"I'm mad at him, not you."

She watches me, then nods.

Picking up her hand, I kiss her knuckles. "One thing that I hate are the injuries on you. I don't like seeing you hurt."

She shrugs. "It doesn't hurt that bad."

I don't believe you.

The dark circles under her eyes catch my attention, and even though I know the answer, I ask anyway. "Did you sleep last night?"

"A little," she says shyly.

"Explain a little."

"Thirty minutes," she mutters.

Without thinking, I straighten my legs and pull her head into my lap—making sure her face is a good distance away from a certain body part.

She peers up at me, her body rigid. "What are you doing?"

I cover her eyes with my palm. "Letting you take a nap."

"It's okay. I'm not sleepy."

"Probably, but you look tired."

"I'll sleep tonight."

"Just close your eyes and relax," I command.

"But—"

"Rose," her name escapes my lips like a melody, sweet and filled with love. I feel like I'm incapable of saying her name with any other emotion, because even her name is too precious for me.

"Yes," she whispers.

"Do it for me," I say.

I half-expect an argument, but she stays silent. Carefully, I remove my hand away from her eyes and find them closed. She isn't sleeping, but at least she isn't wasting any more of her energy.

Any other guy in my position would look away, but I don't.

Seeing her like this warms my insides. The fact that she trusts me and feels safe around me. I never knew what that'd do to me—my heart. Since the first time I saw her, I've been wanting her to get this comfortable with me.

Reaching down, I caress her temple. The scar from that night is there and it will be for a long fucking time. Not wanting to get aggravated over it, I study the rest of her face and quickly realize how much I like her face.

It's not just the face. It's the whole girl.

Not wanting to wake her up, I pull back my hand and watch the sky instead. For a long time, I hated looking at it, but now it feels like someone there is looking back at me and making sure I'm okay.

Mary

"Your mother knows about me!" Rose pales.

I park my car in the driveway and mention it to her, so we don't have to sneak around anymore.

"Yes." My lips twitch in amusement. "Another thing that you didn't tell me about."

She pales further. "I'm sorry. I... I just thought you didn't want me meeting your mother. But at the cafe, she was there, and we started talking. I didn't know what to do, and—"

Leaning over, I kiss her. "It's alright."

"I thought you'd hate me for talking to her—"

"I could never hate you. Remember that."

She opens her mouth but then shuts it. For that alone, I reward her with a kiss.

"But you should've told me," I mumble against her lips.

She sighs. "I know."

I nod. "Let's go inside."

Walking around the car, I help her out and then entwine our fingers.

I lead her inside. Her fingers shake and she moves slowly beside me.

"Relax," I whisper to her as we pass the empty foyer.

"I am."

"You are shaking."

"I'm not."

"Rose," I raise our hands and plant a kiss on the back of her hand. "It'll be fine."

She lets out a breath. "I just want her to like me."

"She already does," I assure her. All I want to do is pull her into my arms and squeeze the anxiety out of her.

"Heath, is that you?" Mom calls from the living room.

Rose stiffens and stares at me with wide eyes.

I clench my jaw as tension gathers beneath the surface.

Before I can say anything, my mother stands in the hallway. She looks stunning in a pastel yellow dress paired with pearl jewelry and white shoes. Her face brightens up when she sees me—a glow that

183

makes her look fuller and younger, so opposite from the version that came here a week ago and almost gave me a heart attack. A megawatt smile appears on her lips as she closes the long distance with hurried steps and engulfs me in a hug.

"You're home," she whispers under her breath.

She is always delighted to find me home. And I always find it strange.

"Yes." I put my hand on her back and pat. The action is full of awkwardness.

Fortunately, she takes the hint and lets go of me rather quickly.

It takes me a second to figure out why.

"Hope, dear." She wraps her arms around my girlfriend and hugs her tightly.

Panicked brown eyes find me and I give her hand a squeeze to let her know that it's okay.

I don't know my mother well, but I know she won't jeopardize it. She knows the consequences will be dire. Because this is huge. I'm letting her meet the girl who's the most important person to me. The person I'm helplessly in love with. The person who's my girl.

If she hurts Rose, we're done forever.

"It's so nice to see you again." Mom smiles.

"Uh, you too," Rose replies shyly.

"I had no idea you were dating my son."

Rose pales further. "I... Yes... I... Uh...forgot."

I cough to hide my laugh. She's adorable when she is like this.

"You forgot?" Mom teases.

In return, Rose squeezes my hand so hard I feel like she'll break my bones. "I'm sorry I didn't tell you. I wasn't sure—I'm sorry—"

"Oh my, you don't need to apologise. I don't mind." Mom touches her shoulder to reassure her. "I'm sure you had your reasons. I understand."

"I'm sorry."

"No need to apologise." She gives her a knowing smile.

Rose nods.

"Now, are you hungry? I made lunch."

"I'm not hungry."

She is hungry but she won't admit it to my mother.

I weigh my options, whether to have lunch with my mother or not. The way she's watching us with that dazzling smile, I know she's dying to know all the details. She assured me she'd be careful, but I feel like her excitement will make her too curious, and she'll start probing us with questions.

And I don't want to make Rose uncomfortable.

"We'll be in my room," I say and give her hand a squeeze. Rose visibly relaxes beside me.

Mom looks gloomy but musters up a smile. "If you need anything, let me know."

I give her a nod and then steer us in the direction of my room.

"Your mother is nice," Rose says as soon as I shut the door and slip on the lock.

"Perhaps," I say as I pick out clothes to change into.

"You're not sure?" She appears in the archway separating my room from the walk-in closet.

I stop in my tracks. "I don't know her that well."

"Do you want to?"

I shrug.

Her inquisitive stare bores a hole in the side of my face. I know she wants to press me for answers but I don't have those. This whole mess with my parents is something I'm figuring out myself. All I keep thinking about is that they're going to leave sooner or later.

They said they're moving back, but there will come a time when they'll pack their stuff and leave. I'm betting it'll take them a month at most.

"I'm planning on changing. I wouldn't mind if you watch."

Her cheeks redden and she steps back. "Uh...I'll wait."

Turning around, she disappears.

I chuckle.

Once I've changed clothes, I join her. She is standing near the couch, still not comfortable enough in my space to do whatever she feels like.

"You can sit down, Rose," I say.

She jostles, finding me behind her.

As she sits down, I stride toward the cardboard boxes that have the stuff I ordered for her.

I look over, and she's busy studying the boxes. She's curious.

A rush of excitement pumps through me, knowing what's inside will make her happy.

Sitting down, I reach for the flat box. Using a cutter, I carefully cut through the tape. The noise slices through the quietness of the room that seems to be brimming with anticipation. Inside, there are two tall side panels, smooth and white, with pre-drilled holes running their lengths. Also the top and bottom boards, the five shelves and a thin fiberboard—the back panel. Next to it is another small cardboard box which contains the hardware pack. There are wood dowels, cam lock nuts and bolts, screws, nails, tiny metal shelf pegs and anti-tip bracket kit and the instruction manual which has information paired with images to build this thing.

I check everything, making sure all the accessories are present before I get to work.

Taking out the planks, I set them neatly on the floor in an organized manner. Then put in the wooden dowels.

"What are you doing?" Rose asks with a frown between her eyebrows. She looks completely clueless. And completely cute.

"I'm building a bookshelf," I reply.

"But why? You don't have books."

Yeah, I fucking don't, because I'm not a reader.

I grab the manual and start to read it to hide my vulnerability. "It's not for me."

Because I can't help it, I sneak a look at her. She purses her lips, still confused as hell. "Then?"

"It's for you."

"But why?"

Putting down the manual, I look at her. "Because your dad fucking destroyed your book wall. He doesn't get to destroy the one thing you love the most in the world."

Her brown eyes fill with sorrow. "You don't have to."

"I know but I want to." I add, "When it comes to you, I can't stop myself from giving you everything that I can."

186

"I'm sorry, I... I don't want to be a burden—"

"You are not a burden, you can never be a burden to me. I'm doing this because I know how much you love books."

She nods. "The shelf will take up too much space."

"I have plenty of space. Don't worry your pretty head about it."

She fidgets with her fingers as anxiety tightens its hold on her. "Are you sure you want to do it?"

"How about you come here and I kiss you to tell you how much I want it?"

22

HOPE

HEATH IS WEARING A WHITE T-SHIRT AND GREY
sweatpants.

And just like that my mind goes blank.

Black. He's supposed to wear black. Not grey sweatpants.

The last time he wore them I was spiraling in lust because he
looked so attractive.

Everything about him is perfect. His handsome face, his amazing
body and his beautiful eyes. I often find myself staring at him because
someone who looks this good seems unreal. And if he wasn't perfect
already, now he's building me a bookshelf. A bookshelf.

A frisson of excitement hums through my blood. I can't help but
gravitate toward him.

The moment I kneel down beside him, his hand comes around and
holds the back of my head. Gently, he pulls my face toward him and
kisses me with such tenderness that I melt into him. Like snow under
the heat of the sun.

I press my palm over his chest and almost get burned with how hot
he feels. He is burning up.

Breaking the kiss, I breathe heavily as I rest the back of my hand
against his forehead.

"You are hot," my voice comes out breathy.

"I know." His rich chuckles pours into me and the sound gets tucked away in some corner of my mind.

I blush. "No—I mean—your skin is hot."

His laughter slowly dies and a smile dances on his lips. "That's because of you. You do *this* to me."

I stare at him, blinded by the sincerity in his gaze.

He removes his hand from the back of my head and lets his fingers aimlessly explore my collarbone. I shiver as electricity zaps through me and goosebumps raise on my arms.

The rough calluses scrape against my skin, gently, as they dip into the neckline of my sweater that isn't deep.

Air bleeds out of my lungs, and I'm panting as if I ran a marathon.

"Looks like I'm not the only one," his voice is low and eyes fixed on me.

I avert my gaze to his chest where I'm holding his T-shirt in my fist with a vice grip.

When his finger goes near my breast, I let out a quiet gasp.

After reading so many romance books, I know exactly what happens. If anything, I know a little too much. However, it's too intense in reality. Those words don't even come close to how I'm feeling right now.

His steady gaze makes me forget my name. His touch makes me forget to breathe. And his heat makes me want to curl up against him and never move.

All of this is too much but I can't bring myself to say no. Because I want this. I want him.

I've wanted him for a long time now.

I'm ready for it.

I know it.

Heath reads the look in my eyes and says, "Rose—"

"I want you."

Shock flashes across his face, as he pulls back his hand. "What?"

I nod. "I want you."

Running a hand through his hair, he exhales. "Fuck. Don't say those words. You don't know what they do to me."

"I mean it," I tell him.

His eyes close. "For fuck's sake."

Doubt plants its seed in me the longer he makes me wait. I can't help but utter the words with deep sadness. "I'm sorry... I didn't know that you don't—"

His eyes open and he glares at me. "No! It's *not* that."

I stare at him with uncertainty.

"I mean it, Rose. I want you. Fuck. I want you so bad, it's driving me insane," he says slowly.

"Then what's the problem?"

"I want you to be ready."

My eyebrows pinch in thought. "I am ready."

"You are not."

"How can you say that?"

"What happened a week ago was a disaster. And just yesterday, your dad hurt you again. I want you to be okay right now and not rush into this to feel better."

A rope ties around my chest at his words. "You do make me feel better."

"I know but this is serious. It is huge."

"It's sex. People have sex," I end up saying without thinking.

He speaks calmly, "Yes, they do. But for you I want to make it special. We haven't even gone out on a date yet."

"I don't want special, I just want you."

He cups my face and his thumbs caress my cheeks in a loving manner. The stir of anxiety swirling in me starts to slow down as he speaks. "Maybe you don't, but I do. I want you to experience everything you've read about in books. The magic of love that you believe in." He pauses. "I've seen the way your eyes light up when you tell me those stories. You look enchanting, as if that kind of love can only exist in books. I want to change that. I want to be the guy you compare your book boyfriends with. Not the other way around."

When I don't say anything, he adds, "As for sex, we've got all the time in the world. Let's take things slowly."

"Slowly?" I whisper.

His lips twitch. "You can barely breathe when I kiss you. What will happen when I get you naked, kiss you everywhere and use my fingers to make you—"

I put my palm on his mouth and muffle his words.

Blue eyes fill with amusement and he stops talking only to grin beneath my hand.

My whole face has turned red.

Taking my palm down, I refuse to look at him. "Let's build this bookshelf."

"Sure, Rose. Whatever you want," he teases me.

For the next hour or so, we work together to build the tall, white bookshelf. The smell of wood is addicting and reminds me of books. Heath does most of the work and barely lets me do anything. I only read the instructions, show him the images and hand him whatever he asks of me.

Seeing him work on something for me makes my heart pound like never before. I can hear his name echo in every beat of my heart.

I'm falling in love with him with every little thing he does.

The worst part is, it makes me so scared.

I've felt fear before, but this is different.

The way I feel for him is so strong and addictive that it has the power to destroy me.

I never thought I wanted love after watching how complicated my parents' relationship was. I didn't want it because to me love is pain. It's not beautiful or sweet.

I was going to stay away from this emotion, but then a blue-eyed boy entered my life and changed everything.

"I think it's ready," he says as he aligns the bookshelf against the wall. It looks perfect next to the ceiling-to-floor windows that offer a spectacular view of the outside—a perfect spot for reading.

"What do you say?" Heath asks as he stops moving it.

Running over to him, I throw my arms around his neck and pull him down for a kiss. I pour all my gratitude, happiness, excitement, and the emotions I'm feeling into that kiss, letting him know how I feel.

"Thank you," I say.

"You're welcome." He smiles down at me.

I love his smile.

"This looks amazing."

"Wait till it fills with books."

"I have my Harry Potter collection. I'll bring it over to fill these empty shelves."

He shakes his head. "No need."

I pull back. "What?"

Untangling himself from my arms, he strides toward the other three boxes. "All your books are here."

"What books?" I'm baffled.

"The ones you ordered in the library with me weeks ago and the ones—" he scowls "—your dad ripped apart."

My pulse accelerates. "How?"

He rubs his neck. "A while back, I took a picture of your book wall so I can read those books."

Inching closer to him, I ask, "Why?"

His gaze flickers to me. "So I can know you better."

"You do."

"There's still so much more that I need to know."

Handing me the cutter, he lets me open the boxes. When I turn over the flaps and see the books inside—the ones I lost—my heart drops into my stomach. With shaky hands, I reach for them and take them out.

The spine isn't creased, the pages aren't filled with annotations and the cover isn't old.

They are not mine. But I can make them.

With my arms full with the twenty books, I walk over to the bookshelf and neatly arrange them on the shelf.

Just seeing them makes me happy.

"Rose, you've got other boxes, too." Heath reminds me.

I unpack the rest of the boxes. By the time I slide in the last book, two whole shelves are entirely filled, and something warm and flurried replaces the despair I felt for losing my books that night.

Enclosing my arms around me, I try to make myself small, to contain this huge feeling that starts consuming me.

I love books.

Mary

"It's okay." He comes up behind me and wraps his arms around me. His face burrows into the side of my neck. "You are okay."

I nod as I stare at the shelf.

"I'm going to fill the rest of the shelves, too."

I lean into him and shake my head. "This is enough."

"No fucking way."

"How will I ever repay you?" I whisper.

Our eyes meet at the same time and it feels like time slows down. Everything around us disappears. It's just the two of us that exist.

"Go on a date with me," he says in a hoarse tone, voice thick with emotions.

"Date?"

He nods slowly, his eyes locked on me.

"Okay," I give him a sweet smile.

His lips twitch until he can't hold in his smile.

23

HEATH

"I NEED HELP," I GRUMBLE AS I PACE IN FRONT OF MY BED.

"Help with what?" Sebastian asks, eating my mom's blueberry muffins on my bed, his face full of delight. Clearly, he loves them, and if he keeps this up, our united front will crack. My relationship with my mother is fairly new. She needs to know I'm not over the shit she put me through for years, that she has a lot to make up for.

My mind is brimming with anxious thoughts; otherwise, I would've said something about it or the fucking crumbs falling off his mouth and occupying my duvet. I don't like mess.

"I asked her out on a date," I announce.

He stops eating. "Really?"

I give him a curt nod.

Closing his eyes, he lets his head fall back. "Finally!"

"What do you mean by that?"

"I feel so happy." He sounds so dramatic.

"Will you just tell me—"

"It took you months to ask her out when you should've done it after meeting her. You were down bad for her since day one."

My face tingles with heat. "That is not true."

"It is," he asserts.

My lack of response makes him grin. He is right. I was a goner for Rose the first time I saw her. I just didn't know about it until later.

My gaze locks on the bookshelf that is lined with romance books. If I pick out one of the bunch, I'd be able to get all the help I need to plan the date. But I want to do something special. Something that makes her happy.

"Wait a second." Sebastian gets up from my bed and makes a beeline toward the bookshelf. "When did this get here?"

"While you were busy eating those damn muffins," I mock.

He throws me a look over his shoulder. "Be serious."

"Yesterday. I built it for my girlfriend."

"What the fuck?" He gapes. "You've never built me shit."

My eyes roll at his comment.

"This looks good, Heath."

"Rose liked it too."

"I'm sure." He smiles. "Also, there are romance books. I bet she can't wait to get to your room to see her books."

"Do you know why I built it?" I ask, my chest getting tight as I remember the reason.

"Why?" He looks back at me.

Anger burns through me like a scorching trail of fire as my fingers curl into fists by my side.

"Her father ripped apart her books," I grit out.

Sebastian goes rigid and his face turns stone.

With a scoff, I continue, "That's not even the worst fucking part. He took away all the money that she made from selling bracelets and hurt her. He hit her so hard that he split her lip."

Tension grips me like a vine and I can hardly breathe.

I can't take it if someone hurts Hope. *I can't.* And knowing there is someone who can get to her and I can't do anything about it makes me sick to my stomach.

How long will this continue?

What is going to happen next?

Is there going to be an end to it?

She isn't safe in that house. It's not a home. It's a cage she can't break free from. Her mother is controlling and her dad is cruel. And together they cause her pain. I can't fathom how she's survived with such parents for this long.

"Hey!" Sebastian shoves me, and I stumble a little as I lose my balance, but I regain it quickly.

"What?" I glare at him.

"You looked like you were plotting someone's murder," he says. "It's her Dad, isn't it?"

"Of course, it's him."

He sighs. "You can't do it and you know that. We have to be reasonable and smart to figure out a way out of this."

"Shut up."

He grabs my shoulder to make me look at him. "I mean it, Heath. You can't do it."

"You can't tell me what to do or not to do."

His green eyes soften slightly. "I know. That's why I'm *ordering* you."

My eyes widen at his words.

Pain crosses his face. "I saw you get behind the bars. I don't ever want to see it again." He takes a deep breath. "There are other ways for us to help her. Not for you to run headfirst into it."

Frustration bubbles like lava under my skin as I think if roles were reversed—which they were a year ago—he would've done anything to save the girl he loves. My best friend has no right standing here and ordering me not to chase after the girl who desperately needs help because she can't be protected from that monster. Someone has to run headfirst to save her and it is me. Because I love her.

I'm starting to realize that where these pesky, annoying things called feelings are concerned, rationality doesn't exist.

The concept of safe and dangerous is fucking lost on me. The only thing I care about is taking care of my girlfriend.

"You do know I fucking love her, right?" I snap.

He nods. "I know and I'm happy for you. But this is a huge problem. We are talking about domestic violence, emotional and physical abuse. And it's not just her father, her mother is as much of a problem."

He couldn't be more right.

A weight so heavy and hard starts to settle on my shoulders, and I can't help but feel like I need to sit down. Rounding the couch, I take a seat, lean my head back, and stare at the ceiling.

I feel lost, worried, and terrified. It's like a fucking cocktail of emotions stirring inside me, and I'm getting drunk on it.

Sebastian joins me and stares at me with a troubled gaze.

Putting his hand on my shoulder, he says, "I'm here for you."

"I know, thanks."

He chuckles. "She's changed you."

Turning my head, I shoot him a glare.

He quickly sobers up. "So, the date?"

"What am I supposed to do?"

"What do you have in mind?"

I shoot him an exasperated look. "That's exactly what I don't fucking know."

He thinks for a minute, then says, "Library?"

I shake my head. "Too predictable."

"She loves that place."

Don't I know it. "I want to take her somewhere she hasn't been to."

"Inside your pants?"

I shove him. "Fuck off. It isn't like that with her."

He laughs. "Oh, so you're keeping it PG-13, huh?"

"I'm being *careful* with her."

Picking up the Doritos from the coffee table, he opens it and starts munching. "And how is it going for your blue balls?"

"Just fucking great."

He nods. "You sound sexually frustrated."

"I'm not," I snarl, my hackles rising in defiance.

I am.

He has no idea just how bad.

"You are." He reads my mind. "I bet the porn isn't helping either."

"Can we not talk about it and instead focus on the date?" I deadpan.

He shakes his head. "It is important too."

"Sebastian, drop it!"

"Have you talked to her about sex? You should because—"

"She said she wants me, but I'm the one taking it slow, because I want to do the right thing."

He pauses as his gaze locks on me. "Did you seriously reject sex?"

Letting out a tired sigh, I nod. "I did."

"Clearly, you haven't done it before because if you did, you'd know that you don't reject a girl—especially a girl like Hope—when she asks for it. Do you know how much courage it takes to even ask for it?" He muses, "Of course there are times when you reject like when she's drunk, high, or sleepy. Basically, when consent is blurred. And yes, consent is *very* important."

My head rolls with all this information.

Reject. Girls like Hope. Courage. Consent.

Despite my brain yelling at me not to ask, I still do.

"So, should I have sex with her?"

He nods. "Yes."

"But with everything happening at her home with her parents. Maybe she isn't in her right mind—"

"She is. She wants you because you're her safe place. She wants to be close to you."

"I want to make it special for her."

I can see that he wants to laugh in my face, but he fights the urge.

Good for him because I can't say I wouldn't hit him. Fine, I understand that it is new for me to talk about this sort of thing. We never talked about girls, feelings, or sex. But that was before Marie and Rose walked into our lives and flipped our worlds upside down. Nothing is the same anymore. And I'm glad it isn't. We needed the change. We needed the good. And those two are good for us. Way too fucking good.

"I think instead of special, you should focus on making it comfortable for her."

I study him in confusion. "Why wouldn't it be comfortable for her?"

He watches me as if I've grown two heads.

When he doesn't answer, I start growing anxious.

For fuck's sake. I know nothing about girls and now I have a girlfriend.

Sebastian finally regains some composure. "*That* is a talk for another time. Until then, don't even think about sex. Because clearly we have a lot to cover."

"Fuck off," I say, embarrassed—I've never been embarrassed in my life before. "I'll look it up on the internet."

He hums. "Yeah, it's better because otherwise I'd be traumatized giving you the talk."

"I know how it's done," I add, letting him know that I'm not a complete idiot.

"So does every other guy," he retorts. "But it's not about us. It's about the girl. We—nope. I'm not going there today. Let's just focus on the date for now."

"Help me out then." I kick my feet over the table.

"Whatever you do, just make sure you guys have a good time."

I grimace. "I want *her* to have a good time."

He nods. "Yes, but you are important too."

I roll my eyes. "You are getting extra annoying today."

"Just taking care of my best friend."

"You don't need to. I'm fine."

"Then I'm gonna make sure you stay that way."

24

HOPE

"Heath asked you out on a date," Marie squeals. "Oh my God!"

I smile, watching her jump in excitement.

We're at her house after school because Heath had something to talk about with Sebastian. He looked grim, so I assume it's something serious. I wish he'd tell me about it since we're in a relationship and people tell each other everything.

Don't be a hypocrite.

You haven't told him how nervous you are about the date.

Marie rushes over to me and grabs me by the shoulder. Excitement is buzzing through her veins. Her hazel eyes, a delicious blend of brown and green, are filled with delirium. "Please tell me this is real and not a dream."

I laugh. "It is real."

"Oh my God! Yes!" she squeals again.

A knock sounds on the door. A second later, it opens, revealing a grinning Camila leaning against the doorframe. She's dressed in a fitted red pantsuit and white heels with red bottoms.

I love those heels. The red bottom is such a nice touch.

I bet they cost a lot.

"Heath is taking Hope on a date," Marie announces, grinning from ear to ear.

Camila lets out a rich laugh, her eyes sparkle with the same happiness as her daughter's. "It was about time."

"I've been *waiting* for this day," Marie adds.

Camila turns to me. "Where is he taking you?"

I get nervous. "I don't know. He didn't say."

"So he's planning."

"He has to take her to an amazing place," Marie argues.

Camila walks into the room. "Now, love, you are right. But it is his decision and I know he'll choose wisely."

"He better. Hope deserves the absolute best," Marie says.

"She does." Camila shoots me a motherly smile. Backing away, she says, "I'm heading out to pick up your father from the airport. I'll be back in an hour or two. If you need anything, text me."

"Okay, bye!" Marie waves and so do I.

When the door closes, all of her attention falls on me.

"Do you have something nice to wear?" she asks.

I wince.

Nothing in my closet is right for a date. I only have clothes that make me feel comfortable but look boring. I've never bought anything fancy—not that I could with the money issue at home. And all the money that I had saved up is gone—I try not to think too much about it.

"Not really." I shrug.

"It's fine. I can come over and help you pick out something."

Panic grips my heart. "No! No. You can't come over."

"Why not?"

"Because I don't want you to get hurt." Those words pain me as I say them. I feel terrible that she can't feel safe in my house.

Her eyes soften in understanding. "I'll be fine. Don't worry about—"

I shake my head vigorously. "You can't come over. Please."

"How else will I help you with the outfit?"

"I don't know."

Marie gets lost in her thoughts.

A few seconds later, she gets up from the bed and walks into her walk-in closet. Taking out one outfit after another, she fills her arms with dresses, cardigans, sweaters, and scarves. The pile builds up so high that it hides her face from my view. Satisfied that she can't find anything else in her closet, she returns and dumps all the clothes on her giant bed.

"That took a while," she breathes out, "but I think I got everything."

I stare at the pile, then her. "For what?"

She meets my gaze. "You can wear something of mine to the date."

"No, I can't," I protest.

"You can."

"This is too much." I don't even glance at the pretty clothes. "I'll find something in my closet."

Marie grabs my hand. "This is not too much. This is just enough. Friends do a lot more for each other."

"I can't, Marie."

"Look at it this way. After school, you come here and change. You look pretty and feel pretty—it is important to feel that way. Then Heath comes to pick you up, and his jaw breaks and he falls to the ground because you look perfect. You guys go out, have fun, and eat at a nice place. And then you come back, change, and go home."

"You've thought this through."

She nods enthusiastically. "I have. This way you'll be safe—" We both hang on to that word, but she recovers quickly. "—and won't have to worry about anything."

"Safe," I whisper. That one word hits me like a bullet.

She stiffens. "I'm sorry. I didn't mean to offend—"

"You didn't."

"Then why do you look sad?"

I sigh. "My parents don't know that I'm going out on a date. I should tell my mom. But I won't because she doesn't like Heath at all."

"Why not?"

"She thinks he's like my dad," I say, not thinking about the fact how openly I'm telling her stuff. Somehow, it's become easier to just say what I want to say.

Marie scowls. "What the fuck? Heath would never hurt you."

"Yes. But she doesn't think so. In her head, I'm making the same mistake as her younger self."

"You are not," she asserts.

I smile.

Swiveling my head, I look at the clothes. They are expensive and the fabric is in beautiful colors and designs. It's like a rainbow burst open and this is the result.

"Do you like anything?" she asks, watching me.

I shake my head.

Despite these clothes looking stunning, not a single article piques my interest. Something that I'd prefer to wear on a date with the guy I love.

"I think I love Heath," I tell Marie without meeting her gaze. "No, I'm sure. I love him."

The room goes quiet and tension fills the room so thickly that it feels hard to breathe.

And then, a squeal breaks the silence as she climbs over the bed and starts jumping.

"You love him!" She throws her arms above her head and laughs so loud that the fact I haven't told my mother—whom I've been close with since I was little—doesn't bother me.

"Oh my God!" She gets down and tackles me into a hug.

Her arms squeeze me hard as she surrounds me with her bright, warm energy.

"I can't breathe, Marie," I wheeze.

"Oh, sorry!" She quickly moves back and sits cross-legged beside me. "I got too excited."

A heartfelt laugh bursts out of me as I straighten up and tuck my legs underneath me. "You're the first person I've told this to."

She grins. "That means I'm special."

I return her grin. "You are. The most special person I've ever met."

Her eyes start to water but she quickly wipes away the moisture, not losing her million-dollar smile. "When will you tell him?" she asks.

"I don't know..." *Never seems like a good answer.*
What am I thinking? I have to tell Heath.

"Are you nervous?" Before I can answer, she says, "You don't need to be. I'm more than sure that he feels the same way."

She can't be serious. "What? No! That can't be true."

She scoffs. "Heath is obsessed with you. If it's not love, then what is it?"

"Just obsession?"

She shakes her head. "It's love."

I shrug, not wanting to get my hopes up. The last thing I want to do is hear he doesn't feel the same way about me. I would be shattered if he told me that he *only* likes me. Maybe it's better that I keep it inside.

"Tell him!" Marie insists, reading my mind. "You have to tell him."

"What if he doesn't—"

"Still, you should tell him. He deserves to know."

I cup my face in my hands as anxiety engulfs me. "I feel so scared."

"Hey!" Marie comes close and wraps her arm around my hunched shoulders. "Don't get in over your head. It's just voices."

I put down my hands and listen to her.

"You should tell him because you have to be honest with yourself," she assures me. "Also, I've known him for more than a year and we're best friends. I'm telling you he's already waiting at the love stop. I'm pretty sure he fell for you weeks ago."

My heart races. "You think so?" I ask in a small voice. Getting my hopes up despite what I told myself a minute ago.

"Yes," she says.

"But how?"

"Because you're an amazing girl and he's so damn lucky to have you," she replies without skipping a beat. As if it's pretty obvious.

"Is there a rule about confessing love on your first date?"

"Nope. But even if there were, who cares? Every love story is different."

I smile. "You're right."

She smirks. "I know."

I giggle, feeling lighter in my bones and excited for the date.

Mary

She leaves my side and stands on the other side of the bed and presses a dress onto herself. "So, let's pick a dress for the date."

"Are you sure?" I hesitate.

She only shoots me a mega-watt smile.

Somehow, that says it all.

25

HOPE

It's Friday evening when I come downstairs for dinner—not because I wanted to, but because Mom insisted. She took the day off from the hospital for Dad. She said the three of us haven't eaten together in a while. What she doesn't know is that I've been trying my best to avoid sitting at the table with him.

The second I got home, she had a long chat with me to not skip tonight's meal. I tried reasoning with her but it was useless. It was like what happened two weeks ago had been wiped off from her memory and she couldn't understand why I didn't want to have dinner with them.

The moment I enter the kitchen, the atmosphere changes. A dense cloud of tension hangs in the air, ready to bring down a storm.

Dad's gaze locks on me like a laser. Hate and anger swirling in those dark irises.

Confusion prickles my head as I start to wonder why he hates me. I've never done anything to him. I get good grades, stay out of trouble, and have a good reputation. What is it that I'm lacking? Why does he look at me like that? What is my fault?

"Hope, don't just stand there. Take a seat," Mom reprimands as she passes close, giving me a quick nudge.

I hesitate, which goes unnoticed by her but not him.

He smirks.

With a troubled head, I sit across from him—not that I have much of a choice. There are four chairs, two on one side and two on the other, facing each other.

"I bet you're hungry," Mom muses, standing over the stove and tasting the gravy off the spatula.

She gets busy with preparing the food and the silence follows.

With each passing second, my heart rate rises until it feels like the organ is beating in my throat and not my chest.

Anxiety wraps around me like an ever-growing vine, its branches getting tighter and fierce. My breathing reduces to shallow pants with oxygen scarcely entering my lungs.

"How's school?" he asks, leaning back in his chair that creaks under his weight. He is tall and built, with strength that can easily break someone like me.

I can never think about standing up to him, because in the end, I'll be the one who gets hurt.

"Good," I mumble and reach for the glass.

He watches me closely. "How are your grades?"

"Good."

His eyes narrow. "Don't be a smartass. Answer the questions clearly."

"Hope," Mom gets behind him so he doesn't see the pleading look she sends me, "tell us more, honey."

My hands start shaking under the table. So I clasp them together, but then my fingers begin to fidget with each other—an itch that refuses to go away no matter how much I rub my skin.

I want to get out of here.

I feel scared.

That storm cloud isn't growing away. It's only getting darker.

Something is going to happen.

Taking a deep breath, I answer him. "School is the same. Um... nothing new." I elaborate, knowing that what I said is basically nothing. The problem is I can't manage my head to function. It's too busy fighting off the anxiety attacks.

He arches an eyebrow. "Got any friends? Or are you still a loner?"

I think of Marie, Sebastian, and Heath. *My friends.*

Everything in me wants to protect them, so I shake my head.

He scoffs, calling my bluff.

"Dinner's ready," Mom chirps and presses a kiss to his cheek. "I made the gravy just the way you like it with the rice."

"Thanks, sweet." He grins at her.

"Do you need help, Mom?" I stand up before she can refuse me. I can't sit still and watch him, not when he looks at me with such a steady, dark gaze that makes goosebumps rise over my arms.

"Yes, she does." He glares at me. "Be useful and help her."

A shiver rolls down my spine. The sensation is so sudden and strong, it further puts me at unease.

Instinctively, my gaze meets Mom's, and she looks at me as if nothing is wrong.

Shoving down the disappointment, I scurry toward the cabinets and take out plates and cutlery. I linger, dragging time out like it might agree to stop for me, but eventually I run out of it. There's only three of us, not six. Returning to the table, I place the plates down one by one, then the cutlery.

Then I'm left with no choice but to sit and eat with them.

She sits next to him and leans over and kisses him.

I avert my gaze and find a spot in the old, weathered table to study.

"We should eat," Dad announces.

Mom fills his plate first, then hers, and at the very end, mine.

It means nothing but it bothers me. She used to fill my plate before hers. But tonight she didn't.

The gesture is small and insignificant, but it bears the mark of change: things are different. Love is different. Our relationship isn't what it used to be. In the past few months, it's changed more than it ever did in the past decade or so.

The clink of the cutlery shatters the silence and the stillness in the room. The noise is as sharp as a needle as it weaves through the storm cloud, making it about ready to rain.

The anticipation nearly kills me.

"Did you see the boy?" Dad asks. His tone is laced with suspicion.

"No," I say, glancing at him for a mere second, then going back to moving the food around on my plate.

"You shouldn't. He isn't good for you," he adds.

He's not the one who's not good for me.

I say nothing.

"You know that, don't you?" he probes me when I don't reply.

I give him a nod.

"Your father is right," Mom chimes in with a blank face. "Boys are nothing but trouble. It's better that you stay away from them."

"If he doesn't, then I'll make him," he reminds me.

A wave of protectiveness washes over me as I tightly hold the fork and think about scratching him with it.

Just as that thought crosses my brain, shame riddles me weak.

I'm thinking about hurting someone when it's something I've never thought about before.

What is happening to me?

Am I changing?

Is that okay?

"That won't be needed," she assures him.

Dad stills. Slowly, he turns his head and faces her. "What did you just say?"

Mom looks up, eyes filled with a splash of panic. "No-nothing!"

The spoon clatters on the table as his hand reaches forward and grabs her hair. He tugs roughly, making her cry.

"Think you are the only one who can make decisions around here, huh?" He yanks her head. "Just because you make money doesn't make you the boss. My word is the law. Do you understand or should I remind you?"

I sit and watch as my whole body goes numb.

"Maybe I should remind you!" Standing up, he starts dragging her toward the sink. "This is all your fault. You make me behave like this," he snaps at her.

"Alex, I'm sorry. I'm sorry," she begs him while crying.

He jerks her head back, making her look up at him. "This is you protecting her, isn't it?"

She shakes her head. "No—"

"You pretend to love her when you used to hate her."

"Stop, please."

"You were the one—"

"Stop it!"

"I see. You haven't told her the truth," he snarls.

Turning his head, he looks straight at me. "It's time you learn the truth."

Those words break my bubble, and I quickly stand up, hoping to help Mom but his serrated glare keeps me rooted in my place.

"Alex, please," she whispers.

He looks me dead in the eye. "You are nothing but a mistake. An accident."

"Alex!" She calls his name to warn him but he slaps her across the face.

"Shut your damn mouth!"

She whimpers, leaning against the sink and staring at the floor.

He stares at me long. Not a flicker of regret or sorrow crosses his face; nothing tells me he'll ever second-guess his words.

"When your mother got pregnant in college, it was a drunk mistake. One wasted night that we don't even remember because we were too intoxicated. No plans or anything," he explains. "I wanted to get rid of you because we were young and had nothing, but she decided to keep you. She said we'd make it work. So I dropped out and started working jobs to support her, but it wasn't enough. Nothing was enough. And then she suggested that we elope. Did that too, but nothing changed."

"Alex. Alex. Alex," Mom keeps mumbling his name.

Dad's gaze burns. "You understand why I hate you. It's because you're a mistake. You weren't supposed to happen," he breathes. "A fucking mistake. That's all you are. *A mistake.*"

Mistake.

Mistake.

Mistake.

That one word keeps looping over and over in my head.

Mistake.

Mary

I wasn't supposed to happen.
Mistake.
I wasn't conceived because they wanted me.
Mistake.
I was born because my parents were drunk.
Mistake.
I'm not a choice or a decision. I'm nothing.
Mistake.
He didn't want me.
I wait for my heart to break, but it doesn't.
It gets eerily quiet inside my bones. No sound or noise. No breaking or mending. Just shattered pieces lying on the floor as blood drips down from my chest, where my heart bleeds.
My chest feels heavy, swollen—like it's been flooded with blood instead of breath.
"Because of you, I didn't get a degree. Because of you, I started working. Because of you, we moved to this fucking town. Because of you, we're in this mess. Because of you..." he keeps talking. He blames me for everything because apparently I'm the root of his problems.
I tune him out and look at Mom, who is watching me.
Truth glistens in her eyes and I don't need to ask her anything.
What he said is true.
"Listen to me!" Dad slams the table and everything rattles.
I jostle and look at him.
His eyes appear dark, although they are light in shade. His face is composed of anger and his mouth is pulled in a scowl.
"What are you looking at?" he snaps.
I shake my head and look down at my lap.
"Alex—"
He turns and raises his hand to hit her.
"Don't!" I yell at him. "Don't hurt her."
Shock spreads like a cold winter breeze through my system, freezing everything and turning it into ice.
But I refuse to just stand and stare this time.
I won't let him hurt Mom.

My hands clench into fists by my side as rage courses through my veins like a stream of molten lava. It melts the ice and disperses the heat, making me move.

Abandoning my position, I rush to her and try to help her sit down. Upon a closer look, I notice her split lip and bruised cheek, which seem to be swelling a little.

Despite everything, I care about her. I know she loves me in her own way and I can't just leave her.

I'm acting purely on my instincts that are tied to her because of the motherly bond. She's done plenty of wrong things, but she also stood by my side plenty of times.

"Mom, are you okay?" I reach for her. "Stop crying, please."

Before my fingers can wipe away her endless stream of tears, she slaps away my hand.

"Get away from me."

I frown, not understanding her one bit.

When I don't move, she shoves me. *Hard.*

I fall on the floor on my back, stunned.

A chuckle bounces off the walls as he walks over to me and stares down at me. "Would you look at that? She doesn't want you either."

I look at her but she doesn't look at me.

Sitting up, I reach for her again. "Mom, I can—"

"Get out." When I don't move, she screams. "Get out of this house!"

Get out of this house.

Surely she means going to my room.

Right?

I sit and stare at her, trying to understand her.

"She said leave," he repeats.

I sit still.

With a sigh, he makes a move to reach for me, but in a flash, she stands up, grabs my arm and pulls me up harshly. Dragging me out of the kitchen, she leads me to the front door and pushes me out on the porch.

"Stay out," she says in a serious tone.

"What?" My voice is thick with disbelief.

Her gaze is sharp as it cuts me. "I said, stay out. You're not staying here."

"What do you mean?"

"I don't want you here." She looks at me, eyes brimming with tears —rage burning behind the sorrow.

I shake my head. "You can't kick me out. I don't have anywhere—"

"*Leave.* I don't care." She screeches, her fingers reaching for her hair. "I can't deal with this. I can't deal with you."

"Deal with what?"

"You," she says slowly.

"Mom—"

"Maedrian, come inside right now!" Dad's voice booms from the inside.

She holds the door, her frame leaning against it as if she can't stand on her own. She looks weak and tired. Bruised and battered.

I didn't think I'd see her like this again.

I thought she'd be safe.

I assumed things were fine between them.

It was all inside my head. Everything is the same.

Things are back to how they were.

THUD.

The door closes and the lock clicks.

For a brief second, I can only stare—paralyzed by disbelief.

Then, raising my hand, I knock. My fist collides with the wood, hoping to land a sharp, echoing rap, but the sound is a soft thud that is barely audible.

Crisp, cold air whips past me, wrapping me in chills that make my bones shake.

I lean against the wall, listening to the silence. A few minutes go by and yelling starts. I can't make out what the words are but it's Mom speaking and she's mad.

Once she calms down, she'll invite me back in.

Kicking me out on the porch was her being—

Being what? I ask myself for an excuse.

Tears prick my eyes and I feel helpless, confused, and cold.

Running my gaze around, I study the neighborhood, blanketed in darkness with sleeping houses. No stray dogs or cats roam the streets, no crying child throwing a fit, and no lights are turned on. No one is awake.

CRASH.

Something breaks inside and more arguing follows. With time, their voices get louder and angrier.

I don't think I can sneak in because they're banging doors and moving around.

A tear rolls down my cheek. Then another. And another.

When another crash sounds in the living room, I jump and rush down the steps and into the driveway.

I look around and analyze the surroundings, feeling panicked out of my mind because I have no idea what to do.

"What are you doing out here, girl?" a familiar voice speaks from nearby.

I find Nadina standing on the porch holding her crane. She's dressed in a nightgown and slippers. Her thin, wavy hair swept away from her face and tied in a braid.

"Nothing." My voice cracks as I sniffle.

Her gaze pins me down, and I feel myself almost breaking under the weight of shame.

Can she tell that I've been kicked out of my house?

I hope not.

She taps her crane. "Come here."

"It's alright. I'm going inside any minute." I offer her a weak smile, the corners tremble with uncertainty as tears burn my eyes.

Her lips press together.

More voices and louder arguments spill out of my house, carrying every word into the street, making me shift from one foot to the other.

I refuse to look at the elderly woman who is boring her gaze into my frame like she can see through my DNA and knows what kind of people made me.

Made me? No. I was something that came about.

A mistake.

That's what I am.

Tears spill down my cheeks and I angrily wipe them away.

"Come here and wait," Nadina says adamantly. "Until one of them comes to get you."

What she doesn't know is that no one is going to come get me.

26

HOPE

NADINA MAKES ME TEA. I'VE NEVER HAD TEA BEFORE.
One sip is all it takes for me to fall in love with it. It tastes sweet and smells earthy with hints of honey and herbs that soothe my senses.

We sit in her big kitchen bathed in dim light and a calming silence. The unfamiliarity of the room pricks my nerves. I'm on edge, my gaze lingering on the old refrigerator that is littered with colorful magnets, a tall antique cabinet filled with beautiful china crockery, and a kitchen table that has a plaid sheet with a flower vase as a centerpiece. The sage green walls blend well with the checkered tiles covering the floor.

There is so much life and color pulsing through this tiny space. I feel like I can breathe properly, not seeing bleakness for once.

"What were you doing outside?" the old woman finally asks, holding a cup and saucer.

I take a sip. "Nothing—"

"Don't lie to me, girl," she rebukes me. Her gaze cuts sharp like a blade.

My stomach hurts, a sudden pang of anxiety poking me like a needle.

"My mother kicked me out," I tell her.

Our eyes meet and I wait to see judgement but I see something else.

A swirl of darkness that is comprised of only fury. "Where are you staying tonight?"

I shake my head.

She hums.

After a moment, she says, "What about that boy who is fond of you?"

She must be talking about Heath.

I blush. "He doesn't know."

"Why not?"

"I don't have my phone with me. I left it in my room before coming down for dinner—" My sentence breaks, remembering what followed afterward. The utter, chaotic mess.

"All the rooms in my house are full," she explains.

I pale. "No. It's alright. I wasn't gonna stay here anyway. I'm sorry if you thought—"

She narrows her eyes and I shut up.

"Just today I sent the couch in the living room for repairs," she says.

I nod, not knowing what to say. She is a stranger to me, but she has been nothing but kind to me.

The fact that she's letting me sit here and treating me to tea is a fact in itself.

"Do you know the number of your boyfriend?"

I shake my head.

With a sigh, she stands up and slowly walks toward the small table next to the front door. Opening a drawer, she takes out a thick book and returns with it.

"Let's see if it has the number we need." She slips on her glasses that are hanging around her neck. They are red in color with an intricate designed frame. They match the color of her long gown.

"What's his full name?"

"Heath Travon."

She flips pages, diligently searching for his contact information as if she has it—which I highly doubt.

"Here it is," she says, her finger pinned at his number.

I check for myself and sure enough his number is scribbled next to his name in a small cursive writing.

"How do you have his number?" I ask.

"I asked him for it."

Before I can ask her about it, she says, "The phone is on the table. Go call him."

I hesitate for a moment, not sure if I want to involve him into this mess, but I don't have anywhere else to go.

Despite my reluctance, I get on my feet and pick up the old phone.

Punching in the number, I press the call button.

Please pick it up.

Please pick it up.

Please pick it up.

"Hello," his low and husky voice speaks.

I clutch the phone in both of my hands. A ball of nervous energy rolling into my stomach.

"Is someone there? If you don't fucking speak up—"

"Uh, Heath, it's me," I croak out, my nerves shaking.

Silence lingers for a second before he speaks, "Rose. Is that really you?"

"Yes."

"Where is your phone? Whose phone is this? What's happening? Fuck. Is everything okay? I'm coming over right now."

I stiffen. "No wait."

"What the fuck happened?"

I bite my lower lip as tears gather in my eyes hearing his voice—it alone breaks my walls and I can't keep it together. "Can you come and get me? If it's okay."

"I'm already in my car." The sound of the door closing filters in.

"Okay."

"Rose, what happened?" Worry laces his tone.

I sniffle, not knowing what to say to him.

"I'm coming for you," he assures me.

"Okay," I murmur.

"Keep talking."

I wipe my nose with the back of my sleeve. "I can't. I'm using Nadina's phone."

"Who is she?"

"My neighbor. You talked to her once."

"The old woman?"

"Yes."

"I'll pay her bill. Don't worry about it. Just keep talking to me."

"Okay."

"How did you end up at her house?"

Tears roll down like a stream. "My mother... Uh...she kicked me out."

"What?" He raises his voice.

"She screamed at me to get out. I told her I don't have anywhere to go but she didn't listen."

"And now you're at that woman's house."

"Yes. She saw me in the driveway and offered to let me wait here until you come."

"I'm three minutes away."

"I'm sorry for calling you this late for something like this, but I didn't know who else to call." I explain to him, feeling so helpless. "I don't have anywhere to go—"

"Rose," his voice is stern, "I'm fucking glad you called me."

"Are you sure—"

"I am."

"Okay."

"And you're wrong. I'm your place. You can always come to me."

I hold the phone tightly in my hands. Relief overcomes my nerves, and I relax a little after hearing those words.

Looking over my shoulder, I see Nadina looking through her phone book. If she is eavesdropping, she doesn't let it show on her face.

"I'm outside," he says.

I quickly end the call and fling open the front door. My heart is beating so fast.

The porch light is enough for me to make out his figure. Heath is walking up the driveway in hurried steps. When he sees me, he rushes over to me and envelopes me in his arms making me stumble back a little.

Getting tucked against his body hits me so hard that the tears start pouring, followed by a sob that cracks open a wound in my chest. Pain flows out freely, as if the walls don't exist anymore.

"Shh, it's okay," he mumbles into my hair. "It's fine now."

Footsteps echo behind us and soon a stare burns into the back of my head.

"You arrived quick, boy." Pride shimmers through Nadina's voice.

"Thank you for taking care of her," Heath says, giving me a squeeze.

"I expect she can spend the night with you and you'll be careful with her," she says with a hint of suspicion.

"I will be," he tells her, then, rubbing my back he adds, "We should get going."

Pulling out of his chest, I wipe away my tears and face her.

Gentle, green eyes stare at me.

"Thank you so much for letting me stay and for the tea. Is there any way I can repay you?"

She stares at me for a long moment, as if she wants to say something, but then shakes her head. There's so much sadness in her eyes. All for me.

Heath grabs my hand and tugs me toward his car. Before slipping inside, I look at my house and find all the lights on. My parents are awake but they didn't come out to get me. Their indifference kills a part of me.

As soon as we leave my neighborhood, he pulls the car over to the side of the road.

Tension coils through the thick air of the car, making the small space feel congested.

An immediate burst of tingles scatter like wildfire beneath my skin. With every pulse of panic they spread faster, leaving me breathless and on edge. I'm so close to having a panic attack.

Never mind. It's already here.

Air escapes my lungs as though the weight of what happened is finally sliding back on me.

The whole scene plays around in my head. Voices, words and actions flicker like a fast-paced movie that I can't stop watching.

It was a drunk mistake
I wanted to get rid of you
That's all you are. A mistake.
Get away from me.
Get out of this house
I can't deal with you.

A sharp sting spreads through my chest, like getting pricked by a thousand needles at once. The pain is excruciating, causing dots to appear in front of my eyes.

"Rose, hey!" Heath's voice filters through my dilemma.

His hands clamp around my wrists and he starts rubbing soothing circles on the inner side, unfurling heat that sears through my shaky senses.

"I can't...breathe," I wheeze out.

"It's okay. I'll help you."

I shake my head, growing frantic and more anxious. "No..." I whisper, ripping my hands out of his hold and clutching my chest. "Air. I need *air.*"

Heath says something, but I can't hear him above the chaos stirring inside me. His words are muffled. And no matter how much I try, I can't focus on his voice.

Voices. There are so many voices.

But the words are the same.

It was a drunk mistake
I wanted to get rid of you
That's all you are. A mistake.
Get away from me.
Get out of this house
I can't deal with you.

A cry breaks out of me, desperate and painful, begging to erase those words from my memory that feel like arrows dug so deep into my chest that pulling them out would kill me.

The pain intensifies in my chest with every short, little breath I draw in. The weight continues pressing down on me. My body feels light and breakable. I can't stand it.

In the midst of the storm, I feel my face being cupped by big, warm hands. Fingers that are rough and calloused. They caress my cheeks, softly and slowly, permeating sparks that burn the ropes of anxiety curled around me. Then, his mouth presses against mine. The shape of his lips, the heat of his breaths, and the tenderness of his movements wash over me with a wave of familiarity so intense and strong that I drown in it.

I stay still, as he kisses my lips. His strokes are deliberately long as they infuse life into me.

His thumbs keep moving over my cheeks, bringing warmth to the skin.

Slowly, my lips start to tingle. Suddenly, an intense rush of sensations erupt, sharp and electric, making the butterflies in my stomach flutter their wings wildly. Just a moment ago, they were swinging around buzzing with nervous energy.

When he pulls back, I gasp, inhaling a lungful of air—that was much needed.

It takes me a minute to realize that my head isn't humming with thoughts and my heart isn't scratching the walls to come out.

"You are breathing." Heath gently leans his forehead against mine. "Thank, fuck." Relief echoes thick in his voice.

I close my eyes and breathe. The whiff of his scent enters me and makes a home inside my lungs. It's his everyday cologne. One that is rich in sandalwood and fresh mint tones. It smells heavenly and addicting.

Something taps the windshield pulling my attention away from him. I glance and see raindrops. A few more fall down. Then, the skies crack open with the booming sound of the thunder and bright flash of lightning that slices through the heavy mass of clouds. Soon, it starts raining freely.

"How are you feeling?" Heath asks, turning my face in his direction.

I meet his worried gaze. Blue eyes that ache for me. It heals something in me to know that at least someone cares about me. "I'm okay."

He tucks a few strands of my hair behind my ear. "Are you hurt anywhere?"

I shiver, as those fingers graze the side of my neck. "No, I'm fine."

"You really mean that?"

"Yes," I answer.

He turns on the heat and adjusts the fans in my direction. Warm air hits me, and it feels oddly comforting.

"You were shivering," he murmurs as he starts the car and flips on the wipers.

"Thank you," I reply.

Heath drives slowly as the rain gains momentum, drumming hard against the windshield. His eyes stay focused on the road as he switches lanes and makes turns.

I've seen him drive before, but I've never noticed how incredibly attractive he looks while doing it. Even in a weather like this, he commands the car with such skill that comes naturally to him.

"Who taught you to drive?" I wrap my arms around me and get comfortable in the seat.

I know he wants to know what happened but I don't want to talk about it right now.

We stop at a red light. The roads are empty and the shops are closed. If he wanted to, he can break the signal, but he doesn't. As if he is stretching the moment, hanging onto the calm before the storm unleashes.

The way his jaw ticks and his hands tighten around the steering wheel, make it clear he's livid.

And that makes me nervous.

I don't like anger. I know what it makes one do.

His head turns as if he can sense my fears. A switch happens instantly. His eyes soften and his face relaxes.

He changes himself for me.

Reaching over, he places his hand on my thigh, as if it's second nature to him.

"Derek," he says.

A jolt of surprise whizzes through me. "Derek?"

He smiles. "Yes."

"I can't believe it."

He huffs out a laugh, but sadness flickers through his eyes. "He wasn't so bad when my sister was around. He was chill, used to smile and laugh with us." He sighs. "I was fourteen when he taught me in our driveway on his old Subaru. It was manual—"

"What's manual?" I ask.

"There is a gear stick so you can switch gears," he explains calmly.

I look down and see a stick. "So this is manual?"

Instead of taking away his hand that is resting over my thigh, he lifts off the one from the steering wheel and points it to the centre console and the handles on the side of the steering wheel.

"It is both."

"Is that possible?"

He nods with a hint of a smile while I try to wrap my head around it. Clearly, I know nothing about cars. Only books.

The light changes to green. Pressing hard on the gas, he goes right and then slows down again.

"What changed Derek?" I blurt.

His hand tightens on my thigh, fingers stretching and reaching the inner side, eliciting tingles that make me shift a little. Heat gathers in the pit of my stomach.

"Emery's death," he says in a grim tone. "They were close. He saw her like a granddaughter and adored her. He wasn't as grumpy or robotic like he is now. He used to be human."

"How was he with you?"

"He was nice. He didn't like me much because of my hatred for my father. He wasn't okay with it. Apparently, he knew why they had sent us here and always said that it was for a reason. I tried to extract that information out of him multiple times, but he never gave it up."

I knew it bothered Heath that his parents left him. It hurt me to see him like this.

Whatever he felt, I felt it a hundred times more. All I wanted for him was to be happy and not feel like he wasn't wanted or that he could be abandoned. He was worth far more than what he was made to feel.

His exterior was tough, but on the inside there was a kind, caring heart—despite being a little purple and bruised from all the pain he was carrying.

"Do you still wonder about it?" I ask.

"About what?"

"The reason why your parents left you."

In a quiet voice, he says, "Always."

Before I can say anything more, his phone starts ringing. We both glance at it. 'Mom' flashes across the screen.

Heath switches it to silent and keeps driving.

But the calls keep coming.

The rain continues to fall as he drives along the winding road that curves around the small hills leading to uptown. On either side, rows of magnificent houses sit, and street lamps cast a warm glow in the sea of darkness. It's past midnight and everyone is sleeping.

He pulls up in front of his house. Rolling down the window, he punches in the code and the gates separate, making way for him to drive. He pulls up in the garage and parks the car beside his sister's car. When he switches off the engine, his gaze locks onto her car and his body goes rigid.

"She misses you too," I say.

His gaze flickers to me and he leans over and kisses me.

Getting out, he comes around and opens the door for me—it's something he always does, but I still haven't gotten used to it.

Lacing his fingers with mine, he kisses me again and then stares down at me.

"We need to talk," he says.

I give him a weak nod. "Thank you for bringing me here. I don't have anywhere else to go—"

"Good. Because I don't want you to go anywhere else when I'm here," he says in a serious tone.

I give his hand a squeeze, because if I open my mouth only a sob will come out.

Heath has no idea how awful I feel right now. If I didn't have him in life, I'd be on the streets, probably sleeping against a tree or in the back of an alley. But that's not even the part that hurts. It's the fact that my mother kicked me out and both of my parents are okay with it. As if they don't care about what happens to me.

They kicked me out.

Pain slices through me like a double-edged sharp sword. A twinge of excruciating pulse, biting deeply.

He steps closer. Cupping the back of my head, he presses a kiss on my head. "It's fine. Don't worry your pretty head about it."

How can I not?

"I've got you, Rose. I've always got you. You can rely on me."

Are you sure?

"It's going to be okay."

I don't know about that.

"You can stay here."

For how long?

When I don't answer, he tips my head back and makes me look at him. His gaze is steady as he studies me. Eyes locked on me in full concentration as if he can read all the words and sentences that I don't speak.

I try to hide from him, but I know I can't.

He's always seen me.

27

HEATH

ROSE IS BREAKING INSIDE. NOT JUST BREAKING. SHE IS fucking losing herself.

I see the haunted look in her eyes—filled with a wild mix of emotions. Sadness, humiliation, and shame.

And it hurts me to see her like this.

I hear a door creak open nearby, followed by footsteps thumping through the quiet hallway just outside—the one that connects the garage to the house.

My parents are awake. From the dozen calls Mom made, it's evident that she saw me rushing out earlier. I didn't have time to tell her not to wait up for me—not that it matters, since she waits for me anyway.

I swivel my head just in time to see my parents standing by the glass doors, wearing confused expressions on their faces.

Hope's back is toward them—for which I'm glad. I don't want them to see her right now. Because I know she is barely keeping it together right now. The last thing she needs is an interrogation.

Mom's distressed gaze stays on us, while Dad frowns, studying me in detail.

"Is there someone behind us?" Rose asks shakily.

She attempts to turn her head, but I prevent her from doing so. "Derek is passing by."

I knew saying his name wouldn't affect her as much as knowing it's my parents who are glued to their spots and refuse to move away.

Much to my dismay, she doesn't believe me. "Why is he staring? I can feel his stare on my back."

I let out a groan. "It's my parents."

Her eyes widen and she looks like she's about to have another panic attack.

For fuck's sake.

I don't want that.

One was enough to make me spiral.

"It's okay. I'll take care of them." I assure her. "Give me a second."

"No! Don't leave me." She grips my arm with a firm grip as tears well up in her eyes again. *Eyes that I love so much.* "I don't want you to go."

"Rose—"

A few tears fall and my heart twists painfully inside my chest.

Without a word, I tuck her in my arms and put my chin on the top of my head.

She's incredibly sensitive tonight. I've seen her panic before, but this is different. She's in so much pain, it's triggering her anxiety.

Bending down, I slide one arm under her knees and the other around her waist, then gently lift her into my arms, pulling her closer to me. Her arms loop around my neck and her face burrows into the crook of my neck, making it impossible for me to read her.

She isn't making noises, but she is crying.

Her tears dampen my black hoodie.

I walk toward the glass doors, not making eye contact with my parents, who look shocked. Mom has her mouth cupped by her hand, eyes wide, while Dad stares hard, questions burning in his gaze. It's a relief that they don't say anything as I move past them.

Rose shakes against me as if she knows they are a few steps away from us.

Picking up pace, I hurry down the hallways and take the stairs that lead up to my room. Once we're inside, I lock the door and set her down on my bed. She doesn't let go of me. So, I sit down with her on my lap and remove her shoes so she can slip under the duvet. She still doesn't move.

"What's wrong?" I ask, lifting her chin.

This time, she doesn't hesitate.

"I don't want to think what your parents are thinking but I can't stop thinking about it," she tells me in a quiet voice. "What will I tell them if they ask me why I'm here?"

"Tell them I want you here."

"In the middle of the night?"

"I can't stay away from you."

She looks up at me and the sight of her shoots an arrow right through my heart. Her eyes are puffy and red-rimmed and her cheeks are flushed with streaks of tears. She resembles a mess—pulled apart piece by piece, barely holding it together. She still looks beautiful. But in a sad kind of way that tugs the heartstrings of my fucking heart.

Just like that, my mood switches and my body turns stone.

"What the fuck happened tonight, Rose?" My tone is hard, laced with anger that I can hardly keep inside.

"A lot," she whispers.

My muscles lock in tension. She doesn't look hurt, but I know her shitty father is the reason for her pain.

Taking a deep breath, she tells me everything. The things her father said make me want to kill him, but then she tells me about her mother and how she practically shoved her out of the house in the middle of the night with no care.

He said I'm a mistake.

They were drunk.

He wanted to get rid of me.

After hearing those words, I feel sick to my stomach. My insides have fused in a knot. With every twist and turn, nausea stirs, and I feel like my dinner is going to come up any second.

"They didn't want me," she sobs. "I was a *mistake*. Something that wasn't supposed to happen."

I hold her close to me. "You're not a mistake."

229

She shakes her head, adamant about it. "He said it. And he sounded so sure."

"Well, he is fucking wrong, so don't listen to him."

She sniffles. "*His words. His voice.* I can't stop listening to it. It's playing in my head."

"Rose," I cup her face in my hands. The look she wears splinters my lungs, making it hard to breathe. "You are not a fucking mistake."

"How can you be so sure?"

"Because you're perfect."

She looks unconvinced. "You're only saying this because you like me."

No, I'm saying this because I love you.

Of course I can't say that to her.

I rub her cheeks with the pad of my thumbs. A slow and gentle back-and-forth motion. "I'm saying this because I *know* you."

Her lower lip wobbles and she throws her arms around my neck and hugs me.

I return her hug, pulling her close to me.

Lightning spills into the room, followed by a deafening crack of thunder. The rain gets harder and louder outside, but the room is still and silent.

"You should get some sleep." I run my palm down her back, calming her down.

"I'm not sleepy," she mumbles into my shoulder.

"Have you had dinner?"

"No, but I'm not hungry—"

"Doesn't matter. I'm getting you something to eat."

With a sigh, she nods. Untangling her arms from around my neck, she gets off me and climbs into my bed. She faces the window and stares at the storm raging beyond the glass. It is terrifying to know that if she didn't have me, she'd be alone and lost in such weather.

"Thank you for letting me stay here," she says.

"You don't need to thank me, Rose." With that, I stand up and press a kiss on her head. "I've got you."

Mom and Dad are in the living room, engrossed in a conversation as I walk past them into the kitchen. I grab a plate and start pulling it

Mary

up with food when they appear in the doorway. It's Mom who steps forward and stands beside me.

"Heath, what is going on?" Her tone is laced with worry.

"Nothing," I mutter as I speed up my movements to escape as fast as I can. The last thing I want is an interrogation.

"Why is Hope here?" she asks.

"Her parents are out of town, and she was alone, so I asked her to stay with me." The lie rolls off my tongue effortlessly. I just hope she believes me and doesn't prod me for details.

Of course I thought wrong.

"But she was shaking and crying," she adds.

"There was a power shutdown in her area and it got her scared." Another smooth lie.

Dad's watchful gaze burns a hole in the side of my head. Questions brimming under the surface that I'm sure he wants to ask, but is waiting for Mom to finish.

Quickly, I place the plate in the microwave and lean against the counter, waiting, avoiding eye contact with my parents at all costs.

Mom approaches and stands in front of me. "I know something is wrong," she says softly.

My gaze lifts and meets hers. The second it does, I feel like she can see right through me. Despite my hatred and resentment, and the thick walls I've built between us, we are blood. I'm connected to her.

"Nothing is wrong," I say confidently.

Doubt lingers in her eyes.

Dad steps behind Mom and puts his hand on her shoulder in reassurance. His eyes cut to me. "We know she's the reason you got arrested."

Color drains from my face.

My mind goes entirely blank.

Reaching behind me, I hold the marble counter with a firm grip to steady myself.

For fuck's sake. My parents were the last people I wanted to know.

The non-serious look in his eyes tells me that he isn't lying. He knows what happened. Somehow, he has the details.

But how?

231

With a heavy gulp, I try to wet my parched throat.

"What the fuck do you mean?" My tone is low and dark as it slices through the veil of tension suspended between us.

"She is the reason—"

"You're wrong. She is *not* the reason," I grit out.

The instinct to protect her comes naturally. My body reacts before my mind and heart can decide.

"You don't need to lie to us."

"I'm not."

Dad's eyes soften for a second. "Why don't you tell us what is really going on?"

"We know you're in trouble," Mom chirps in.

There is a lot of 'we' going on as if they have talked about me for long hours. Almost as if they care about me.

Mom moves closer to me. "We can help you."

I scoff. "I don't need your help."

Her face crumples, the glimmer of light vanishing from her eyes.

Looking at Dad, I say, "And nothing is going on. Whoever gave you this information, they are fucking wrong."

Dad sighs heavily. "Then why don't you tell us what happened?"

"I beat up a man because he pissed me off," I reply. At least, that bit isn't a lie. Hope's dad made me so angry that I didn't hesitate to climb over him and hit him like a madman. I regret I didn't do some serious damage. Like break his hand or fingers so that he couldn't touch my girlfriend ever again. Maybe I should have hurt his tongue so that he wouldn't spew bullshit to her that makes her feel small and worthless. Because his fucking words hurt her more than his hits ever did.

Dad arches an eyebrow. "A man who is the father of your girlfriend."

My blood goes icily cold.

Tension wraps around my body like steel chains, tightening with every ragged, fast breath that I inhale. My muscles ache because of how tightly wound up they are, my jaw locked in its place, and the centre of my chest burns with rage.

My fists shake, the tremors impossible to control. "What did you say?"

His lips press together. "We know what happened, son."

Anger flares through me as I push off the counter and straighten up. "You don't know anything."

He nods. "I did some research and found out everything."

My jaw goes slack. "You hired someone to investigate me?"

He shakes his head. "I hired someone to find out what happened that got you into trouble."

"And that sounds right to you? To get into my business?" I snap, heat surging through my veins.

"It isn't his fault." Mom quickly jumps in. "It's mine. He looked into it because I was worried."

"Not just you, Mia Cara," Dad says just as his gray eyes lock on me. "I am worried, too."

Those words hang in the thick smoke of tension that has always been there when we are in the same room. Over the years, it has become darker and denser, clouding the view completely so that we don't see each other.

The coldness in his eyes melts away. "Getting that call from your friend and hearing that you were locked up nearly gave me a heart attack. I left in the middle of a meeting, one I had worked for two years, got home and told your mother. We packed nothing. Just grabbed important stuff and got on the plane."

"I didn't ask you to come," I grumble.

"I'm glad you didn't," he counters. "Because it's not something that you should ask for. It's our responsibility to be there for you."

I grind my molars so tightly, I feel like I'll break them.

The fact that I don't have a fucking answer makes me furious. Because what he just said makes my chest hurt. It makes me realize that perhaps they give a fuck about me—something I don't care about.

"She is here because something happened at home," Mom says sorrowfully. "And you brought her here to keep her safe."

I glare at her, hating how quickly she put it all together—it wasn't hard, considering they knew why I was at the police station.

The microwave pings, cutting through the silence in the room, but I don't move.

Mom and I stare at each other for a long minute.

Finally, I look away.

"Bring her down." Her voice carries a command.

"What?" I frown.

"We need to send her back home."

I frown harder. "What the fuck?"

"Your mother is right," Dad speaks in a curt tone.

I glare at both of them. "I'm not sending her back."

"You need to," Dad asserts.

"Her parents must be worried about her," Mom says.

A scoff leaves past my lips. "It's her mother who kicked her out."

Mom lets out a loud gasp, her hand reaching for the island to steady her. Dad quickly reaches for her and wraps his arm around her.

"Wh-what?"

I run a hand through my hair, frustration making me annoyed. "She has nowhere to go so I brought her here." Narrowing my eyes, I add, "And she isn't going back. Especially not tonight."

"How could they do this to her?" she asks. "What is going on?"

I press my lips together in silence. I've already said enough.

Squeezing past them, I grab the plate from the microwave and a spoon and leave.

28

HOPE

HEATH TAKES A LONG TIME AND I SIT ON HIS BED WATCHING the relentless rain drench the town. The endless pitter-patter of the raindrops brings a calm to the restless storm churning inside me.

I've spent time in this room before—multiple times—yet spending the night here makes my nerves jittery. It feels like a ball is jumping between my heart and stomach, growing faster with each bounce. And all I'm doing is waiting for it to crash and burn.

What feels like forever, the door finally opens, making me sit straight.

He walks in, holding a plate of rice and a glass of water. Setting it on the nightstand, he takes a seat beside me and looks at me with those blue eyes that make my heart flutter.

Leaning over, he kisses me softly. I melt into him, surrendering myself because I feel safe with him.

Maybe it's the fact that it's late at night or perhaps I've been abandoned by my parents, but I just let it be. I don't let myself think about anything.

"You okay?" he asks.

"You asked me that earlier."

He smiles. "Just making sure."

I nod. "I am."

Reaching for the plate, he places it on my lap and hands me the spoon. "Chicken rice. Mom made it."

"Thank you." My stomach squeezes in hunger at the sight of food that looks delicious.

I take a bite and chew quickly. The flavor dissolves into my mouth bringing a joy inside. "It tastes good."

"Really?"

I offer him a bite and he eagerly takes it. "Fuck, this is good."

"You seem surprised."

He shrugs. "Can you blame me? I haven't spent much time with them."

"What about now?"

He groans. "I'm still avoiding them."

A sad smile tugs on my lips. "I bet they aren't as bad as my parents."

Heath's stare burns a hole in my face as I keep my head down and eat.

Uncomfortable silence fills the little space between us.

"I don't know about that," he says quietly, "but they've hurt me by ignoring me and my sister for years. They didn't hurt us with words or physical violence, but their ignorance was just as bad if not worse."

I nod, feeling awful. "I'm sorry."

He shakes his head. "You don't need to be sorry."

"You say they don't care, but your Mom, when I talked to her at the cafe, seemed like she genuinely cared about you and wanted to know more about you."

"And did you tell her?"

I set aside the empty plate and reach for water. "No. I knew you wouldn't want me to."

"Good choice."

"I know you," I say softly.

His eyes brighten even in the dark. "But I know you more."

It is true. He knows me better than I know him.

The fact bothers me and I decide that I'm going to learn more about him, as much as I can.

Setting down the now-empty glass on the nightstand, I sit straight, not knowing what to do.

Heath, unaware of the anxiety that consumes me, picks up the empty plate and glass and puts it on the coffee table. When he comes back, he takes the other side of the bed and gets under the covers. Then, he shifts closer until we're sitting shoulder to shoulder.

Heat infuses into me, having his rock-solid body pressed against me. His scent envelopes me, pulling everything inside me toward him. The tug is so strong it's hard not to gravitate toward him and get closer to him more than I ever have.

Ludicrous thoughts fill my mind and my skin warms.

My pulse quickens.

The little space between us shrinks with each shallow, slow breath that I inhale.

His hand reaches for my hair, and he tucks a few strands behind my ear. The slight brush of his fingertips makes me shiver.

I meet his gaze and an electric current sizzles through me. In the dim golden light of the nightstand lamp, his eyes appear beautiful. The hue of blue is so rich and bright in color that it reminds me of a peaceful ocean. I realize that I wouldn't mind drowning in him.

"Do you have any idea how scared you got me tonight?" he murmurs, his fingers playing with my hair. "I lost my mind when you called me."

"I'm sorry."

He shakes his head slowly. "I don't need your sorry. I need you to be okay."

"I am okay." I force myself to be brave enough to press my palm over his chest. His heart beats wildly fast. A rhythm both powerful and rapid. "With you, I always am," I say.

His gaze goes heavy as it lays on me with a tangible force. The weight of it diminishes the space between my lungs and I can hardly breathe.

Is no breathing an option?

Because I sure am heading there.

Heath stays still, his eyes locked on me, but the desire burns brightly within him. It's the way his gaze never wavers or the way his breathing becomes deep and rugged.

I glance away just long enough to watch his throat work, a slow, painful bob.

He is holding back because of me. Because he thinks I'm not ready.

Truthfully, I don't know if I'll ever be ready. Things aren't going to change at home. But one thing is for certain. I want him.

Without thinking, I push him back against the headboard and straddle his lap.

My fingers quiver and my stomach tightens, but I refuse to back down.

Before he can stop me, I lean down and kiss him. I move my lips against his slowly and sweetly, taking my time to memorize the shape of them and how they taste.

Heath stiffens for a moment, then pulls me down with his hands on my hips and his mouth focused on devouring me.

In the silence of his room, with the rain tapping against the windows, we kiss for a long time, not leaving a single place. His breath is warm and minty as it infuses into mine and fills me up.

Finally, he moves to the side of my neck when I can barely feel my lips. However, the tingles are there, sparking under the surface and inducing lust into my veins.

His mouth is gentle and hot as it peppers kisses over my skin, stirring heat into the pit of my stomach.

"Please tell me to stop," he begs. "Because tonight I won't if you don't ask me to."

"No, don't stop," I plead.

I feel his hands climb up a little until they reach the hem of my sweatshirt. Raising his head, he meets my gaze, a question brimming in them.

I give him a nod.

Very slowly, he lifts it off my body until it's completely gone.

Quickly, I shield my chest because I'm not wearing a bra. If I had any idea that I'd be here tonight, I would put on my best one—the one that would qualify as decent, because before today, I didn't even care about how important that is.

Heath places his hands on my hips, his fingers rubbing circles over my bare skin. The touch is new and makes me lose my mind. His eyes don't steer toward the area I'm trying my hardest to hide.

I know I lack in that department. After all, I'm skinny.

"You are beautiful," he says in a voice that is full of conviction. As if it isn't a compliment but a fact.

"These aren't," I gesture to him.

"They are to me." There is no speck of a lie in his words.

I fold my arms tightly over my chest, desperately hiding everything. Embarrassment washes over me like a bucket full of cold water, making shivers race down my spine. I've never felt more vulnerable.

"Rose," he calls me softly, eyes locked on me.

This was a huge mistake.

What was I thinking?

That's right. I wasn't thinking.

I just reached for him because I wanted him.

"Hey." His lips meet my collarbone and I tremble.

I can't do this.

It is too real.

"Baby," he murmurs, tipping my chin back so we're staring at each other. "Let me see them. Let me see you."

"Are you sure?" I choke.

He nods.

Taking in a stuttering breath, I slowly remove my quivering arms, all the while keeping eye contact with him. When my arms land in my lap, I let out another shaky breath that shakes my entire body.

Heath touches my back with one hand and draws me closer to him. "These are fucking beautiful, just like the rest of you."

A gasp escapes my mouth, the second he kisses me there.

Pleasure rushes through me and I can't keep my head straight.

I get lost in him, his touch, and his soft kisses.

We lay in bed awake. My back is toward him, but I can feel his gaze burning a hole in me. I bite my lip to hide my smile as I think about all the lewd things that he just did to me. At the same time, my breasts hurt a little. But it's a good kind of pain.

I want it again.

"Rose," he says. "I know you aren't sleeping."

I don't move a single muscle.

"Your breathing is loud," his tone carries amusement.

I quickly clamp a hand over my nose. "No, it's not."

The covers shift and then his arm wraps around my waist and he plasters my back against his hard, warm chest.

"You're a terrible liar," he murmurs into my hair as he nuzzles his face into my neck.

I stop breathing.

"Breathe, baby." He squeezes me.

There is that word again. One that makes a thousand butterflies flutter in my stomach in excitement. When he used it earlier, I was too caught up to process it. But now, it's the only thing I can think about.

He gives me a squeeze to pull me out of my thoughts.

"What are you thinking?"

"Nothing."

"That's not possible."

I sigh, knowing it is futile. "Should I go home tomorrow?"

He stiffens. "No."

"Why not?" I whisper.

"Because they don't get to fucking throw you out like that. I can't believe they did it." His tone is full of anger. "It was late at night and raining. Anything could've happened to you if I hadn't come to get you."

When he says all those things, my chest hurts. Pain spreads like poison, dissolving into my blood and sinking into my bones. The ache is so deep and intense it knocks the air out of my lungs.

I was abandoned by my parents.

That sentence hits me like a bullet, shattering my entire world in seconds.

"I have nowhere to go," I murmur.

"The fuck not," he grumbles. Gently, he turns me around so I'm facing him. He cups my cheek in his palm and looks intently at me. "You'll stay here with me. I'm not letting you go."

"But your parents—"

"They can fuck off."

I purse my lips. He's not thinking logically.

Things would have been a lot different if his parents weren't here. I could consider staying here for a day or two until Mom declared that I could come back—but will she, though? Questions start piling up in a stack, one by one.

Is she looking for me right now?

Is she worried about me?

Is she thinking about whether I'm safe or not?

Disappointment fills my heart because I don't have the answers.

And I'm someone who likes to have the answers. Whether its derivatives in maths, chemical equations in chemistry, research in biology or theories in physics. I like it when I know the definite solution. The uncertainty of anything bothers me. It triggers my anxiety, not knowing the unknown.

"You don't need to worry about my parents. They won't bother you. But if they say anything, just tell me, okay," he says.

I give him a weak nod.

His mother seems nice, but I don't know anything about his Dad. I wonder what he is like? The only thing I know is that Heath hates him a lot.

"I'm going to take care of you," he promises.

That makes me burrow my head in his chest. I don't want him to see the way tears blind my vision because not knowing what's going to happen next is killing me from the inside.

In the midst of it all, I do something that is so stupid.

"I love you," I say, without thinking.

Heath's fingers dig into my hair as his whole body tightens.

"What?" he asks in a raspy, low voice.

"I said, I love you," I tell him.

The tension hangs in the air, and our ragged, fast breaths fill the tiny space between us. It's so quiet that you can hear a pin drop.

It's a miracle he can't hear my heart racing.

After a long moment, he says, "That's my line, Rose."

I look up at him in bewilderment. "What?"

"I love you."

He loves me?

He loves me.

Our gazes connect and our hearts beat at the same rhythm.

Something inside me that was broken mends.

"Heath—" I whisper, my hand reaching for his T-shirt. He changed into it, saying he gets hot under the covers. I feel the scorching heat of his skin through the thin material of his T-shirt. He is burning.

"I thought you only liked me," I whisper.

He smiles in the dark. "I do like you, but it's more than that. It has been for a while."

"Since when?"

"Since the first time I saw you."

I gasp. "That long?"

He nods. "I was captivated by you the moment I caught you staring at me through the window."

"But you were glaring at me."

"I was, because it bothered me that one look at you and I forgot to say everything I wanted to." He chuckles. "You looked so beautiful that day."

My cheeks redden. "I wasn't wearing anything special."

"It wasn't the clothes. It was the girl."

I clear my throat, feeling warm inside. "I fell for you when I started trusting you."

"So it wasn't my good looks?" he teases.

"No, that's not what I'm saying. I mean, you are handsome and your face is pretty—"

"Just pretty?"

"—and your body—"

"My body?"

"—it looks good—"

He bursts out laughing, the sound warm and bright like the first ray of sunshine on a frosty, cold morning. His whole chest shakes, the strong vibrations traveling through my palm, into my skin. My hand twitches as if to grab and hold them forever in me.

"For fuck's sake," he mutters. "I work out for hours, do boxing, and you think my body looks just good?"

Of course, it doesn't look just good.

It looks delicious.

He draws me closer and wraps me up in his big, muscular arms that make me feel safe. We've been this close before, but this is different. It feels oddly cozy to be this close with the person you love.

"Remember, I asked you out on a date?" He rubs my back. "Would you like to go with me?"

"A date."

"Yes, Rose. A date."

"Where would we go?"

"Anywhere you want to go."

"I'm fine with anything." I just need you with me.

Heath starts drawing soothing circles on my back, the movement so careful and gentle it lulls me to sleep.

"I've never been to an aquarium," I mumble absentmindedly.

"Aquarium?"

I nod, my eyes get heavy and fog wraps around my thoughts.

Before I know it, I'm falling asleep.

29

HOPE

THE MOMENT MY EYES OPEN, A JOLT OF PANIC SHOOTS through me, sharp and paralyzing, like ice in my veins. It's the fact that I'm waking up in a room that isn't mine. Instantly, an emptiness settles into my bones as last night's events roll back like a bad memory.

I slowly sit up and look around. The blinds are drawn to keep the sunlight out and the space is bathed in quietness and darkness. It's comforting.

Heath isn't here. I can't feel his presence anywhere in his room. Strange, how I can now just know when he's nearby. It's like my body knows him in ways that I didn't even know.

It's because you love him.

The digital clock on his nightstand blinks in red digits. 10:17 am.

I haven't slept this late in months. In fact, I haven't slept peacefully in a while. For the first time, I didn't wake up because of a bad nightmare or due to the shivers that'd come because of the cold winds drifting in through my broken windows.

Sliding off the bed, I carefully make it, trying my best to make sure there aren't any wrinkles.

"Oh dear, you don't have to do that," a familiar voice speaks from behind me, making me stop.

I find Heath's mother standing in the doorway, looking stunning in an expensive red dress that fits her perfectly. Paired with diamond jewelry and heels, she resembles a model.

"I don't mind."

Her gaze softens as she steps into the room and fills the air with a lightness, but the knot in my stomach does not uncurl.

"How did you sleep?" she asks.

My whole face turns red. "I slept...okay."

She grins, as if she knows that I slept with her son in the same bed. My blush deepens.

I wrap my arms around myself and smooth my arms to ease the trembling nerves. Before she can speak, I say, "You don't have to worry about anything. Nothing happened between us. I promise."

A giggle bubbles out of her. "I'm not worried about that." She turns serious. "I'm worried about you."

My eyebrows pull together in a frown. "Why?"

Without saying a word, she takes a step forward, and I immediately retreat—purely on instinct. The action doesn't escape her attention and she stops.

My chest caves in from the anxiety that hits me like a train. Air knocks out of my lungs, all because I can't get my body under control. Especially, in front of someone I want to like me.

"I'm sorry," she quickly moves back.

"No!" I whisper. "I-I don't know why I moved. I—"

"Did it without thinking."

I stare at her in shock.

"Why don't you come downstairs and have breakfast with me?"

My stomach tightens. "Where's Heath?"

She smiles. "He left early with Sebastian and Marie."

I nod.

"Freshen up and come downstairs." That sounds more like a command than a request.

AFTER WASHING MY FACE WITH JUST WATER—HEATH USES A charcoal facewash and charcoal doesn't suit me—and brushing my teeth with a spare toothbrush that I find in one of the drawers, I fix my hair and plaster on a smile.

I'm still dressed in sweatpants. Not an ideal outfit when you're about to have breakfast with your boyfriend's mother. I'm definitely not impressing her today. All I want is for her to like me.

Practicing a five-minute breathing technique, I leave the room and walk down the hallway. I feel so anxious that I have to use the banister to descend the stairs—the chances of me falling down are very high.

The closer I get, the more nervous I become.

I've met her before and I know she's nice, but that was before she saw me getting carried away in her son's arms and spending a night in his room. I hope she believes me that we didn't do anything and I'm not corrupting her son.

The only thing we've done is kissing and a little bit of touching, but only the upper half.

My cheeks flame up at the reminder and I press my cold palms against my cheeks to cool them down.

I desperately need the cloak of invisibility.

Since I know where the kitchen is, I find my way to it without getting lost in the maze of rooms.

I draw in a deep breath before entering and see his mother near the stove. She's frying pancakes and humming a song in a sweet melody.

I almost turn around to leave when she says, "Take a seat, Hope."

I should've known. My chances of escaping awkward situations are always slim.

Walking toward the stool, I sit down and try to keep my back straight. I read somewhere that it oozes confidence.

"Do you like maple syrup on your pancakes?" she asks.

"It's fine," I say.

"Are you sure?"

"Yes."

"Someone told me you only like chocolate."

Butterflies soar in my stomach. "I do, but the maple syrup will be just fine."

She stacks up three pancakes and places the plate in front of me.

Moving around, she places another plate that has a couple of sandwiches. Finally, she brings a plate of omelettes with bacon, toast, and blueberries on the side. She takes it as she sits across from me.

Grabbing the chocolate syrup, she sets it next to my plate.

"You don't need to stop being honest with me. If you like something, say it. Don't be afraid of anyone," she advises.

"Thank you," I mumble.

"You certainly weren't afraid to speak your mind when you first met me. I admired that about you. I can see why Heath likes you."

He loves me.

I almost blurt, but realize it's probably best if he tells her himself.

Grabbing the chocolate syrup, I pour it over my pancakes and take a small bite. They melt into my mouth and the sweet taste is heavenly. But they are not like my mother's. She makes the best pancakes.

Just thinking about her swells my throat, making it hard to swallow the food.

The reminder of last night once again circles my head and my barriers grow weak at keeping my wandering thoughts locked.

"How are the pancakes? Do you not like them?" she asks. "I can get you something else."

"No!" I shake my head. "No, they taste perfect."

She frowns. "Then why do you look sad?"

"I... Um..." She just said to be honest with her. What should I tell her? That I miss my mother and her pancakes. That I could have them right now if I were home, but I'm not because she kicked me out.

"It's okay if you don't want to talk about it," she adds, taking in my silence. "There are a lot of things that we can't just share with someone we barely know, dear. Though I want to know you."

"What do you want to know?"

She sighs. "There's this one thing I want to know. I don't know how to approach this subject without sounding intrusive."

"It's okay, you can say it." I take a bite.

She takes a bite and chews painfully long before saying, "Do you often stay over for the night?"

"No, this was my first time."

"But you hang out in his room?"

I nod.

She lets out a loud breath. "I'm just going to say it because I'm growing anxious."

What she doesn't know is, I'm growing anxious too.

"Are you kids having sex?"

My face pales.

Before I can answer, she continues, "Because if you are, you need to be safe. I can go with you to see a doctor and we can—"

"We're not having sex, Mrs. Travon," I blurt.

She pauses. "Really?"

"Yes." My face is brick red. "We've only kissed."

"Okay," she says slowly as if she doesn't believe me.

"I promise. We've kissed a few times."

Plenty of times.

Not that I'm going to say that.

"I see." She takes a sip of the juice. "Okay, I believe you. All I'm saying is, be careful. At this age, hormones get crazy and you do things you don't want to."

I nod, feeling too uncomfortable to have this conversation.

"Now, keep eating. It's important to have a healthy breakfast and you need meat on your bones, dear."

Silence fills the room as we both quietly finish off the food from our plates. When I take my last bite, she advances a bowl of blueberries and raspberries in my direction.

"Here, have a couple of these. They are good for your health."

I comply and eat a few of them even though my stomach is full.

"Can I ask what happened that made you come here last night?"

I freeze. The blood turns so cold in my veins that it resembles ice.

Her eyes bore into me, sympathy shimmering in them.

I knew this was coming. I knew I couldn't avoid this conversation. But it still sends me underwater, drowning me in anxiety.

She stares at me quietly, giving me all the time in the world.

Footsteps thump in the hallway. A second later, a man appears in the doorway. He's tall, built, and dressed in a fine, expensive suit. His face is sharp and carved with granite and his eyes are a shade of light gray that resembles graphite.

One look at him and I can tell it's Heath's father.

He enters the room and the atmosphere changes. It grows thick and heavy, making it hard to breathe. The air shifts with his strong demeanor, which is quite intimidating.

His eyes lock on me and narrow a little.

A bead of sweat slithers down my back as those eyes study me. They remind me of my dad.

Without a single thought, I get off the stool and walk around the island to put distance between us. My hands start shaking and my chest moves rapidly with fast, labored breaths.

A gasp fills the room and I glance at Heath's mother, who watches me with tearful eyes.

"I need to go," I whisper but don't move.

"No, wait!" She quickly stands up and looks behind her at the man whose face softens the second he sees her. "This is my husband. He is completely harmless."

She drags him to the stool and makes him sit down while I press my back against the counter.

"Hope, dear. It's fine," she says.

My hands do not stop shaking.

"He is not going to hurt you. You're safe here," she says with conviction.

I look at him and find him still watching me. However, his gaze doesn't seem like an arrow piercing into my skin anymore. It's lost its sharpness the second he sees his wife and the way she tries to mend this situation.

"I'm Carol and this is Xavier."

I stay silent, taking them both in. They're both incredibly beautiful and insanely rich. Everything about them screams money and it makes me nervous. I come from a struggling household where I had to skip dinners because we didn't have money. Seeing them, I realize they would never accept me.

It's a miracle their son somehow fell in love with me.

Carol runs her fingers through his hair and the tension drains from his body like a tide pulling back to sea. He relaxes and pulls down her hand and kisses her knuckles.

"See, you don't have to be afraid of him." She shoots me an

encouraging smile. "Why don't you sit down and we have a quick chat?"

I quickly shake my head. "No. I need Heath. Can you please call him? Please."

She looks miserable. "I can do that, but if it's okay with you, maybe we should talk first—"

"Please," I beg her.

"Hope—"

It's then he speaks in a deep voice. "We know what happened weeks ago."

Color drains from my face. I have to hold the counter to not turn into a puddle on the floor from shame.

I want to go.

I want to leave.

I want to disappear.

They know.

Did Heath tell them? I know he would never, but what if... My stomach clenches at the thought of betrayal. But can I blame him? I'm the reason why he was at the police station. I'm the mistake that cost him a record. I'm the problem.

Tremors dance under my skin.

"We also know why you're here," he adds.

Those words make me sick.

No. That can't be right.

They can't know why I'm here.

I heard him wrong.

He is lying to me.

I keep telling myself that, but the way those two pairs of eyes look at me, I know my answer.

I move but barely make a step because my feet are shaky. I stumble over and almost fall to the ground, but grab the counter at the last moment.

Tears pool in my eyes as I feel like I'm standing naked in front of them, letting them see every scar and bruise on my body. Everything I want to hide, they can see it. And I hate how helpless I feel.

"Oh dear," I hear Carol, and a few seconds later she appears beside me. "It's okay. You're okay." She wraps me in her warm arms and tucks me against her chest. The switch flips and I turn into a statue.

I don't know what to do or what to say.

I go numb.

"You're gonna be okay, love," she tells me softly, rubbing my back with such tenderness that it melts my rigid stature.

"Calm down."

"You are safe here."

"It's alright."

"Stay here as long as you want."

"Everything's going to be okay."

It takes me a while to calm down and stop shaking. I pull away from her embrace and put distance between us, refusing to meet her worried gaze.

The room is cloaked in silence and tension with unspoken words. I can practically hear their hundreds of questions and it makes me distressed.

I tug on my sleeves.

"Sit down with us for a moment," Carol says. "We just want to talk."

I look at both of them and slightly nod my head.

We leave the kitchen and walk into the living room. They sit on the sofa and I take a seat opposite them.

"What happened last night?" Carol asks in a soft voice.

My tongue glues itself against the roof and it takes everything in me not to get up and run away. These people are linked to the guy I love. I can't avoid them or hide from them. But it physically overwhelms me to share about my family life with them.

"I... I'm sorry I'm here. I understand it's your home and I can't just come here and —"

"That's not an issue, dear." She gives me a genuine smile. "You can always come here because you're someone close to Heath."

I nod.

"I'm asking you this because of the way you arrived. It was raining and late at night and you were crying... Something big must have happened."

I tightly clutch the ends of my sweatshirt, trying my best not to lose it.

"My mother... She didn't want me to stay. She kicked me out," I tell her in a low, quiet tone. "And I didn't have anywhere else to go."

I hesitate to meet her gaze and when I do I see tears glisten in her eyes.

"I'm sorry. It won't happen again," I add hurriedly.

"No! No." She tries to rise but her husband grabs her arm and shakes his head. Understanding flows between them as they stare at each other. One look and they know what the other one is saying.

She takes a deep breath. "You can always come here. We don't mind at all."

I don't believe her but I nod anyway.

"I'm sorry for troubling you. It wasn't my intention." I feel so awful for bringing my problems to their doorstep.

"It's no trouble, dear. We're just worried about you," she coos. "How can your mother do that? I don't understand." Anger carries in her tone.

I fiddle with my fingers, hesitating to tell them the truth.

Just do it.

Heath loves you.

Even if these people won't like you and judge you.

I realize I don't have anything to lose. I have someone who will be there for me anyway.

Love pulses through my veins and gives me strength that I wouldn't have found otherwise.

"My parents had a huge fight and my dad hurt my mom. I tried helping her and she wasn't... She didn't like it and asked me to leave."

Carol and Xavier stare at me with shocked expressions. More tears brim in her eyes and she presses her hand against her chest.

It's Xavier who asks, "When you say fight, you mean your father physically hurt—"

I give him a shaky nod.

He presses his lips together in silence.

"That's why Heath got involved that night. My father attacked me and he was in my room and saw it happen. In order to protect me, he hit him. It wasn't his fault. It is mine." I clasp my hands together in my lap in desperation. "Please don't be mad at Heath; he was just trying to protect me. My Dad called the police and he pressed charges against Heath."

"Your father attacked you?" Carol asks with a shuddering whisper.

"Yes, but I'm fine. You don't have to worry about me."

"How can you be fine?" Tears fall down her face.

"It's okay."

"It is not," she protests, looking miserable as if the thought of me getting hurt aches her.

"It happens..." I murmur.

She starts weeping and her husband wraps his arm around her.

Guilt climbs around my heart like a vine, its branches tightening at the fact that I'm the reason behind her tears.

"How long has this been happening?" she asks.

"A few months."

"Did Heath know?"

"Not until that night. I didn't want him to know about it. I knew he'd get into trouble because of me."

"I'm sure he doesn't regret it. He likes you a lot," his mother assures me.

"But I don't want him to get hurt," I say.

The front door opens, and a few moments later, Heath appears.

"What the fuck is going on here?"

His gaze locks on me.

30

HEATH

ROSE IS SITTING WITH MY PARENTS IN THE LIVING ROOM—A sight that sends instant worry through me.

In seconds, I cross the room and stand beside her. My gaze searches every inch of her face and drowns in the depth of her eyes—they look calm but tension is streaming through her muscles. She is sitting straight and her fingers are fidgeting with each other, which is always a sign that she is spiraling.

"Rose, are you okay?" I ask her softly, cupping her chin and tilting it up. "Did something happen? Did they do something? Tell me."

Anger makes my skin hot, and my head fills with dangerous thoughts. I don't spare a single look at my parents, knowing I'd lose it.

I'm worried about my girlfriend.

The girl I fucking love.

"I'm okay," she says. Then she adds in a low, quiet voice, "I had to tell them."

My eyebrows pinch. "Tell them what?"

She gulps. "Why I'm here and why you got arrested."

My body goes rigid as a stone, but I force myself to stay calm.

"You didn't need to," I murmur, gently brushing my thumb over her cheek.

For fuck's sake.

My parents did it. They cornered her and forced the truth out of her.

Turning my head, I send them a glare. "You just couldn't fucking help yourselves, right?"

Mom looks at me with puffy eyes. "What?"

"You had no right to talk to her."

She appears perplexed.

"When I said I didn't want to tell you, it fucking meant I didn't want you to know. You talked to her when I wasn't home to get to me." I leave Rose and take a step toward my parents. A hand wraps around my wrist and pulls me back.

"Heath!" She comes around and stands in front of me. "Don't."

She stares at me with those soft, innocent brown eyes that make my knees weak.

Fuck. Does she have any idea how much they affect me?

"I told them. They didn't force me."

I find that very hard to believe.

"It doesn't matter. You don't need to explain yourself to them. They don't need to know," I grit out.

She squeezes my wrist and steps closer to me. "Please, calm down."

"I'm calm," I grumble.

Of course, I'm not calm. How can I be?

Mom crumbles at my accusation. "We didn't force her. We're just trying to help."

Heat burns through my chest. "We don't need your help. Stay out of our business."

"But—"

I shoot her a deadly glare and she shuts up.

They know.

They fucking know.

My fingers curl into fists and shake with tremors that are difficult to stop. I can't believe they did it. They were sniffing around me just to know the answers they wanted, and when they didn't get them from me, they went to the person who's close to me.

The strike of betrayal cuts so deep and close to my heart, it makes the back of my eyes burn.

I thought they were getting to know me.

How stupid I was.

Rose squeezes my hand tightly, pulling me back from the abyss of darkness that whispers my name. A dense, thick cloud swirling in anger, sadness, and grief that loves to follow me around.

"Please, calm down." Her bottom lip trembles and it breaks my resolve like a lightning strike hitting the ground and destroying everything in its wake. My emotions settle down as my attention narrows on her. "They just wanted to know. They didn't force me. I told them because this is their house and I'm someone who's intruding—"

"You're here because I brought you here. *I want you here.* You're not intruding."

"That's not how I feel," she murmurs.

I twist my wrist out of her hold and lace our fingers together. "You are safe here. I'm not going to let anyone hurt you."

She nods. "They are not at fault. Please don't be mad at them."

I press my lips together in a thin line in disagreement.

"Heath." Mom stands up and comes near us. Instinctively, I bring Rose behind me.

"What do you want?" My anger returns in full force.

She watches me with such an intense look in her eyes, it feels like she can see right through me. And I hate it. I fucking hate it. I don't want her to get close to me. Because when she leaves, it's going to hurt. I refuse to let myself surrender to that pain and loss. Especially when I know it's inevitable.

"I just want you to be okay," Mom says.

"I'm okay."

"You're in trouble."

"I'm not."

Her eyes momentarily drift to Hope, and that fucking action coils tension around my muscles.

"You need to take her home."

I scoff.

Looking at my girlfriend, she asks, "Hope, does your mother know that you're here?"

My blood boils at the mention of that woman.

"No," she replies.

Mom glances at me.

"She should go home before her parents come knocking on our door," Dad says from his perch on the sofa. "She is underage. It would be a problem if they figure out she's here and you're involved."

I glare at him. "She isn't leaving."

He watches me for a moment. "It's the right thing to do."

"Fuck the right thing. I don't care," I protest.

His lips press together in disagreement.

"They are right," Hope murmurs. "It's time I go home."

My jaw ticks and my body seems to be pulling apart at the seams just by hearing that suggestion.

Take. Her. Home.

That house is a building, not a home.

"I know you don't want to do it, but it's the right thing to do," Mom suggests in a soothing, calm tone, hoping to placate me.

I run a hand through my hair, the strands flying in every direction with how frustrated I am.

No one in this room knows that today, of all days, I can't take her home because I've planned a date for her.

Last night, when she said that she wanted to go to an aquarium, I couldn't sleep the entire night. I kept thinking about how that's the one place she wants to go. As soon as morning came, I grabbed my things and went to Sebastian to plan it all out. Only to come home and find out that my parents had cornered my girlfriend and made her spill out the secrets I had no plan of sharing. And on top of it, they're asking me to drop her home—the last place I want her to be.

"We should go," Rose repeats.

Not saying a reply, I grab her hand and pull her out of the room. I take her to the garage. We stand next to my car but I make no move to open the door. Because I don't want her to fucking leave.

"Thank you for letting me stay—"

"Don't say it."

She cups my cheek. The action makes me shudder. The touch of her warm skin makes me meet her eyes. "You are always so good to me. Sometimes, I think I don't deserve it," she says.

"You deserve more. Far more." I lean down and kiss her. Immediately, my body relaxes, the tension evaporating and pleasure settles into my bones. They ache with the need to do things to her that only reside in my head.

Last night was enough. She was enough.

But I want more. I always want more when it comes to her.

Holding onto the thread of restraint, I pull back and press my forehead against hers, breathing hard.

She has her eyes closed and her hands are pressed against my chest.

"I was going to take you out on a date today," I confess.

She looks at me, shocked.

"I had it all planned out."

"A date?" she whispers. Then a tiny smile blooms on her face. "Really?"

I nod and pull her closer by her waist. My hands fit so perfectly over those curves that I can't help but trace them. "Yes."

"Where?"

"It's a surprise."

She sighs. "If you don't tell me, what am I supposed to wear then?"

I grin. "You'd look beautiful no matter what you wear."

She flushes.

I tuck a few strands of her hair behind her ear and let my fingers linger by the side of her cheek. She shivers a little and a low gasp leaves her lips. I love seeing how much I affect her.

I touch her and she softens.

I kiss her and she melts.

I hold her and she relaxes.

Those little things make me fall deeper for her, knowing I'm the only one who makes her let her guard down so she can let me in. Her trust is the most precious and valuable thing I own.

"Don't go home. Go on the date with me," I plead.

She frowns. "What about my parents?"

"I say let them fuck off but I know you're not that kind of person."

"My mom must be worried." She pauses for a moment. "I think."

I can see that she is second-guessing herself. Even if I convince her to go on the date with me, she won't enjoy herself. Her mind would linger toward her home and her parents.

"I can take you back if that's what you want."

She nods quickly.

I help her into the car, then get in myself.

Once we hit the road, I entwine our fingers and set our joined hands on her thigh. Every now and then, she squeezes my hand and every single time I look over to make sure she is okay.

She is not.

One look at her face and I can tell.

It takes us ten minutes to arrive at her place. I park the car around the block and cut off the engine.

Rose makes no move to step outside, which only makes me worried about her.

I give her hand a gentle squeeze and she faces me. "I'm coming with you."

A look of panic washes over her. "No, you can't. My parents will get so mad."

"I can't let you go inside alone."

She shakes her head. "You can't come with me. My dad... He'll hurt me and my mom will get so mad at me. She doesn't like you."

In other words, she is saying she hates me.

Fucking great.

Both of her parents resent me.

"What if you don't come out?" I ask, rubbing circles on the back of her hand. "What if something happens and you need me?"

Doubt crosses her face but she gives me a weak smile. "I'll be okay."

That's not fucking enough.

"I'm coming in if you don't text me in five minutes."

Rose gets out of my car and starts walking down the road. My gaze stays locked on her like a hawk. I can't look away from her thinking if I do something might happen to her.

When she stands on the porch, she looks over at me for a second before knocking on the door. I watch her wait there longer than it fucking takes for someone to open the door.

She knocks again. Again. Then again.

But no one comes.

Even from afar, I can see the look of heartbreak on her face.

She walks around to the windows and what she sees makes her step back. She stands there for a long minute before turning around and walking down the road toward me.

Without saying a word, she slips inside and pulls up her knees to her chest. Burying her face in her arms, she quietly sobs.

Unbuckling the seatbelt, I reach over and wrap my arm around her. Pressing a kiss to her head, I give her a squeeze, letting her know that I'm here.

"She was there. She saw me..." she croaks out in a weak voice that shoots pain through me.

It hurts me to see her like this.

"Why didn't she let you in?" I ask.

"I don't know," she whispers. "She saw me and turned her head as if she didn't know me."

"Fucking hell," I mutter under my breath.

"Dad was there too, but he didn't see me. The TV was loud so I think they didn't hear me knock on the door."

We both know that's not true. Her mother saw her. If she wanted, she could have let her in, but she didn't.

I wonder what her fucking excuse is. She is choosing her husband over her daughter. What kind of sick mother is she? And she doesn't care that Hope is homeless right now. She has nowhere to go. Isn't she worried about where she spent the night or where she's staying?

How cruel can parents be?

"I don't know what to do..." she murmurs.

"Do what?" I tuck her hair behind her ear to get a better look at her but her face is burrowed deep in her arms.

"Like where am I going to go now? Also, my phone, bag, clothes and everything is in my room. I have nothing with me."

"You're going to stay with me." That makes her lift her head and look at me. Seeing that beautiful face with tear-streaked cheeks and red-rimmed eyes yank at my heartstrings. I find myself filled with so much anger it makes me want to confront her parents.

But it's also that face that holds me back because her pain creates an ache in me so deep I feel it in my soul.

My chest feels so tight that it becomes hard to breathe. Like I'm taking my first breath after spending an eternity underwater.

Using my thumb, I wipe away all her tears and then cup her chin. "Don't worry about my parents. I'll take care of them."

"But they said—"

"I know, but trust me, okay?"

She chews on her bottom lip, clearly not convinced of the idea.

After the stunt my parents pulled this morning, I don't trust that they'll stay away now that they know everything. It'll be hard to keep them at bay when it comes to my life. They're already making decisions about whether Rose should stay at the mansion or not.

I need to talk to them about it.

But that'll have to wait.

"Let's get out of here for today," I say softly.

"What?"

"Remember that date. Let's spend the day together."

"I don't think I can—"

"Be with me today, Rose. I'll take care of you."

The wheels start moving in her head.

"Or we can go back to my place, if that's what you want."

The wheels stop.

Raising her hands to her face, she wipes away all her tears and pats her cheeks clean. Taking a tissue from the box sitting on the dashboard, she sniffles and cleans herself. Then she tames her hair and finally looks at me.

"I'll go with you on the date."

My face softens. "We don't have to if you don't want to."

"I want to." Reaching over the centre console, she grabs my hand and her fingers settle on the middle finger. She moves the silver ring back and forth, as if doing so keeps her steady.

"Right now you're the only one I have."

Kill me.

Just fucking kill me, Rose.

Those words make my chest hurt. A throbbing pain pricks my heart like a needle.

Cupping her face in my hands, I press a long kiss against her forehead. "You will always have me, Rose. I love you."

Tears glisten in those eyes, but she blinks and pushes them back, fighting herself to stay strong.

She doesn't need to.

I've got her.

She can shatter into a million pieces and I'll put back every single one. She can lose herself and I'll find her. She can break down and go crazy and I'll hold her and bring her back to me.

That's how deep my feelings run for her.

I can do anything for this girl. Anything.

She shivers and murmurs in the tiny space between us. "I love you too. Much more than the limit."

"Not possible because I love you more."

Grabbing the jacket from the backseat, I wrap it around her trembling shoulders. I rub my palms down the length of her skinny, long arms, hoping to suffuse some heat into her.

When she doesn't stop shivering, I pick up her hands, engulf them in my big, warm palms, and meet her gaze.

It doesn't take a genius to know that what just happened has shaken her world.

"What's wrong?" I ask.

"I don't know. I can't stop shivering..." she says, confused.

The vents are directed at her, blasting hot air, but the chill in her bones is too cold to melt.

"Everything is going to be okay." I kiss her hands. "You have nothing to worry about."

She takes a deep breath but her teeth clatter together.

That breaks my resolve, watching her disassemble little by little.

Pulling away from her, I slide my seat all the way back and then pick her up and put her in my lap. Wrapping my arms around her, I press her tightly against my chest.

"Baby," I say in her hair.

She nuzzles her face in the crook of my neck.

I cup the back of her head and slowly sink my fingers in until they reach her scalp. Gently, I knead her head and mutter, "Look at me, Rose."

Titling her head back, she looks at me. Her sad, scared eyes meet mine. "There you are," I say, getting lost in her gaze. "Focus on me and my voice."

She nods.

"It's okay..." I coo as I run my palm down her back in an attempt to calm her down. I've never seen her react like this before. And she's been through some shit.

"Come back to me," I plead in a desperate tone that sounds foreign to me. I don't beg anyone for anything. But seeing her like this is tearing my heart apart. Bones crack. Blood leaks. I can't contain it all inside me.

We stay like this for what feels like an hour.

She stays on my lap with her body curved into mine as if she wants to infuse herself into me—I want her to make me a part of her. Her face is tucked in my chest. I know she's awake because she plays with the threads of my hoodie and focuses on getting her breathing under control.

Silence has always felt comfortable with her. But today, it becomes air in which we both can breathe.

My hand unconsciously runs up and down her back, the motion helps me soothe my erratic nerves.

After a long time, she asks, "Can we go on the date tomorrow?"

"Yes," I agree quickly.

"Are you sure?"

I tilt her chin up and make her look at me. "I'm sure."

Her teeth work on her lower lip and I free it before she draws blood from it.

"What is it? Talk to me, Rose."

"I'm sad."

I nod, encouraging her to keep going.

She gulps. "No matter what I do, I can't stop thinking about the fact that my parents don't want me in their house. They kicked me out as if I didn't mean anything to them. Especially my mom. I wasn't expecting her to meet my gaze and pretend like I'm nothing to her."

Pain flashes over her face and her eyes appear gloomy.

She is stuck inside her head—a place she likes to visit often—and keeps playing back what she saw.

"Yes, I can stay with you, but I want to go home. My home."

Fuck. Those words sink into my flesh like claws.

She truly feels like she's been abandoned.

I know the feeling but this is different.

She's lost her home.

"I'm sure she'll let you in after a while," I say.

"Maybe."

"She will," I assert. She has to.

Before she can argue with me, my phone pings with a message. The chime breaks the tension and pulls our attention toward the text.

Blondie: When are you bringing her over?

"What does she mean?" Rose asks.

I grab my phone and type out a reply.

Heath: In fifteen minutes.

"She offered to help you get ready for the date," I explain.

"Really?"

I give her a nod, then roll my eyes. "She went on and on about how she'll make you the most beautiful girl in the world—" I look deep into her eyes. "Which you already are."

A soft flush spreads across her cheeks.

She looks lovely.

My phone starts ringing and it's a call from Marie.

I attend the call and her first words are, "I want to talk to Hope."

"No greeting for me?"

"I made you breakfast and gave you brilliant ideas for the date."

"You told me all the things not to do on the date, including kissing."

Rose lets out a giggle.

"That is because a date is about spending time together rather than making out."

I roll my eyes. "You're the last person who should be saying that."

"What! No. I didn't make out with Sebastian."

"You did. I know it because he told me."

"Ugh! Why can't guys keep a secret?"

"Why can't girls keep a secret?"

She lets out a groan. "Put her on the phone."

I hand my phone to my girlfriend and she takes it.

"Hi, Marie... I'm fine... Yes, I'm with him for the weekend... I'm sorry I didn't tell you.... Yes...No, we are not today... No... Uh, no... You don't have to... I have some money... Okay, I'll ask him... No, wait, you don't have to... Are you sure?... Okay, see you."

She hands me back my phone.

"Marie is coming to pick me up."

I groan in annoyance. "Why can't she steal her fucking boyfriend and not my girlfriend?"

"Because she wants to check up on me."

"I told her you're fine."

"And she said she wants to see me for herself." She fidgets with the strings. "She offered for me to stay at her house."

"Not fucking happening. You're sleeping with me."

I loved having her in my arms and watching her sleep. It was peaceful seeing her toss her worries aside and rest for a few hours. She looked so calm and I wanted that look to stay on her face forever.

"She said we can have a girl sleepover. I've never had that before," she says in a low voice.

I clench my jaw at the thought of letting her go tonight. "Then you should stay the night with her. I'll pick you up in the morning."

She stares at me. "Are you sure—"

I cup her face in my palms and smack a kiss on her lips. "I'm always sure, Rose. You don't have to ask me every time."

"People can change their minds."

It doesn't take a genius to know what makes her say that.

I press another kiss. "Not me. Never me."

31

HOPE

Marie is waiting at the curb outside her house when Heath pulls up. She rushes over to my side and tries to open the door, but it's locked.

She sends a glare through the window at Heath, who smirks.

"Let her go. She is staying with me." Her voice is muffled but we hear her.

He leans over the console and says, "In your dreams, Blondie."

"What? No!"

"Yes."

I turn to him, and his gaze quickly shifts to me, then to my lips, and back to my eyes. "I'll be okay."

He scowls. "I know." He runs a hand through his hair. "I just don't want to let you go."

A smile tugs on my lips and I lean forward and kiss him. "I'll be with you for the whole day tomorrow."

His tense expression softens a little as if the thought consoles him.

A bang raps on the window and we both see Marie staring at us, waiting.

I shoot her a smile before facing Heath. "I'll see you tomorrow."

He rolls his eyes and presses a button that unlocks the car.

I'm about to open the door when he cups the back of my head and pulls me in a long, deep kiss that I feel in my toes. They curl as he devours me, plunging his tongue into my mouth but being careful not to overwhelm me. His heat sears through me, burning everything else until he's the only thing in my head.

The kiss is hungry and full of anger, as if the thought of letting me go tears him apart at the seams.

When he breaks the kiss, I can barely feel my lips.

"I'll call you later," he murmurs and tucks my head behind my ear. "Have fun with her and don't worry about anything."

How he can talk after a kiss like that is beyond me. I can't even breathe properly.

"I love you," he says.

My heart jumps. "I love you too."

With that, I get out of the car and shut the door.

Marie quickly envelops me in a hug and suffuses her warmth into me.

Leaning up into my ear, she says, "That was a hot kiss."

Blush spreads over my cheeks.

I sneak a glance at Heath and he's watching me.

A grin splits on my face and he shoots me a wink, then drives down the road.

"Finally, he's gone." Marie lets go of me and puts her hands on her hips. "I was afraid that he wouldn't let you go and I wanted him to let you go. He's too much in love with you."

"He is," I say.

Her eyes widen. "What?"

"Last night he told me he loves me."

"Oh my God! I can't believe it." She starts jumping. "Oh my God! It happened."

I start laughing seeing her like this.

The fact that he loves me makes her so happy. I've always wanted this sort of friendship.

The metal entrance door slides and a man steps out. He's tall, lean, and handsome. Dressed in a navy blue suit and polished shoes, he starts walking toward us, his eyes lock on Marie. Upon close proximity, I notice his features. His eyes are the same color as hers—hazel, a beautiful blend of brown and green—and their nose and lips also look the same.

With a chuckle, he nears us. "Lia, what got you so happy?"

Marie stops jumping and tries to stay still as she explains to him, "Heath loves Hope. He told her. He finally told her. I'm so happy."

He grins before turning to me. "I assume you're Hope Hanson. My daughter's best friend."

The man is so handsome that it renders me speechless.

Heath and Marie both have insanely beautiful parents. It's intimidating.

"Uh, yes," I mumble.

"I'm Issac Anderson, Marie's dad. It's nice to meet you." He seems like a kind, warm person. "Don't be alarmed when I say that Marie has told me a lot about you."

"No, it's fine."

Marie snuggles up to her dad and wraps her arms around his waist. "My dad is my fourth best friend."

Issac chuckles. "Fourth? I didn't know I've moved so far down the list."

Marie turns serious. "I have different categories. You're number one in the parent-best friend category."

"But overall, I'm fourth."

She thinks for a second, then nods.

Another chuckle, then he says to me. "Apparently, Heath is on the third spot, you stole the second spot and the first spot belongs to Sebastian."

"Sebastian came before her and I love him a lot," Marie justifies.

Her dad playfully rolls his eyes. "Yes, I know. Just don't remind me."

"You can't pretend he doesn't exist."

"But I can pretend that you're single and I don't have to worry about you being with a boy."

"You're good friends with the boy."

That shuts him up and Marie giggles and turns to me. "He pretends he doesn't like him but he does. They play checkers whenever he's over."

"He's a decent player."

"He's beaten you more than you've beaten him."

"Precisely why I don't like him."

Marie lets go of her dad and loops her arm with me. "C'mon, let's go inside. I made chocolate cookies with Mom."

We wander inside the property and walk down the long driveway. Issac tells me that I'm always welcome here and should make myself at home. He also mentions the countless stuff Marie made her parents buy for me over their travels. I feel embarrassed about it, but as if he can read my mind, he tells me that it's because she truly cares about me. She never asks them to bring her stuff. It's always for other people.

When we enter the mansion, Camila grins and hugs me.

"Hope, you're back. You should come here often," she advises.

Marie tugs on my hand. "We'll be in my room."

Her parents laugh at her eagerness.

I give them a polite smile, then follow Marie to her room. The state of it makes me gasp.

There are clothes and shoes everywhere. It looks like someone broke into her room and searched through all of her stuff.

"Excuse the mess," she mumbles as she rushes over to the bed, collects all the dresses, tops and jeans and dumps them on the floor without a thought. "You can sit."

I carefully make my way over to the bed and take a seat.

"What happened here?" I gesture around.

She grins. "I was looking through my stuff to help you get ready for the date."

I sigh. "Tomorrow."

"He texted me about that. What made you change your mind?"

My gaze drifts around the room, avoiding her curious, worried stare. She knows something is up. I just don't know how to tell her that I've been kicked out of my home.

She has loving parents and a safe home.

I wish I had too.

The fear of where I'm going to stay is eating me alive from the inside. Heath has offered to let me stay with him, and knowing Marie, she will do the same, but I feel like an intruder. Their homes aren't where I belong.

Marie touches my hand. Her touch ignites a spark of warmth inside my veins, burning away my anxious thoughts and fears.

"You can talk to me, Hope," she says softly, as if reaching a wounded bird. "It's alright. You know I won't judge you or anything."

"It's not that."

"Is it Heath? Is he pressuring you?" She adds without skipping a beat, "You don't have to worry about it. Tell me and I'll kick his ass."

A laugh bubbles out of me. The way Heath cares about her, he'll probably let her hit him.

"No, he would never do that," I try to calm her down.

Worry lines mark her forehead. "Then what is it?"

I have to tell her.

She's my best friend.

My chest aches as I force in a long, deep breath. As I let it out, I tell myself that it will be okay. At least I have these people in my life. I'm trusting them not to abandon me—it takes a lot of courage for me to do that.

"Last night, my parents got into a huge fight. My dad told me that I was a mistake, that they never planned on having me. He wanted my mother to get rid of me, but she didn't—"

"What?" Tears shimmer in her eyes.

My lips tremble seeing her sadness. "My dad—"

"No, I got it, but what do you mean? You're not—" Marie lets out a sob.

I quickly reach for her and she wraps me in her arms.

"You're not a mistake," she chokes out. "He's wrong."

I rub her back, calming her down.

It's hard not to believe something when it's said with such conviction.

And my own father said those words.

He meant it and I believe him.

"Mom jumped in to shut him up but he hit her and she got hurt. I moved to help her, but she backed away from me. Then, she gripped my arm and pushed me out on the porch and said not to come home."

Marie's cries get quieter as she listens and clings to me.

"I stayed with my neighbor. She called Heath for me." I hug her tightly. "I spent the night with him."

"You can stay with me, as long as you want," she tells me in a muffled voice.

A smile breaks out on my face. "I will, but he is insistent that I stay with him."

"Of course, he is. He loves you."

"Yes," I whisper.

"What else happened?"

"He told me he loves me, which is crazy. I never expected him to fall in love with me. I thought he only liked me."

Marie huffs out a laugh and pulls back to wipe her tears away. "Loving someone means liking them a whole lot."

"I love him too. I told him," I rush out.

"I'm glad you told him. He needed to know. You're the only person who's made him feel anything after Emery's death. He was a walking shell, angry at the world and hating himself. He hated everyone—he still does—but you're his exception."

I'm his exception.

"He's the only person who's made it easy for me to trust him."

She smiles.

"And I love how he makes me feel safe. I've never felt safe before because of the home I grew up in. I watched my father hurt my mother, and it was terrifying. He hurt her with such ease and made sure that she was afraid of him, but still only loved him." I fidget with the ends of my sweatshirt, feeling my chest fill with so much air. "That's the kind of love I've seen. The one I read about in books was fictional and unreal. To me, love was beautiful, trapped inside books. But ugly in real life."

Marie reaches forward and grabs my hand. Just having her close to me gives me strength. "Now you have the kind of love that you once believed in."

"I love Heath a lot. It scares me sometimes."

"You'll be okay," she assures me quickly.

The pain gathered inside me is because of the fear of losing him. I have someone who listens to me, cares about me and fights for me. I've never had that before. Heath is my best friend. I can talk to him and he pays me attention. Whenever I'm wrapped in his arms, the rest of the world goes quiet—even the wild thoughts in my head. He makes it easy to believe in love that I wished for but thought I would never find.

Now all I want to do is protect him.

"Did you sleep in his room with him?" Marie asks excitedly.

My cheeks turn red. "Yes."

"On the same bed?"

I nod.

"How was that?"

"It was good." With shaky hands, I tuck my hair behind my ear, making it so obvious that there's more.

Marie smirks. "So you guys just slept?"

"Not really... We..."

She screeches. "Oh my God! I knew it. What happened? Tell me."

"We kissed me and then he..." Heat flushes over me. "...he took off my sweatshirt—"

She grins too widely and buzzes with excitement. "And?"

"He kissed my..."

"What?"

"Breasts."

"Did you like it?"

I nod, biting my lip to hide my smile.

Marie tackles me in a hug and I can't help the laugh that escapes me. "Oh my God! I'm so happy for you."

"Happy that we moved past kissing?"

She makes a noise in disapproval. "Actually, there's more. I know intimacy is a big thing for you. I'm happy that you trust Heath enough to let him see you. Of course, he'll be happy either way, but this is about you being comfortable with him."

"He was patient and so gentle. And when his mouth—"

"Okay, too much information, Hope."

I huff a laugh.

Pulling back, she sits beside me on the bed. We both lean back against the headboard and grab the chocolate cookies she made for me with her mom. Silence lasts for only a few minutes before Marie breaks it. Because it's her. She has always had a lot to say—and I love listening to her.

"Did Heath tell you where he's taking you for the date?"

"No."

She smirks. "I know!"

I quickly turn to her. "Tell me."

She shakes her head, a playful smile playing on her lips. "It's a surprise."

"Still, I want to know so I can decide what to wear."

"Oh, don't worry about that. I'll help you."

"Um..."

"Trust me, you're going to love it," she assures me, then reaches for the remote on her nightstand and turns on the TV. "We should watch something together."

Before I can respond, she beats me to it. "Do you have a show in mind? No wait—I have the list." Scrolling through her phone, she opens the notes app and shows me the long list with the title, 'Shows I want to watch with Hope.' "Pick a random one."

I quickly peruse the list and settle on the show named 'The Queen's Gambit.'

Marie nods in approval and starts the show on the TV.

"Have you watched it before?" I ask her.

"I did a while ago. It's a great show and I love it."

As episode one plays, I watch it with great interest, deeply immersed in the storyline and the character. For the first time, Marie is quiet beside me and eats the cookies while passing me the plate every now and then. Being with her makes me forget everything at home and only focus on the show that portrays the difficult childhood of a little orphan girl. Seeing her alone brings tears to my eyes, but I keep them at bay.

Hours go by as we hit play on episodes and keep watching.

By the time we finish, it's dark outside and the world is quiet.

"That was brilliant," I sit up and my muscles ache.

"I want to be like Beth. Super intelligent and intimidating."

"*You are.* You are amazing, Marie."

"You're only saying that because I'm your best friend."

I shake my head. "I don't have to be your best friend to know that. Your light shines brighter than anyone I've ever met."

"I have a light?"

I nod confidently.

"Wow, that makes me feel like I'm a star."

I smile genuinely. "You are."

The sparkle in her hazel eyes matches her wide grin.

She looks beautiful.

"Then you're the moon. Just being with you brings me peace and you're so beautiful."

I smile. "Now who's being biased?"

"Definitely me." She wraps her arms around me and pulls me in a hug.

The room is drowning in darkness except for the light coming from the TV as the credits roll and music plays at a low volume. Heat comes from the vents in the ceiling and makes the room feel like a warm, cozy cocoon.

Just then, the realization hits me: once again, I'm not in my room tonight. I'm sleeping somewhere new.

My room is my sanctuary and I miss it.

I wish I could go back there.

"Hope." I find Marie staring at me with worry swimming in her eyes. "What's wrong?"

I gulp, pushing down the heaviness that threatens to climb my throat. "Are you sure I can stay the night here? I don't want to bother your parents. Did you ask them? Were they okay with it? I can leave—"

She gives my hand a squeeze. "They're more than okay with you being here. You don't have to worry about anything at all."

I nod. "And you?"

She grins, shutting down my stupid thoughts. "I *love* that you're here."

I can see it. The sincerity in her eyes. And it makes me wrap my arms around her and hug her tightly. "Thank you for everything."

"You don't have to thank me. I'm always here for you."

"Me too. If you ever need me."

"I always need you." Then, she adds. "Because you're my only girl best friend."

"You're my only girl best friend, too."

After a few seconds, she says, "Guys don't understand us."

"They don't."

"They're so dumb."

"And mean."

"But they love us."

———

I BARELY SLEEP AT NIGHT, TOSSING AND TURNING ON MY side while Marie sleeps peacefully with her arms and legs spread like a starfish. She likes to occupy space, while I stick to my side and don't move that much. It happened over time. When I was little and my parents fought, I'd freeze in one position and wouldn't move. My body would lock in place and my blood would go cold as I'd listen to them scream at each other and then the quiet sobbing of my mother. Every time I wanted to go down and comfort her, but something in me—a pull as strong as the force of gravity—would hold me back. Deep down, I was afraid that Dad would hurt me—which he has. Multiple times now.

Seeing the unfamiliar walls and ceiling makes dread grow in the pit of my stomach. I am safe here, but it doesn't feel like home.

It's early in the morning and the quietness makes my brain wander.

What are my parents doing? Are they sleeping or worrying about me? I got my answer yesterday when I visited them, but still, I wish that they're missing me and want me back.

Surely, they don't plan on kicking me out forever.

They will ask me to come back at some point.

Right?

The uncertainty gnaws at my insides like a parasite, eating me away with wild, strange thoughts that cause my anxiety to triple.

My heart sinks into my stomach.

I glance at Marie and she's sleeping soundly. Not a worry on her face. She looks at peace.

I wish I were like her.

Brave. Happy. Safe.

But I'm not.

My life is a complete mess. Now things have gotten even more complicated.

Hundreds of thoughts surround me and sleep arrives in full force.

Slowly, it lures me and before I know it, my eyes shut on their own.

32

HOPE

"Are you sure?"

Marie nods. "Yes."

"Maybe I should wear something else." I glance at the outfits lying on her bed. Each one is better than the other. They all belong to famous brands and look gorgeous.

"Nope. This looks beautiful on you." She smiles. "Look in the mirror again."

Turning my head, I stare at myself. The simple red dress loosely hugs my figure and reaches a little below my knees and strapped in white heels that are only an inch tall. My hair looks shiny and perfectly curled into soft waves that cascade down my back, pinned back from the front with a few strands falling over my face. I have very light makeup on, but the dense mascara makes my eyes pop.

"This isn't too much, right?" I ask hesitantly, even though I like how I look. *I really like it.*

Marie's grin holds a sparkle. "No, this is just the perfect amount of too much to give Heath a heart attack."

Heat rushes to my cheeks at the mention of his name.

"We don't want that," I speak lowly.

"We definitely want that," Marie protests. "He better forget how to speak when he sees you."

I roll my eyes. "That won't happen. Heath is the most confident guy ever."

She hums in dismissal. "That was before he met you and fell in love."

Drawing in a deep breath, I settle a hand over my stomach to calm down the butterflies that are fluttering around in excitement.

"You okay?" she asks.

I nod.

"C'mon, sit down." Marie clears her bed—by that I mean she dumps all the clothes on the chair and it becomes a huge pile—and makes me sit down. "You look nervous."

"I am," I croak out. "I can hardly breathe."

Grabbing my hand, she gives me a squeeze. "You'll be fine. He'll take care of you. Have fun today."

"I don't even know where he's taking me."

She presses her lips together as if trying not to say anything.

I playfully nudge her. "Give me a hint, at least."

Marie shakes her head. "No, I made him a promise. I take my promises very seriously."

"But you can nod as I make some guesses, right?"

That makes her pause. "That isn't fair."

"What isn't fair is, I have no idea where we're going. It's nine in the morning and nothing is open at this hour."

"Well..." Marie clears her throat. "Nope. I can't tell you. Just trust him, okay? You're going to love it."

Trust him. I can do that. So easily. I nod absentmindedly.

My mind starts spiraling as it finally sinks in.

I'm going on a date with Heath Travon.

The guy I'm hopelessly in love with.

No matter what happens today, I know I'll be okay because I'll be with him.

Just thinking about Heath washes over me in a wave of calm. Like the stunning blue in his eyes, I transport onto the shore of a peaceful, beautiful ocean where the water kisses my feet and I stand tall. I'm not afraid of the waves taking me away with them or the storm drowning me. I'm afraid of no one or nothing. And that bravery doesn't feel foreign. It feels like it was always there, buried deep inside me, but he helped me dig it out.

"Now let's talk about something very important." Marie reaches over and pulls something out of her nightstand. "Keep this."

She offers me a small packet and my eyes widen.

It's a condom.

"Marie!" I stand up and throw it back at her.

"Keep it." She pushes it in my direction.

"Oh my God!" I cover my face with both my hands.

"It's better to be safe."

"Please stop talking."

"I'm being a good friend."

"We are not going to do it."

"You never know. Your feelings are new. Sex can happen."

"It won't happen."

"Just don't do it in the backseat. It's uncomfortable. And for your first time? Nope. Not the best place."

My whole face is red. "It isn't happening. He hasn't even seen me naked."

"He's seen you half naked." I can hear the smirk in her words.

I peek at her through my fingers, and sure enough, she looks smug. "That doesn't count."

"Oh, it does. Now you need to see the other half."

I choke on my saliva.

Just thinking about seeing Heath beyond his perfect abs makes my pulse race.

Marie continues, "Tell him to go slow. And also, don't forget foreplay."

At this point, shutting her up is impossible.

Heath better be here in the next second—

The doorbell rings and we both freeze.

It's him. I can feel it.

"Let's go."

We leave her room and descend the long staircase. Each step causes my heart to drop a little lower and my breath gets stuck in my throat.

By the time I reach the floor, there's a tight knot tied in my stomach that refuses to loosen. It tightens the closer I get to the door where he is standing on the other side of it.

Marie leans against the wall, making herself hide from his view. She gestures to me to open the door.

Without letting myself think too much, I reach for the handle. And there he is.

The sight of him sends a jolt through me.

I watch as his eyes lock on me and make me forget how to breathe.

We stare at each other, holding our breaths and not uttering a single word.

For the first time, Heath appears speechless as he stares at me.

A smile touches my lips. "Hi."

That one word breaks the spell, and he clears his throat, appearing flustered. "Hi."

He quickly hands me something and I reluctantly look away from his blue gaze to find that he got me flowers. Fresh, bright lavender bouquet that is small and fits perfectly in my arms. The sweet fragrance enters my nose and puts my nerves at ease.

"I love these flowers," I murmur, staring down at them. "How did you know?"

"You told me once," he says nonchalantly as if whatever I tell him, he tucks it away in a safe in his mind.

I hug the bouquet and keep it close to my chest. "Thank you—"

When I look at him, his gaze is slowly making its way down my body. Heat sears through me as I watch him let his eyes wander over my figure and linger on places that make sparks burst inside me. I try my best not to shift on my feet or fidget with my fingers and stay completely still—it's a nearly impossible task.

Heath openly and hungrily checks me out, but in a way that isn't strange or creepy.

I quickly peruse him. He's dressed in all black. The black T-shirt grips his muscles tightly. His silver chain sits on top of it, but looking at it after last night, all I can remember is how it felt against my skin when he kissed—not the time for those thoughts. I see the rest of him and find a shiny, new watch on his wrist. There's also the bracelet that I made for his birthday. It's always there. He never takes it off. The rest of him looks the same. Black jeans and black Converse. But he looks insanely attractive and handsome.

By the time I look back at him, he's already staring at me. Air whooshes out of my lungs and a smirk tugs on his lips. He takes a step forward and closes the distance between us. Air crackles and I can't find oxygen to breathe.

Raising his hand, he runs his fingers across my jaw, then my cheek. His touch is soft and light like a feather, but it permeates tingles.

The morning air breezes past us, and I shiver and he steps even closer.

Leaning his head down, he stares deeply into my eyes. "You look perfect, Rose."

My pulse quickens.

"So beautiful, it took my breath away," he adds softly.

"Thank you," I say. Averting my gaze from his eyes—because they are staring at me with so much love—I stare at his chest. "You look great."

"Just great?" he teases.

"Uh, no, not just great. Handsome, too."

"Great and handsome." He chuckles. "That sounds like a fucking compliment, baby."

Baby. I melt hearing that nickname.

"We should get going," he says, reaching for my hand. "Do you have everything you need?"

I nod, holding the shoulder bag that Marie gave me. She filled it with a few cosmetic products, tissues, and money—I tried to fight her over it but she said it's important that I'm not empty-handed.

Before I can say goodbye to Marie, she pops up beside us.

"Okay, off you go now." Then, turning to Heath, she says, "Take care of her or else I will kill you."

He arches an eyebrow. "With what, exactly?"

"My car."

He scoffs. "Not possible. You love it."

"I love Hope more."

I shoot her a smile and she envelopes me in a hug. "Call me if you need me."

"She'll be fine with me." Heath rolls his eyes.

Marie doesn't let go of me and turns her head to say to him, "I know."

Heath tugs me and we get down the porch stairs to where his car is parked in the driveway. Like always, he opens the door for me, and I slide in.

Once inside, I set the bouquet in my lap and gently touch the petals of the flowers. I love that he bought me flowers. It's something I only read in books.

"Rose," Heath gets inside, "put on your seatbelt."

As soon as I'm done, he starts the car, turns on the heat, making sure all the fans are directed my way. Then he looks over at me and offers me his open palm. It takes me a second to realize that he wants to hold my hand.

With a giddy smile, I put my hand in his. Quickly, he laces our fingers together and sets our hands on my thigh and gives it a squeeze.

Then he hits the road.

IT TAKES ME FIFTEEN MINUTES TO FIGURE OUT THAT HE isn't taking me anywhere here.

We are going out of town.

I've never been out of this place, so the nerves hit me when I see the unfamiliar road that stretches long and wide with acres of fields on either side of it. We cross a few cars and trucks as Heath drives with complete control with one hand on the steering wheel. He is at complete ease and makes it look so effortless.

He spares me a glance as if he can feel my gaze. "Are you okay?"

"I'm fine," I rush out.

"You're squeezing my hand a little too tight."

With a gasp, I loosen up my hold on him, but he only tightens his hold on me.

"What's wrong?" he asks, his voice on alert.

"I've never been out of town," I say.

"Really?"

"Yes."

"Why not?"

"My parents couldn't afford it." Just saying that turns my mood sour. A lump gathers in my throat like a rock.

As if he can sense my emotions, he starts drawing circles on the back of my hand. The action is soothing and calms my quivering nerves that can't help but think about being homeless. I've been trying to shove back that thought as far away as I can, but it keeps coming back.

"Did you want to go?" Heath asks, diverting my mind.

"Yes, especially when people went on school trips and came back with things that looked so special." I smile, remembering those times. Every time the school trips happened, I'd be hit with a pang in the chest knowing I couldn't go because my parents wouldn't allow it. My mother wanted me to study all the time. The only other thing that I did besides studying was reading.

I didn't fall in love with reading because it was something different than studying.

No, I fell in love with it because it let me travel worlds and understand emotions, all the while I was sitting in my small room. Through words and characters, I got to experience happiness, sadness, adventure and so much more. Even though it was all fictional, it felt so real.

"I never went on school trips," he confesses. "I hated everyone."

I laugh a little. "You still do."

With a smirk, he looks over at me. "Yes, but not you. You are someone I love."

"I love you too," I say.

He faces the road, but a tiny smile hangs on his lips. "If you went to the city, what would you buy?"

"Is that where we're going?"

He nods.

I cup my mouth with my other hand to hide my shock, but I know it's apparent on me.

Heath has no idea how long I've waited to go there. To see the world that exists outside Bellmare.

"I'd buy books," I say, replying to his question.

He chuckles. "Besides books."

"I don't want anything else."

A smile lingers on his face as if he truly understands me.

Which he does.

33

HEATH

I LOVE THIS GIRL.

I know I already do.

But it's like I'm falling for her every second more that I spend with her.

Everything about her consumes me like a drug until she's all I can think about. My head is filled with her words, her voice, her laugh and glimpses of her smiles that she gives to me so easily. The way her pretty brown eyes twinkle at the sight of me, as if seeing me makes her happy and how she softens when she's in my arms, as if the weight of the whole world slips away from her shoulders.

Lifting my foot from the gas, I slow down, knowing she doesn't like it when I drive fast. Having her mind relax is important to me. Because God knows she doesn't let it rest with her overthinking.

The car feels too quiet and small with her presence. The scent of lavender flowers is suffocating the tiny space, but I wouldn't have it any other way.

I look over at Rose and find her sleeping. She's curled up on the seat and is holding the bouquet in her lap and my hand.

Marie told me that Rose didn't sleep. She woke up once and found her just lying there, staring out the window. Probably occupied in her head with her thoughts.

Parking the car on the side of the highway, I let go of her hand and get out to grab my blanket from the trunk. There's also my jacket I know she'll be needing tonight when it gets cold. The weather has changed quite a bit and it is getting chilly these days. I don't want her to feel cold when she's with me.

Slipping back inside, I carefully lean her back against the seat. When she doesn't wake up, I take the bouquet and handbag out of her hold and put them in the back. I drape the blanket over her and make sure every part of her is covered—even her sexy legs that I can't help but admire. They look delicious in that little short dress that fits her so beautifully.

I'm about to move back, but pause when I look at her face. She looks so peaceful, more than she has after what happened.

The urge to touch her face and kiss her bubbles underneath my burning skin, but I shove it deep down. I don't want to wake her up. She needs rest because today is going to be exhausting. I planned everything keeping her in mind. Because I want her to have the best date.

She deserves it.

Still, not being able to hold myself back—because I love the fucking bones of this girl—I tuck back the curl that kisses her face so gently that I wish it were my lips instead.

For fuck's sake.

What is happening to me?

It's like I'm forever stuck to her by the glue.

It's her or no one else.

WE'RE TEN MINUTES AWAY FROM THE DESTINATION WHEN Rose stirs. Her eyes flutter open and she finds me staring at her.

I'm stuck in a traffic jam, and I'd rather watch her than the long lane of cars.

I tuck her chin up and rub my thumb over her chin. "Sleepy head."

She stays put. "I'm sorry I fell asleep."

I narrow my eyes. "You should be. I was having fun talking to her."

Her eyes widen and she quickly sits up. Remorse flashes across her face and she grabs my hand. "I don't know what happened. I—"

Pulling her to me by the chin, I bring our faces closer. "I'm teasing you, Rose."

Her eyes look sad. "I'm sorry—"

"You don't have to be."

She shakes her head. "I love talking to you and I wanted to talk to you. But I didn't sleep much last night." She hits me with those beautiful, magical eyes of hers that got me into this trouble. "I don't know what happened, but being here with you made it easier for me to sleep."

My chest feels tight, hearing her say that.

"You can fall asleep on me anytime," I tell her. Moving my hand from her chin to her cheek, I caress her with my knuckles. "I love it when you get comfortable with me and trust me."

The horn blares from behind us and I have to let go of her.

But the fact, her cheeks turn a little bit red tells me everything.

Fortunately, the lanes keep moving and I'm able to drive us closer to the destination.

When I glance over to check up on her, I find her face pressed against the window as she stares out at the busy streets, bustling crowds, crowded shops, and tall buildings. Her eyes are filled with wonder and so much excitement that I can't help but smile.

We pass a huge bookstore and she stares at it with such longing that I want to park right in front of it and take us inside. It takes everything in me not to change plans. Where we're going, we have to be there on time before it closes.

Besides, this particular bookstore is on the list anyway. We're just coming to it later.

I roll into the parking lot and Rose gasps when she reads the giant roof signs that says—

"Aquarium!" She grins so big it wakes up the butterflies in my stomach.

"Yes," I say, and park the car in the empty parking slot. It appears to be a little crowded and that annoys me. If it were up to me, we'd come on a weekday to avoid people and roam around freely. But bringing her this far on a weekday would've been difficult. In fact, it would've been impossible. If the situation with her parents hadn't happened, we wouldn't even be here.

While she grabs her stuff from the back, I get out and stalk over to her side and open the door for her.

She hits me with a grin that makes it so hard for me not to kiss her like I need air.

Kiss comes at the last. Sebastian's words ring in my head.

I find it fucking stupid because we're in love and have kissed plenty of times but according to him, it matters.

Make sure she has a good time or else I will kick your ass. Marie's warning comes to the front of my mind.

Clearly, I'm off my game today because I'm hearing their voices in my head. Usually, they're the background noise.

"I'm so excited," Rose gushes as she takes my offered hand and tightly holds it. "I can't believe you made it happen."

"Believe it," I drawl out.

"Thank you," she says and stares at the building with sparkling eyes and dazzling smile.

Just seeing that look on her face, I want to give her the whole world.

Rose looks so beautiful it makes my heart race. I can feel every beat like a drum in my ears. I'm scared that if she hears it, she'll know how much she affects me.

Before meeting her, I didn't know just how strong and powerful love is.

Ever since I've fallen in love with her, my world rotates on its axis a little crooked. Everything seems different and new.

And she's changing me too.

Rose slowly drags me along with her to the entrance area that is bright and open. Her eyes take in every single detail while mine are locked on hers like a hawk. I don't want to miss anything.

I quickly buy us tickets and check us in.

We pass by a lot of gift shops that have sea creatures-themed things like stuffed toys, T-shirts, mugs, jewelry, and so much more.

I cast a glance at my girlfriend, checking if she is interested, but she is busy assessing the inside of the building with a huge smile.

My fingers tighten around hers, making sure there's a firm grip that won't let her get lost as we weave through the eager, loud crowd.

"Wow," Rose breathes, her voice hushed as we step into the expansive hall. The air is cool and thick with the scent of saltwater. Around us, small tanks glisten under the soft blue light, each one containing a vibrant world of fish—colorful, darting between swaying plants and smooth rocks.

She slowly walks over to the tank nearest to us and bends down to look at the fish.

We're surrounded by people with noise floating all around us, but a quiet descends on me as I stand next to her and watch the tiny creatures as they leisurely swim by us.

Then we move along to the next tank that has shrimps scuttling through the calm, translucent waters. Their bodies are adorned with bright colors and they look amazing as they weave around the rocks and algae.

For a split second, I sneak a glance at Rose and get mesmerized by the way the blue light paints her face like a gentle caress. Then, a soft smile carves up on her face, making her look breathtaking.

My blood races, a steady thrum beneath my skin, and I hold my breath.

She lets out a playful giggle, and I hear it so clearly and precisely in a room that is packed with people, because to me, only she exists. Only she matters.

From there, we move from tank to tank, and my eyes stay fixated only on her. She laughs, smiles, and giggles. Not knowing I'm storing all those sounds in my head to listen to later.

We follow others as they enter the dim tunnel and an immediate hush falls over. The air goes quiet and the world turns blue as if we're trapped underwater in a glass cylinder. A lone Manta Ray nears us above and Rose shifts closer to me. Not taking my eyes off it, I let go of her hand and wrap my arm around her waist, bringing her closer to me.

She inhales sharply when the Manta Ray glides over the top of our heads, unbothered and disinterested in the pair of eyes staring at it with sheer bewilderment. Its shadow falls over us and I pull her closer as we both watch it, holding our breaths.

"Oh my God," she whispers.

"I know," I mutter.

She meets my gaze with a smile. "That was so exciting."

On instinct, I lean down to kiss her, but retreat at the last moment. For fuck's sake.

I have to wait till the end of the date.

Something else catches her attention and she slips out of my hold, grabs my hand and drags me deeper into the tunnel. And I let her.

Pressing her face against the cold glass, she gapes at the massive sharks that glide around gracefully. They move with such confidence and ease as if they own the waters around them. Rose seems hypnotized by them.

As we move down the long tunnel, more Manta Rays swim over us and we crane our necks every time to catch a mere glimpse of them.

"Look, Heath," that's all she says before she's tugging me to the right. Turning to me, she shoots me the biggest smile I've ever seen on her. "Jellyfish!"

Before I can reply, she faces it and touches the glass as if to touch it.

Stepping forward, I stand beside her.

"Look!" she says, pointing to the sea turtles that come close to us as if greeting us. There's this one in particular that can't stop staring at my girlfriend.

I narrow my eyes on him, hoping he'll get the hint, but he only swims near.

"Oh, hi," Rose speaks with such softness and sweetness in her voice it evaporates my anger.

But remnants of it linger when that fucking turtle doesn't back off.

Rose laughs and says, "I love it."

I do not.

A second later, a shoal of fish bursts past them—their colors so many and beautiful—and all the turtles separate as if to make room for them.

Rose waves at the turtle, then turns to me. Her expression drops. "What's wrong?"

I let out an annoyed sigh. "I don't like that turtle."

"What?"

I just stare at her. "He was watching you a little too much."

A few seconds pass, then her lips wobble and she's laughing openly. I fight the urge to scowl.

"Are you jealous of a turtle?" she asks between her delicious laugh.

This time, I can't withhold my scowl and narrow my eyes at her.

Sea creatures float over to us behind the glass, just as Rose steps into my space. Her delicate, pretty face gets closer to me. A rugged breath leaves my lungs.

Fuck.

This girl is so beautiful that it knocks the air right out of me, like I've forgotten how to take a simple breath.

"You don't need to be jealous," she tells me. "I only want you."

I only want you.

Those words keep turning over and over in my head, a relentless mantra I can't put a stop to.

I only want you, too.

Rose gets closer, until her chest brushes against mine. The contact sends a rush of heat through my system, and an ache settles deep into my bones to infuse her inside me.

"Besides, a turtle can't take me away from you." She grins.

I lean my head down and stare at her. The world fades away into a blur of colors, noises and distant murmurs, and she is the only one who has all my attention.

My expression smoothes out, and my body relaxes, the burning sensation in my chest disappearing.

"No one is taking you away from me," I tell her.

She grins wider and my lips twitch until a smile is forming on my lips.

This girl knows how to make me smile.

34

HOPE

HEATH AND I SPEND HOURS AT THE AQUARIUM, STUDYING the sea creatures and wandering around as we explore. We make a quick stop at the cafeteria and grab ice cream. Heath gets blueberry and I get chocolate, and then we make our way to where starfish are in a touch tank. Instructors stand nearby, offering guidance on interacting with the creatures while emphasizing the importance of being gentle and mindful.

I inch closer to get a better look when a guy's elbow swings in the direction of my face. Before it can make contact, Heath catches it and gives him a hard shove. The guy turns with a mean glare.

"What?!"

Heath traps me against the tank, with his arms on either side of me like a barrier. Looking at him, with a flare of anger in his burning blue eyes, he says, "Keep a good fucking look around yourself. Your elbow was about to hit my girlfriend."

The low, rough tone of his voice makes the guy swallow. He's shorter and skinnier than Heath. If they were to throw punches, there's no doubt Heath will do serious damage to him.

Without a single glance, he scurries away from us.

"Asshole," Heath mutters under his breath.

"Maybe it was an accident."

He brings his face down to my right so he can look at me. "Don't see the good in people. Some are just fucking bad."

A rope tightens around my gut and tugs hard.

I'm sure he only meant that in the context of that guy, but I can't help but think about my parents. I see the good in them because I love them. Is that wrong? I love them so much, but why does it hurt?

"Do you want to touch them?" Heath asks, breaking down my thoughts.

It takes me a few seconds to utter the reply. "Um, no..."

He frowns and studies me with his curious eyes that have seen right through me since day one.

"Want to get out of here?"

I nod, leaning my back against his chest.

We stay like that for a few minutes, watching the starfish, then move as the crowd gets thicker around the tanks. Everyone seems eager to feel the starfish, but I'm not. How I see it is, they look calm being alone. They don't want wandering hands on them, a touch that would disturb them. They just want to be.

Heath interlocks our fingers and maneuvers us out of the crowd safely.

At the exit, there are many gift shops that are overflowing with souvenirs.

My gaze drifts over the shelves—everything looks irresistibly cute. Then, it lands on a star necklace, and for some reason, I can't look away from it.

"Do you want to eat? I know a great place—Rose, are you listening?" Heath gives my hand a squeeze.

I shake my head, bringing my gaze back to him. "Yes. You were asking—"

He looks in the direction where I was staring at and I watch as his eyes narrow in thought. They seem to be searching for something.

"What is it that you want?" he asks finally.

A delicious curl unfurls in the pit of my stomach. "Nothing."

He looks down at me and my breath gets stuck in my throat.

His blue eyes are so soft, they make me believe they're the exact way the love look in romance books is described—gentle, calm, and full of warmth.

"Rose," and then he says my name. "If you want something, we can get it. We can get anything you want."

My pulse flutters under my skin and my skin turns flush.

I melt from the inside.

"I thought we could get something," I say. "I like a necklace. It looks pretty. But if it's too much, we don't have—"

He is already tugging me in the direction of the shop I saw the necklace at. When we stop at the counter, I can't help but stare at it.

Heath notices. *Of course, he does.*

Not wasting a single second, he buys it. It costs more than it does in Bellmare, but it doesn't matter to him. He hands the owner a few bills and turns to me.

"Anything else you want to buy?"

I study the keychains and their prices. It's the only thing I can buy here because it's cheap. Marie gave me a lot of money, but I don't want to use it that much. I want to spend what I can return to her. Although knowing her, she won't take it.

I see a simple H-letter shape keychain that catches my eye. It's small and silver in color and has no design on it. Exactly how he likes it.

"Can I get this?" I ask the owner and he starts taking it out of the bunch.

Heath reaches for his wallet but I stop him.

"Let me, please." I hand the money and grab the keychain.

Dangling in front of him, I smile. "Do you like it?"

His eyes avert to the keychain, then back at me. "I love it."

I grin wider.

Slowly, he takes it from me. His thumb caresses the entirety of the letter with such gentleness, my skin heats up. "It reminds me of you."

"How?"

"That's how your name starts. The name I love."

He chuckles as I blush.

As we step outside, the late afternoon air hangs around us, and the sun is slowly sinking toward the horizon, casting a warm glow over the parking lot. The sky is painted in a perfect blend of orange, red, and pink hues.

A cold, icy breeze whips past us, and I quickly wrap my arms around myself.

"Time to go."

I stand next to the passenger door, waiting for him to open it, but he jogs to the trunk and pulls out a black jacket. Striding back to me, he helps me put it on.

I laugh as I notice how big it looks on me. Yet the warmth and the scent of it just make it feel right.

Peeking up at him, I meet his gaze. "Is something—"

"It looks perfect on you."

Heath drives us to a pizza place where we have the best pizza I've ever had. We talk about school and share memories from childhood—the happy ones. Towards the end, when the sky starts getting dark and the room grows a little quieter. Sitting in the tucked-away corner of the room, he tells me about his sister in a way I've never heard him speak before. He describes little things about her and all the ways that she drove him crazy, but also made him love her anyway. It's like he's letting me know her on a deeper level. He also explains how she got cancer and the time he spent at the hospital with her. We don't talk about our parents, because it's a heavy topic that neither of us wants to get into.

At the end, the waiter serves us molten lava chocolate cake.

Heath passes me the spoon. I devour it slowly, enjoying every second.

While savoring it, he asks me more about my wishes and I tell him.

It's not like he's gonna make every single one of them true.

But sharing them with him feels enough.

"ARE YOU SURE I CAN GET THAT MANY BOOKS?" I ASK HIM for the seventh time.

Heath looks at me over the tall pile of books. "Yes, I'm sure. Now grab more books. I can still see you."

The minute we arrived at the bookstore, he told me to buy enough books that the pile would make it difficult for him to see me.

I thought he was joking, so I picked a single book and handed it to him. Then I just walked around, touching the books I've read—greeting the characters—and the ones I can't wait to read someday.

I was so in my element that I forgot he was watching me and swiping away those books and making a pile.

After what felt like half an hour, I turned around to check on him —it's only then that I remembered that I'm not alone and he's here too —and saw the pile and almost let out a squeal.

Heath just nudged me to keep going.

And that's exactly what I did.

We end up buying twenty books and when he slides his credit card across the counter, I try hard not to pull it back.

He carries my books to the trunk and puts them in.

We sit in the parking lot, eyes locked and breathing softly.

His blue eyes look so intense and dark in the shadows. I notice how his hair is tousled, strands flying in all directions like he's run his fingers through it a hundred times. But somehow, it still looks perfect. And his face... The edges are sharp and chiseled, making him appear striking.

Heath is the most handsome guy I've ever seen.

After seeing his parents, I get why he is the way he is. They're both insanely beautiful.

The longer I stare at him, the more I think about his beauty.

The space feels too tight and small and my brain can't stop thinking.

I can fit on his lap, or maybe I can straddle him, perhaps....

Go home. Now.

"Uh, we should go back," I mutter, turning around with my heart racing. Heat has crawled up to my neck, spreading like a slow burn. The warmth fills my cheeks and I can feel it prickling all the way to the tips of my fingers.

I grab the seat belt with shaky hands and try to click it into place but I just can't do it.

"Wait," the low timbre of his deep voice sends a shiver down my spine.

Gently, he takes it from my hands and effortlessly does it.

"Thank you," I murmur, staring at his chest and not his eyes.

He tilts my chin up and our gazes collide. "My eyes are up here."

"I know," I croak out in panic.

A smirk twitches his lips, then he leans closer in all seriousness. "The date has ended."

"Not until you drive me home."

A chuckle breaks out of him. "That's when I'll get my kiss?"

"You can get it here, too." The words leave my mouth before I can think.

Heath glances down at my lips and smirks devilishly. "Give it to me, then, Rose."

Not letting myself overthink, I place my palm over his cheek, an inch closer to him. His hot, labored breaths caress my lips and I shudder. But I keep moving, decreasing the distance between us until there isn't any.

Our lips meet and sparks burst inside me.

It's like the first time. The emotions and the intensity.

Heath groans and delves his fingers into my hair and brings me closer to him. With that, his lips move harder, kissing me deeply until I feel it in my soul.

Heat washes over me and everything inside me turns to liquid warmth.

When his tongue grazes the edge of my lips, I part them—hesitant, nervous—and he meets me there, slow and gentle. I can't help but melt into him.

The world narrows to this moment. Just us.

We kiss for a while, until he focuses his attention on the side of my neck. A gasp escapes me and I hold his shoulder for support. My nerves quiver with the jolts that he sends through me, every time he places a hot, wet kiss on my skin.

"You smell so good," he murmurs softly.

I'm wound up too tightly by the effect of his touch that I can't let out a single word.

"And you're so beautiful, Rose."

"I love you," he says, and tilts back his head to look at me.

"I love you too."

For some strange reason, saying those words causes a twinge of sharp pain to slice through my heart. The fear buried inside me, that something bad is going to happen to destroy this, resurfaces. And it starts stirring into a whirlwind.

Heath pecks my lips, then starts the car and drives us away from the city. But that fear lingers.

35

HEATH

MONDAY MORNING, I PARK MY CAR AROUND THE BLOCK.

"I can go," Rose says, from beside me.

"No. I don't want you inside that house." I declare. Whenever she is there, she only gets hurt. And I don't fucking want that. Last time was enough.

"But—"

Reaching over, I kiss her to shut her up. It works because she goes soft against me. "I'll be out of there in no time."

Worry swims in her eyes. "You shouldn't be going. If my parents see you... They'll get mad."

My chest tightens, seeing her concern. But I'd rather I get hurt than her.

"They won't know."

With that, I'm out of the car. As I hurry toward her house, I notice how in this neighborhood, her home is different. Others have neatly trimmed lawns and blooming gardens, hers contains wild, long grass that needs to be mowed. The porch looks old and rickety, its floorboards scraped raw and its stairs creaky. And the inside is as broken as the outside.

The house is the perfect reflection of what goes on the inside.

I don't want Rose here. She deserves better than this and them.

Anger builds up inside me and I curl my fingers into fists.

I need to stay calm.

In and out.

That's the plan.

Going around the back, I climb to her room like the previous times I've done. Yanking up the handle of the window, I pull it up and slip inside quietly. The second I land on my feet, I take in her room. Everything seems to be glued to its place. Meaning, no one's been here.

Taking light steps, I walk to her bed and grab her phone and charger. Next is her school bag and some of her clothes. As I stand in front of her wardrobe, my hand freezes over her bra.

Now that I know how she looks without it, I don't want to take it with me. But I know her, she'll get stressed and I don't fucking want that.

With a grumble, I take a bunch of her clean undergarments and quickly zip the bag.

I'm about to toss in her Converse when the doorknob jiggles.

An icy cold chill runs down my spine. Not a single muscle moves in my body.

"I know you're in here." I hear her mother speak as she steps inside and closes the door.

If I move, she'll know.

Silence hangs so thick in the air that I'm afraid even my breathing might be too loud.

"It's better if you come out." She warns, and her voice gets closer as she appears in my vision. She's dressed in her hospital scrubs and sneakers. Her uniform is wrinkled and has a small tear and her shoes are dirty and worn.

"I don't have time to play games, kid." A slight turn to the left and she'll see me.

Kid.

Is that what she calls Rose?

Before I can think, her head turns. Our eyes meet.

Tension winds through my muscles, drawing them taut.

I can't breathe with how tight my chest feels.

But I refuse to lower my guard around this woman.

She has the advantage of inflicting pain on me and getting away. I won't do anything to hurt her because she's a woman. But it doesn't make me hate her any less.

Her eyes narrow to slits and her face becomes a mask of fury.

"What are you doing in my daughter's room?"

I hike up her backpack. "Getting her stuff."

"Why?"

I glare at her. "Because you kicked her out and all her stuff is here."

Something flickers through her gaze for a very short moment. If I wasn't studying her, I wouldn't even have caught it. "So, she's staying with you."

A scowl plasters itself on my face. "She wouldn't be if you hadn't abandoned her."

She takes a step back as if my words hit her. "I didn't abandon her," she whispers.

"You did. You kicked her out of her home," I argue.

"I didn't want to."

"But you did," my voice is tense. I can barely hide my fury.

She gulps and squares her shoulders. "I don't expect you to understand."

I scoff. "Trust me, I don't want to." Taking a step forward, I add, "You're just like him and that's all I need to know—"

"I'm not!" Tears fill her gray eyes—the color so different from Hope's. "I'm not like *him*."

My lips press together to not aggravate her. She could call in that husband of hers and I don't want to look at his face and not pummel it.

Besides, this time my anger is directed more at her than at him.

She is the reason why my girlfriend is heartbroken.

Her own mother abandoned her. If she hadn't asked me to come, she'd be on the streets right now and dealing with freaks.

The thought of it all lights a furious, burning heat within me. The fire is so fierce that it can burn anything.

"I'm not like him," she repeats as tears rush down her cheeks.

No, you're much worse.

"I love my daughter," she says.

Then why do you hurt her?

"I didn't mean to do it."

But you did.

I dump the blue Converse into the bag, then face her.

All I want to do is walk away from this woman. But so many questions circle my head. I can't let them go even if I want to.

Why do you let your husband hit her?

Why do you manipulate her?

Why do you stay with him?

Why do you love a monster?

Why do you do nothing?

Why. *Why. WHY!*

So many "whys" cluster in my head, but there's one that keeps poking at me.

Why did you kick her out?

The rational thing to do is leave in the middle of her mumbling, but for some strange reason, my feet stay glued to the floor. Images of Rose crying and utterly miserable flash before my eyes. I look back at the weekend and all I remember is her sadness. Despite the date that cheered her up, when we came home, she cried in my arms and then fell asleep. I held her the entire night, not moving at all, because I didn't want to wake her up.

My self-control starts to wither away at the thought of it.

Tension wraps around my body like a vine, tightening with every passing minute.

I can't leave without knowing.

So I lift my head and study her face. Her eyes are red, with dark circles shadowing them, and sadness is written clearly across her features.

"Listen, I care a lot about your daughter, despite what you think." My words capture her attention instantly. I keep going. "I know you don't particularly like me, which is fine because I don't fucking like you either."

I narrow my eyes at her. "But I want to know one thing and I want the answer."

She stares at me in waiting.

"Why did you kick her out of her own home?"

She closes her eyes, hiding away all her emotions from my sharp gaze. My jaw ticks at her tactic.

For fuck's sake.

Her bottom lip trembles, and she slowly looks at me. "I did it to protect her."

"Protect her?" I ask, a little too aggressively,

"Yes." She nods. "Alex was saying all these things, secrets that were supposed to stay hidden from Hope. She didn't need to know that we were drunk when we... She didn't need to know that her father suggested that we get rid of her. She didn't need to know that for a week, I hated that I was pregnant because all I felt was dread. All I could think about was that my nursing career was over. I can't be a mother and a student. I needed to make a decision.

"Which I did. When I got my first ultrasound and saw her, I knew I wanted her. That I would do anything for her. So I convinced Alex to keep her. But..."

A hiccup breaks out of her, but she quickly recovers as if she needs to let these words out of her. "I knew he loved me and it took months for him to come around to the idea of having a kid."

Looking up at me, she says, "That night, I recognized the hate and anger in him. I didn't want Hope to get hurt by it, so I asked her to leave." A tiny, empty smile hangs on her lips. "And I knew you'd come for her. Since I've noticed that you're awfully fond of my daughter."

That's because I love her.

She continues, "Believe it or not, all I've ever done is to protect Hope. I made sure I was the target of his hits and the victim of his anger. I'd get her to leave the room so she wouldn't get in his way. I tried my best, but then he came back and started hurting her."

"He's been abusing her for months," I grit out.

She nods. "I know. I've seen the marks."

"And what did you do about it?"

She stays silent and it pisses me off.

Her sob story doesn't mean anything to me because the person I love is getting hurt because of her actions and choices.

What she needs to do is leave him.

MENDED

"Maybe the person you should kick out is your husband," I suggest.

She shakes her head. "He won't leave me. He loves me."

Surely, she is fucking joking.

"And the worst part is, I love him and hate him at the same time."

She is on my shit list.

I scowl. "You need to make a choice. If you don't leave him, your daughter will keep getting hurt."

A few seconds pass and she doesn't utter a word.

Anger floods through my veins, seeing her like this.

Sidestepping her, I open the window and leave, not looking back at her at all. She pissed me off enough that I didn't continue the conversation with her.

I jog back to my car and slip inside. The second Rose sees me, her face brightens up.

"You're back," she says, engulfing me in a hug. Her delicious warmth and sweet scent wraps me entirely and my anger dissipates.

I run my palm down her back. "Of course, I'm back."

She holds onto me for a while before letting go of me. Her eyes search mine for answers. "Did something happen?"

"No."

Relief washes over her. Then she asks, "Did anyone see you?"

"No."

The insightful conversation I had with her mother needs to stay under wraps. I will tell her about it, just not now.

She bites down on her lower lip, worrying it between her teeth. "Did you see anyone?"

"No. The house seemed empty." The lie rolls off my tongue so easily. Because I don't want her to get hurt.

She nods. "My parents must be at work."

Your mother wasn't. She looked as if she knew I'd be there.

"Here's your bag. I tossed in as many things as I could."

"Thank you." She unzips it, grabs her Converse and slips them on. When she reaches again for something else, she sees her bras and turns red.

"Did I pick the right one?"

304

She quickly zips her bag. "They're fine."

"I made sure there was a red one because it'd look fucking sexy—"

"We're running late for school." She looks absolutely flustered.

And I fucking love it.

"About the panties—"

"Heath!" She faces me with a face burning red.

Leaning over the console, I get close to her. "Yes, Rose."

She stares at me, dumbfounded.

I arch an eyebrow. "You were saying something?"

She looks down and stares at my chest. "Can we not talk about my...bras and panties?"

"So you're saying you don't want to know what color I prefer?"

I prefer all the colors.

Not that those things will stay long on her when I have my hands on her.

Her tongue flicks across her lips as her breathing grows heavy. "What color do you prefer?"

A slow smirk curls across my lips. "Don't you think I have to see a few options before I can decide on one?"

Innocent brown eyes meet mine and my pulse races.

"I don't have a lot of options." Her tone holds something buried deep: embarrassment.

Tilting her chin up, I say, "You have enough to make me weak for you."

She watches me closely while her overthinking kicks in.

Cupping her face in my hands, I add, "Don't listen to the voices in your head. Listen to me."

She nods.

Looking into her eyes, I try to be fully honest with her. "You're so beautiful that every time I look at you, my heart starts beating fast."

"Really?"

I nod. "I love everything about you. The color of your eyes, the shape of your lips and the contours of your face. I love how soft and wavy your hair is. I love your body and the curves that make me lose my mind. And when I saw you naked that night...I didn't know what to do at first. All I wanted was to spend hours memorizing your skin and the way you react to my touch."

She blushes hard. "It was a little dark."

"I saw you. And I *loved* what I saw."

"But I'm skinny—"

"I love your bones."

"And the size of my—"

"They are perfect to me."

Her lips press together, no further argument leaving her mouth.

I press my lips softly against the corner of her mouth, then her jaw, then the spot right below her ear and side of her neck that always makes her melt.

I'm starting to learn the places that make her go completely weak and surrender to pleasure.

Rose turns her head so our lips can meet and I end my torture.

I fight a smile at her eagerness, and comply.

The second we kiss, heat rushes through my system. I'm burning up. Not just with the urge to pull her into the backseat and explore that sweet, pretty mouth of hers that has me obsessed, but also to take things further.

Rose shivers when I cup the side of her neck and pull her closer to me. A low noise escapes her as I kiss her deeply, taking my time with her.

When she seems to be on the edge of losing all the oxygen in her lungs, I unlock our lips.

Her quick, short breaths fan over my chin.

"School... Late..." she croaks out.

I grin.

School should be the last thing on her mind after the kind of kiss I gave her.

Letting go of her, I put on her seatbelt and press a kiss to her cheek.

Then we're off to school.

I'M FUCKING PISSED.

Mary

It's been weeks now, but the people at school still stare at us like we're paintings in the museum. Their eyes watch us with so much interest.

I don't care about people, but my girlfriend does.

She caves in when the attention narrows down on her in a room.

She meets people's eyes more than mine and she walks closely to me as if she wants to hide in me.

I shoot everyone a death glare, and their eyes avert, but there are some stubborn people who just can't mind their own fucking business.

As usual, I walk Hope to her class. Before backing away, I lean down and place a quick kiss on her lips.

Of course, it's not enough for me. And I want a good damn kiss. But the way she wants to be by herself tells me that I should think about her.

I know this is hard for her.

She's gone from not being noticed to now being stared at. People are seeing her. She is not invisible anymore, as much as she likes to believe that she has an invisibility cloak—she told me about it and I felt like I just got to know her more.

The night we came back from the date, I took her to Marie's place because she wanted to be with her. I scowled for a whole minute before she kissed me and gave me a hug.

A hug.

She gave me a hug and I strolled back to my car and drove back home with a big ass grin.

With Hope not being at my place gave me an opportunity to tell my parents to back off and hold their concerns in for this weekend. I knew I was going to have a long, important conversation with them and I was dreading it. It'd be filled with words that I didn't want to hear. They were adamant about being involved in my life. Which was ironic, since they had been absent for nearly two decades.

Sometimes I wonder what's the reason? Why did they leave? How could they be so cruel?

And my brain has tried to come up with answers to assure me that it wasn't because they didn't love me or didn't want me.

Giving my head a shake, I get to my class where Sebastian waves at me. I give him a nod and slide into the chair that he's saved for me.

I want to keep Rose.

Not like an object, but as my person.

Because when she's next to me, I can relax, knowing she's safe.

No one will understand how much I used to worry about her—I still do—when I saw bruises and marks on her that weren't an accident but inflicted upon. I spent hours, days, and weeks trying to find the person who was the reason behind them.

Every day, I got excited to see her at school, but also felt my stomach tied in knots when I'd see her sad eyes and the evidence of abuse.

It'd make me want to break the rules and just protect her.

This feeling has grown a million times.

It's worse than before.

I don't want to let go of her.

A pen taps against my temple and my chain of thoughts breaks. I find Sebastian studying me. "You okay?"

I nod.

"Everything good?"

I nod again.

He narrows his eyes. "Are you insane?"

I start nodding, then midway shake my head.

He slams his palm on the table. "I knew it! Your head is somewhere else."

More like *with* someone else.

"I'm fine, Sebastian," I assure him.

"I didn't ask that, Heath."

We stare at each other for a few seconds and I feel like he can see everything just by looking at me.

"Trouble in paradise?" He arches an eyebrow. "From what Marie told me, you guys had an amazing time. Hope loved it."

I know she did. It was written in the bright, beautiful, bold colors of the way she smiled and looked at me.

"The date was perfect," I say.

"Then, what's the problem?"

My jaw ticks as the thought crosses my mind. "I met her mother this morning."

His green eyes fill with surprise. "You're kidding, right?"

I shake my head. "I went to her room to grab her stuff and she came in. It was almost like she knew I'd come."

"Maybe she did. Mothers are freaky like that." He shivers a little as if a distant memory revisits him.

I don't ask him because I don't want him to remember. Some things should be left buried.

"She said she made Rose leave in order to protect her." For some reason, it makes sense. Because if she hadn't left, her dad would've attacked her next.

What she did was wrong, but it kept Hope safe.

"From her dad?" he asks.

I give him a side eye. Who else?

He scowls. "What I'm trying to say is, she couldn't have done anything to protect Hope and realized that it's better if she just left?" He pauses. "That sounds fucked up. So as long as her Dad lives in that house, she's not safe. Not even if her mother is there. She can't do anything to protect her. So where is Hope supposed to live then? It's her home."

"She can stay at my place," I suggest.

"Not for long. Your parents already know what happened. They asked you to take her back."

"Well, they can fuck right off."

He sighs. "We need to think—"

"There's no thinking. She isn't going back."

"Heath—"

"No, Bash. You have to understand—"

A streak of anger contorts his face. "And I do, but she is sixteen. Her parents can cause big problems for you if you don't think with your head."

My chest swells from the impact of his words.

The classroom quietens as the teacher enters. Sebastian turns around in his seat without another word. But I know he's got a lot more to say.

I just can't bear to hear it.

Because deep down, I know he's right.

36

HOPE

THE SCHOOL DAY HAS ENDED AND I'M NEAR THE LOCKERS TO put away my textbooks. There's no way I can take them with me. They won't fit in my bag and I don't want to clutter Heath's space.

"Give me those," he demands, as he walks beside me.

Before I can reply, he takes the heavy, thick textbooks from me and holds them as if they weigh nothing. They probably don't, when he has those huge, defined muscles that carry more weight than these.

"You don't need to," I tell him.

He doesn't spare me a glance. "I need to because you're my girlfriend."

The butterflies dance in my stomach.

"Um, thank you," I say shyly.

Accepting his acts of kindness is still hard for me.

We reach my locker and I quickly open it so he can put the books inside. But he doesn't.

I look at him. "Why aren't you putting them in?"

He quirks up an eyebrow. "Because you need them to study."

"It's fine. I can use my notebooks. They have my detailed notes, anyway."

"Not the recent topics. So I'm taking these with me to my place so you can study."

Panic grips me. "No! You don't have to. It's fine."

Heath leans down a little and bores his eyes into mine. "Do you remember what I said when you came to school after that weekend?"

I try to sort through my memories of that day, but everything is a blur. All I remember is the fear and anxiety that crippled me. And him. I remember him holding me and becoming my safe place.

But the words are fuzzy in my head.

"I... "

"I said, 'I've got you.'"

Air escapes my lungs, hearing those words again.

I've got you.

Those three words crack me from the inside, because now that I'm truly on my own with no support from my family. He's the one I can rely on. He's here with me, asking me to depend on him.

I nod, biting the inside of my cheek.

His eyes soften. "Grab anything that you want or need. I'll carry it. There's plenty of space in my room for your stuff."

I nod again.

He cups my cheek and tilts my head back a little so I'm only focused on him.

Blue eyes stare at me with so much love, they nearly drown me. "Don't overthink, Rose. There's nothing to second-guess here. I love you and I'm not going anywhere. No matter what happens."

My nerves loosen, and the tightness in my stomach unravels.

Since the morning, I've been feeling so down. Seeing Heath enter my home and come out with my stuff wrecked me. I was hoping perhaps my mother was waiting for him to ask him if I was alright, or my dad threatened him to bring me back. But none of that happened. They weren't there. They don't care.

It's hard to understand.

Because my head and heart both keep rejecting the idea.

Heath brushes his knuckles over my cheek, bringing me back to him. "Do you need that biology textbook?"

"No, I don't—" A thought crosses my mind. "Do you need help with biology?"

A smile breaks onto his face and he pulls back his hand. "What? You're gonna tutor me?"

"I can help you."

"I'm terrible at it."

"It's fine. I'm good at it. I can teach you."

He grabs the textbook and closes the locker.

We walk together into the parking lot where Sebastian and Marie are already waiting. He casually leans against the black McLaren, dressed in a dark green hoodie and black pants. A smile hangs on his lips and his eyes are locked on Marie, who is talking animatedly about something. She's wearing a yellow sweater and jeans with her self-painted sneakers.

Once we get closer, their conversation is audible.

"...he was so rude to me, but since he was on my team, I had to save him." She sighs heavily. "I hate when guys underestimate me. I'm a good player and I can kick their ass."

"Give me his ID," Sebastian says calmly, but his eyes appear a bit tense.

"Why?"

"No one disrespects my girlfriend and gets away with it." He slips his hands out of his pockets and sets them on her waist as he tugs her toward him.

"I handled him," she argues.

"I know, and I love you for that. But I want to teach him a lesson, anyway."

"What if he tells all the players in the world to stay away from me because I have a scary boyfriend?"

I fight the urge not to laugh. Marie has a wild imagination.

Sebastian seems to be holding back a laugh as well, but stays serious. "That's even better."

"Then I won't have people to play with."

"Fine, I will be less mean to him."

Marie grins and hugs him.

Sebastian wraps her in his arms and buries his face in her neck.

"Now don't start making out on my car," Heath grumbles from beside me.

Marie turns in Sebastian's arms and smirks at Heath. "It won't be the first time."

Heath narrows his eyes on her. "You better wash my car this weekend, then."

"You make out with Hope in your car."

My cheeks warm up. I sneak a glance at Heath and he looks tongue-tied, which is a first.

Untangling herself from Sebastian, she comes over and throws her arm around my shoulders. With a grin, she asks, "Do you want to stay over at my place?"

"No, she doesn't." Heath answers before I can.

She ignores him. "We can have a movie marathon and—"

"You are not stealing my girlfriend, Blondie." Heath removes her arm and brings me to her chest. "I need her."

"For what exactly?" She quirks up an eyebrow at him.

"None of your business."

"It is. She is my best friend."

"And she is my girlfriend."

"Okay, settle down, you two." Sebastian comes behind her and presses her back to his front and sets his chin on the top of her head. "Let's ask Hope."

All at once, three pairs of eyes focus on me, and my nerves coil.

I look at Marie, her eyes sparkling with stars, then at Heath, whose fierce gaze burns as if being apart from me is unbearable.

"I'm fine anywhere," I say.

Sebastian shakes his head playfully. "You gotta pick."

I can't make a choice.

Because the truth is, I like staying with both of them, but I miss home. I admit I hate living there most of the time. All I feel is fear and anxiety, but it's also the place that is mine. No matter how comfortable, cozy, and homey their mansions feel, a part of me misses my old bedroom.

"Look, if it isn't the girl whose dad reported her boyfriend." Jason, a football player on the team, makes a comment as he walks past us with his group of friends.

I stiffen and spare a glance at him. His eyes hold amusement, as if what happened to me is funny and not a serious matter that ruined my weekend.

It's been weeks now, but if he is talking, then others must be too.

No one has said anything to my face, but I've heard whispers in hallways and classrooms. People watch me with gazes full of questions that make my skin crawl.

"What the fuck did you say?" Heath reacts fast.

Jason stops abruptly with a smile dancing on his face. Five of his friends stand behind him, forming a circle. "You heard me."

"I want you to say it to my face."

He grins. "Rumor has it your little girlfriend's father—"

Heath grabs him by the collar and yanks him closer in one powerful move. "Shut your fucking mouth."

"What? Did that hit a nerve?"

Heath glares at him with such bitterness, it's a surprise that he doesn't crumble into dust.

Sebastian sidles up beside him and makes him let go of the guy. "Don't do it."

Jason grins. "People have been talking about it. Everyone knows."

My heart stops beating.

Everyone knows.

Why didn't I think of it? Of course, the word got around.

"How was the night in the cell?" Jason prods.

Sebastian places himself between them and backs up Heath. "He is lying."

We all know he isn't.

"I'm not. Henry's dad was on duty that night." Henry is in our grade. He's lanky and has braces and has many friends because he's smart. Unlike me, people like talking to him.

"Heath," Sebastian warns him but Heath's eyes are locked on Jason. "Let's go."

Heath pulls Jason to him once more. "You listen to me, asshole. If you don't shut your fucking mouth, I will break your teeth."

Jason scoffs. "I'm not afraid of you."

Heath narrows his eyes. "You should be."

"What do you think of yourself?"

"I'm someone who'll make your life a fucking hell if you bother my girlfriend again."

Jason throws the first punch, making Heath stumble.

On instinct, I move toward him but Marie grabs my arm and pulls me back.

"No, stay back," she says to me.

"You've always pissed me off." Jason is onto Heath and throwing punch after punch. He dodges a few, but those that land make my stomach empty.

Sebastian attempts to help Heath, but the other guys jump in and he gets busy fighting them off.

"We need to help them!" I tell Marie frantically.

She shakes her head. "I know how you feel but we can't."

"Why?"

"Because it'll piss them off if we get hurt."

Feeling like my hands have been tied behind my back, I helplessly watch them fight.

Heath manages to pummel Jason to the ground and break his nose. Then, he hurries to Sebastian, who seems to be struggling a little.

"What the hell is going on here?" I hear one of our teachers walking into the parking lot. "Stop right now!"

All the guys listen to him.

"All of you, in the office now," he demands, staring at them.

His gaze narrows on us and he adds, "You two get home."

"Yes, sir," Marie speaks for both of us.

"Start walking!" he barks, and the entire group falls into motion at once.

Heath turns back and gives me a reassuring nod but it does nothing to make me feel better.

Trouble follows me.

Those words play on repeat in my head.

First the cell, now the office. I'm always getting him into trouble. Why am I like this?

"C'mon, Hope." Marie gives me a nudge toward her car, and somehow I manage to load my things in and then climb in myself.

"It's okay, they'll be fine," she tells me as she grabs my hand.

"What if they get suspended? What if—"

"Nope. We're not doing it. We're not going to think about the future. Just focus on the present."

"The present says they're in trouble because of me," I burst out, the weight of guilt sinking deep into my bones like spikes.

"Hey! That's not true." She gives my hand a squeeze. "If those assholes said something about me, they would've done the same."

"And you'd be okay with that?" I ask, my voice choking.

She shakes her head. "Of course not, but I also know that we protect the people we care about."

The slow, quiet thrum of anxiety flows underneath my skin, permeating tremors in my fingers.

"I don't want to get Heath into trouble."

Marie shoots me an encouraging smile. "That's inevitable." She pauses. "Because he loves you, he's always going to step in to make sure you're safe. It's something that you have to be okay with."

I nod, absorbing her words.

"I used to feel the same way you're feeling right now. Guilt, right?"

I nod again.

"It's okay to feel this way because this is new to you. You've never had someone who jumped in without thinking. Someone who wanted to protect you. Someone who cares a lot about you."

I hear everything she says, but one question keeps circling in my head. "What if it becomes too much and he leaves?"

Marie bursts out laughing. "That isn't happening. He isn't going anywhere because he's obsessed with you."

A reel plays through my head, highlighting everything we've been through. He stayed when he didn't need to. And now he's here because he wants to.

I trust Heath with everything in me.

I need to trust his love, too.

Because the way he loves me isn't like how my parents love each other. This love is different. It's kind, patient, and safe. It's the opposite of what I've seen my entire life, but exactly what I've read about my entire life.

"Heath loves you more than anything," Marie says with a grin.

"I love him too. A lot."

She smirks. "You tell him that when he comes back to you."

"I will."

MARIE AND I ARE SITTING IN HER ROOM, EATING COOKIES that her mom made, when my phone rings.

One glance and I see his name across the screen.

Marie grins as she watches me take the call.

"Hi," I say before he can speak.

"Hi."

Just the sound of his voice fills me with an unexpected sense of peace

"Are you okay? What happened?" I rush out.

"I'm fine. Everything's fine. Don't worry your pretty little head about it."

"They didn't suspend you, right?"

"No."

"You promise?"

He chuckles. "I promise."

Marie nudges me and shoots me a 'I told you' look. Then, her phone starts ringing, and she goes into the bathroom to talk to her boyfriend.

"Seems like you were worried about me," Heath teases.

"I was. I couldn't stop thinking about—"

"I'm fine, baby."

Relief wraps around me, and I feel like I can breathe again.

"Are you okay?" he asks.

"I am."

"I'm coming to pick you up. Grab your stuff."

Five minutes later, I'm in his car, and we're going to his house.

For once, his parents aren't home. I'm scared to face them again, especially after the last conversation we had. They know what happened. I can't bring myself to tell them that I won't be a problem for their son. That it's my family, not me. I love their son and want to be with him.

They have to understand.

Heath grumbles all the way to the bathroom, where I take him so I can apply ointment to his wounds. There's a small cut on his bottom lip and a few scrapes on his knuckles. As I work on him, he stays quiet and watches me. I try to be as gentle as I can be.

Once I'm done, he picks up my hand and brushes a soft kiss on my fingers and mutters, "Thank you."

I'm pretty sure my heart stops beating.

Taking my hand, we return to his room, where he shows me the huge pile of books that I bought in the city and suggests I put them on the shelves.

It's late in the evening when we finish arranging all the books onto the bookshelf. He helps me, then leans against the wall and watches me like a hawk.

I blush under his unmoving, steady gaze that says I'm the most captivating thing in the world and he can't look away.

"I can't wait to read them all," I say, admiring the books that line the shelves. There are so many. My book wall is nothing compared to it.

Thinking about it sends a pang of pain through my chest. At least these books will forever be safe.

"You should pick one to read," Heath says dryly.

"I will tonight." I'm determined to finish them in no time.

"Not tonight."

I face him. "Why not?"

Stepping away from the wall, he strides in my direction in slow, deliberate steps that make me freeze on spot.

Once he's close, his heat wraps around me.

Placing his arms on either side of me, he cages me. "Because tonight you'll be too busy with me."

My breath chokes. "What?"

A smidge of a smirk twitches the left side of his lips. "I'm going to kiss you now."

The next second, his lips are on mine, sparks explode, shooting heat and tingles everywhere. As he deepens the kiss, my toes curl and I can feel every nerve ending in me light up at once.

My back hits the shelf with a low thud.

I shiver when his big, warm hands touch my hips and he gently presses himself onto me.

The gesture knocks the air out of me because I can feel him.

A fire ignites, and heat gathers in the pit of my stomach, making it impossible to stay still and not squirm.

Slowly, he takes my hands and moves them above my head, where he pins them gently with only one hand. Bringing down the other, he cups my jaw and angles my face in such a way that when he kisses me, it's like he's touching my soul.

We kiss long and hard, until we're both panting.

"I'm going to touch you," he rasps.

His hand keeps my wrists pinned above, and the other slowly makes its way under my sweater.

A shiver races through my body, and he senses it.

His eyes stay locked on me; just looking into them fills me with trust.

Heath touches my skin, his knuckles softly caress, he makes small circles on my stomach.

My breath catches and I lean into his touch.

"Is it okay?" he asks, his touch staying in the same place.

I manage a small, unsteady nod.

"Words. I need words, Rose."

"Yes," I whisper.

A sly, mischievous smile spreads across my face at my boldness and his fingers inch upward.

Heat coils through my body, setting my skin alight. Beads of sweat gather at the base of my spine and my blood feels warm inside my veins.

"Can I take it off?"

I pause. A thought crossed my mind that night when I sat on his lap and let him see me. I wriggle my wrists a little, and he gets the message. In a flash, he lets go of them and places his hands on either side of my waist—not touching me.

"I want to see you."

A frown appears on his face. It takes him a whole minute to comprehend what I meant.

When the meaning dawns on him, a chuckle escapes him, the sound light and easy as it sends the butterflies in my stomach into a frenzy.

"You know, you've seen me before."

I blush hard. "That was different."

"How?"

"I was merely admiring you."

"And now?"

My cheeks flush with heat. "Now I can touch you."

His gaze holds mine for several seconds before he takes my hand and leads me to the couch. Sitting down, he silently gestures for me to straddle him.

I place my knees on either side of him and settle into his lap, acutely aware of every inch where our bodies press together.

A curl of heat unfurls in the pit of my stomach. A new feeling that I've never experienced before.

Heath places his hands on my hips and moves me closer to him.

A soft gasp slips from my lips as I rub against him unintentionally.

His expressions tighten and I have a wild guess why.

Then his eyes soften. "Do you want to take my shirt off?"

I avert my gaze to the black T-shirt that clings to his body, the fabric stretching perfectly over his muscles, drawing my attention unwillingly.

"No, you do it," I say, knowing I won't be able to do it.

Sitting upright, he extends his arm to the back and reaches for the T-shirt. In one fluid movement, he lifts it, removes it from his body, and tosses it beside us.

My eyes take in every inch of his upper half. His chest and shoulders are packed with muscles, each curve defined. The dips of his abs create a perfect six-pack, his toned shape adding to the appeal of his strong physique. A little lower, and the faint shape of a V catches my attention that disappears into the band of his trousers.

I quickly avert my gaze from it.

"Go ahead and touch me," Heath demands.

Lifting my hand, I press it in the middle of his chest where the strong, healthy beat of his heart vibrates. Upon my touch, it picks up pace and the rhythm pulses against my palm.

"This is what you do to me," he tells me.

"Make your heart race?"

His lips twitch. "And some other things."

"Like what?"

Taking my hand, he slowly moves it down his chest. His skin is burning hot and feels tight and smooth as it stretches over his prominent and sculpted muscles. As we near his stomach, the meaning behind his words start to sink in.

He stops my hand just above where the waistband of his trousers rests.

We both freeze, knowing well enough where this is going.

"This is natural because you're my girlfriend and I love you."

I nod, my face probably resembling a red brick.

"We're not going to do anything until you say so."

Before I can tell him that I want him, there's a knock on the door. And then the door opens.

"Oh my God!" Carol stands in the doorway, her face full of surprise.

My face pales.

I scramble off, rushing as far away from Heath as I can, while he remains motionless, sitting exactly where he is and watching his mother with an annoyed expression.

I want to disappear.

37

HEATH

"What is going on here?" She glances at Hope, then me. "Were you guys—"

I roll my eyes. "Nothing happened."

Grabbing my T-shirt from beside me, I slip it on and sweep a hand through my hair, trying to shake off the tension.

"But—"

Standing up, I glare at her. "I said nothing happened."

Disbelief lingers in her eyes, and worry etches onto her face—for what, I don't know. She found us in a compromising position, so what? It's not like this kinda stuff doesn't happen between teenagers.

She shifts her gaze to Hope and I hate it.

Walking in her direction, I plant myself in front of her, hiding her from her peculiar gaze.

"I thought you weren't coming home," I say, finding those words so strange. For years, I lived without them, never really bothered by when they showed up or disappeared. Because in the end, they never stayed.

But now it's different. They come back when they go out. It's a mundane thing that doesn't even matter, but it holds so much meaning. All my life, I only watched them walking out of the door.

"I was going to stay with your Dad in the city, but I came back." She pauses. "I didn't want to leave you alone again."

My heart clenches. "You didn't have to come back."

Her face softens. "I know, but I wanted to."

We stare at each other for a moment.

"It doesn't matter. I'm always alone here." Words leave my mouth before I can think.

"Maybe that can change now," she says in a gentle tone.

"Too fucking late," I murmur.

Hope grabs my hand and squeezes it. The storm of anger and frustration stirring within me begins to fade, its intensity slowly draining away.

Mom gives me a weak smile. "Can we talk downstairs?"

I narrow my eyes. "About what?"

She arches an eyebrow. "About what I saw."

"You saw nothing," I grumble.

Her lips twitch. "Come downstairs. I want to talk to you both."

My mouth opens to argue but she exits the room.

"She hates me," Hope cries out from behind me, her voice full of panic.

Taking her wrist, I guide her around until she's standing directly in front of me. With my palms, I cup her face and lean down, kissing her nose.

"No one can hate you, least of all my parents."

"I think your Dad does."

"He hates everyone. The only person he likes is my mother."

She bores her gaze into mine. "I don't think that's true. He cares about you."

A surge of surprise hits me. "What?"

She places her hands on mine. "He seemed worried about you when he suggested that you take me back so my parents wouldn't cause problems for you."

"He said that to hurt me."

She shakes her head. "No, he didn't. He was looking out for you."

With a sigh, I decide not to argue with her over this. She doesn't know my father like I do. He's known to be cold, ruthless, and powerful worldwide. And that's exactly how he is at home. I only know that side of him, but lately he's been interfering in my matters, and that is every bit strange. Because all my life, he's kept a wall between us. He acted like he didn't care about me and that's buried deep inside me.

The same goes for my mother. She might not have been cruel but she has always kept distance between us.

They're both the same.

I asked Hope's mother why she made her leave and she gave me a reason. I wonder what reason my parents have for abandoning me. Why did they dig a hole in my chest that has never filled? I've tried to stuff things into this hole—making up excuses and conjuring up reasons—but nothing fits into it. It's like a puzzle piece I keep inserting, but the corners are jagged or the size is too small.

"We should go downstairs." Rose tugs me out of the room and I follow her.

My head has been in shambles since I had that conversation with her mother. In her own twisted, unreasonable way, she tried to protect her daughter. I hate her and what she said hasn't changed my mind or anything, but it makes me think. Perhaps there is a will that drives people to do things, and just because you don't know about it doesn't mean it doesn't exist.

Hope thinks about why her mother kicked her out of nowhere, but she's unaware that her mother was protecting her in her own strange way. I want to tell her, but she'll start overthinking, and for a little while, I want the machines in her head not to overwork. She cares about people and gives them the benefit of the doubt—something she shouldn't do. She should stay away from people who hurt her, but I know she isn't that kind of person. I was mean to her in the beginning, because of how she made me feel, and took it out on her in words that were cold. But she still talked to me, stood in front of me and was kind to me—all the things that she didn't have to do. She was nice to me and wasn't afraid of me. Her reluctance to not back down made me like her. And because she's beautiful. The most beautiful girl I've ever seen.

We get to the floor and she stops in her tracks. I feel the tremors running through her hand from where she is holding mine.

I give her hand a squeeze, which makes her look up at me. "Relax. It's okay."

"What if she—"

"Nothing is going to happen because I'm here with you."

Doubt flickers through her gaze and pierces my heart like an arrow. Titling her chin up with my other hand, I say, "Do you trust me?"

"Yes." She doesn't even think.

"Then trust me when I say everything will be okay."

Interlocking our fingers, I raise our joined hands to my lips and place a soft kiss on the back of her hand.

She smiles and I feel my heart grow a thousand times more. It's rare to see happiness on her face. But those fleeting moments are like shooting stars and I savor every one.

We walk into the kitchen, where Mom is. Still dressed in her designer dress, she stands on the stove, stirring the ladle in the pot with the steam wafting off.

"Sit down. I'm making chicken soup," she says, throwing a smile over her shoulder.

Hope sits down on the stool, her timid gaze locking on me.

I slide into the seat next to her and lean down to whisper in her ear. "Do you want chocolate?"

"No, I'm fine. I don't want you to go out and leave me alone here."

A frown embeds between my eyebrows. "I won't be going out."

She studies me. "Um, you don't eat chocolate, so you can't have it here."

"I don't eat it, but you do." I abandon my seat without a second thought, heading straight for the drawer where the chocolates are kept. I grab one, quickly return to my seat, and settle in.

"You keep chocolates in your house for me?" Surprise laced in her voice.

"I keep a lot of things here because of you," I tell her.

Her eyes soften and gratitude fills them. "Thank you."

A wave of discomfort washes over me. I feel unworthy of her because she is too good and deserves the absolute fucking best. But I want to be that person for her, so I keep trying.

"Yeah, whatever," I mutter, running a hand through my hair as heat prickles the tip of my ears.

"You really are something," she whispers underneath her breath, but I hear it.

No, you are something. I want to say.

"Make sure you don't eat the entire thing. People say my chicken soup is the best," Mom interrupts us and we both turn to her. She has a teasing smile playing on her lips that screams trouble.

The three of us are in the same room and my stomach churns with anticipation. I don't know what she's going to say. All I know is, I don't want her to hurt my girlfriend.

"I'm sorry." Hope quickly closes the chocolate bar and sets it on the island.

Disappointment twists Mom's features. "No, it's alright. You can have it."

"Are you sure?"

She nods. "Absolutely. The soup is going to take a while, anyway."

Getting the assurance from her, she reaches for the chocolate bar and takes a small bite, then covers her mouth as she devours it.

"So, how was the date?" Mom asks, glancing between us.

I shoot her a glare for bringing it up.

"What? You didn't tell me anything. I'm curious."

"I didn't tell you for a reason."

She smiles, unbothered by my reply. "Well, I'm asking Hope."

Hope snorts, drawing my attention back to her.

We make eye contact.

You don't have to tell her anything if you don't want to.

I don't mind if you don't.

I sigh and give her a nod, letting her decide whatever she wants to share with my obnoxious mother.

"We went to an aquarium," my girlfriend says with pride.

Mom grins, staring at her starry-eyed. "How was it? What did you see? Tell me everything."

Rose talks excitedly about our date; I sit and listen, absorbing every word. The joy in her voice fills me with quiet pride, reassuring me I did well. Giving her the best first romantic date was exactly what I wanted.

327

I've fallen hard for her.

And it's not just that I've lost my head. I've also lost my control and senses.

Only she matters to me.

I watch my mother closely, studying how she absorbs everything Rose tells her. She looks genuinely happy that we're together and had a perfect date.

The weight in my chest shifts a little, making it easier to breathe. The hate and resentment I possess for her morphs into ashes by some small portion.

Seeing her care for the person I care about the most makes me hate her a little less.

"When are you going on the second date?" Mom asks.

Rose blushes and looks over at me. "Um..."

"Soon," I answer for her.

Mom nods and I notice there's a glimmer in her eyes. "So, the reason why I asked you two to come downstairs is—"

Hope stiffens beside me.

I shoot my mother a look not to continue. But of course she does.

"—because of the position I found you two in."

I close my eyes, knowing an embarrassing conversation is heading my way.

"I certainly didn't hope to see you like this," she mutters.

"We weren't doing anything!" Rose blurts.

Mom arches an eyebrow at her. "It didn't look like that."

"I was just admiring Heath because he has a nice body—" she cups her mouth, eyes wide in panic.

My lips twitch in amusement.

Mom looks like she's about to burst out laughing. "Well, I'm glad you think that about my son."

Hope turns all sorts of red.

Mom snickers. "So you're saying I have nothing to worry about?"

Hope shakes her head. "No."

A long moment passes before she says, "Have you guys had sex?"

You can hear a hairpin drop with how silent the room is. Tension hangs in the air and it's suffocating to breathe.

Sex.

My mother is talking about sex.

For fuck's sake.

All I want to do is escape this conversation, but Hope is glued to her seat with her cheeks flushed and hands held together in her lap.

"No," she tells her.

Mom looks at me. "We've never talked about this, but I need to know—"

"It's none of your business."

"It is," she says softly. "I'm looking out for you. At this age, kids catch all sorts of diseases because of sex. And I don't want you to—"

I groan, feeling awkward as fuck. "Please stop talking."

"—get sick because I didn't step in."

"You don't need to step in. I'm fine. No sex is happening in my life."

"Are you sure?"

"Yes."

"You're not lying to me, right? It's not something that you should lie about."

I glare at her. "I'm telling you the truth. No sex."

Mom watches me for a minute before letting out a sigh of relief. "Thank goodness. I'm too young to become a grandmother."

I roll my eyes at her dramatics.

"Can we leave now?" I ask.

She shakes her head and faces Hope. "I've already had this conversation with you, dear. I hope you remember what I said."

Hope nods while I stare at her in confusion.

My mom has talked to her about sex. When?

"You both are too young for this. Wait a couple of years and don't forget to use protection. If you're too shy, I can go and buy—"

"No need. We'll buy it ourselves when we have sex," I grit out.

"Which won't happen for a while," Rose adds.

I look at her, and she looks all red and fidgety.

Leaning down, I whisper in her ear. "Are you okay?"

She glances at me and gives me a nod shyly.

"There's something else too," Mom declares in a curt tone which is so unlike her. "There are a few rules that I need you to follow whenever Hope is here."

"Rules?" I huff out a laugh.

She nods.

"Why bother when you won't be staying?" I argue.

A flash of pain crosses her face and she grips the island for support.

Guilt simmers in the pit of my stomach, but I discard it.

"I'm not going anywhere," she says.

"Yeah, sure." I roll my eyes.

Her expressions turn sad. "I mean it. I'm staying."

We stare at each other, and for the first time, I realize that maybe she's telling the truth.

"I want to spend more time with you. I want to know you. I want to be there for you." She takes a deep breath, grounding herself. "I want to repair our relationship."

"What's broken doesn't get mended."

She nods. "I know, but I want to try anyway. Love mends all that's broken."

I shoot daggers at her for annoying me.

Despite the fact that I don't want to believe her, I do anyway.

"You're expecting too much," I grumble.

She smiles softly, but doesn't say a word.

Getting off the stool, I pour myself a glass of water and chug it down. I walk to Hope's side and lean against the counter near her. Without my mother noticing, I slide my hand onto her lap, gently untangle her clasped hands, and take one in mine. I softly trace circles on the back of her hand, hoping to calm her racing thoughts and distract her from the worry consuming her.

Just then, Mom says, "I have two simple rules. Always keep the door open and don't do whatever it was that you were doing today."

"Alright." I think about her rules and agree anyway. Because we both know I won't be following them.

She starts working on the soup while Hope and I watch her in silence.

Ten minutes later, I notice Hope's shoulders shivering a little. She quickly wraps her arms around herself, but her thin maroon sweater does very little to provide her heat. Without a word, I leave the room to grab my jacket for her. When I come back, I find a smile on her face, as she stares at my mother, who's now standing near her and speaking in a hushed tone.

Mom notices when I step closer to them and I hear her say, "I'll show them to you."

"Show her what?" I grumble as I slip my jacket onto my girl.

Rose turns to me with a grin. "Your childhood pictures."

I look at Mom in confusion. "We don't have them."

She shakes her head. "We do. I have so many photo albums and videos."

I frown. "That's not possible."

"It is. I've kept them safe with me for years."

"I don't believe you."

Mom smirks. "I brought those along with me. Do you want to see them?"

I nod, because I'm curious. I thought my childhood wasn't recorded but looks like Derek and Kelly made sure that wasn't the case. And my mom has kept all those memories safe.

The urge to know *why* she's done that begins to eat me again.

I want to know why she wasn't there for me throughout my childhood. Why she wasn't the one who took the pictures and recorded those videos.

I want to know everything.

Mom serves us soup and joins us.

"Do you guys like it?" she asks with a hint of worry in her voice.

"Yes, it's delicious," Rose says quickly.

Mom smiles at her, then glances at me in question.

"It's fine," I mutter. The soup is fucking good but I won't tell her.

"There's plenty. You can take more if you want," she offers.

I hum in response and she just smiles.

IT'S LATE AT NIGHT WHEN I CLOSE THE DOOR TO MY bedroom.

Rose is sleeping peacefully on my bed, curled up in my hoodie and on my side of the bed, after tossing and turning for an hour. She couldn't settle down, so I tucked her into my arms and whispered words of reassurance that helped her calm down. I know she doesn't want to stay here. She wants to go home—the last place I want her to be.

I lean against the wall and run a hand through my hair.

She had a great time with my mother earlier, when they were going through the photo albums that contained my entire childhood. Mom wasn't lying. She had the albums and videos. I stood near the sofa where they were sitting and watched them—not the photos. Because the question why she has them kept bothering me.

I rush down the stairs into the living room to see if the albums are on the table, only to find my mother still there. She glances up at me and her hand freezes from where it is flipping through the album.

She watches me for a quiet moment, then speaks quietly, "You're up."

"I couldn't sleep." I walk deeper into the room.

"Me neither," she says.

For some reason, I sit next to her and she notices. She spares me a quick look before turning back to the album in her lap. We both pretend it isn't a big fucking deal when it is.

"Dad will be worried knowing you aren't sleeping."

"That's why I didn't pick up his call. It's better if he thinks I'm asleep than knowing I'm sitting alone and flipping through my children's photo album."

"You aren't alone," I mutter.

She pauses and looks at me. Her face softens. "I'm not, now that you're here."

Discomfort pricks my skin, making me clear my throat and look away from her.

"Dad only loves you." The words are out of my mouth before I can think.

"Is that really what you think?"

I nod.

"That's not true. He loves you."

332

I roll my eyes. "You don't need to assure me with a lie. I can handle the truth."

Mom sets the photo album aside on her lap and reaches for another one. This one is old and worn, its front cover creased and the edges slightly torn as if it's been opened and closed a million times.

Without a word, she flips it open. The first photograph shows a pregnancy test with two red lines; beneath it is a picture of my parents smiling at each other. My eyes move to the second page, where my dad is kneeling in front of my mom, kissing her stomach.

Page by page, she shows me a short reel of her pregnancy—each moment capturing how elated my father was, always smiling, always leaning down to kiss her belly.

Finally, we reach the part where they're in the hospital. Mom is holding me in her arms, and Dad is kissing my forehead. There's another photo where his fingers are gently brushing my hair, and he's looking at me like I'm his entire world. That look in his eyes is raw and captured candidly. There's nothing fake or pretentious about it.

"He has loved you even before you came into this world," she says in a loving tone.

Something heavy sticks to my throat, making it hard to swallow those words.

"He was so happy when he found out that he was going to be a Dad. And when he heard your heartbeat for the first time he squeezed my hand so hard while staring at the screen." She laughs a little. "He was always kissing my stomach or rubbing it to make sure you were okay inside. He may not say it, but he loves you so much."

"Then why did he abandon me?" I mumble, my voice sounding broken.

She studies me closely. "We didn't abandon you."

A spark of anger lights up. "You sent me here while you were living in another country. What do you call that?"

Pain flickers across her face. "It's complicated."

My eyebrows dip. "How is it complicated?"

She breaks eye contact. "Please know we didn't do it because we don't love you. It was something else."

"I want to know it." I push the matter.

She abruptly stands up. "It's late. You should go to bed."

"For fuck's sake. How long are you going to hide this truth from me?!" I snap. "For years, I've wondered why my parents left me. I thought maybe I did something wrong and you guys didn't want me—"

"That's not the truth!" she cries out. Her blue eyes fill with deep sorrows and locked secrets.

"Then, what is the fucking truth?"

She opens her mouth, and my chest tightens, thinking she's finally going to give me the answer. But then, she closes it and turns her back on me. "All you need to know is, we did it to protect you."

Air fills my lungs and I feel like I'd burst at any moment.

We did it to protect you.

Protect me from what?

Instead of giving me an answer, she's left me with an even bigger question.

I've heard this same answer twice in a day from two different parents.

What does it mean?

Mom leaves the room in a hurry while I stand there in the pile of my memories she's kept like her most prized possession. I know if I pick up any other album besides the one she showed me, I wouldn't find any more pictures of us. It'd be just me or Emery.

My hands curl into fists.

I want to know what happened.

And I will find it out.

38

HOPE

A FEW DAYS LATER, WE'RE AT SCHOOL, BUT INSTEAD OF classes, we're all attending a bake sale, which is part of one of Heath's business projects. The football field is packed with stalls set up by the business students, buzzing with the energy of the entire eleventh and twelfth grade. Last year, I didn't attend because being in the crowds isn't my thing and I also had no one to support.

But this time, it's different.

I have a boyfriend who looks every bit as grumpy as he checks the stall, making sure everything's in order and organizing things on the table for the people. If it weren't for the grade and Sebastian's begging, he wouldn't be doing this at all. Regardless, I find it so sweet seeing him manage everything so effortlessly. He is cool, calm and collected while I'm a ball of nerves because I want today to go well for him. I want him to make a lot of sales.

"Are you sure you want me here?" I ask him for the third time, sensing so many questioning eyes on us.

"Yes," Heath says, meeting my gaze before going to work.

"What about Sebastian?"

"He's going to attract the crowd to our stall."

"And Marie?"

"She's with him."

"So, we're alone." I look around in panic.

"Why, Rose? Are you nervous to be alone with me?" he asks with a smirk.

I turn red, remembering how things have been between us lately. "No, that's not it."

"Then?"

"I just…" I cast another glance around and find those curious eyes still locked on me, making my skin crawl with ants. "You know, I'm terrible at confronting people. What if I mess up? And I don't want to mess up. This is important to you and I—"

Stepping closer to me, he cups my chin and tilts it up. "You're going to be fine. Don't worry, I'm here with you."

"I'll hand you stuff and pack it."

"I can handle that, but if that's what you want to do, then you can do it."

"I want to help you."

He smiles and I can't help but smile too.

Leaning down, he kisses me. "You don't need to help me. Just be here with me and it'd be enough."

"I can pack stuff. I can do it."

He grins and kisses me again. "Okay, Rose. Okay."

A rush of confidence flows through my veins, and the nervous energy thrumming in my blood quiets down.

I pretend it's only him and I. And no one else.

It seems to work as I take the blueberry muffins from the box and neatly put them on the tray. Heath's mom made them fresh in the morning. We were having dinner the other night and she mentioned how she'd heard there would be a bake sale taking place and if he were a part of it. At first he refused, saying it's not something he likes to do, but only I knew what was the reason. At a bake sale you're supposed to bring home-made stuff and Kelly has been visiting her family, so Marie, Sebastian and I were going to make everything but she suggested that she wants to do it and for some reason Heath didn't say a word more.

Marie and Sebastian made banana bread, cinnamon sourdough, and lemon bars. Heath and I prepared chocolate and vanilla cupcakes, chocolate chip cookies and brownies. It was the most fun I've ever had, making all those things with him while his mother helped us along. For a moment, my chest stopped aching and my sorrow seemed to disappear. I felt comfortable inside those walls and room that were so different from the kitchen I had grown up with the people who had raised me.

Since the night Mom kicked me out, I haven't received a single phone call or text from her. My fingers hover over her contact, lingering there, but never quite lowering enough to press the screen.

I've stayed with Heath for more than a week now but it still feels like a strange place to me.

Carol hasn't said anything to me about leaving and Xavier has been working in the city so I haven't seen him. It'd be a lie if I say I'm not dreading his arrival. That man holds power in the room. The air shifts at his command. I'm sure the minute he comes back, I'd be out of his mansion and even Heath wouldn't be able to do anything.

That thought makes it hard for me to sleep at night. And Heath has to hold me in his arms and talk to me until he's the only thing I'm thinking about. Sometimes I fall asleep just listening to his voice, but there are moments when we talk for hours, and with each conversation, I understand him a little more. He tells me about Emery and I tell him about my childhood. Both topics only bring us pain and sadness, but saying the words out loud somehow makes it hurt less. Something broken inside us mends and the gaps between the walls fill.

I know I'll never be the same if this bond between us ever breaks.

I'd never loved another guy like I love Heath Travon. I'd never trust him like I trust him, and I'd never give myself to him like I've given myself to this guy.

Maybe I'm too young and my emotions are heightened, but I know what I feel. This love is just the kind of love I've read about in books. The kind of love stories I believe in.

It's always going to be him.

"Are you guys ready?" Marie asks, sprinting toward us before stopping at the table. "I talked to people, well, Sebastian did because he has better social skills than me. We convinced a few people to come to our stall, however they all looked scared when I said Heath will serve you."

"What the fuck is that supposed to mean?"

"It's just the way your face looks."

I bite my lip to hide my smile. I know what Marie is doing.

"What is wrong with my face, Blondie?" Heath scowls.

Marie rolls her eyes. "To serve customers you have to put on a smile."

"I'm not smiling at strangers."

"You have to."

"I won't," he grumbles and focuses on writing something down in his notebook.

Marie turns to me with a smirk. "Hope, this grinch will scare our customers away and we can't have that. So why don't you smile at—"

"She is not smiling at random people," Heath says.

"She can speak for herself," Marie argues.

They both look at me and I shrug. "I can do it if it means we win."

Marie grins and gives me a thumbs up. "Yay! We're starting in five minutes. Good luck!"

Then she's running in some other direction.

A heated stare burns into the side of my face. I turn and find Heath gazing at me with an annoyed expression. "You don't have to smile at fucking strangers."

I laugh. "Why not? It's just a smile."

He shakes his head, looking down at his notebook. "It's not just a smile."

"What do you mean?" I step closer to him.

He scribbles something in his notebook, then looks up at me, his eyelashes gently framing bright blue eyes that look stunning in the sunlight.

"You have a beautiful smile, Rose. It was one of the reasons why I became so crazy about you."

I blink, taken aback by his admission.

He drags a hand through his hair, not looking at me. "I don't want others to fall in love with you. I want it to be only me."

"I'm sure that won't happen. No guy has ever approached me before."

He sighs heavily. "If they do, I will break their jaw."

I wince. "That'd be painful."

He nods. "Exactly."

After our conversation, people begin to stop by our stall. It's only girls who linger across the table, eyeing my boyfriend, but he spares them no glance. If anything, he's focused on helping me pack their orders and ringing them up quickly, keeping the momentum going. As they leave, the disappointment is clear on their faces.

I almost feel bad for them.

A few guys make their way to our table and Heath stiffens beside me. I glance at him and he's glaring at them.

Clearing my throat, I shoot them a tiny smile and show them around the table.

"I'd like a few blueberry muffins," a guy with dark brown hair and good looks says, meeting my gaze.

"Sure." I turn around to grab the bag, but my face collides with a wall of muscle. Heath stretches his arm around me, grabbing a few muffins and packing them into a box swiftly, all while my face is pressed against his chest. "Here you go."

The guy pays, and Heath quickly rings him up and they're gone.

I rub my nose and peek up at him. "What was that?"

Heath takes my hand, brings it down from my nose, and inspects it himself. "What was what, Rose?"

"You know what I'm talking about," I say.

His lips twitch as he caresses my nose, the itch soothes. "I just served a customer."

"The customer *I* was going to serve."

"Too bad, I was quick," he pecks the tip of my nose.

"You don't have to be jealous."

"I'm not."

I frown. "Why's that?"

"Because no one is taking you from me."

"You sound confident."

"I am." He smiles down at me.

I roll my eyes and a chuckle breaks out of him.

Wrapping his arms around my waist, he kisses me slowly and sweetly.

Once we break apart, I raise my hand and try to mimic a smile on him by stretching the muscles on the side of his lips. "Smile more today."

"I smile at you, does that count?"

I nod.

Then a thought pops into my head. "Don't smile too much at the other girls, though."

Heath bites down on his lower lip. "Other girls?"

I nod. "They were all waiting for you to look at them."

"I didn't even fucking notice because I was too busy looking at you."

I blush so hard I have to press my cold hands to my cheeks.

Heath laughs and it's one of those rare moments when he looks completely free and full of happiness.

"Lovebirds, keep it moving," Marie calls out as she passes by our stall.

I quickly step away from Heath, standing next to him. "Let's do it."

The day goes on, and we almost sell out of everything on our table. Surprisingly, a lot of people visit our stall, but they don't engage with us much. Later, Marie finds out the reason why people kept coming was the blueberry muffins, which sold out in no time. After that, the lemon bars and chocolate chip cookies followed close behind.

By the time the sky becomes a beautiful canvas of sunset hues, we're tired and hungry. I lean onto Heath who wraps his arm around my waist and holds me up. His jacket is missing from his shoulders and is on mine as it keeps me warm.

Marie is leaning against Sebastian, who supports her—her back resting against his chest.

The third-place trophy sits between the four of us.

"I'm so exhausted," Marie complains.

"It's okay. You can rest as soon as I get you home." Sebastian kisses her head.

"I don't think I'd be able to walk to my room."

"I'd carry you."

"Piggy back ride."

"I know. You hate the other."

I look at Marie in question.

She chuckles. "You heard him right. I hate it when he lifts me in his arms. I like the piggy back ride because I get to hug him and talk to him super quietly."

"You are anything but quiet, baby." Sebastian sets his chin on her head. "But I love you anyway."

"I love you too."

Heath grumbles from behind me. "Please go home and get a room, Blondie."

Marie groans. "I'm way too tired to have sex right now."

"Then go to sleep."

"I will."

"Just fall asleep right here."

"No, I want to talk about today." A grin appears on her face. "It was so fun."

Sebastian nods. "It was. I thought we'd make no sales but people still came to our stall."

I look up at Heath and smile at him.

He catches me looking at him and leans a little in my direction. In a quiet voice he says, "What?"

"You did great today."

He stares at me for a moment. "You did great, too."

I shake my head. "It was all you."

"I don't think so." He tucks a few strands of my hair behind my ear. "When it got busier, you were packing those orders and even talked to people—which you hate. But I knew you could do it."

I smile. "I felt safe because you were near me."

"No, you just found the courage to face one of your fears."

That makes me stop and think about what he just said.

Strength always comes from within and somehow I was able to find it in me today. I wonder if there is more of it in me.

"Hope, you said your birthday is in November," Marie states.

"Uh, yes," I mutter.

Heath arches an eyebrow at me. "You didn't tell me."

I soften my gaze. "It never came up. Also, I don't celebrate my birthday."

Before he can speak, Marie jumps in. "We will celebrate your birthday this year."

"For once, I agree with Blondie," Heath speaks.

I can't believe it's November already and my birthday is next week. I was going to let that day pass but Marie remembers little things. I told her about it one time and it looks like she's been counting down the days.

"I will make sure it is fun," Marie chirps.

I frown. "You don't have to do anything. It's fine. I don't want to burden—"

"It's happening!" She interrupts me.

"But—"

"No buts."

With a defeated smile, I nod and she grins. Sebastian steals her attention as he asks her about something. I'm too distracted by the hand rubbing circles on the side of my stomach to listen to their conversation.

"You didn't want to celebrate your birthday, that's why you didn't tell me," Heath says in a curt tone.

My stomach twists as I slowly face him and find him already looking at me with a sharp look. "I... It's not. I just..."

"I wish you had told me," he grumbles.

I straighten up, fully facing him. "No, it's not like that. I just... I've never celebrated my birthday because buying me presents and cake seemed like too much for my parents and growing up I wanted to do everything to not burden them in any way. Maybe before, when I was very young, it used to feel like a special day to me, but once things started getting rough at home, it just became an ordinary day for me. My mother would wish me and that was it. My dad didn't really remember. I'd spend my day at school and reading books. There was nothing about it that made me think of it as anything more than ordinary."

Heath cups my face. "It is a special day, Rose. Because it is your day."

"My day?"

He caresses my cheeks with the pads of his thumbs. "Yes. It belongs to you."

I've never thought of my birthday as anything other than a normal day. I didn't get presents or blow out a candle to make a wish. Nothing ever happened, and before I knew it, the clock would turn twelve and it was the next day.

"It's fine, really." I find myself saying those words.

He stares at me for a long moment. "No, it's not. This year and every year after, we're going to celebrate your birthday and you're going to have an amazing time and get a lot of presents and a big fucking chocolate cake."

"What are you talking about?" Tears prick the back of my eyes.

"You're going to have a special day, Rose because you're special to me."

I want to look away from him, because the way he gazes at me with such an intense stare makes it hard for my heart not to bleed from pain. It's like he's cut open a wound I never knew was there.

Bringing his face closer to me, he aligns our gazes. "I'm going to give you the best birthday present and the most delicious chocolate cake."

A few tears slip down my cheeks and he gently wipes them away. I sniffle as I say, "You don't have to."

"I want to."

I open my mouth to argue with him, that he doesn't need to give me anything. Having him in my life is enough. It's the best birthday present for me. But he silences me with a kiss.

I press my hands against his chest and he groans.

"Get a room, guys!" Marie teases with a giggle.

I quickly break the kiss and push him back.

"Make sure to use protection," Sebastian adds.

"Fuck off," Heath grits out.

Both of them burst out laughing and I can't help but smile.

"Don't listen to them. They're idiots," he tells me, wiping away any traces of my tears. "It'll happen whenever you're ready."

I give him a grateful smile and he wraps me up in his arms.

39

HEATH

DAD IS BACK HOME AFTER BEING GONE FOR A WEEK. IT'S late in the evening and Rose, Mom and I are sitting in the kitchen eating casserole. As much as I dislike her, I can't lie, her cooking is the best. Her food tastes delicious, and I'm always going back for seconds. Now that Kelly is on leave, Mom prepares every meal, and I'm always wandering into the kitchen to see what she's making, despite my reluctance to keep distance between us.

"You're back!" Mom brightens up like a sunflower at the sight of him. Abandoning her seat, she rushes over to him and embraces him in a tight hug. And then...they're kissing.

Rose turns her head as fast as she can and pretends not to hear them, but the flush covering her cheeks says otherwise.

As for me, I just fucking pretend that my parents aren't obnoxiously in love with each other.

"I missed you so much," Mom speaks in a hushed tone.

"I missed you too, Mia Cara. More than anything," Dad replies in a soft tone.

It's so quiet in the house, it's impossible not to hear them.

"Come sit with us. I made your favourite." Taking him by the hand, she drags him into the kitchen and makes him sit in the seat next to me.

He pauses by the stool and our eyes connect. Like always, he's wearing an expensive, pristine suit, this time a dark charcoal one that fits him like it was tailored just for him, complemented by a shiny watch on his wrist. "Heath," he says in the same tone he just used with Mom.

I nod in greeting and go back to eating my food.

"Hope."

The second he says her name my body stiffens. Tension wraps around my tendons and my spine straightens as I set down my fork to see what he'll do.

"Good evening, Mr. Travon," Hope's voice quivers as she addresses him.

I glare at Dad, warning him not to be rude to her or else I'd cross the line and say something worse to him.

Much to my surprise, he stares at her with a twinge of softness. "You can call me Xavier."

Hope nods and goes back to playing around with the food on her plate.

Dad sits next to me and watches Mom as she prepares a plate for him. He thanks her and kisses the back of her hand when she gives it to him. She grins big and sits down next to him.

The four of us eat at the kitchen island that is smaller than the dining table in the other room. I've always resented that table because of how ridiculously long it is and how it is perfect for a meeting rather than a family table. Having spent a lot of time with Sebastian and Marie, I like to eat at a small coffee table. There is less room for distance and more conversations.

"So, I heard you came in third at the bake sale," Dad says nonchalantly.

I freeze, completely taken aback by his statement. I wasn't expecting him to know about it.

"I made him my blueberry muffins. They sold out."

"Of course they did. They're perfect," he praises her with ease as if he's done it a million times before.

His compliment brings colors to her face and she looks so lively now that he's here. The one week he was gone my mother didn't smile or talk the way she's doing right now.

"It was a group effort. We didn't win because of me alone. I had my girlfriend and friends who helped me," I tell him.

Dad looks at me with deep understanding. "I'm surprised to see that you realize it wasn't you alone. That's the quality of a good leader."

I narrow my eyes. "What are you trying to say?"

"I'm saying, I'm impressed with what you did at the bake sale." He pauses and gulps slowly. "I'm proud of you."

The room suddenly resembles an ice chamber, the cold so sharp and intense it freezes every cell in my body.

My heart stops beating for a second, not believing what I just heard coming out of his mouth.

I'm proud of you.

I've never heard those words in my life before. Especially from him.

Since I became a teenager and learned how he's abandoned me, I've only ever hated him. And when Emery got sick, I found another reason to hate him for. I didn't want anything to do with him—I still don't. But for some stupid reason, him saying those words to me, knocks the air out of me and I feel like I can hardly breathe.

"And you made good profit. Well done," he speaks in an even quieter voice, as if saying those words is new to him.

I cast a glance at Mom and she's smiling hard.

"Thanks," I mutter, my voice all rough and gravelly.

"You're taking business as an elective, why?" Dad asks.

"Because I like it," I reply as if it isn't obvious to him.

"I thought you'd be pursuing boxing. Derek mentioned how passionate you are about it. Enough to sneak out and fight matches at illegal, underground places."

A flicker of anger flares up beneath my skin, making me look at him in fury.

"I know what I'm going to do in life," I reply in a tight tone.

Dad spares me a glance and frowns. "I didn't mean it as a jab. I was just saying I know what you've been up to. Still, I think it's dangerous, and you shouldn't get involved, but you fight anyway because you genuinely love the sport."

"I love boxing but I won't be pursuing it. I want to pursue a degree in business," I say.

Dad seems content with my answer. "As you should. You have the spark."

Mom puts her hand on his and looks at me. "Do what you love. It's important that you're following your heart."

Dad sighs but doesn't say a word to disagree with her.

She looks over at Hope. "What about you, dear? What do you plan on doing?"

I take a bite and then look at her.

Hope has almost finished half of her plate, but now that all the attention is on her, she puts down her fork and focuses on my mother. "I don't know, really. My mother wants me to become a doctor but I don't think it's for me."

Mom shoots her a reassuring smile. "Just as I told Heath, do what you love."

My girlfriend nods just to agree with her.

"Heath said you love books. Maybe follow that career path. There's so much you can do."

A real smile graces her face. "That'd be a dream come true."

Mom laughs, seeing her enthusiasm. "You should definitely make that dream a reality. I can tell just from the light in your eyes that you love books more than anything in the world."

"I do. But I also love your son," she says without thinking.

A second later, the smile wipes away from her face, and her entire face turns bright red.

My parents stare at my girlfriend in utter shock, while I can't help but grin at her honesty.

She fidgets with her hands and refuses to meet their curious gazes.

"I love her, too," I say, ending her embarrassment, and not caring that my parents hear me. "More than anything."

Rose lifts her head and holds my gaze. Sincerity and vulnerability swim in those pretty brown eyes.

"I've known it for a while," Mom says confidently, making us both look over at her. "It was the look in your eyes when you talked about her. I could tell this girl was special to you."

Then Dad says, "And I suspected this was serious because you spent a night in the cell because of her and you had no regrets."

At the time, I didn't realize it, but I was already in love with her.

I had fallen hard for her, so hard that I had lost my fucking mind.

I knew she was trouble the moment I met her. One look and I was captivated.

"I would do anything to protect her," I say out loud.

"You might have to, considering her parents are going to knock on our door at any minute," Dad says in a grim tone.

The air grows thick, making it hard to breathe. Tension hangs over us like a heavy curtain.

"I'll deal with them," I warn him.

"The right thing to do is to send her home — "

The stool scrapes against the floor as I abruptly stand up. "She is not going home. How many times am I going to say this?"

Dad opens his mouth to argue with me, but Mom grabs his arm and stops him.

His gaze moves to Hope. "I'm just looking out for my son."

I rake a hand through my hair as I gather patience from every corner of my body to deal with this conversation.

"I know," Rose says softly. "I'm truly sorry for bringing my troubles to your doorstep. I don't mean to. It's just... I don't have anywhere else to go. With Heath..." She looks at me. "It's easy to stay here because I trust him a lot."

Taking a deep, slow breath, she adds. "I've decided to go back because I worry about him too. I don't want him to get into any more trouble because of me. I'm sorry."

Mom looks about ready to cry and Dad's sharp features show concern.

"Heath has done a lot for me. More than I deserve. I would never do anything to hurt him." Her voice sounds so broken.

It aches me.

"Stop! You don't need to convince them," I tell her. "You're staying here because I want you to and you'll continue to stay here because I say so."

"Heath — "

I grab her hand and squeeze it. "It's either this or I sleep in my car in front of your house because knowing you're in there with him waiting to hurt you haunts me."

"This is a serious matter, son," Xavier says in a placid tone.

I meet his gaze. "I know."

"You should let me—"

"No. I'll handle it."

"You need guidance to wisely handle this situation, not — "

"What I fucking need is your support and nothing else!" My chest heaves as I talk to him. "I need to know that you have my back, not that you're trying to sabotage my relationship with the person I love."

His lips thin. A flicker of hurt crosses through his gray eyes.

"That's not what he's doing," Mom states.

"But that's how I feel," I tell her. "I've already lost someone I love, I don't want to lose this person."

Mom closes her eyes and Dad says nothing.

Without saying another word, I guide Hope out and take us to my room.

The sound of the door click is so loud as it cuts through the tension buzzing between us.

"I'm sorry about my dad."

"No. You don't have to be. He's right."

I scoff. "He's not. He's just trying to ruin this."

She steps closer, forcing me to look at her. "It's been more than a week now. I should go home now."

My fingers curl into fists at the thought of letting her go inside that house. "They don't want you."

My words slash her a sword. Pain contorts her face, twisting her features in a way that I want to take back my words.

I reach for her but she steps back. "Rose. I didn't mean it like that — "

"No. You're right," she whispers.

"No! I'm not," I grumble.

"That is the truth, isn't it?" She wraps her arms around herself. "They don't want me. That's why they kicked me out, and no one's checked up on me."

The secret buried inside me stabs like a knife. I know I need to tell her about my conversation with her mother. I just hope she doesn't hate me for keeping it from her.

"I met your mother the day I went to get your stuff. Somehow, she knew I'd be coming," I start.

Her eyes widen and her mouth hangs open.

I keep going. "She said the reason why she kicked you out was to protect you from that man. Not because she doesn't love you. If anything, I feel like in her own twisted way, she loves you."

She stares at me.

I move toward her and wrap my arms around her. A shiver runs through her body, and a gasp escapes her lips.

"She really said that?" she asks, sounding stronger than I expected her to be.

"She did." I run my hand down her back and gently tuck her against my chest.

There are other things she told me, but if I share them, she might break and I can't do that. What her mother said shook my core and made me upset. Rose would take it hard.

"I thought she hates me," she says.

"She doesn't."

"What am I supposed to do now?"

I set my chin on the top of her head. "I don't know, baby. But whatever you decide, I'll support you."

40

HOPE

"Are you sure you want to do it?" Heath asks.

"Yes, but I'm nervous."

"I can come with you."

I quickly shake my head. "No. I don't want them to see you."

"Your mom already knows that you're living with me. This information will be brand new only for that man."

"You don't call him my dad," I say.

Anger burns in those blue eyes. "Because he doesn't deserve to be called that."

I purse my lips, not knowing if I want to agree with him or not.

It's late at night, and we're parked at the end of the block, with a clear view of my house. The lights are on, and shadows dance behind the curtains drawn at every window. They're both home.

Nerves hit me, and I can't stop the tremors that race down my leg, all the way to my foot, which starts tapping on the floor.

Heath notices, puts his hand on my leg, and presses hard. "Rose."

I can't make myself look at him. All I keep staring at is that house. *My home.*

"What will happen if I go in there?"

His hand tenses over my leg, and his gaze bores deep into the side of my face.

"I don't know. That man is home so the outcome would probably be bad."

I know what he means.

Clawing deep through me, I look for enough courage to face the wrath of my father when I walk in through the door.

I don't find it because he truly terrifies me.

"Baby," Heath calls, rubbing soothing circles on my thigh.

I avert my gaze from the house and look into his beautiful eyes that resemble a calm sea.

"I don't think you should go in there," he says.

I let out a shaky breath and press a hand to my heart. "But..."

"We'll come back later when he's not home and you can talk to your Mom alone."

I nod, because if I go in there right now, I don't think I'd make it out safe. Dad will hurt me or Mom for some stupid reason, and I can't risk that. Besides, I don't think I can stand still when he looks at me with those dark, evil eyes. That stare makes my skin crawl and heart race.

"Let's go somewhere." Heath grabs my hand and laces our fingers together.

"Okay." I muster up a tiny smile and he leans over and kisses me.

I relax into him, letting go of the tension swirling through my body.

With our joined hands on my thigh, he drives with the other hand on the wheel, and music plays softly in the background. It's a song by Chase Atlantic.

Pulling my feet up, I curl up on the seat and watch him drive. He's in full control, and his precision at making turns and smoothly switching lanes makes him look incredibly hot.

It takes me a minute to notice that he's aimlessly driving around, not going anywhere specific.

I don't say a word.

The quiet hum of the engine, the faint hint of his cologne, and the peaceful atmosphere in the car help me relax.

Before I know, I'm thinking of anything but home—it moves somewhere in the back of my head.

Heath is all I can focus on. He consumes my thoughts and senses.

He's wearing a pure black hoodie, and he looks so good in it.

"You're staring at me, Rose." He teases when he stops the car at a red light.

I quickly look away, but he squeezes my hand, bringing my attention back to him.

The smirk on his lips makes my heart skip a beat. "You can stare all you want, because I do too."

My cheeks heat up at his blunt flirting. I should get used to it, but I don't think I ever will.

"I wasn't really staring..." I lie.

His lips twitch like he's fighting a smile. "What were you doing then?"

Now I'm trapped.

Raising our joined hands, he kisses the back of my hand and puts them back on my lap. "I know you're fucking obsessed with me, Rose."

"That's not—"

"So you're not obsessed with me?" He arches an eyebrow at me.

"I am," I speak in a very quiet voice.

With a chuckle that sends butterflies soaring in my stomach, he presses hard on the gas and drives down the straight road that I know leads to his secret spot.

When we arrive, he helps me out of the car, making me wear his thick, plain black jacket and zipping it up for me.

It's mid-November, and winter has arrived. Each day, it gets colder and colder.

"Maybe we should sit inside my car," he mutters under his breath.

"This is fun." My teeth chatter together.

"Rose, you're shaking a little," he grumbles.

"I'm warm. I promise."

"I'm worried that you might get sick."

I step closer to him, and he quickly rests his hands on my waist, pulling me closer.

"I'm fine, really."

He sighs and fog curls around his breath.

I smile up at him and his features soften a little.

"I brought you here to look at the sky. During this time..." His voice fades as I turn my attention to the sky that is full of stars.

It looks like someone has sprinkled buckets of glitter across the black canvas of the sky. The stars shimmer and blink, shining brightly in the night.

The sight is so exquisite it leaves me speechless.

My breath catches in my throat as I stand there, completely in awe.

"I used to come here a lot to look at it," he explains as he looks at me.

"It's beautiful," I say, staring up at the sky.

"It is." His stare is fully locked on me.

That makes me face him and the look in his eyes shakes my entire system. It's so intense.

I find myself standing on my tiptoes, wrapping my arms around his neck.

His hands tighten on my waist and he tilts his head down and presses his forehead against mine.

"I want you to know that I've got you no matter what happens," he says in a thick, gravelly tone, as though he's engraving each word into stone. "I'm not going anywhere. I want you, and nothing in the world will change how I feel."

"I know," I reply.

"And I love you," he says with a smile.

Lately, I've noticed he smiles at me more often. I'm beginning to recognize the way his smile lines appear or how his eyes brighten with joy. It's one of my favorite things about him.

"I love you too," I tell him with a grin.

"Good, because if you hadn't, I would've done anything to make you fall in love with me."

I raise a little and kiss him. He melts against me and gently pulls me closer until our chests are pressed and our hearts are beating together.

He kisses me slowly, sweetly, and with such tenderness that I can't help but get lost in him.

Under the starry sky, we kiss until our lips go numb and every nerve in my body tingles.

Breathless and panting, we stand so close that there's no space between us.

"I got you an early birthday present," he announces out of nowhere.

"What?" I blink.

Letting go of me, he strides to his car and grabs a box from the glove compartment. He jogs toward me, stopping in front of me, looking a little nervous as he runs his fingers through his hair.

"Here it is," he whispers, handing me the small black velvet box.

A frisson of excitement rushes through me as I take the box from him and slowly open it. Inside sits a shiny silver necklace with a rose pendant.

"I got it custom-made," he adds.

The necklace looks stunning.

I trace the rose charm and feel my chest tighten.

"It's rose because that's what I call you and what you mean to me —someone very important to me," he speaks again.

My throat seems to have swollen up with the emotions, but I force the words out. "I love it."

"Really?"

I nod and look at him to assure him. "Yes, and knowing all that just makes it even more special to me."

Gently, I take it out of the box and hold it in my hand. "Will you put it on me?"

"Uh, sure." This is the first time I'm seeing him out of his element. He never loses his composure.

I hand him the necklace and turn around. I feel him close behind me as he brings the necklace around my neck. "Your hair, Rose."

I shiver at his proximity. "Uh, yes." I quickly gather my hair and lift it up.

Then he works on locking it, while my heart thumps furiously against my ribcage.

"It's done," he mumbles, his voice husky.

I touch the charm and the cold metal reminds me of him.

With a deep breath, I turn around.

Even in the dark, I can clearly see how his eyes lock on the necklace.

"It looks pretty on you," he says, lifting the charm and caressing it with his thumb.

"Thank you."

He nods.

"Now I wear a chain just like you."

"Yeah," he murmurs, before leaning down and kissing me again.

41

HOPE

November 20th. It's my birthday today.

The day starts as ordinary until Heath opens his eyes and sees me awake. He hovers over me, his arms on either side, supporting his weight. His hair is flying everywhere and his eyes look a little sleepy, but he looks strikingly handsome.

"Happy birthday, Rose," he says and kisses me softly.

"Thank you," I say, caught in a daze, as someone other than my mother wishes me.

"Today's your special day." He smirks down at me.

I nod, feeling all sorts of strange emotions at what might happen today. A pit of darkness grows in my stomach.

Heath balances on one hand and uses the other to cup my cheek. His thumb caresses the skin underneath my eye. "Your pretty eyes are my favourite thing."

"They're just plain brown."

He shakes his head. "They're anything but plain. Sometimes, when the light hits them, they look like honey; other times, they resemble chocolate. And I don't like either of those things, but when I see them in you, I go crazy."

My heart races.

He grins and kisses me again. "Let's get school over with so we can have the party later tonight."

With that, he gets off the bed and stretches. The plain black T-shirt does nothing to hide the way those back muscles move and shift.

"Party?" I ask, sitting up.

"Yes. Marie is organizing it here," he says and runs a hand through his hair.

Knowing Marie will be in charge of my birthday party, I'm sure it'll be full of colors and fun. The most fun I've ever had.

Heath walks into his walk-in closet and comes out carrying two shopping bags. He sets those down in my lap and stands straight with his arms folded over his chest.

"I got you something." He gestures to the bags.

With a frown, I reach for the bag and look inside. There are clothes.

Slowly, I pull out the white cable-knit sweater that feels so soft, along with a jean skirt and a green scarf. In the other bag, there are knee-high brown boots—the kind of boots I've never worn before.

"This is too much," I say.

"It is not. Marie agrees since she helped me shop."

I feel conflicted, realizing he bought all this for me, and I know it must have cost him a lot since they're brand new. The tags are still attached, and I don't have the heart to flip them over and check the price.

"I told you, today is special, and the people who love you are going to do everything to make it special for you."

I nod, feeling too much all at once.

"Get ready, we have a few stops to make before school."

Before I can ask him, he's already walking toward the bathroom.

———

WE SNEAK OUT OF THE HOUSE BECAUSE HEATH THINKS IF we see his parents, they will say something and ruin my day—my special day.

I can't help but smile all the way to the garage, finding it so endearing that he wants me to have the perfect day.

When I get in his car, there is a bouquet of lavender flowers and a few chocolates in the backseat.

"Is that for me?' I ask, unsure.

Heath reaches for them and puts them in my lap. "Of course it's for you."

"How did you even get these? When did you leave?"

Heath starts the car and drives out onto the main road. "I placed the order and had Sebastian deliver it to me."

"I need to thank him." I caress the flowers.

"You need to thank me first," he complains.

With a laugh, I reach over and press a kiss to his cheek. "Thank you."

The car slows down quickly until we come to a complete stop in the middle of the road.

Heath takes a deep breath. "Please warn me next time before you do that."

I nod with a huge grin, seeing the tips of his ears red. It's a rare sight when he gets flustered.

It takes us fifteen minutes to get to school, and the moment we arrive, I feel the urge to hide. People watch us and talk about us, and it's uncomfortable. Heath is used to the attention and is good at ignoring it, but not me. I've never been in the spotlight, always living in the corners.

I'm still thinking about this when the door to my side opens and Marie stands wearing a huge grin.

"Happy birthday!" She envelopes me in a tight hug as I get out of the car.

"Thank you," I murmur in her soft pastel pink sweater, paired with jeans.

She pulls back excitedly. "I have planned a great party for you. You're going to have so much fun. I have also—"

"Don't spoil it for her," Sebastian says sweetly as he sidles up next to her.

Marie pauses and thinks. "You're right."

Sebastian's green eyes meet mine and he grins. "Happy birthday, Hope."

"Thank you." I return his grin. "I heard how you delivered the flowers and the chocolates for Heath. Thank you. It was kind of you."

He chuckles and opens his mouth to speak, but Heath cuts him off first. "No need to thank him, Rose."

Sebastian smirks and looks down at me. "You're welcome. If you ever need help with anything, you can ask me."

"She won't need it," Heath mutters.

I ignore Heath and speak to Sebastian, "I'll remember that."

He winks at me, and I laugh.

"You're lucky you're my best friend, or I would've given you a black eye and told you to wink like that again," Heath reminds him.

Marie makes eye contact with me and mouths, "Guys."

Sebastian stays relaxed, the mischievous glint of humor swimming in his eyes. "Cool down. I see her like a little sister."

Heath sighs. "I know."

"Still, you can't help the jealousy." Sebastian teases.

"Okay, let's go inside." Marie loops her arm with mine and starts walking in the direction of the entrance.

"What's that?" she asks as we enter the hallway.

"What?" I meet her gaze but she's looking down at my necklace.

"Is that a rose? Did Heath get it for you?"

I smile and give her a nod. "He said it's my early birthday present."

Marie squeals in enthusiasm. "That's so cute."

The bell rings and we get separated because we have different classes. I'm taking out my textbooks from my locker when Heath comes over and leans against the locker next to mine.

"You look beautiful today," he says, staring at me with a soft gaze.

A blush creeps up my skin, and I try to distract myself by locking the locker. It's not the first time he's said it, but it still makes me feel special every time.

I hug the heavy textbooks to my chest. "Shall we go?"

He nods, offering me his hand.

Like every day, we make our way to my classroom first. He talks to me about the biology he has today, and I quiz him with a few questions

360

to keep the answers fresh. After two weeks of living with him, he's gotten much better at it. Like everything else, he's good at his studies too. It turns out he just needed to understand a few things and memorize a lot to score well. The problem is, he hates the subject in general.

After a short kiss in front of the classroom, he leaves for his class.

I enter and sit in the back.

My phone buzzes in my back pocket. I take it out and see a text from Mom.

Silence rings in my ears and it gets so quiet.

She has texted me.

With a lump in my throat, I click on the message preview and there it is.

Mom: Happy birthday, Hope.

Those three words hit me like arrows.

Then, the silence breaks, and the noise of the classroom rushes in, reminding me I'm at school, not alone.

I type out a reply, but don't send it. It sits in the drafts as I put my phone on silent and slip it into my bag.

I wait for the remorse to hit me, especially after knowing what Heath told me, but I can't find it in me to be nice to her. I understand she did it to protect me, but there are a million other ways to do that. Kicking me out and making me live somewhere else isn't the answer.

The classes go by, and soon, it's lunchtime. We head to a diner where Heath orders me a chocolate smoothie and Marie gets me fries. I start to realize that Marie and Heath have turned it into a competition to see who spoils me more. Sebastian grins as he watches them. I end up eating everything they order to keep them happy.

By the time we return for the rest of our classes, my stomach aches. But my heart feels warm with gratitude for all the love in my life.

42

HEATH

Instead of having the party in the living room, we organize it in my room to have privacy. Any interaction with my parents is to be avoided at all costs. I don't want them to upset Rose and ruin her day. My mother might not say something rude, but I can't trust my father.

Marie and Sebastian decorate my room while I drive around with my girlfriend to kill time.

"Why aren't we going home?" she asks for the third time. I'm sensing she is picking up that we're up to something.

Marie and Sebastian better hurry the fuck up.

"I have to buy a few things," I lie.

"What things?"

"Protein powder."

"Didn't you buy it a few days ago?"

I sure as fuck did. "I spilled the entire bottle the other day."

"What?" She sounds worried.

I nod as I pull up into the parking lot of the department store.

Hope hesitantly unbuckles her seatbelt. She doesn't believe me.

I get out of the car and come around to open the door for her. She steps out and wraps her arms around herself, staring at me with those innocent eyes.

"What is going on? I feel like something is wrong." Panic rings in her voice.

I grab her hand. "Nothing is wrong, I promise."

"But I have this strange feeling that something bad is going to happen."

I frown, seeing her troubled eyes.

"Nothing is going to happen, Rose." I study her closely.

She stares at me for a long moment, then nods.

Taking her hand, I let us in.

Hope is on edge the entire time, and I try to calm her down but the wheels in her head keep rolling. I know something is bothering her, but even she can't figure out what it is.

We walk out five minutes later with a protein powder bottle that I don't even need. Because of Dad, I've stopped fighting at the underground. But turns out he already knew about it. It's strange how he never brought it up on phone calls. Not that I'd have stopped if he'd asked me to.

These days, I only go to the gym. It's my only outlet for frustration.

And sexual energy.

Having Rose so close to me all the time has given me permanent blue balls. It's a miracle that I'm functioning properly and not dying from pain.

Sebastian likes to tease me about it.

Asshole.

The sky gets dark and it's only five. Streetlights light up and people start walking toward their homes.

My phone pings with a message. It's from Blondie.

Blondie: All set.

I let out a sigh of relief and drive us home as fast as I can.

When we get home, I take Rose to my room. She looks relaxed now, which is exactly how I want her to be. I don't want anything to ruin her day.

"Go on." I gesture for her to open the door.

She gives me a questioning look but pushes it open.

"Happy birthday!" Marie and Sebastian shout, wearing party hats and holding confetti cannons.

My room is minimally decorated with white and blue balloons and a few other simple touches.

Marie sets aside the confetti cannon and lifts the chocolate cake from the table. Sebastian lights the candles, and together, they bring it over with wide grins.

I close the door behind us and lock it.

Rose laughs as she sees the cake.

"Blow the candles and make a wish," I say to Rose as I wrap my arm around her waist to hold her steady.

Rose glances at me, then closes her eyes and blows out the candles.

Sebastian and I clap the loudest. He hands her the knife, and she carefully cuts the cake.

"Thank you," she whispers, her eyes shining with tears.

"You're welcome," Marie says, looking like she's ready to cry.

Later, the four of us sit on the floor around the coffee table, enjoying the cake. I have a small piece, mostly because of Rose, who's busy devouring a huge slice I can't even imagine finishing.

"Okay, present time," Marie announces and reaches behind her to grab a bag. "I'm first."

"Why?" I ask her.

"Because I said so. If you wanted to be first, you should've spoken up."

I roll my eyes.

Rose takes it with a soft expression on her face. "You didn't have to, Marie. This party was enough."

"I wanted to. Besides, I've had this for so long. I especially made this for you."

With a curious face, Rose puts her hand into the bag and pulls out a pink hoodie. She opens it, and there's a quote on the front that makes her smile.

"You wrote my favorite line, and there are sparkles and stars, too. They match the book perfectly."

Marie wears a smug expression. "I know."

Rose hugs Marie and thanks her.

Next up is Sebastian, who gets her a lot of reading supplies like bookmarks, tabs, highlighters, and pens. Rose gushes over them and thanks him with a hug.

I'm the last.

"What did you get, Hope?" Marie asks.

I ignore her and slip my hand into my jacket pocket, where her present is tucked away. Taking it out, I hand it to Rose, who gasps.

"You made me a bracelet on my birthday so I thought I should do the same."

"But how did you make it?"

I shrug. "I was always watching you when you made them."

She examines the bracelet, its blue with white beads and star charms I added because they remind me of her. It was tough making it in secret. I'd skipped gym hours to work on it. A few times, I'd slip the string, and the beads would scatter everywhere, forcing me to start over. But when I was done with it, I knew she'd love it.

Rose slips it on and grins. "It looks pretty," she whispers.

Looking up, she cups my cheek and pulls me in for a kiss. "Thank you so much."

Gratitude shines in her eyes because she knows how much time and effort it takes for one to make it. "You don't—"

A loud noise comes from downstairs, grabbing my attention. Moments later, shouting follows.

"What's going on?" Marie whispers.

I know for a fact it isn't my parents. They've never raised their voices at each other.

"Wait here." I get up to check.

"I'll come." Sebastian gets up too.

We both step outside my room and hurry downstairs.

As we both turn, we see a familiar face in the foyer, standing toe to toe with my father.

Alex Hanson.

"Call my daughter down. I know she is here!" Alex shouts at my dad, furious.

Dad looks down at him with a cold stare that sends a chill down my spine. Seeing it, Alex backs up a little. "I assume you're the asshole who made my son spend a night in the cell."

"He shouldn't have interfered in my family matters."

"You mean, protect your daughter from you?" Dad retorts calmly.

"She's my daughter. I can do whatever I want with her."

Sebastian puts his hand on my chest to keep me from going over and pummeling his face. "Stay put," he warns me.

Dad narrows his eyes at him as if he is the dirt beneath his shoes. "Do *what* exactly?"

Alex glares at him. "I know she is here. You've kept her here for far too long."

"She's staying here because you and your wife kicked her out," Dad explains to him, not one bit affected by the evil look he's giving him.

"Well, now we want her back."

Dad straightens up. "Why?"

Alex steps closer. "You listen to me, rich prick! Give me back my daughter or else I'll have the police at your door in a minute."

Dad studies him. "I don't think you know who you're dealing with." He moves forward, making Alex step back in fear as he is taller and more muscular than him. "I can have you in jail in less than a second for disrespecting me."

"Xavier—" Mom speaks from around the corner and Dad looks over at her. That's when he sees me.

And Alex does too.

"You asshole!" He takes one step and Dad grabs the back of his neck and slams his face into the nearest wall.

"Don't even think about raising a hand on my son. I will break it," Dad warns him in a menacing tone.

"What do you think—" Alex croaks out but stops when he sees someone behind me.

I swivel my head and there is Rose standing with Marie. She resembles a statue with how still she is standing. Color drains from her face and her eyes fill with fear.

"It's time to go," Alex tells her.

Rose nods, her hands fisting by her sides, and they shake.

Walking past me, she nears him and looks at my father. He lets go of Alex and steps back.

The second he does, Alex raises his hand and hits her across the face right in front of us.

My feet move, and even Sebastian can't hold me back.

I get close enough to reach him, but Dad steps in my way, blocking me like a wall.

I'm shaking with so much anger, it gets to my head. I can't think fucking straight.

"Move," I snap at him.

He shakes his head, knowing fucking well that I can't get past him because he is equally strong as me.

Then, that asshole's fucking voice enters my ears. "You were staying here all this time while your mother and I were worried for you."

He's fucking lying.

They were not worried for you.

For fuck's sake. They didn't even care, least of all him.

"I'm sorry. I'm sorry..." Rose weeps and her entire body shakes.

Grabbing her arm, he yanks her with such force, and they start walking outside.

"Move," I grit out to Dad.

"No."

"I said fucking move," I snarl.

"No."

"I said move, Dad!" My voice echoes in all the corners of the mansion with how loudly I yell those words.

My chest is heaving and my breaths are fast and short. I resemble a wild animal imprisoned for life.

They must still be outside. I can get to them. I can save her.

Those words keep echoing in my head.

In desperation, I push against my father to reach for her, but he endures my attempts, unyielding.

"I said move!" I grit through clenched teeth.

"Heath, you need to calm down," he tells me in a placid tone.

I give him a shove and stare at him with so much hatred. "Calm

367

down?! You want me to fucking calm down after what you just saw. Did you not see how he hurt her? Are you fucking blind?"

Every word bounces off the wall and echoes.

I can hear Sebastian standing behind me, reaching for me. But I fucking hope he doesn't.

I'm too livid right now to talk to anyone.

"I saw what happened, but if you go after him right now, you'll spend another night in the cell," Dad tells me, studying me with those gray eyes, "and I can't let you do that."

"Let me do that? It's my fucking life."

"And I care about you."

I frown deeply. "Care about me? You're fucking kidding, right?"

He shakes his head. "I had my reason for staying away."

I scoff, my eyes burning from all the pent-up rage. "I'm warning you for the last time. *Move.*"

He doesn't reply.

"Whatever fucking happens now is on you."

Wiping my nose, I swing my arm back and aim a right hook at his face. Much to my surprise, he catches it mid-swing, his grip like iron. Before I can even react, he twists my arm with punishing force, the pain sharp and instant. In one fluid motion, he drives me back into the same fucking wall where he had pinned Alex Hanson.

"Xavier, let him go!" Mom cries out.

"Carol, get me a glass of cold water, please," he says instead.

I try to wrestle my arm out of his hold, but he is strong. "Let me go!"

"I will once you calm down and listen to me."

"Listen to you! Are you fucking crazy? Nothing you say is going to make me hate you less."

"I know but we need to talk."

"Talk! I don't want to fucking talk to you." I clench my teeth. "Because of you, another person in my life is going to die. You hear me. She's going to die if you don't let go of me right now."

"He's not going to kill her," Dad says with such confidence that my body believes him.

"You don't know that."

"I know his kind. He won't kill her. But he will kill you if you don't calm down and think with your head."

Turning to my friends, he says, "You both should go home. Heath and I have a long conversation that is overdue."

Sebastian looks at me. "I'll be in your room."

I nod.

Once he leaves with Marie, I turn my neck and glare at my dad. "Let go of me."

"If I do, you won't listen to me."

I groan in frustration. "I don't believe a single word that comes out of your mouth. So even if you speak, it doesn't fucking matter."

A long moment passes before he asks, "Do you really blame me for Em's death?"

"Yes," I grumble.

That's when he lets go of me. I turn around to attack him, but what I see is a face full of despair.

"I deserve that," he whispers.

Mom comes with a glass of water. Her eyes are red and her cheeks puffy. She hands it to me, then faces her husband and glares at him. "If you ever do that to him again, I will never speak to you."

Regret flashes through his eyes. "Mia Cara—"

She faces me. "Here, drink this."

I take the glass from her even though I don't want to.

Dad sighs. "Not that you care, but I think you should know that I feel guilty about leaving you. Before Emery...and after her death. It's my fault that she died. Maybe if I had been here, she wouldn't have died."

I gulp down the water. The cold water seems to help me calm down. "It's too late to feel remorse. What was supposed to happen, happened. I won't lie and say I don't blame you, because I do. If you hadn't been so hungry for money and power, maybe things wouldn't have been so awful in our lives."

"I wanted you two safe. To live somewhere where no one could find you two and hurt you. To have a normal childhood. I have a lot of enemies. People are greedy for the reputation, power, and wealth I've built over the years through hard work. All the—"

"Spare me your sob story. I'm least interested in it." I hit a nerve as his face hardens.

"How about some truth?"

That piques my interest.

"What about it?" My stomach ties in a series of knots.

Mom stares at him, and he meets her gaze. They share a silent moment before he turns to face me. "The reason why we left you and Emery in this town. The truth that I've always hidden from you—"

"Will you just fucking tell me?" I raise my voice, getting agitated with every miserable second that passes.

Dad swallows hard. "Shortly after you were born, your mother and I attended this important company party. We could've skipped it. At least, I wish we had..." He clears his throat, and for the first time, I see him nervous. If there's one thing I'm certain of, it's that my dad isn't afraid of anything or anyone. At least, that's what I've come to believe from the little time I've spent with him.

"The party started at eight and was supposed to end by eleven. We left you at the penthouse, sleeping. Your mom made sure you were fed so you wouldn't wake up hungry, and she left some milk for you in the kitchen in case you did. Paulina, our maid, was the one who looked after you for those few hours. It was only for a short time, so we left without worrying." His face turns serious.

"When we came back, you were gone. We checked the cameras, and it turned out Paulina had taken you. We had no idea how she got past the building's security, but somehow, she did. Your mom was in agony, weeping and screaming the second she saw you weren't in the room. I called some of my best men to search for you, but we couldn't find you that night."

Silence disperses in the room, and tension gathers within the concrete walls.

My heart is racing in my chest and my mind is carefully holding onto the details he's giving me.

I feel something stir inside me, reaching out to him, an invisible thread connecting to him.

"That night was the worst night of my life, son. The stress and fear I felt that day was nothing I had experienced before. It was a fucking nightmare I never thought I'd have to live through." We lock eyes, but I quickly tear my gaze away from him, unable to hold the weight of his words.

"Police were at our door, and their men were searching for you. You were only three months old—so small, but so loud." He smiles, and for the first time, I see him like this—soft, almost vulnerable.

"My security team was on the search too, but nothing came up until the morning. Paulina called me, demanding ransom and some favors. She wanted five million dollars, her brother released from jail, fake IDs, and passports. I was able to fulfill all of her requests except for bailing her brother out. He was facing some serious charges, and getting him out wasn't going to be easy."

My heart climbs up to my throat.

"I didn't want to get him out. Believe me, I didn't. I hated being in a position where I had to do that. Later in the afternoon, she sent me a video of you, lying cold, only in your underwear, with winter just around the corner. You could've gotten sick, and I...I had to make a choice."

I sweep a hand through my hair to relieve some of the tension stirring inside me.

Mom wipes her tears but stays quiet otherwise.

"I put my best lawyers to work, paid a hefty amount of money to anyone and everyone I could so they'd let him go. All the while, I felt filthy for doing something like that. But I had to. You were with that psychotic woman who was... hurting you." His voice drops, almost a whisper.

"By ten that night, I'd given her everything she demanded. She dropped you off on a bench in the park naked. I rushed you to the hospital, and you were fine. I drove back home to your mom, who was overjoyed to see you. She held you that entire night and day, not putting you down for a second. It was maddening. She kept you close, terrified that someone might take you away again."

I'm too stunned to utter a single word. Too surprised and bewildered to form even the simplest sentence. My mouth is dry, as if the words just won't come.

"When Emery was born, we left you two in this town to hide you away, making sure you'd be safe, away from us... Away from me. Because of me, you got kidnapped. I couldn't risk a repeat. So I didn't think twice and sent you both here."

"Is this the truth?" I ask, my eyes searching his face. He doesn't look like he's lying.

"All of it," he says, his deep voice heavy with meaning. It touches my heart, and I step back, the weight of his words settling on me.

"And you never thought to tell me?" I accuse him as anger swims through my veins.

"I did. Multiple times. But every time I looked at you, I realized I had to set a criminal free. That you were kidnapped because of me. I was consumed with guilt and rage. And that's why I never visited you. I distanced myself, speaking only when it was absolutely necessary."

I burst out laughing. Humor cripples my sides and squeezes my heart as I crack. I can't believe he let me hate him instead of telling me the truth.

"I can't believe you. You let me hate you for years. Just because of this. You could have told me. You should have told me!" I shout at him but he doesn't even flinch.

He sighs. "And let you know that I had let you down? That in order to save you I did something I hate myself for every single day? That my money and hard work couldn't offer you basic security and a life that should have been normal for you? Maybe I should have told you. But I'm glad I didn't."

I walk over to him, my fists clenched. "Why the fuck are you saying this?"

"Because nothing will change the way you hate me. Or extinguish the fire that burns for me inside you. Now that I've told you the truth... You hate me more, don't you?"

I want to say yes. I want to scream that word at him, but somehow, I can't find the courage to spit out that three-letter word. The pain of the past and the raw truth of the present hit me like waves crashing in my stomach, mixed with an intense fury I can't contain. I don't know what to do with him. Or what to say to him.

"I'm not a good man. But I've tried my best to keep you away from evil. Even if it meant you being away from me and hating me."

Mary

I stay still and silent.

"You can hate me all you want, Heath. But I'll always protect you. Always look out for you. You're all I've left anyway."

"Emery died because of you. You weren't there," I whisper the words that have always haunted me.

Dad nods. "I know I'm the reason. And I carry the guilt and blame with me every day. She was my daughter, after all. You can't imagine how I felt when I saw her in that hospital bed, hooked up to wires, sleeping. The rise and fall of her chest was the only reassurance she was still alive. But it was also the truth— she was there because of me."

He meets my gaze, his voice rough. "I'm not a good father. I know that. I've failed you and Emery countless times. I hate myself for it all. I blame myself for everything. I deserve the way you treat me, the way you talk to me, or look at me. I deserve it all."

Tears prick at my eyes, and I resent myself for showing any emotion, any weakness to him.

For him.

But I can't help it.

"But you're also all I've got left. The one child who's alive and well. I want to make amends, Heath. I want to make things right."

I chuckle and shove him away from me. "Make amends? You just held me back from saving the girl I fucking love."

He frowns. "I held you back to protect you. That man was drunk and angry. He would have hurt you to get back his daughter."

"Now he is going to hurt her," my voice breaks. My eyes fill with tears, and for the first time, I feel more helpless than I ever have in my life. "I can't fucking lose that girl. You don't understand."

"You just love her."

I run a hand through my hair. "No, I don't just fucking love her. She is the reason why I'm a better person. She is the reason why I'm not in darkness. And she is the reason why I want to fix things between us because she believes you two really love me."

Dad watches me and his eyes hold so much sorrow and regret. "I can save her if you stay here."

My body goes rigid. "What?"

He takes out his phone and scrolls through it, his fingers moving quickly. "I'll send someone there to keep an eye on things. If it gets too much, he'll step in. But there's one condition: you stay here. Because I know evil when I see it. I don't want you going anywhere near him."

I can barely get a word out. "Do you mean that?"

He pauses, glancing up at me before giving a slow nod. "You said you don't just love her. If that's true, then she must mean a lot to you."

"She does."

"Then I'll help you, but you have to listen to me." He gives me a stern look.

It takes everything in me not to roll my eyes or give him a sharp reply.

"Can I trust you, Dad?" I ask.

He freezes at that word, his throat tightening as he gulps hard. "You always can, son."

43

HOPE

DAD SHOVES ME INTO AN OLD CAR AND DRIVES US HOME.
The whole ride, I stay absolutely still. I can't feel the right side of
my face; it stings, but I'm numb. No tears slip past my cheeks and no
sound comes out of my mouth. The pit of darkness that started
growing in my stomach earlier begins to shrink, but it doesn't go away.

I knew it.

I knew something bad was going to happen tonight. I just never
expected Dad to show up at Heath's house. How did he find out about
it? The only person who knew was Mom.

I sit like a statue beside him, scared that any little movement will
tick him off and he'll attack me.

The fear I used to live with all the time went quiet in the past weeks
I spent with Heath. I forgot to flinch or watch my every step. But now
sitting in this car with him, it comes back in full force.

I'm afraid of my own shadow.

We arrive home quickly as he speeds through the streets, running
every traffic signal without a second thought.

I keep my mouth shut and don't utter a single sound as he drives
fast.

Getting out of the car, he slams the door hard and barks at me to
get out.

I force myself to stay calm as I oblige.

My eyes catch a glimpse of Nadina's house and I see her looking at me through the window. Before I can pass her a smile, Dad grabs my wrist and starts pulling me toward the house.

Once inside, he shoves me hard and I hit the wall.

"I brought her home," he shouts.

"What?" Mom comes out of the kitchen and pales when she sees me.

Her eyes fill with sadness and fear but she schools in her emotions. "Hope, what are you doing here?"

I only stare at her.

It's been weeks since I've seen her.

The last time I did, she kicked me out and told me not to come home.

It was late at night, and the silence outside was suffocating, so deadly quiet.

I'd never felt fear and uncertainty like I did that night. It wrapped around me, thick and heavy, and I couldn't escape it. I was scared. So scared.

As we stare at each other, it all comes back and a fire lights up in my heart.

I don't reply to her and avert my gaze from her.

"I found her in a mansion. That boy she has been whoring around with is a rich kid," Dad snaps. "Tell me, how long have you been fucking him?"

"Stop it!" Mom intervenes.

Dad frowns and looks at her. "What did you just say to me?"

Mom steps away from him.

"That's what I thought." He smiles, then turns his attention to me. "Now, you are going to answer some of my questions."

He takes a swig from his bottle and starts walking toward me.

In panic, I start backing up, then break into a full sprint up the stairs, desperate to get away from him. I know I'm as good as dead tonight. He's not going to let me live after finding out I stayed at a boy's house for weeks.

His loud thumps weaken the floorboards of the stairs as they creak.

The horrid sound sends chills down my spine.

Before I can open my bedroom door, he catches me and slams me against the wall.

"Alex, let go of her!" Mom hurries toward us.

"Stay back! Bitch." He throws his bottle at her, but it misses, shattering into sharp shards at her feet.

"Don't hurt her," she begs, eyes filled with tears.

Dad smiles. "Hurt her? I'm going to kill her." He fixates on me, and his eyes look so dark. "I will punish her for leaving us and staying at his house. I told her to stay away from him. I told her what would happen."

"I'm sorry. I'm sorry. I'm sorry," I beg him as fear fully consumes me. I can feel my heart scratching the walls to escape.

Anxiety swirls like acid in my stomach and burns everything. All the happiness and joy I experienced today burn away into ashes, forming a pile.

"You are sorry!" He grabs my hair and gives a good tug, making me scream out. "I told you the rules and you disobeyed me. Just like your fucking mom."

"Alex! Let go of her."

"And what did you tell his family, huh? You think you're clever for snitching on me?"

I shake my head but he doesn't allow it.

Dad drags me by my hair and makes me face Mom. "She's told his family about us and you know what happened. That scoundrel's dad threatened me."

He tightens his grip on me and I wince.

"He threatened to break my hand." He chuckles dryly.

My tearful eyes connect with Mom and she looks devastated. I didn't expect her to feel this way for me. I thought she wanted me to get punished because she's always hated Heath.

"She thinks she is safe now that she's told him and his fucking family," Dad mocks.

"Alex, please calm down. Let's talk about—"

"Talk about what?" he yells at her.

Mom flinches. "No, I mean, you don't need to hurt her. I will talk to her and it'll be fine. She'll stop seeing him."

Dad shakes his head. "No, she won't listen. Your blood runs in her veins."

"She will listen. I will talk to her," Mom softens her voice and steps over the glass to get to us.

He scoffs. "There is nothing to talk about. We need to—"

"I said I will talk—"

At once, he lets go of me and reaches for her. "You're talking a lot today."

A painful noise escapes from her throat where he's holding her.

The image cuts through me, and a sharp, piercing pain spreads through my chest.

My senses go haywire and my entire system shuts down.

This is exactly how he held her that night when he nearly killed her.

A throbbing pain starts in my head, and I can't stop it from consuming every corner of my head.

You have to do something.

Stop it.

He's going to kill her.

Do something.

Do something!

DO SOMETHING.

My feet move before any other thought crosses my head.

A voice whispers in my ear. *The next time he hurts you, I want you to hurt him, Rose.*

Heath had said that to me once and I discarded his words because fighting someone isn't in me. I don't have the courage, strength, or will to hurt someone. I can only take a beating.

But in that moment, my body fills with so much bravery that I manage to shove him away from Mom. She falls to the ground and gasps loudly as if she was seconds away from dying.

Dad turns around, his gaze locking onto me with such a heated glare that it's a miracle my bones don't disintegrate under its weight.

"You little—"

"I hate you. I hate you so much," I choke out those words.

His eyes widen and he grows angrier.

"What did you just say to me?" He extends his arm to grab me, but I manage to dodge, slamming my hands hard against his chest to make him stumble. He loses his balance, stepping directly onto the glass shards with a harsh crunch.

A groan escapes his lips as the glass shards embed in his feet. He tries to pull away, but in his panic, he steps back and trips over the first step, tumbling down the stairs with a loud crash. A thump and then it's quiet.

"Oh my God!" Mom whispers from beside as we both stare down at the body. The unmoving body.

An eerie silence fills the house and the air turns cold.

He's dead.

A long moment stretches by before the shock fades and the adrenaline burns out, leaving me standing there, trembling.

"I did it. I killed him," I choke out, registering what I've done.

My hands start shaking and dots dance in front of my eyes.

"Hope, listen to me!" Mom snaps at me. "You didn't do anything."

I shake my head. "No! I...I pushed him. I did it—"

"—to save me," she finishes in a hard tone, trying to break my panic.

She cups my face in her palms and forces me to look at her. "You saved me."

"But—"

"That's what happened."

I stare at her long and hard.

"You. Saved. Me," she repeats.

I keep shaking but she brings me to her chest and hugs me tight.

"I'm so sorry. I'm sorry."

"Shh... It's okay. Everything's going to be fine."

What happens next is a blur. I fall into a trance, surrounded by people moving and speaking, but their voices and faces blend into the background. I can't focus on anything.

My hands fidget uncontrollably, twisting together, and my throat feels like it's been sealed shut with a heavy stone.

I feel shaky, out of place, like my own skin doesn't fit anymore.

It's as if all the peace and calm have been stripped from me. I'm buzzing with some strange energy I can't shake, unable to find any ground to steady myself.

Through my blurry vision, I watch Mom take control of everything. She calls an ambulance and handles the body, arranges for it to be removed, and cleans up the bloodstains. She answers a lot of questions and with confidence, making it seem like it was an accident. She even takes care of the glass shards, like it's all just another task to be done.

After all that, she helps me into bed and tucks me in, whispering reassuring words to me, but I can't seem to calm down.

Will I stay like this forever?

Will the reminder of what I've done keep coming back to me?

Will I be normal again?

The answers to those questions seem to be out of my reach as I watch the ceiling for long hours.

44

HOPE

In the middle of the night, I hear the creak of the floorboards outside my door, and my body tightens. I sit up in fear that he's back.

The door opens, and Heath stands there, my mother just behind him. She whispers something to him before quietly leaving us alone.

He steps into the room and sits on my bed without a word.

We just stare at each other, the silence thick between us, neither of us breaking it.

My chest feels heavy as my heart yearns to reach for him.

Tears fill my eyes and a few slip down my cheeks.

"Someone once told me, 'You don't ask for a hug. You just take it.'"

That's all it takes for me to leap into his arms, the dam finally breaking as I cry my heart out in his chest. Sobs wrack through me and I shake so hard that he has to hold me tight to contain me.

"Shh... It's okay. Your mom told me everything."

"Heath, I—"

"You didn't kill him."

"But—"

"*You didn't*, Rose," he tells me in a hard tone.

The words don't land but they linger somewhere in me. Maybe someday I'd believe them, but tonight the guilt is too much.

"I've got you," he says softly.

We spend the rest of the night like that. He holds me, and I cry into him, letting the weight of everything spill out. At one point, I tell him what happened and he listens to me.

I know something inside me is broken forever, a fracture that can never be mended, but I know love will heal me. It has to.

EPILOGUE
HOPE

ONE MONTH LATER

IT IS A BRIGHT DECEMBER MORNING, WITH WARM RAYS OF sunlight softening the cold edge of the air. Clouds drift across the sky, attempting to shield the world from the sun's penetrating light. But they forget that light cannot be stopped—it always finds a way to break through.

Life has changed.

It changed the day *that* incident happened.

Everything is fundamentally altered within me. I didn't only see death but also caused it. The guilt, the shame, the pain, all of these emotions mixed and stirred an earthquake in me. I crashed and hit the ground harder than I ever have before and I broke into a million pieces and lost a few.

What happened after that night is a blur of events. Everything that followed afterwards happened at a swift rate. But my memory has images etched to it that flicker through my consciousness from time to time.

I shiver as a foggy picture of me shoving him flashes before my eyes, making me stop in my tracks.

A gasp leaves my lips.

"Hey, it's okay. You're okay," Heath quickly murmurs against my temple as his arm wraps around my waist and he gently pulls me to him. "Relax."

I take a deep breath.

"Maybe it isn't a good day to be here," he says, worry laced thick in his voice.

I quickly look up at him. "No! It's fine. *I'm* fine. I just remembered... something."

He stares at me with his blue eyes, which *know* how to read me. "We can go back anytime you want."

I shake my head. "I want to be here."

With a sigh, he lets go of my waist, interlocks our fingers.

We walk deeper into the cemetery where Emery is. This is my second time coming here. The first time I was here, we buried him; he's on the other side of the cemetery, and we won't be going there. At the mere thought of him, all those conflicted emotions stir. Guilt, so much guilt, fills my chest that it makes it hard to breathe.

I can't believe I did it.

I killed him.

I'm the reason why he's not here anymore.

Just as those thoughts enter my head, a soft voice says, 'It isn't your fault.' *It's Heath.* He's told me that every day, multiple times a day, ever since that night. And everyone else, too.

But it's hard to believe it.

Brave isn't something that I am. I've always been a coward. All I know is fear and panic.

That day, I became someone else.

Seeing him hold Mom like that just snapped something in me. My body moved before my mind could think. Anger consumed with such intensity that it incinerated the fear and panic into ash, until all that remained was a streak of fearless strength that compelled me to fight him.

I know what I did was wrong. *So wrong.*

But I'm safe. Mom is safe. Although, she doesn't think that way.

Ever since that day, she's become reserved, quiet, and peaceful. She doesn't mourn him or miss him. Perhaps, in some corner of her brain, she is relieved that he is gone. She doesn't have to watch her step or be mindful of her words anymore. She can be herself. But she's lost the person she loved because of me. In her robotic behavior and fewer words, she does blame me for it; however, she has never uttered those words to me.

The gap between us has now increased further.

"Are you still cold?" he asks, distracting me from my thoughts.

"No." I smile, snuggling into the jacket he gave me. "Your jacket is pretty warm."

"Good," he murmurs. "We're almost there."

I squeeze his hand, knowing he needs the support.

For months, I waited for Heath to make the move because I didn't know if he'd be okay with me meeting his sister. She means a lot to him. There isn't a day that he doesn't think about her. His parents, too, who have made it a mission to make their house a home. Now it's filled with life, laughter, love, and photographs of their children—it bothers Heath to see his baby pictures everywhere. I always pause to admire them.

His relationship with his parents has evolved. He eats meals with them, talks to them, and spends time with them. I occasionally find him in the kitchen with his mother baking blueberry muffins and chatting with her. It's cute seeing him help her around. As for his dad, things are a little tough between them, but the animosity that he used to feel for him is gone. He doesn't actively hate him or avoid him. In fact, he sometimes visits him in his office and leaves after hours.

I wanted him to get closer to them because they seemed sweet and caring, but it wasn't my choice. Also, I didn't know them like he does. I only knew what he had told me, and it wasn't the good stuff, and that made me apprehensive and cautious.

That has changed, too.

Now they invite me over for dinner, talk to me, and let me stay the night. Which is most nights, considering my only option is to return to an empty house and sleep alone. Mom tries her best to stay out of the house most nights.

"We're here," Heath says with a heavy pain laced in his words.

Before us is a white, gleaming marble grave. My eyes trace the name engraved in the stone. Emery Anne Travon. My chest caves in.

Crouching down, he gently wipes the dust from the grave, then places the fresh, beautiful gardenias.

"Hey Em, look who I brought with me today." He pauses. "This is Rose, my girlfriend." With every word, the enthusiasm in his voice drops, and at the word 'girlfriend', his voice is almost a painful whisper. Then, in a choking tone, he adds, "I miss you. I *miss* you a fucking lot."

I place my hand on his back, hoping to give him some strength.

I rarely see Heath break down or be vulnerable or weak. He's always strong, with a tough exterior that barely lets anything in or out. To see him like this, so emotional that even speaking is hard for him, yanks my heartstrings in the most brutal way ever.

With a quiet huff, he wipes his nose and sniffles, gathering himself once more. Color returns to his skin, but his eyes remain heavy with sadness.

"She loves you and is proud of you," I say.

Heath cranes his neck to look up at me. "You think so?" he asks hesitantly.

"Yes. And I'm sure she misses you, too."

He chuckles, and a soft look graces his face. "Emery, you see this girl. She's the one I was talking about. I love her. You once told me that love is beautiful, well, you were fucking right. It is beautiful."

I smile, staring at her grave. This person is the most important person to him.

Also, Heath talks to her about me.

"You were always right, Em," he whispers as he stands up and sidles up next to me.

"Can I say something?" I ask, and he gives me a nod.

"Hi Emery. I'm Hope and I—"

"Nope, she's Rose," he interrupts.

I smile, my cheeks tinting a deep shade of blush. "I'm happy to finally meet you. I wish you were here so I could actually meet you. I think we'd have been good friends. I saw your photo in his room and I want to tell you that you're pretty." I have no idea what I'm saying. All

I know is, Heath said, 'Just say whatever you feel like saying,' so that's what I'm doing.

"And I love your brother. He treats me right." I lean into him, and he wraps his arm around me. "He is my safe place."

"And you're *my* safe place," he murmurs against my temple.

We stay for a while talking to her. Heath informs her that it is strange how his parents are mending their relationship with him and how annoying he finds it—which I don't think he does. He also tells her about school, friends, life, and me.

It's around noon when we leave the cemetery.

My feet stay rooted in their place by the gates as if something calls for me to visit his grave. *Guilt.*

Heath studies me. "Do you want to go?"

He's giving me a choice, despite the anger and hatred he feels for him.

Gathering whatever little courage my body possesses, I make myself move to not give in to it.

It isn't your fault.

"Yes." I get inside the car as he holds the door open for me.

He lingers by the door, his eyes fixed on me.

A cold breeze slices through us, effortlessly cutting through the uncomfortable tension.

With a soft thud, he closes the door and, a few seconds later, joins me.

As we drive away from the cemetery, I go away with a heart that feels lighter than it did a month ago.

LEAVE A REVIEW

Hope and Heath's story has ended! Thank you so much for reading Mended. It means a lot to me that you continued the story and finished it. I hope you had a good time reading it.

Please leave a review on Goodreads, Amazon or any other platform of your choice. I'd be grateful to you.

Love, Mary

KEEP IN TOUCH WITH MARY

www.authormary.com

ACKNOWLEDGMENTS

To my readers — Thank you so much for all your love and support. Because of you I get to do what I love!

To Mirah — Thank you for everything. Your feedback always helps me to make the book better.

To Bri — You're one of my close friends. Your constant support keeps me going.

To my brother — I love you. My therapist, my best friend, my favorite person in the whole wide world. Thank you so much for being my number one supporter and for everything else.

To the Book Community — Ah! You guys have changed everything. I can't thank you enough for your posts, messages, Instagram stories, edits and reviews. You guys are the best and I'm so glad that I got to meet you. Thank you so much for all that you've done for me. It means the world to me.

Love, Mary

Made in United States
North Haven, CT
28 April 2026

10578124R00243